FEARBOOK CLUB

RICHARD ASHLEY HAMILTON
writer

MARCO MATRONE
artist & colorist

DAVE SHARPE
letterer

MARCO MATRONE cover
DAVE SHARPE logo design
CHARLES PRITCHETT book design
MIKE MARTS & **CHRISTINA HARRINGTON** editors

CREATED BY RICHARD ASHLEY HAMILTON

SEISMIC
PRESS

For Max & Ben.
I love you so much, it's scary.
— RICHARD ASHLEY HAMILTON

To my father, thank you.
—MARCO MATRONE

Thank you, Bonnie, for all of your
support and love! I wouldn't have
made it through without you.
— DAVE SHARPE

SEISMIC PRESS IS AN IMPRINT OF

MIKE MARTS - Editor-in-Chief • JOE PRUETT - Publisher/CCO • LEE KRAMER - President • JON KRAMER - Chief Executive Officer
STEVE ROTTERDAM - SVP, Sales & Marketing • DAN SHIRES - VP, Film & Television UK • CHRISTINA HARRINGTON - Managing Editor
TEODORO LEO - Associate Editor • MARC HAMMOND - Sr. Retail Sales Development Manager • RUTHANN THOMPSON - Sr. Retailer Relations Manager
KATHERINE JAMISON - Marketing Manager • KELLY DIODATI - Ambassador Outreach Manager • BLAKE STOCKER - Director of Finance
AARON MARION - Publicist • LISA MOODY - Finance • RYAN CARROLL - Director, Comics/Film/TV Liaison • JAWAD QURESHI - Technology Advisor/Strategist
RACHEL PINNELAS - Social Community Manager • CHARLES PRITCHETT - Design & Production Manager • COREY BREEN - Collections Production
SARAH PRUETT - Publishing Assistant

AfterShock and Seismic Logo Designs by COMICRAFT
Publicity: contact AARON MARION (aaron@publichausagency.com) & RYAN CROY (ryan@publichausagency.com) at PUBLICHAUS
Special thanks to: ATOM! FREEMAN, IRA KURGAN, MARINE KSADZHIKYAN, KEITH MANZELLA,
ANTONIA LIANOS, ANTHONY MILITANO, STEPHAN NILSON & ED ZAREMBA

AFTERSHOCKCOMICS.COM/SEISMIC   Follow us on social media ▼ @SeismicComics @SeismicPress @SeismicPress

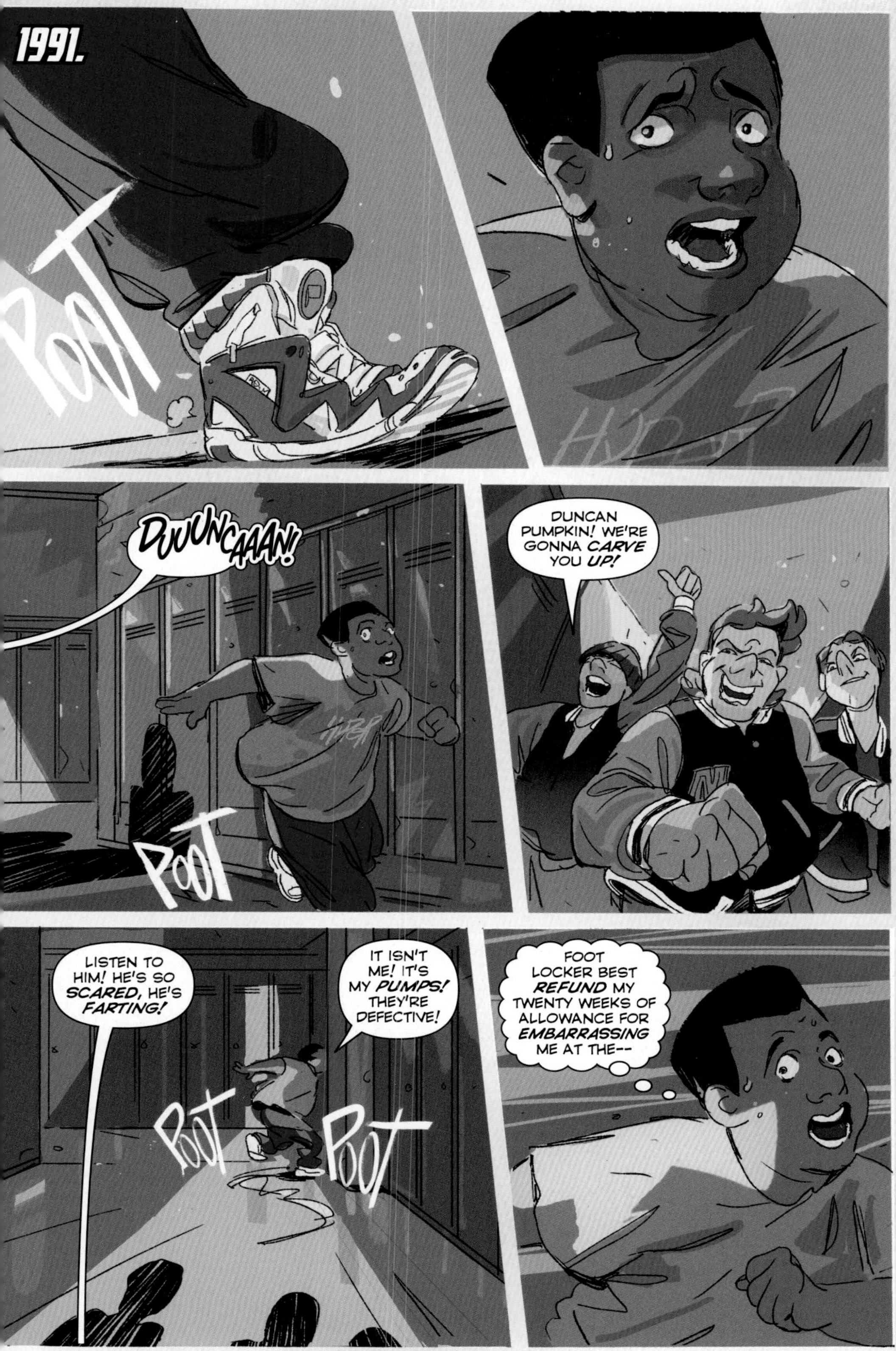
1991.
POOT
DUUUNCAAAN!
POOT
DUNCAN PUMPKIN! WE'RE GONNA CARVE YOU UP!
LISTEN TO HIM! HE'S SO SCARED, HE'S FARTING!
IT ISN'T ME! IT'S MY PUMPS! THEY'RE DEFECTIVE!
POOT
POOT
FOOT LOCKER BEST REFUND MY TWENTY WEEKS OF ALLOWANCE FOR EMBARRASSING ME AT THE--

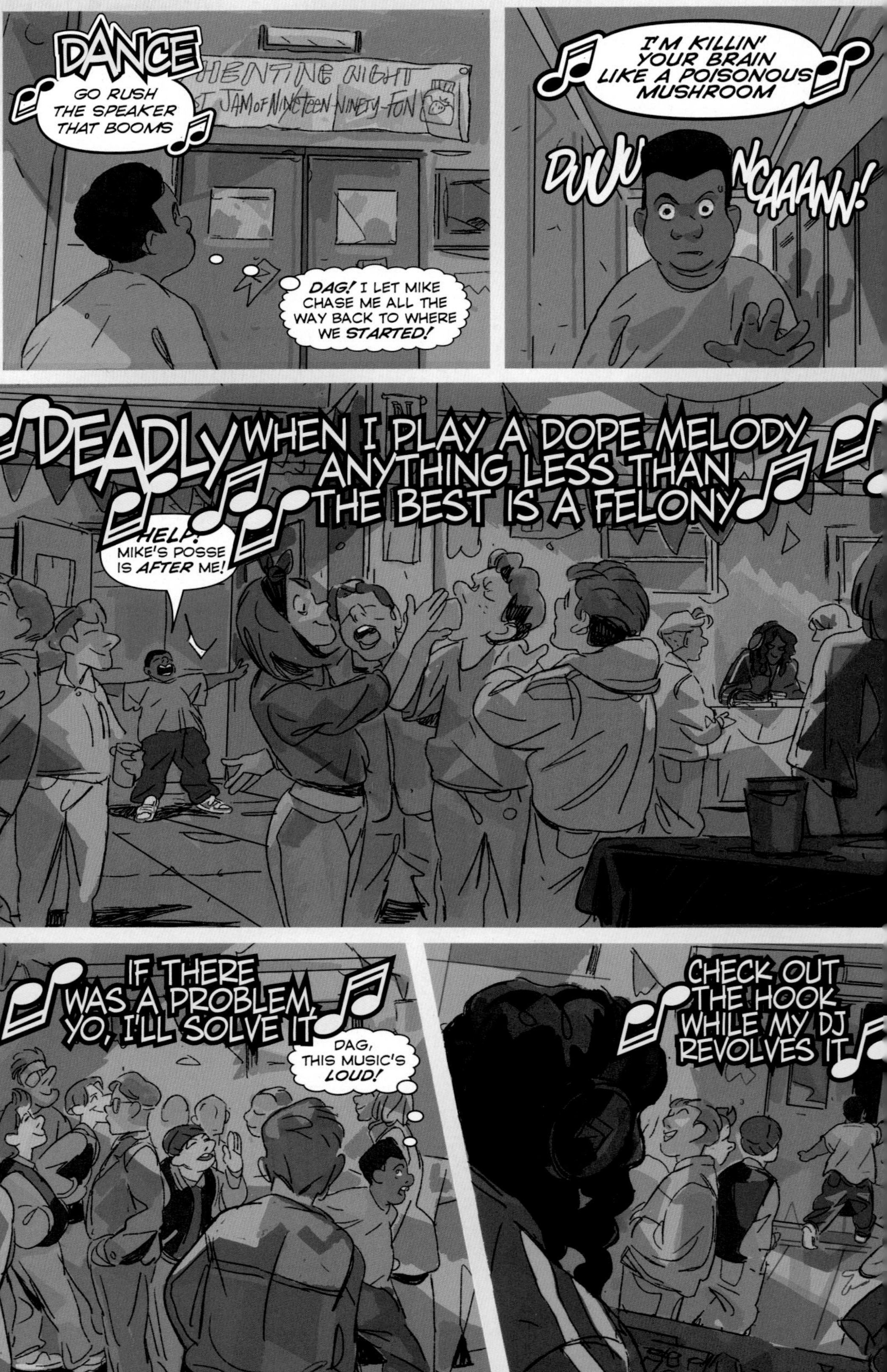
DANCE
GO RUSH THE SPEAKER THAT BOOMS
JAM OF NINETEEN NINETY-FUN
DAG! I LET MIKE CHASE ME ALL THE WAY BACK TO WHERE WE STARTED!
I'M KILLIN' YOUR BRAIN LIKE A POISONOUS MUSHROOM
DUUU
NCAAAANN!
DEADLY WHEN I PLAY A DOPE MELODY ANYTHING LESS THAN THE BEST IS A FELONY
HELP! MIKE'S POSSE IS AFTER ME!
IF THERE WAS A PROBLEM, YO, I'LL SOLVE IT
DAG, THIS MUSIC'S LOUD!
CHECK OUT THE HOOK WHILE MY DJ REVOLVES IT

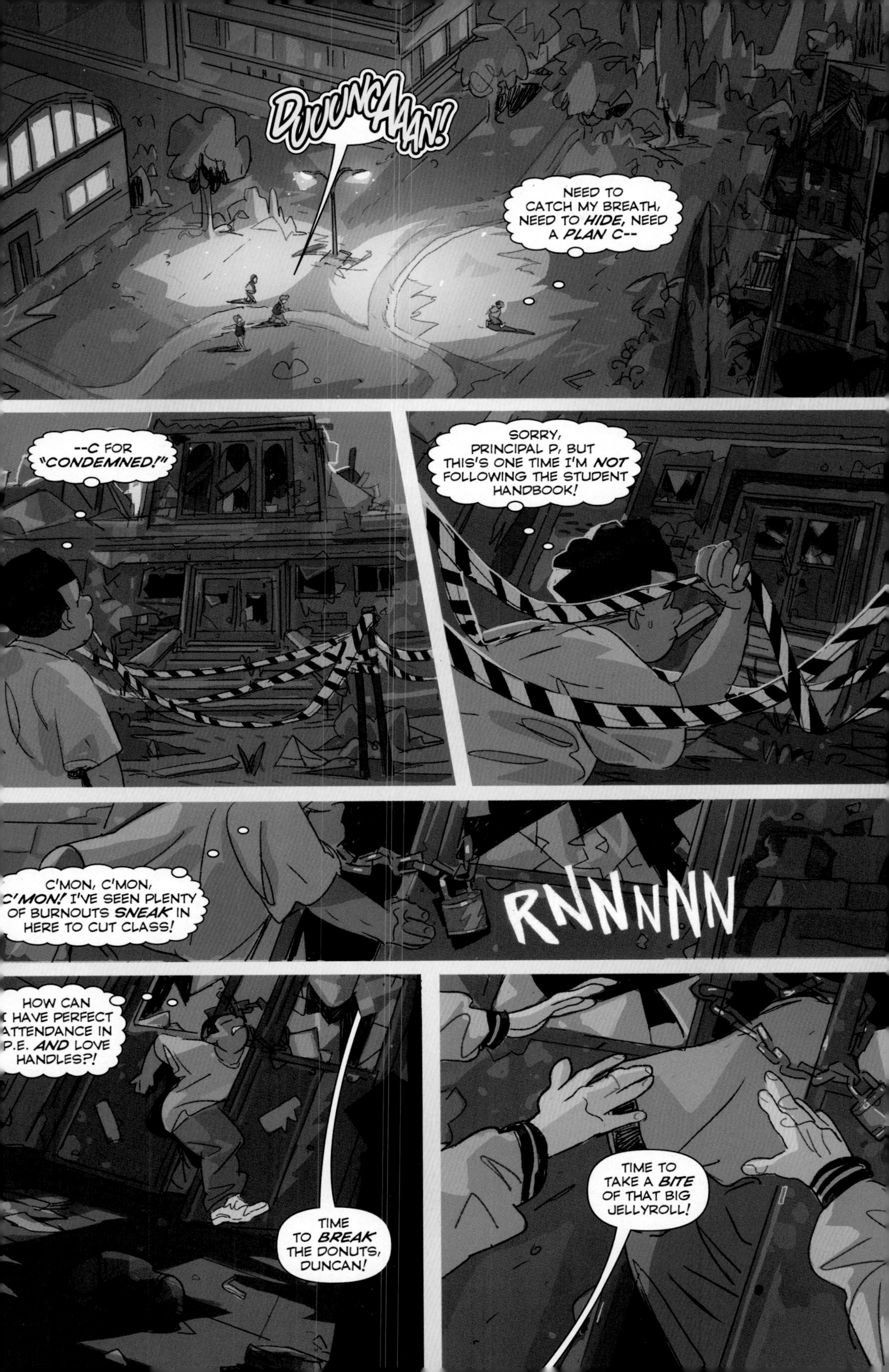
DUUUNCAAAN!
NEED TO CATCH MY BREATH, NEED TO *HIDE*, NEED A *PLAN C*--
--C FOR "*CONDEMNED!*"
SORRY, PRINCIPAL P, BUT THIS'S ONE TIME I'M *NOT* FOLLOWING THE STUDENT HANDBOOK!
C'MON, C'MON, *C'MON!* I'VE SEEN PLENTY OF BURNOUTS *SNEAK* IN HERE TO CUT CLASS!
RNNNNN
HOW CAN I HAVE PERFECT ATTENDANCE IN P.E. *AND* LOVE HANDLES?!
TIME TO *BREAK* THE DONUTS, DUNCAN!
TIME TO TAKE A *BITE* OF THAT BIG JELLYROLL!

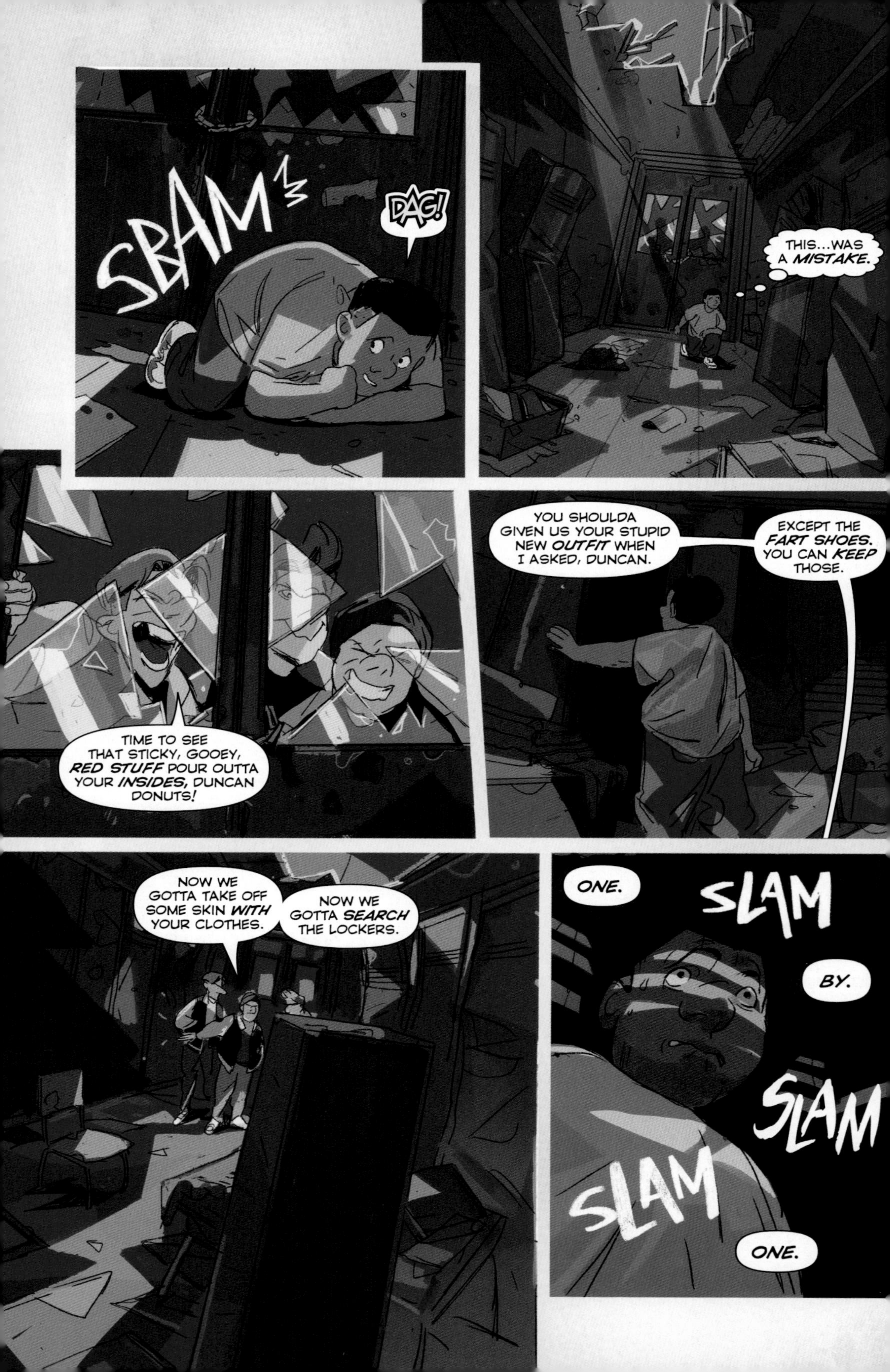
SBAM
DAG!
THIS...WAS A MISTAKE.
TIME TO SEE THAT STICKY, GOOEY, RED STUFF POUR OUTTA YOUR INSIDES, DUNCAN DONUTS!
YOU SHOULDA GIVEN US YOUR STUPID NEW OUTFIT WHEN I ASKED, DUNCAN.
EXCEPT THE FART SHOES. YOU CAN KEEP THOSE.
NOW WE GOTTA TAKE OFF SOME SKIN WITH YOUR CLOTHES.
NOW WE GOTTA SEARCH THE LOCKERS.
ONE.
SLAM
BY.
SLAM
SLAM
ONE.

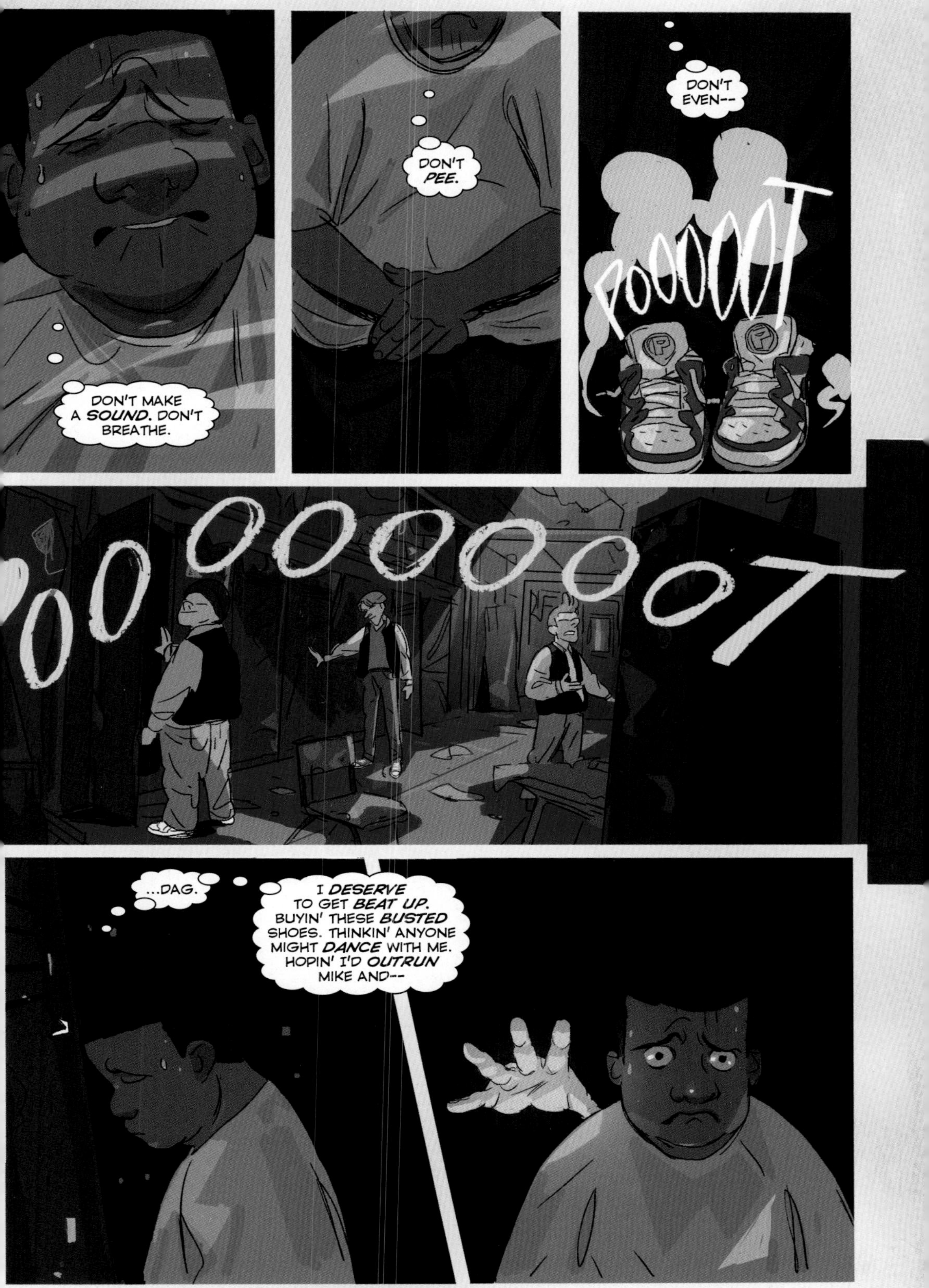
DON'T MAKE A SOUND. DON'T BREATHE.
DON'T PEE.
DON'T EVEN--
POOOOOT
POOOOOOOOOT
...DAG.
I DESERVE TO GET BEAT UP. BUYIN' THESE BUSTED SHOES. THINKIN' ANYONE MIGHT DANCE WITH ME. HOPIN' I'D OUTRUN MIKE AND--

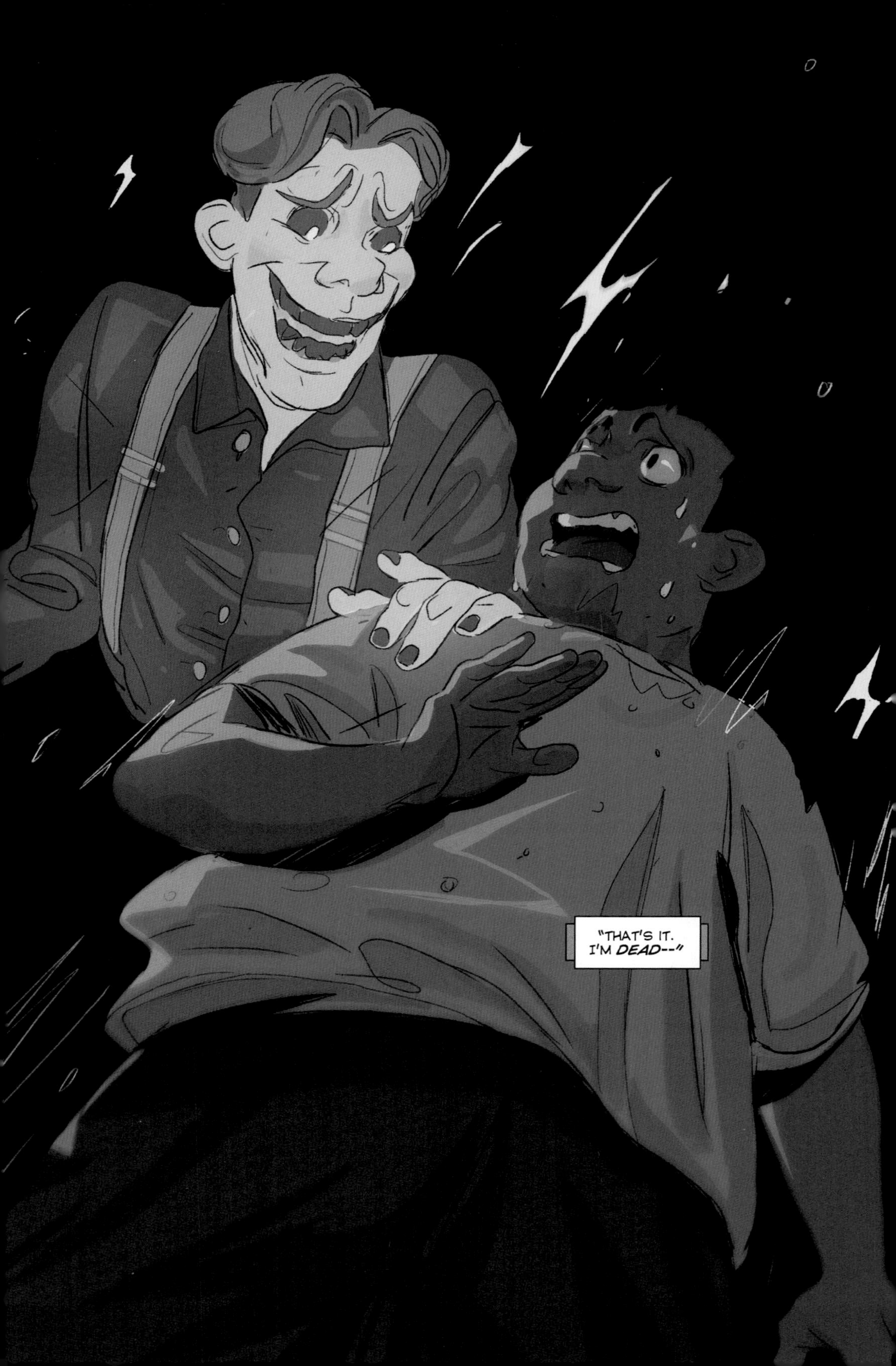
"THAT'S IT.
I'M *DEAD*--"

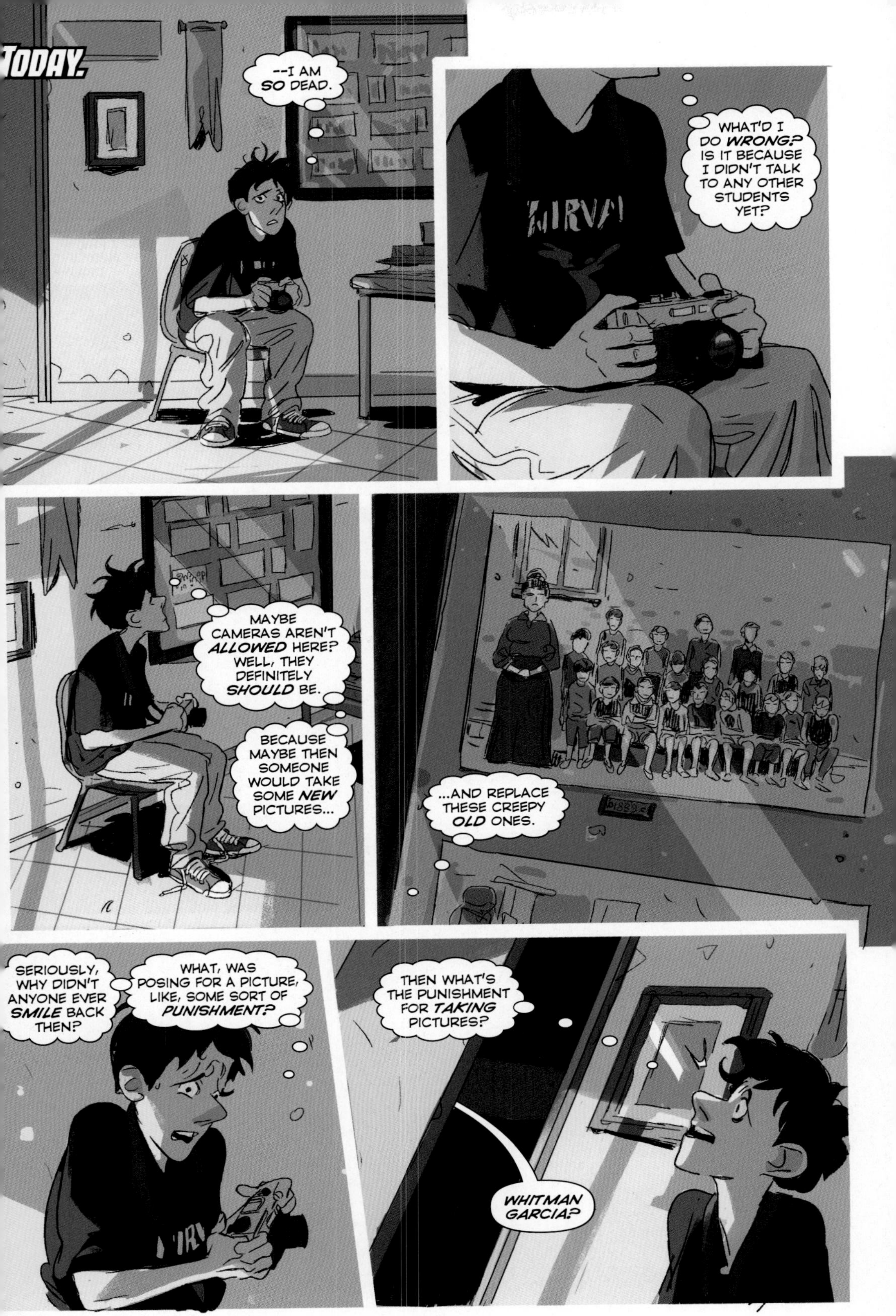
TODAY.
--I AM SO DEAD.
WHAT'D I DO WRONG? IS IT BECAUSE I DIDN'T TALK TO ANY OTHER STUDENTS YET?
MAYBE CAMERAS AREN'T ALLOWED HERE? WELL, THEY DEFINITELY SHOULD BE.
BECAUSE MAYBE THEN SOMEONE WOULD TAKE SOME NEW PICTURES...
...AND REPLACE THESE CREEPY OLD ONES.
SERIOUSLY, WHY DIDN'T ANYONE EVER SMILE BACK THEN?
WHAT, WAS POSING FOR A PICTURE, LIKE, SOME SORT OF PUNISHMENT?
THEN WHAT'S THE PUNISHMENT FOR TAKING PICTURES?
WHITMAN GARCIA?

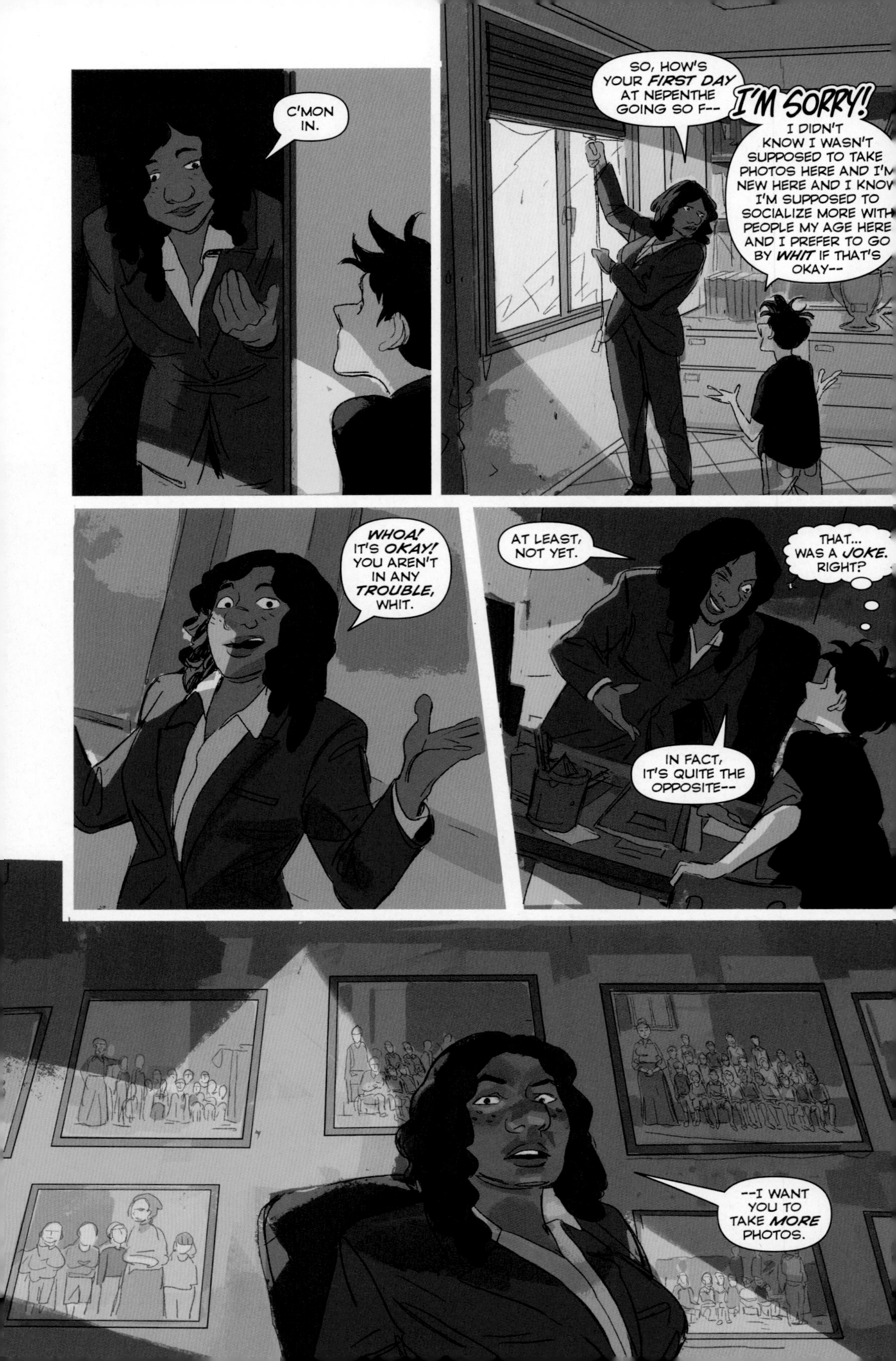
C'MON IN.
SO, HOW'S YOUR FIRST DAY AT NEPENTHE GOING SO F--
I'M SORRY!
I DIDN'T KNOW I WASN'T SUPPOSED TO TAKE PHOTOS HERE AND I'M NEW HERE AND I KNOW I'M SUPPOSED TO SOCIALIZE MORE WITH PEOPLE MY AGE HERE AND I PREFER TO GO BY WHIT IF THAT'S OKAY--
WHOA! IT'S OKAY! YOU AREN'T IN ANY TROUBLE, WHIT.
AT LEAST, NOT YET.
THAT... WAS A JOKE. RIGHT?
IN FACT, IT'S QUITE THE OPPOSITE--
--I WANT YOU TO TAKE MORE PHOTOS.

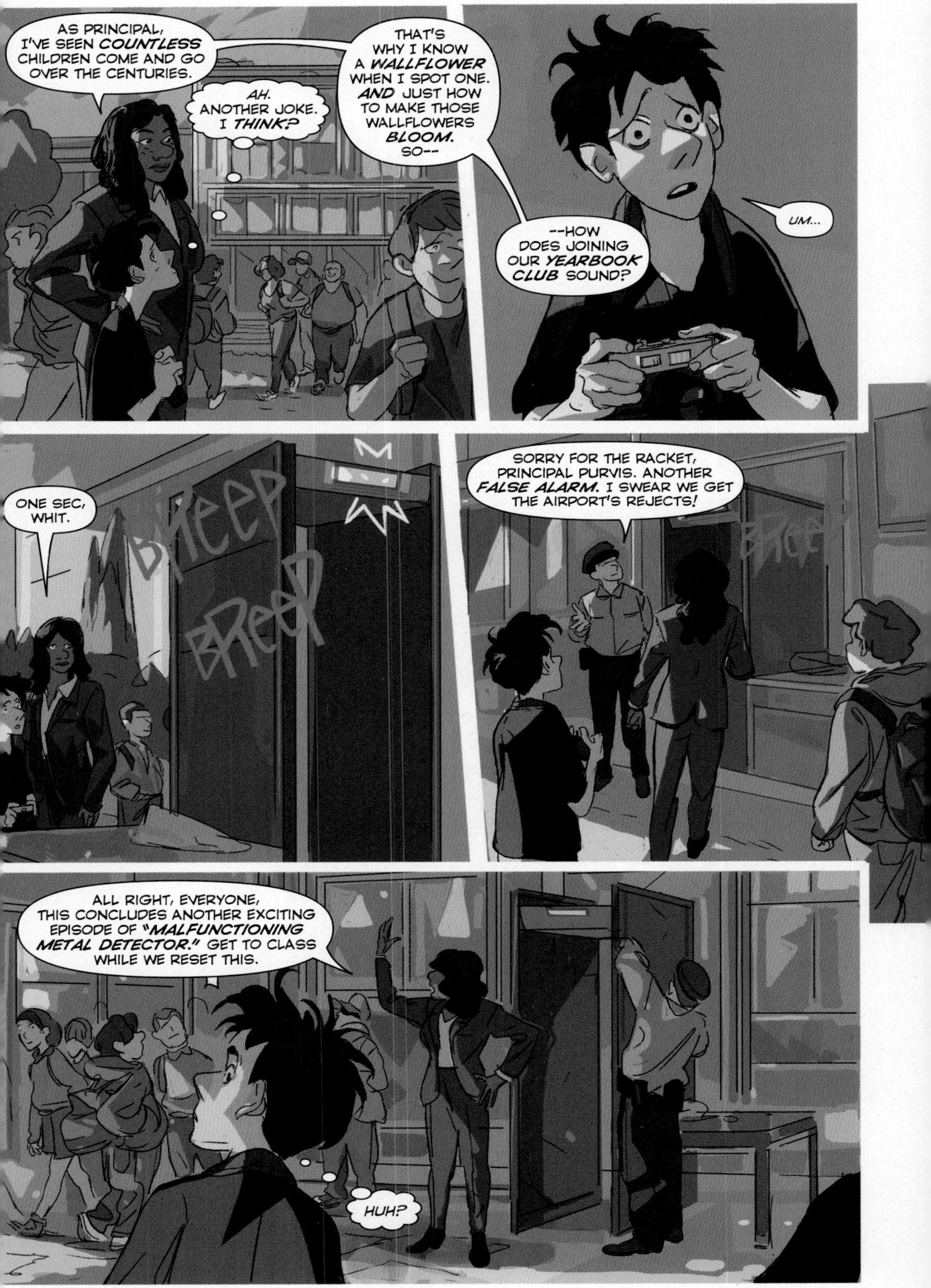
AS PRINCIPAL, I'VE SEEN COUNTLESS CHILDREN COME AND GO OVER THE CENTURIES.
AH. ANOTHER JOKE. I THINK?
THAT'S WHY I KNOW A WALLFLOWER WHEN I SPOT ONE. AND JUST HOW TO MAKE THOSE WALLFLOWERS BLOOM. SO--
--HOW DOES JOINING OUR YEARBOOK CLUB SOUND?
UM...
ONE SEC, WHIT.
BREEP BREEP
SORRY FOR THE RACKET, PRINCIPAL PURVIS. ANOTHER FALSE ALARM. I SWEAR WE GET THE AIRPORT'S REJECTS!
BREEP
ALL RIGHT, EVERYONE, THIS CONCLUDES ANOTHER EXCITING EPISODE OF "MALFUNCTIONING METAL DETECTOR." GET TO CLASS WHILE WE RESET THIS.
HUH?

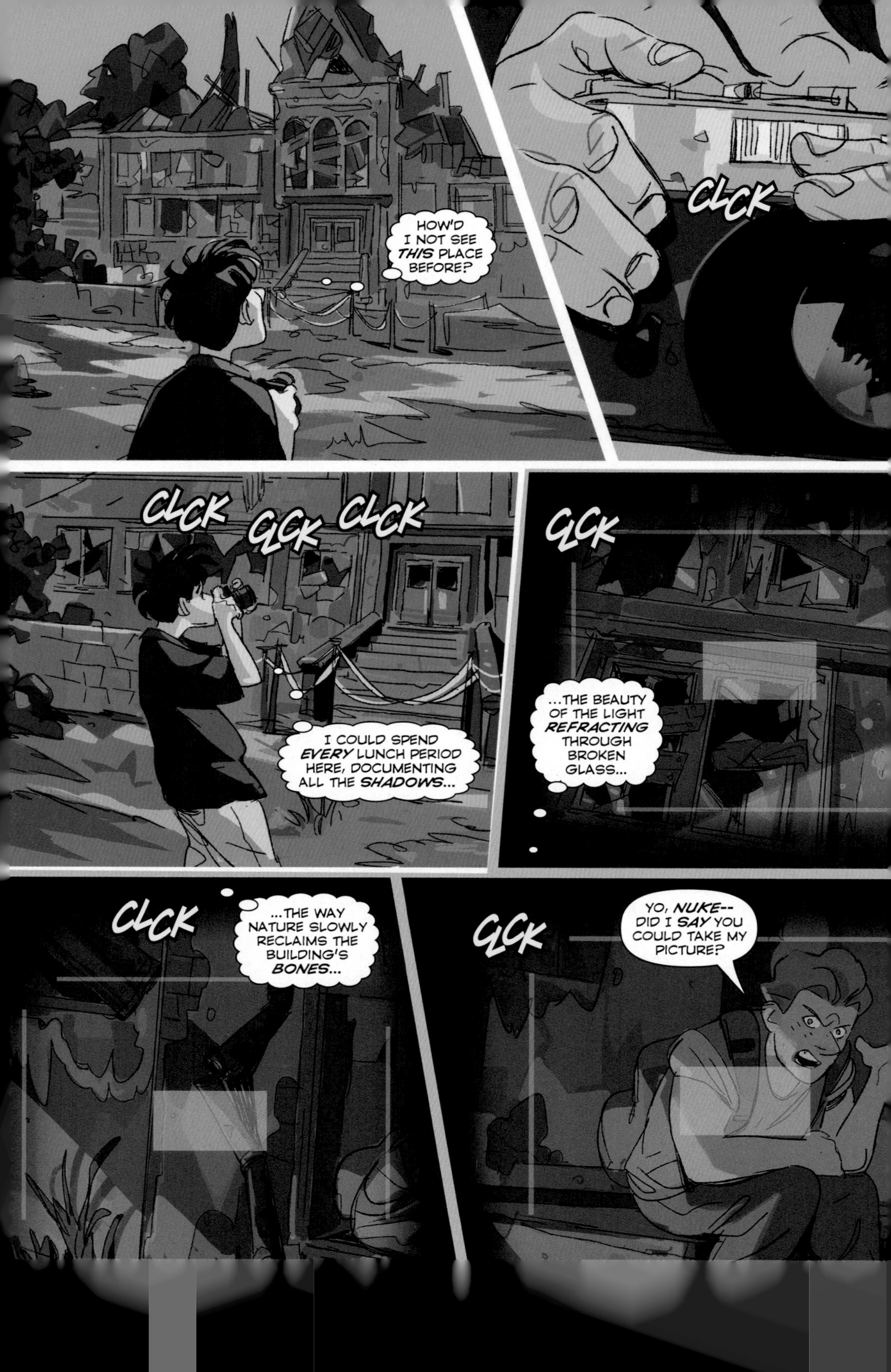
HOW'D I NOT SEE *THIS* PLACE BEFORE?
CLCK
CLCK
CLCK
CLCK
I COULD SPEND *EVERY* LUNCH PERIOD HERE, DOCUMENTING ALL THE *SHADOWS*...
CLCK
...THE BEAUTY OF THE LIGHT *REFRACTING* THROUGH BROKEN GLASS...
CLCK
...THE WAY NATURE SLOWLY RECLAIMS THE BUILDING'S *BONES*...
CLCK
YO, *NUKE*-- DID I *SAY* YOU COULD TAKE MY PICTURE?

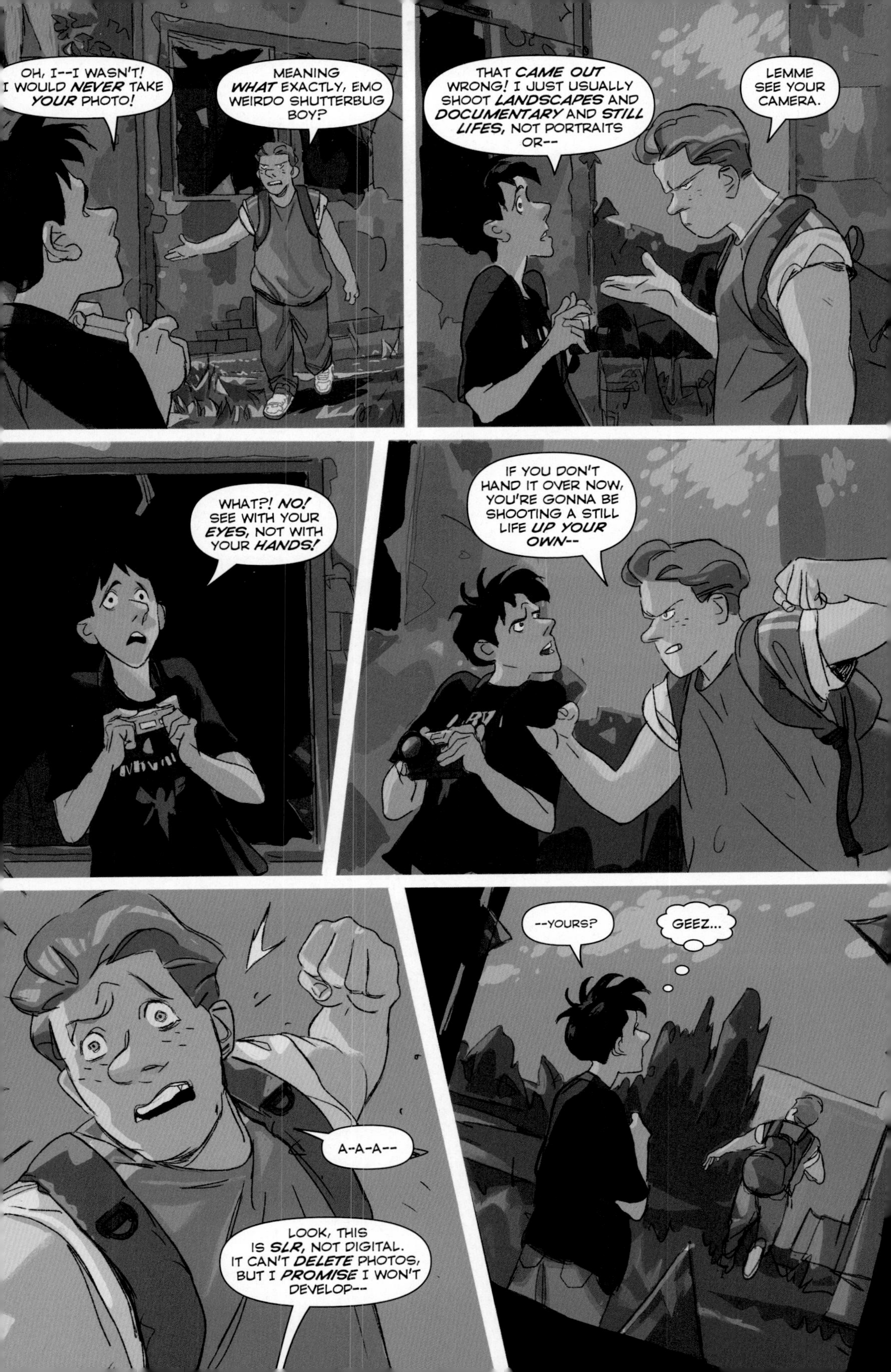
OH, I--I WASN'T! I WOULD NEVER TAKE YOUR PHOTO!
MEANING WHAT EXACTLY, EMO WEIRDO SHUTTERBUG BOY?
THAT CAME OUT WRONG! I JUST USUALLY SHOOT LANDSCAPES AND DOCUMENTARY AND STILL LIFES, NOT PORTRAITS OR--
LEMME SEE YOUR CAMERA.
WHAT?! NO! SEE WITH YOUR EYES, NOT WITH YOUR HANDS!
IF YOU DON'T HAND IT OVER NOW, YOU'RE GONNA BE SHOOTING A STILL LIFE UP YOUR OWN--
A-A-A--
LOOK, THIS IS SLR, NOT DIGITAL. IT CAN'T DELETE PHOTOS, BUT I PROMISE I WON'T DEVELOP--
--YOURS?
GEEZ...

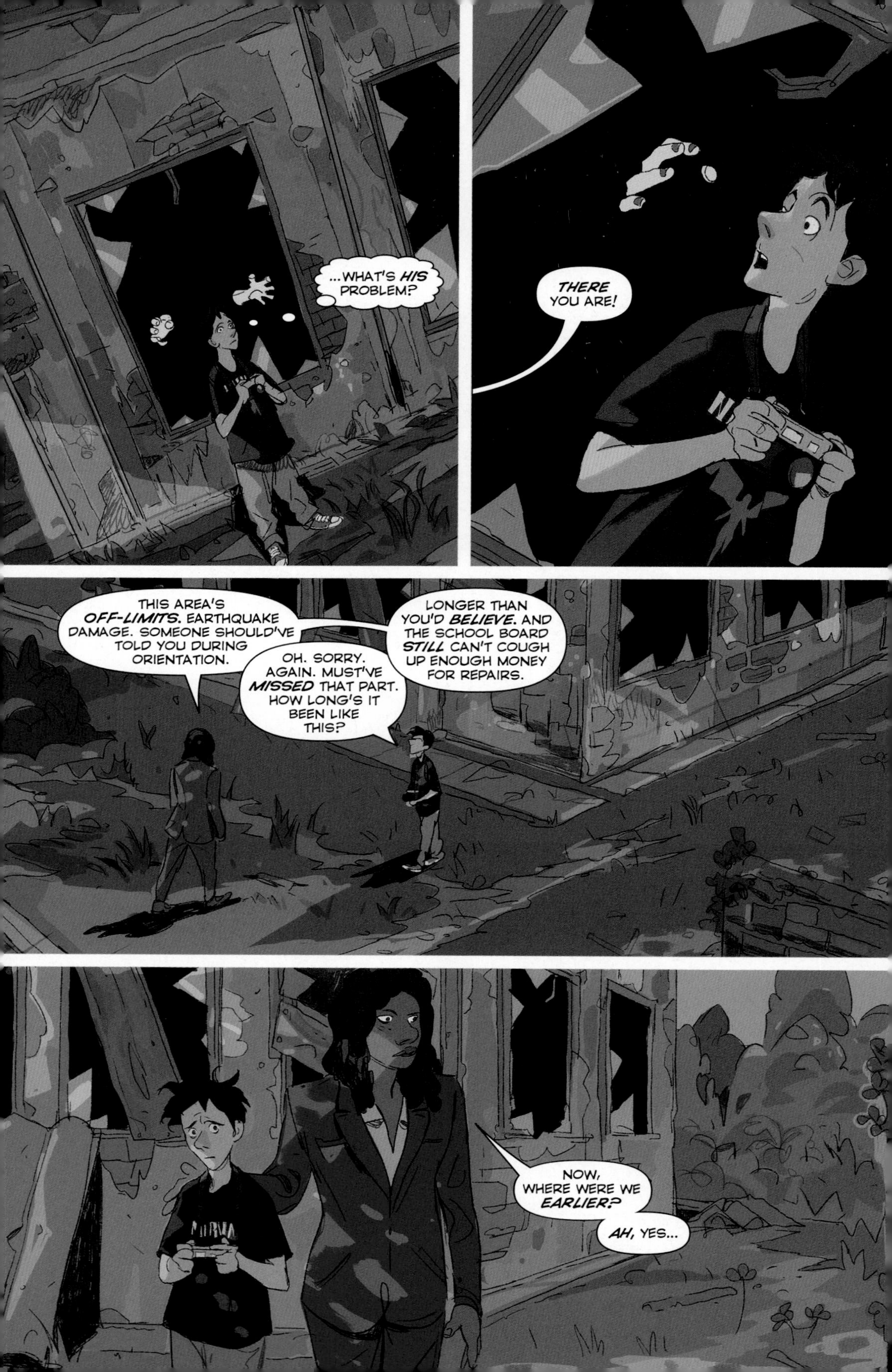
...WHAT'S *HIS* PROBLEM?
THERE YOU ARE!
THIS AREA'S *OFF-LIMITS.* EARTHQUAKE DAMAGE. SOMEONE SHOULD'VE TOLD YOU DURING ORIENTATION.
OH. SORRY. AGAIN. MUST'VE *MISSED* THAT PART. HOW LONG'S IT BEEN LIKE THIS?
LONGER THAN YOU'D *BELIEVE.* AND THE SCHOOL BOARD *STILL* CAN'T COUGH UP ENOUGH MONEY FOR REPAIRS.
NOW, WHERE WERE WE *EARLIER?*
AH, YES...

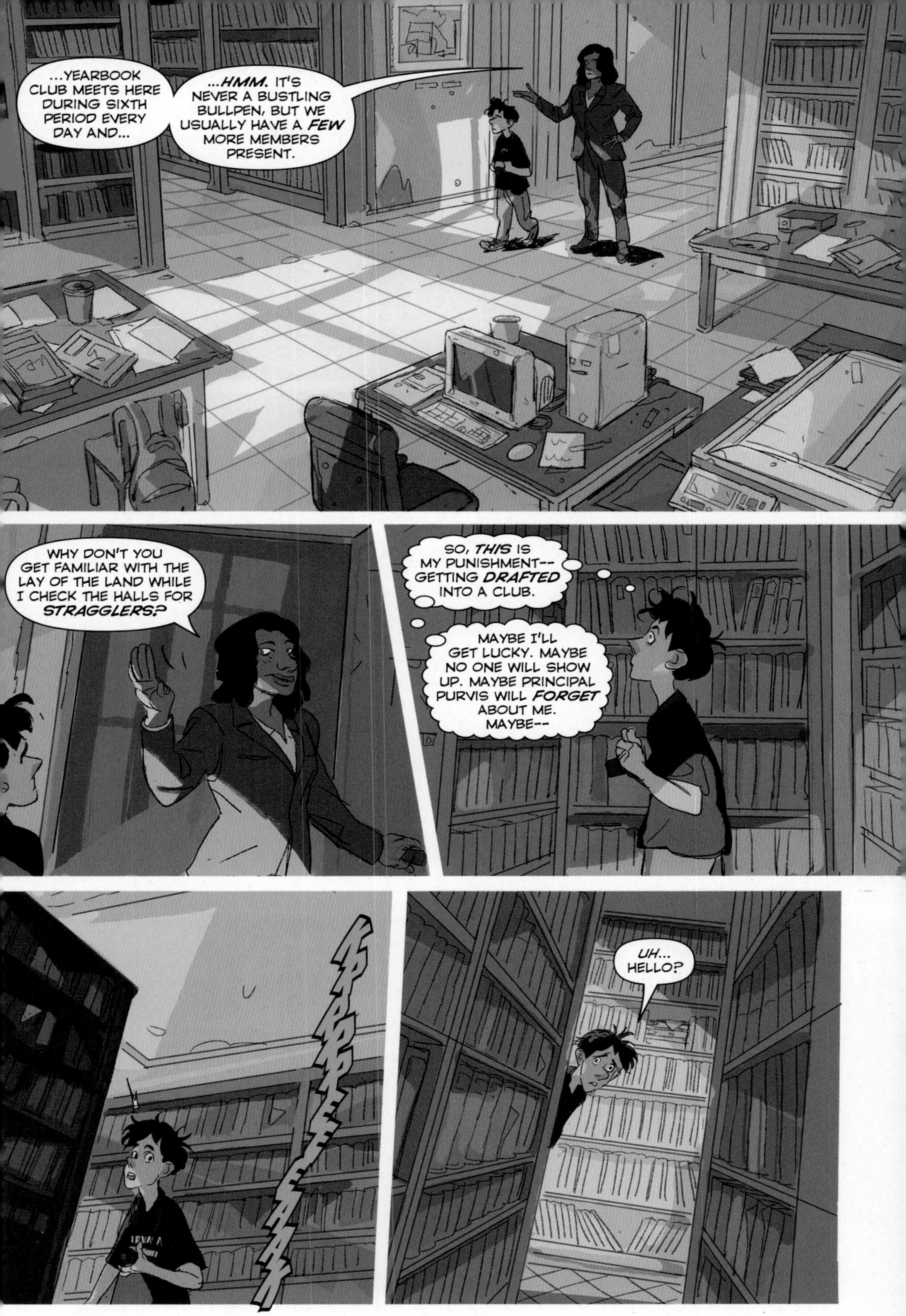
...YEARBOOK CLUB MEETS HERE DURING SIXTH PERIOD EVERY DAY AND...
...HMM. IT'S NEVER A BUSTLING BULLPEN, BUT WE USUALLY HAVE A FEW MORE MEMBERS PRESENT.
WHY DON'T YOU GET FAMILIAR WITH THE LAY OF THE LAND WHILE I CHECK THE HALLS FOR STRAGGLERS?
SO, THIS IS MY PUNISHMENT-- GETTING DRAFTED INTO A CLUB.
MAYBE I'LL GET LUCKY. MAYBE NO ONE WILL SHOW UP. MAYBE PRINCIPAL PURVIS WILL FORGET ABOUT ME. MAYBE--
UH... HELLO?

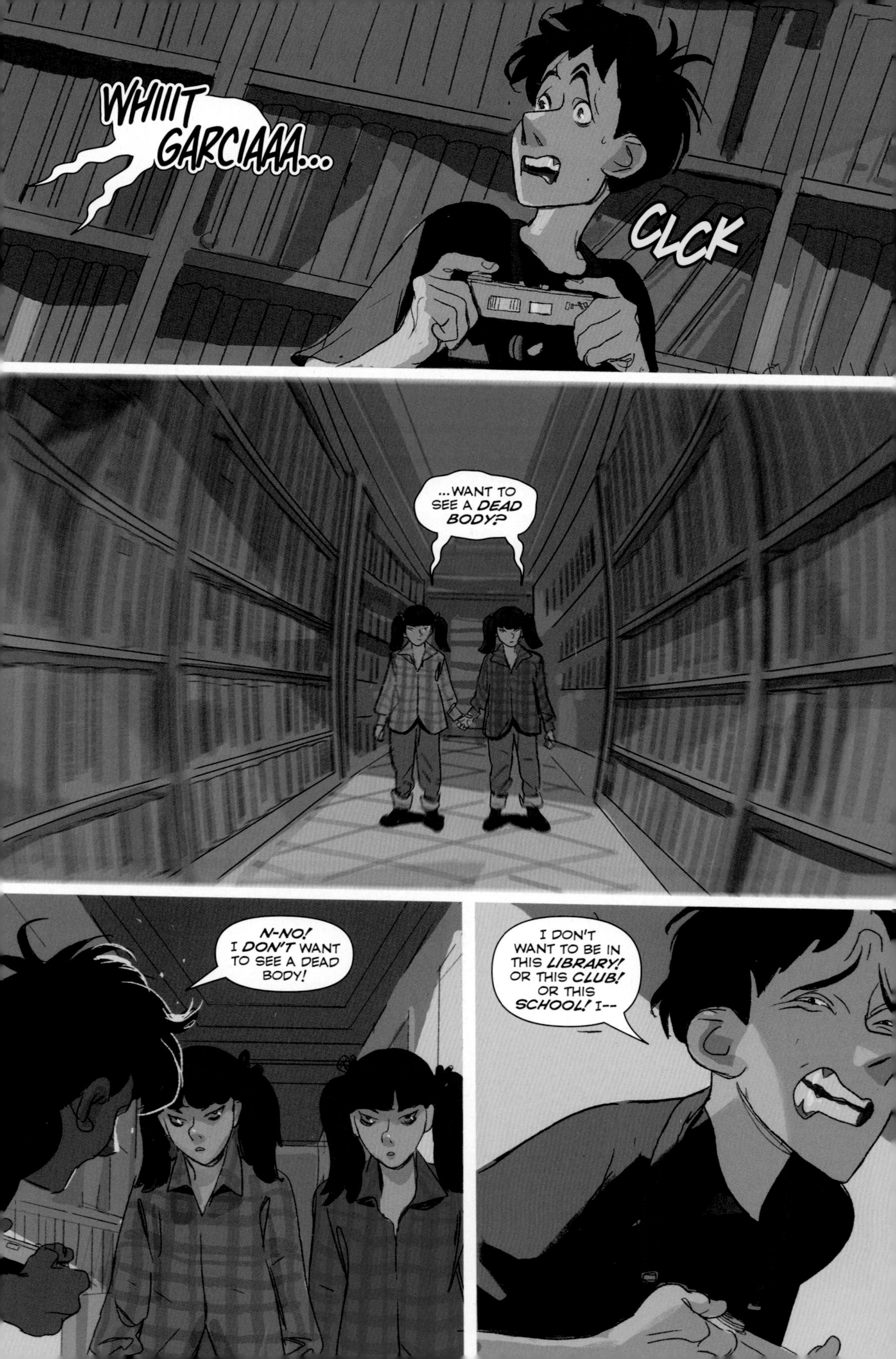
WHIIIT GARCIAAA...
CLCK
...WANT TO SEE A DEAD BODY?
N-NO! I DON'T WANT TO SEE A DEAD BODY!
I DON'T WANT TO BE IN THIS LIBRARY! OR THIS CLUB! OR THIS SCHOOL! I--

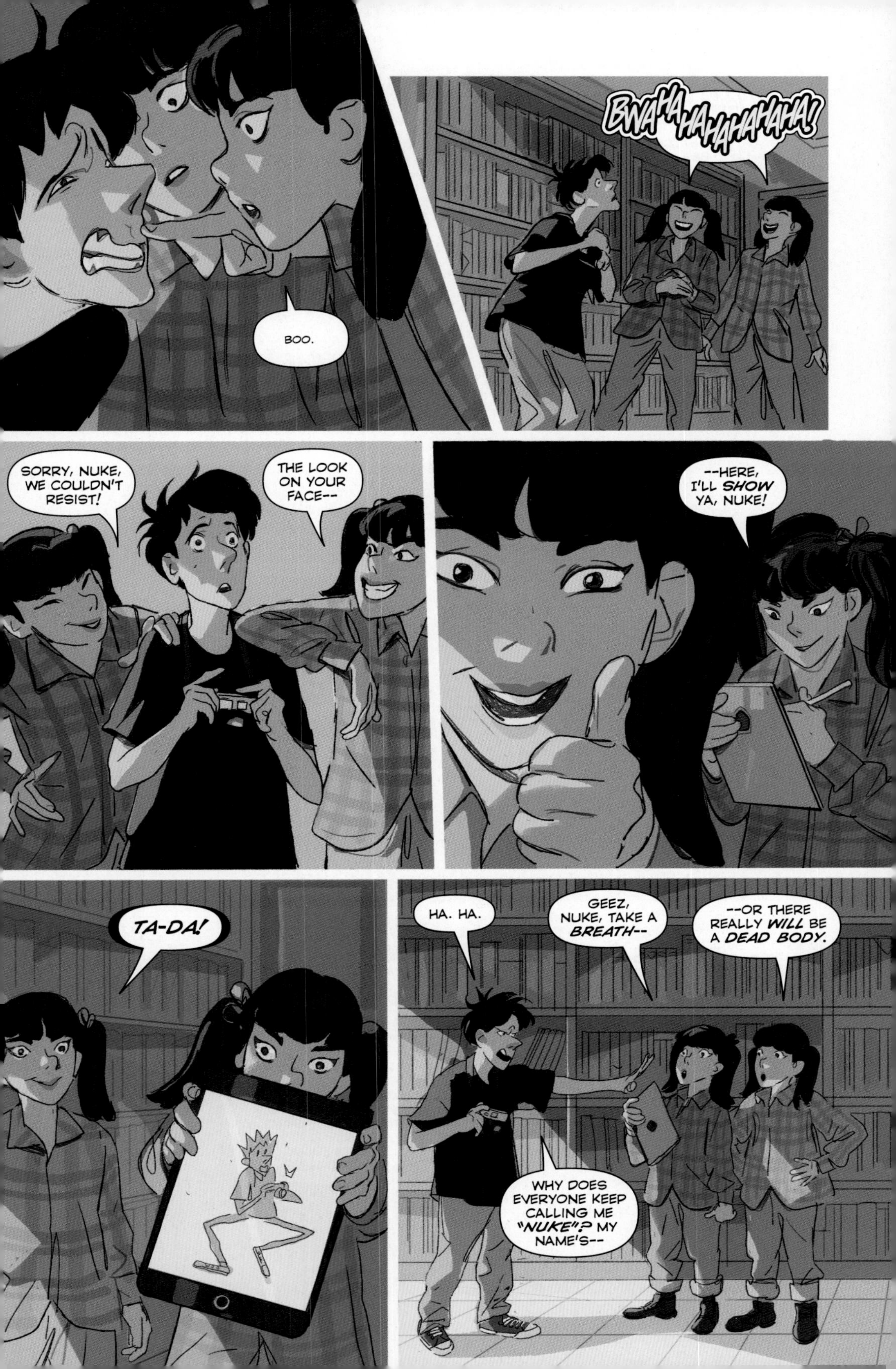
BOO.
BWAHAHAHAHAHAHA!
SORRY, NUKE, WE COULDN'T RESIST!
THE LOOK ON YOUR FACE--
--HERE, I'LL *SHOW* YA, NUKE!
TA-DA!
HA. HA.
GEEZ, NUKE, TAKE A *BREATH*--
--OR THERE REALLY *WILL* BE A *DEAD BODY*.
WHY DOES EVERYONE KEEP CALLING ME *"NUKE"*? MY NAME'S--

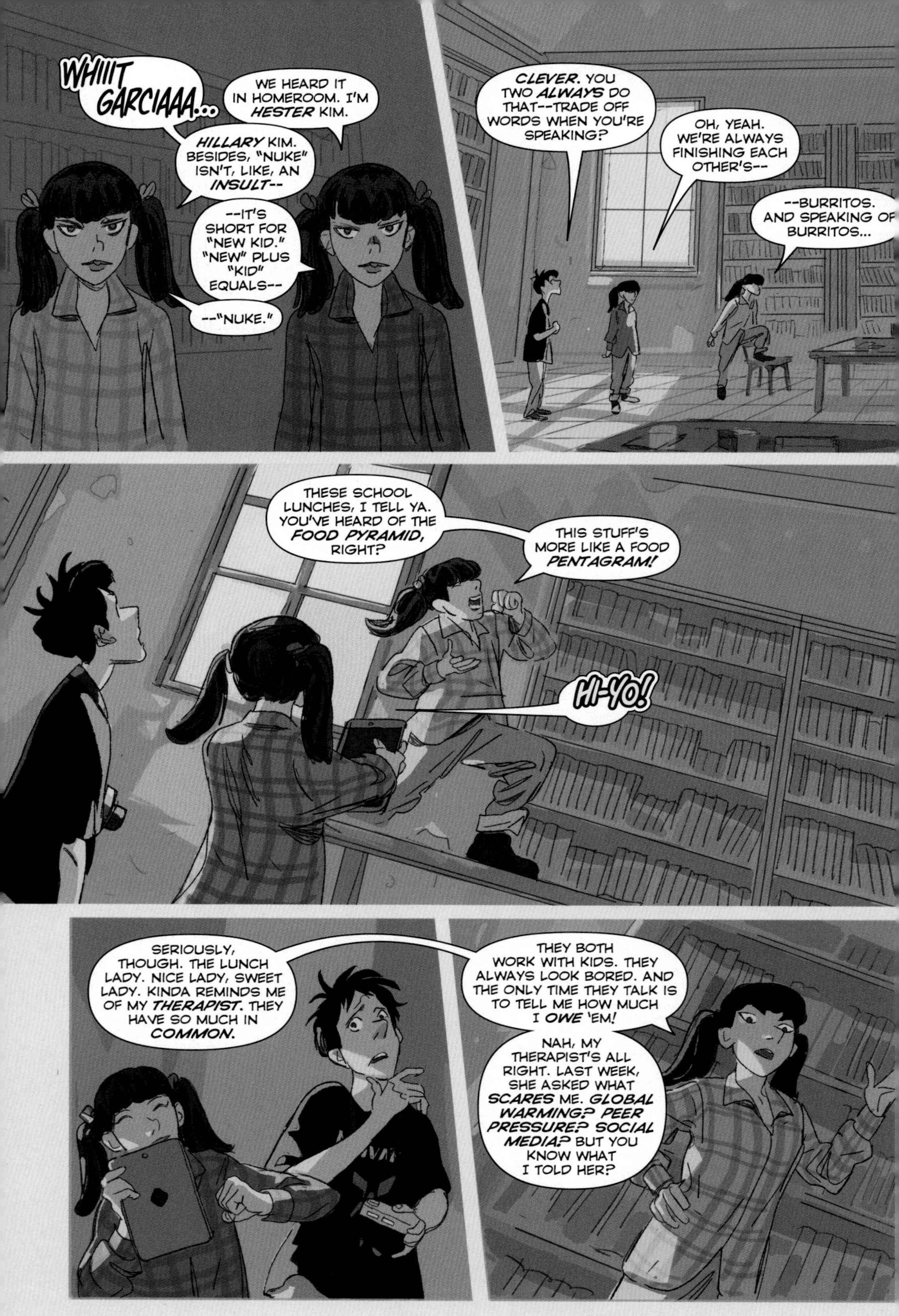
WHIIIT GARCIAAA...
WE HEARD IT IN HOMEROOM. I'M HESTER KIM.
HILLARY KIM. BESIDES, "NUKE" ISN'T, LIKE, AN INSULT--
--IT'S SHORT FOR "NEW KID." "NEW" PLUS "KID" EQUALS--
--"NUKE."
CLEVER. YOU TWO ALWAYS DO THAT--TRADE OFF WORDS WHEN YOU'RE SPEAKING?
OH, YEAH. WE'RE ALWAYS FINISHING EACH OTHER'S--
--BURRITOS. AND SPEAKING OF BURRITOS...
THESE SCHOOL LUNCHES, I TELL YA. YOU'VE HEARD OF THE FOOD PYRAMID, RIGHT?
THIS STUFF'S MORE LIKE A FOOD PENTAGRAM!
HI-YO!
SERIOUSLY, THOUGH. THE LUNCH LADY. NICE LADY, SWEET LADY. KINDA REMINDS ME OF MY THERAPIST. THEY HAVE SO MUCH IN COMMON.
THEY BOTH WORK WITH KIDS. THEY ALWAYS LOOK BORED. AND THE ONLY TIME THEY TALK IS TO TELL ME HOW MUCH I OWE 'EM!
NAH, MY THERAPIST'S ALL RIGHT. LAST WEEK, SHE ASKED WHAT SCARES ME. GLOBAL WARMING? PEER PRESSURE? SOCIAL MEDIA? BUT YOU KNOW WHAT I TOLD HER?

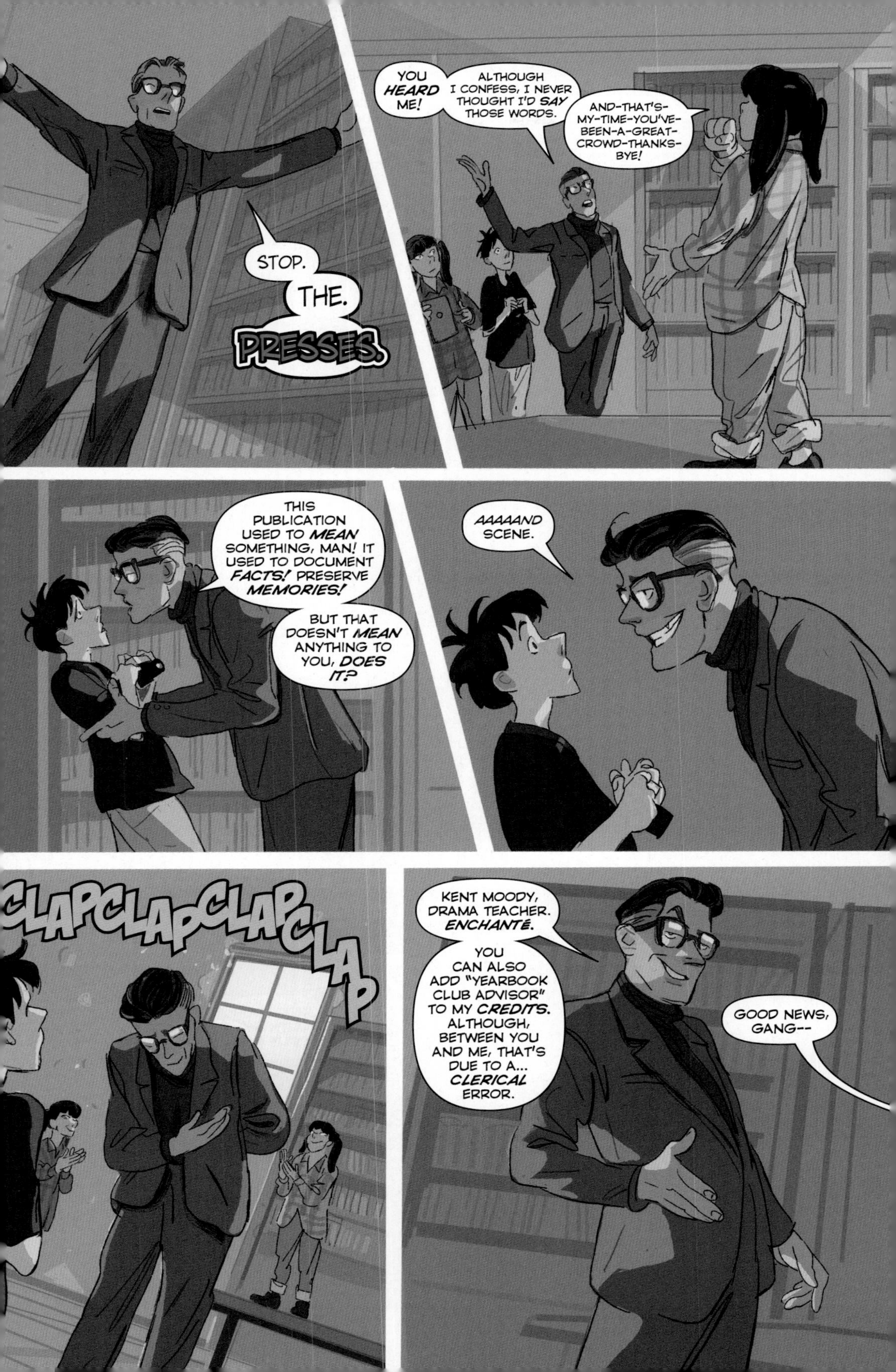
STOP.
THE.
PRESSES.
YOU HEARD ME!
ALTHOUGH I CONFESS, I NEVER THOUGHT I'D SAY THOSE WORDS.
AND-THAT'S-MY-TIME-YOU'VE-BEEN-A-GREAT-CROWD-THANKS-BYE!
THIS PUBLICATION USED TO MEAN SOMETHING, MAN! IT USED TO DOCUMENT FACTS! PRESERVE MEMORIES!
BUT THAT DOESN'T MEAN ANYTHING TO YOU, DOES IT?
AAAAAND SCENE.
CLAPCLAPCLAPCLAP
KENT MOODY, DRAMA TEACHER. ENCHANTÉ.
YOU CAN ALSO ADD "YEARBOOK CLUB ADVISOR" TO MY CREDITS. ALTHOUGH, BETWEEN YOU AND ME, THAT'S DUE TO A... CLERICAL ERROR.
GOOD NEWS, GANG--

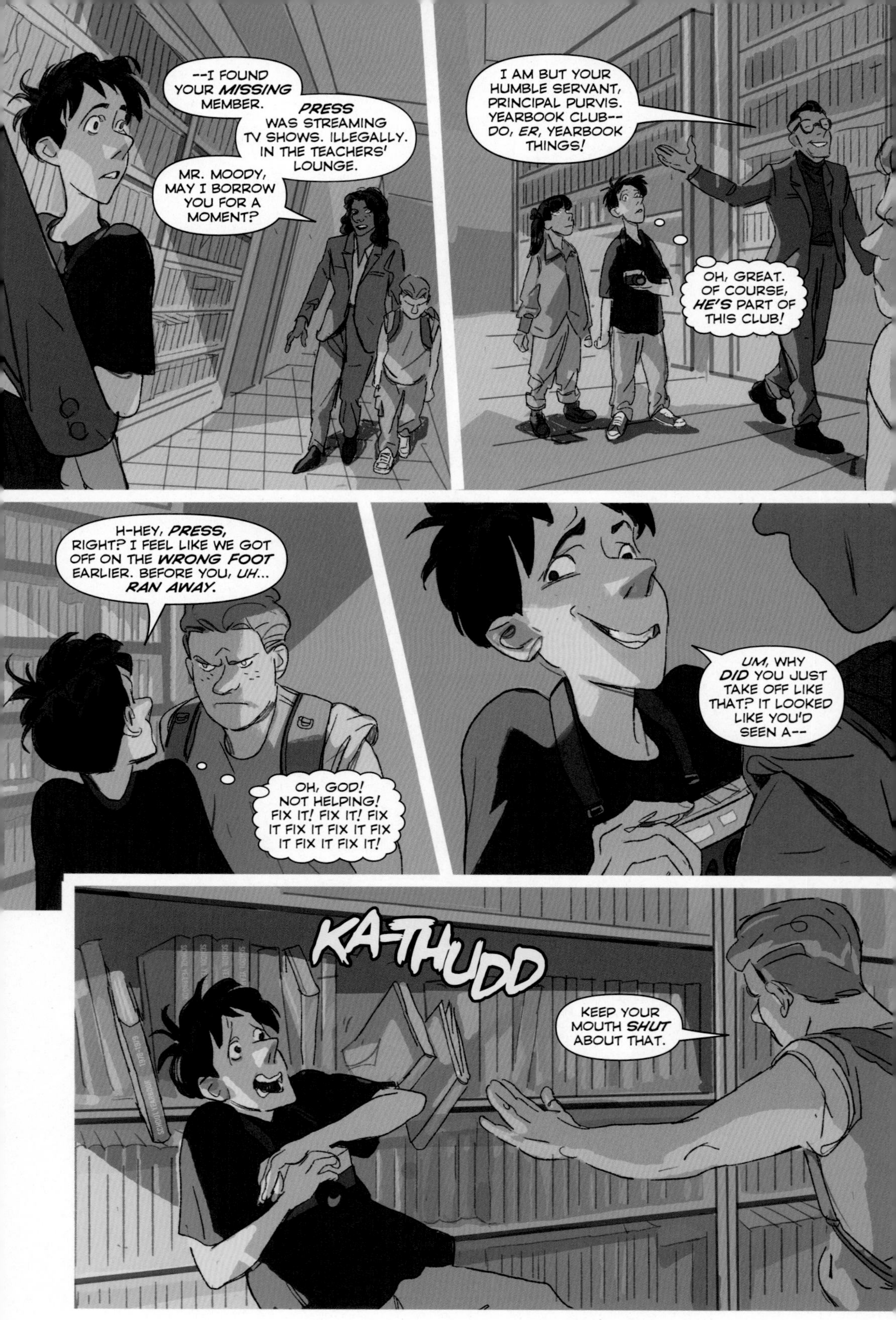
--I FOUND YOUR *MISSING* MEMBER.
PRESS WAS STREAMING TV SHOWS. ILLEGALLY. IN THE TEACHERS' LOUNGE.
MR. MOODY, MAY I BORROW YOU FOR A MOMENT?
I AM BUT YOUR HUMBLE SERVANT, PRINCIPAL PURVIS. YEARBOOK CLUB-- DO, *ER*, YEARBOOK THINGS!
OH, GREAT. OF COURSE, *HE'S* PART OF THIS CLUB!
H-HEY, *PRESS,* RIGHT? I FEEL LIKE WE GOT OFF ON THE *WRONG FOOT* EARLIER. BEFORE YOU, *UH*... *RAN AWAY.*
OH, GOD! NOT HELPING! FIX IT! FIX IT! FIX IT FIX IT FIX IT FIX IT FIX IT FIX IT!
UM, WHY *DID* YOU JUST TAKE OFF LIKE THAT? IT LOOKED LIKE YOU'D SEEN A--
KA-THUDD
KEEP YOUR MOUTH *SHUT* ABOUT THAT.

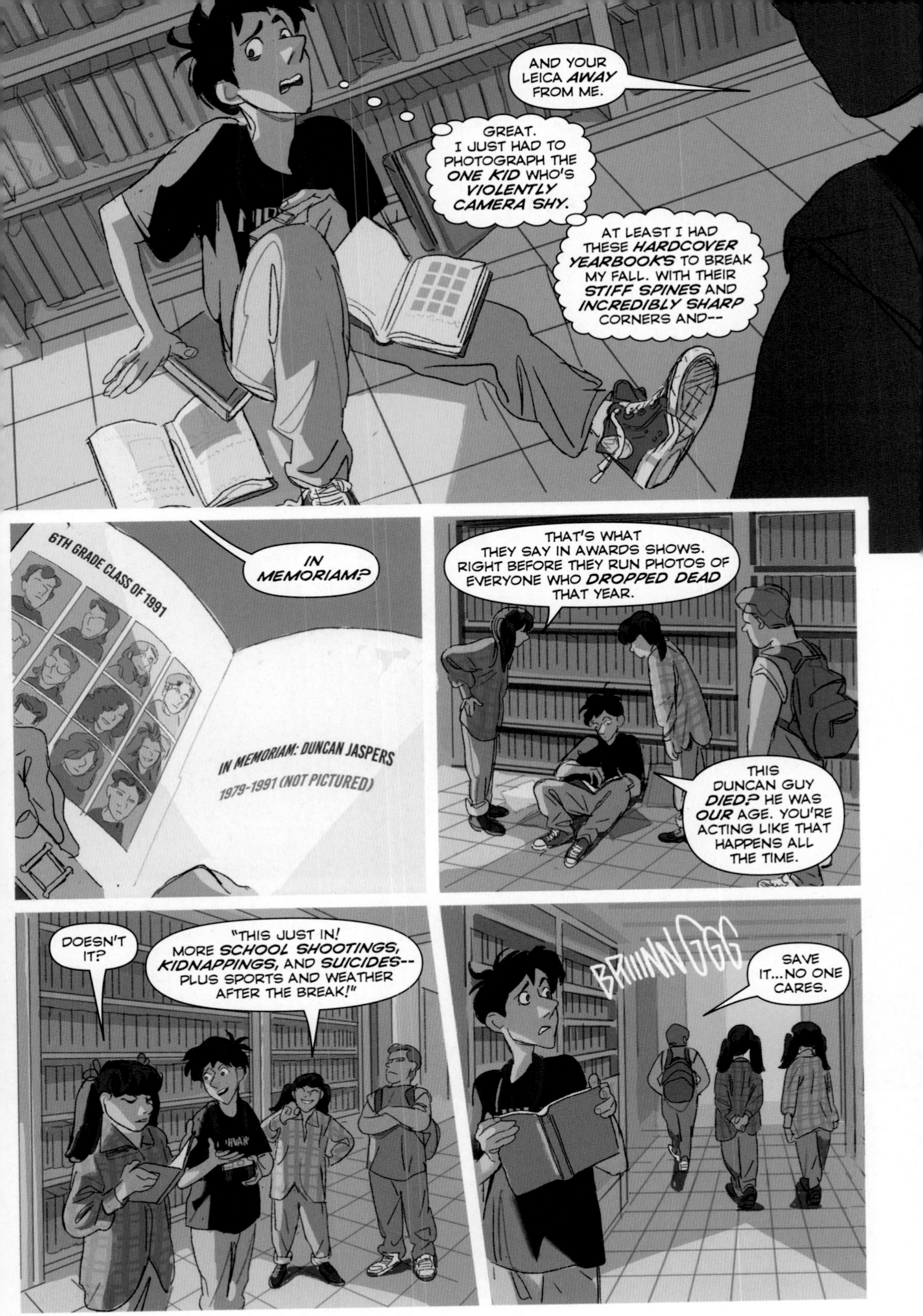
AND YOUR LEICA AWAY FROM ME.
GREAT. I JUST HAD TO PHOTOGRAPH THE ONE KID WHO'S VIOLENTLY CAMERA SHY.
AT LEAST I HAD THESE HARDCOVER YEARBOOKS TO BREAK MY FALL. WITH THEIR STIFF SPINES AND INCREDIBLY SHARP CORNERS AND--
6TH GRADE CLASS OF 1991
IN MEMORIAM: DUNCAN JASPERS
1979-1991 (NOT PICTURED)
IN MEMORIAM?
THAT'S WHAT THEY SAY IN AWARDS SHOWS. RIGHT BEFORE THEY RUN PHOTOS OF EVERYONE WHO DROPPED DEAD THAT YEAR.
THIS DUNCAN GUY DIED? HE WAS OUR AGE. YOU'RE ACTING LIKE THAT HAPPENS ALL THE TIME.
DOESN'T IT?
"THIS JUST IN! MORE SCHOOL SHOOTINGS, KIDNAPPINGS, AND SUICIDES-- PLUS SPORTS AND WEATHER AFTER THE BREAK!"
BRIIINNGGG
SAVE IT...NO ONE CARES.

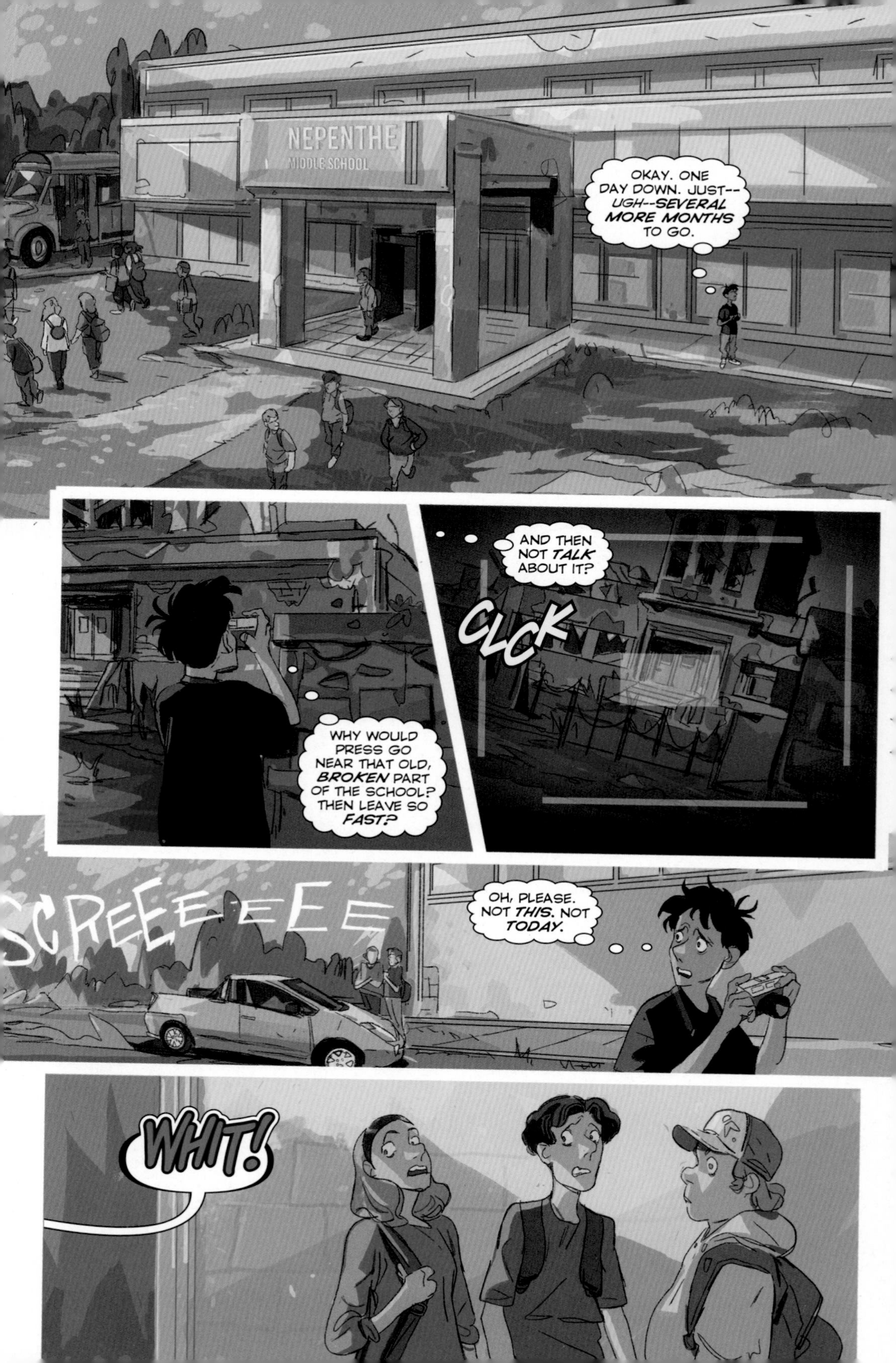
NEPENTHE
MIDDLE SCHOOL
OKAY. ONE DAY DOWN. JUST-- UGH--SEVERAL MORE MONTHS TO GO.
WHY WOULD PRESS GO NEAR THAT OLD, BROKEN PART OF THE SCHOOL? THEN LEAVE SO FAST?
CLCK
AND THEN NOT TALK ABOUT IT?
SCREEEEEEE
OH, PLEASE. NOT THIS. NOT TODAY.
WHIT!

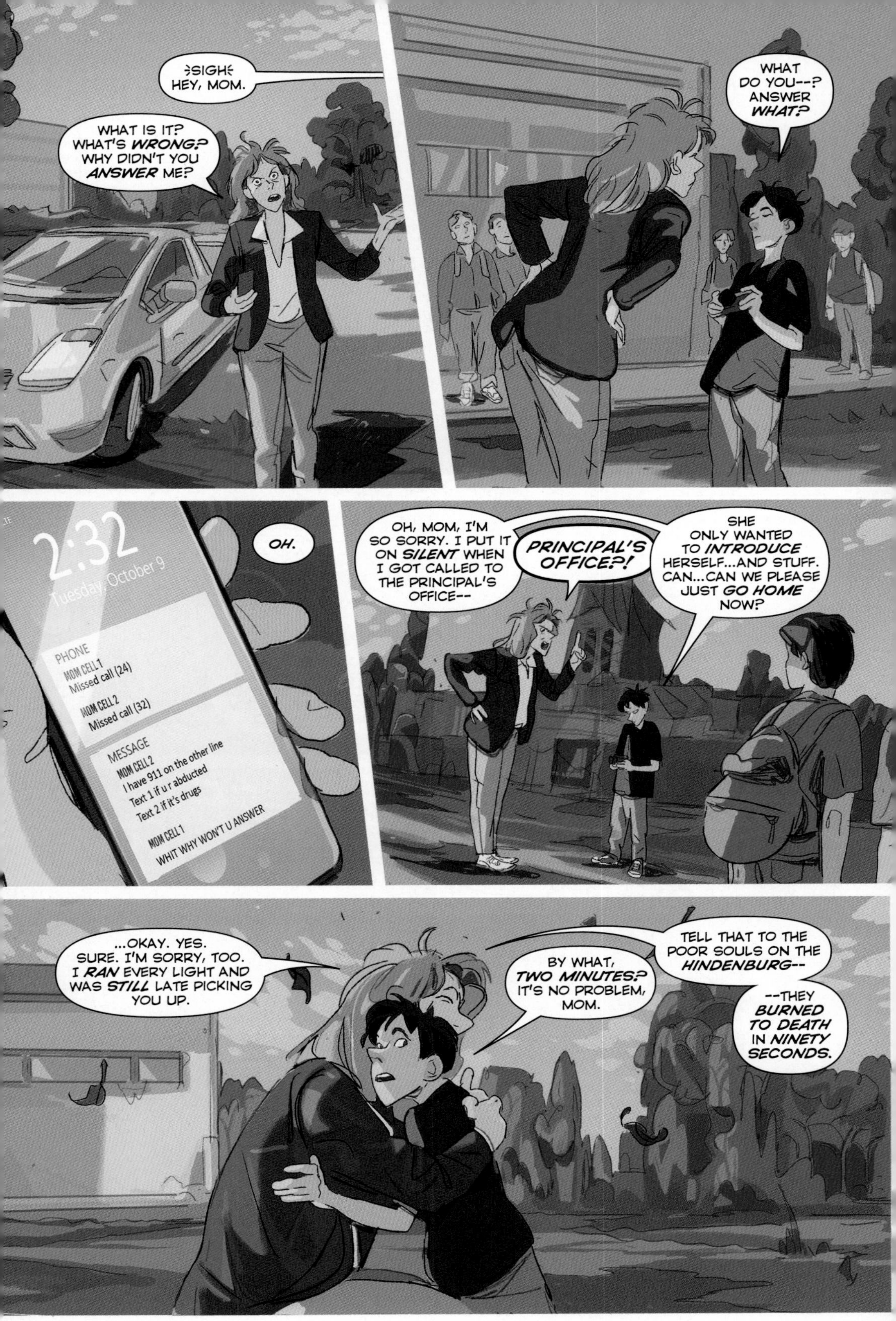

⁓SIGH⁓ HEY, MOM.
WHAT IS IT? WHAT'S WRONG? WHY DIDN'T YOU ANSWER ME?
WHAT DO YOU--? ANSWER WHAT?
2:32
Tuesday, October 9
PHONE
MOM CELL 1
Missed call (24)
MOM CELL 2
Missed call (32)
MESSAGE
MOM CELL 2
I have 911 on the other line
Text 1 if u r abducted
Text 2 if it's drugs
MOM CELL 1
WHIT WHY WON'T U ANSWER
OH.
OH, MOM, I'M SO SORRY. I PUT IT ON SILENT WHEN I GOT CALLED TO THE PRINCIPAL'S OFFICE--
PRINCIPAL'S OFFICE?!
SHE ONLY WANTED TO INTRODUCE HERSELF...AND STUFF. CAN...CAN WE PLEASE JUST GO HOME NOW?
...OKAY. YES. SURE. I'M SORRY, TOO. I RAN EVERY LIGHT AND WAS STILL LATE PICKING YOU UP.
BY WHAT, TWO MINUTES? IT'S NO PROBLEM, MOM.
TELL THAT TO THE POOR SOULS ON THE HINDENBURG--
--THEY BURNED TO DEATH IN NINETY SECONDS.

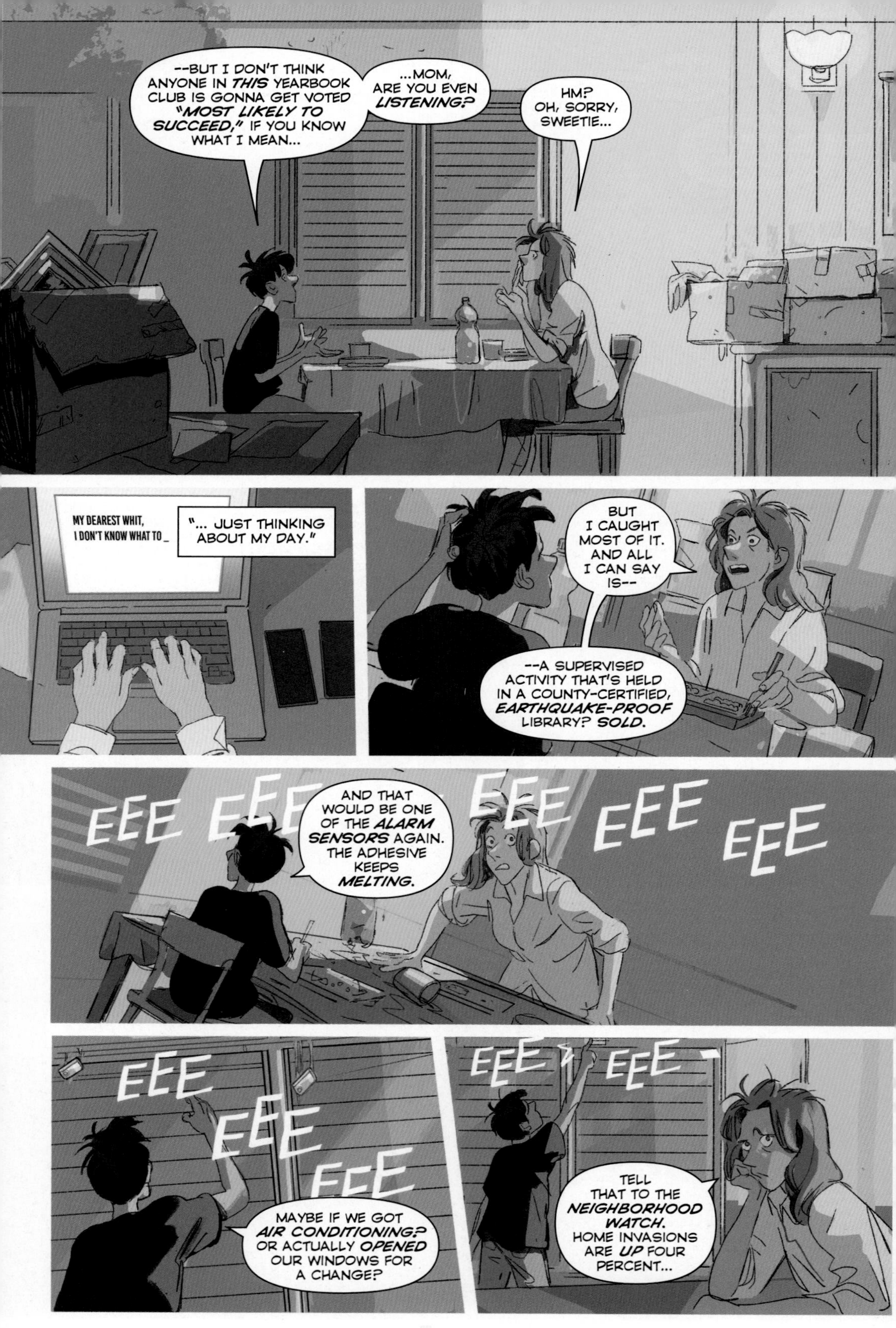
--BUT I DON'T THINK ANYONE IN THIS YEARBOOK CLUB IS GONNA GET VOTED "MOST LIKELY TO SUCCEED," IF YOU KNOW WHAT I MEAN...
...MOM, ARE YOU EVEN LISTENING?
HM? OH, SORRY, SWEETIE...
MY DEAREST WHIT, I DON'T KNOW WHAT TO _
"... JUST THINKING ABOUT MY DAY."
BUT I CAUGHT MOST OF IT. AND ALL I CAN SAY IS--
--A SUPERVISED ACTIVITY THAT'S HELD IN A COUNTY-CERTIFIED, EARTHQUAKE-PROOF LIBRARY? SOLD.
EEE EEE
AND THAT WOULD BE ONE OF THE ALARM SENSORS AGAIN. THE ADHESIVE KEEPS MELTING.
EEE EEE EEE
EEE EEE EEE
MAYBE IF WE GOT AIR CONDITIONING? OR ACTUALLY OPENED OUR WINDOWS FOR A CHANGE?
EEE EEE
TELL THAT TO THE NEIGHBORHOOD WATCH. HOME INVASIONS ARE UP FOUR PERCENT...

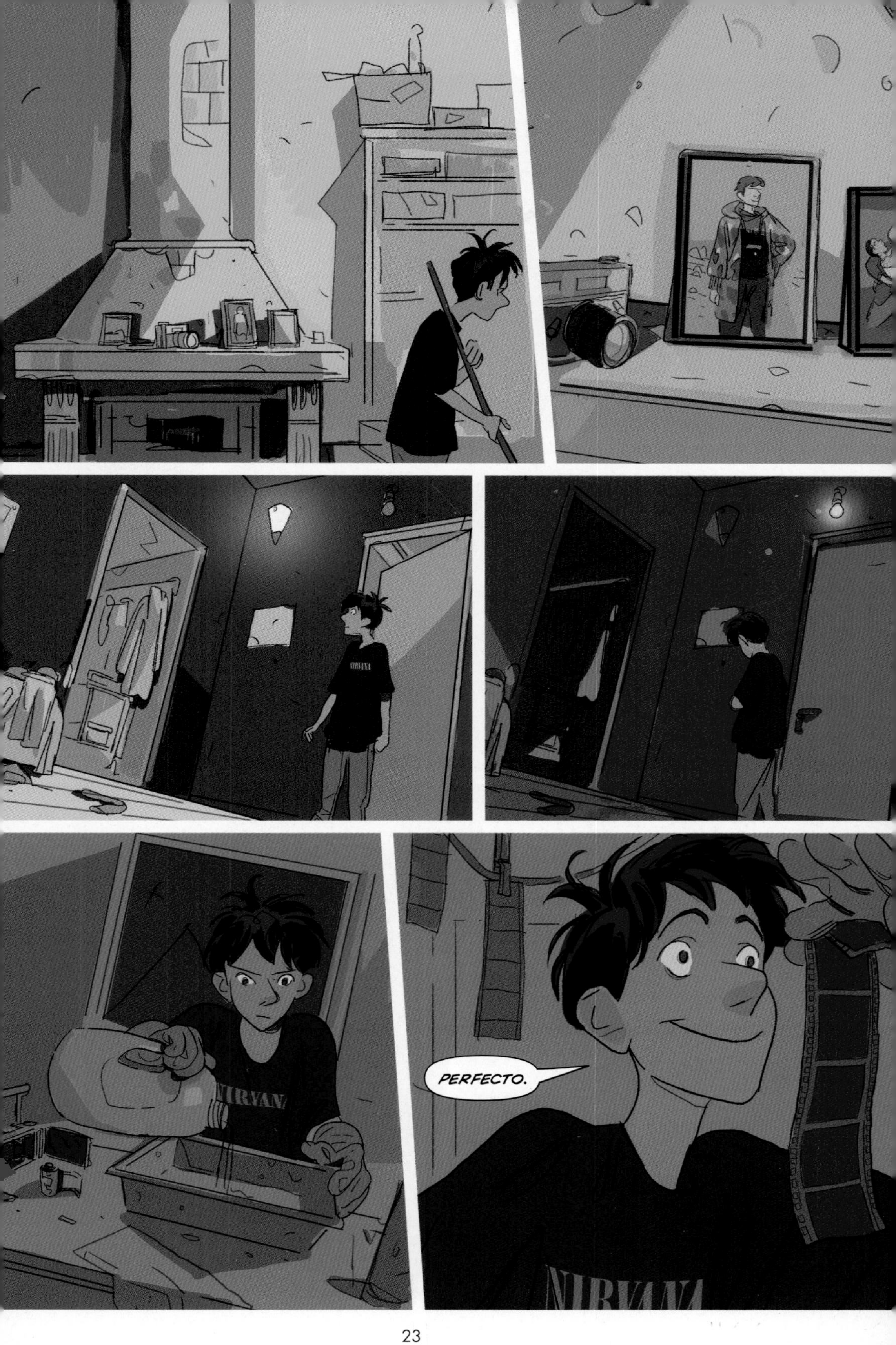
NIRVANA
NIRVANA
PERFECTO.
NIRVANA

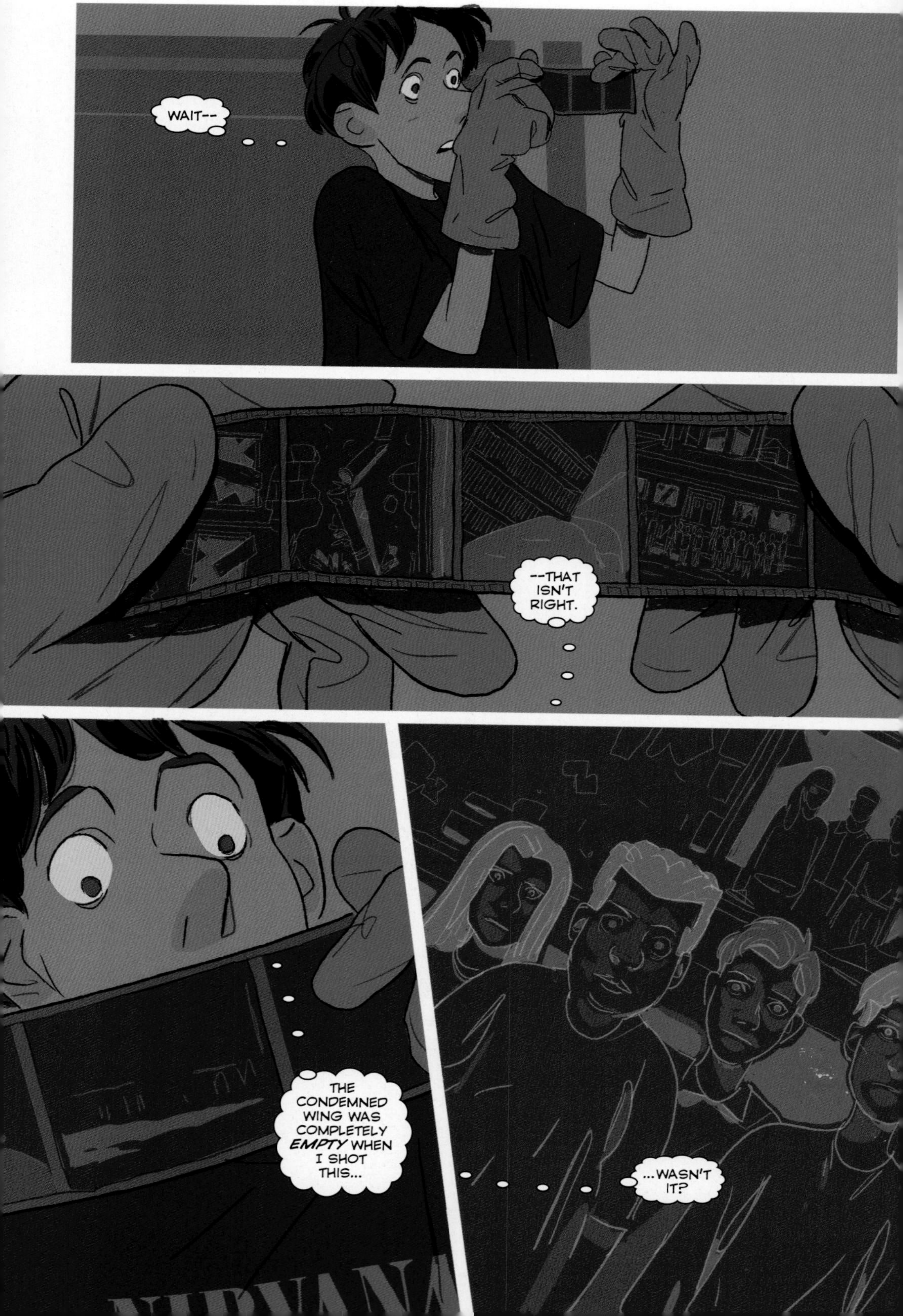
WAIT--
--THAT ISN'T RIGHT.
THE CONDEMNED WING WAS COMPLETELY *EMPTY* WHEN I SHOT THIS...
...WASN'T IT?
NIRVANA

IS **HOME SCHOOLING** AN OPTION?

WHIT, WEREN'T YOU JUST COMPLAINING ABOUT HOW **UNCOMFORTABLE** OUR APARTMENT IS?

NEPENTHE MIDDLE SCHOOL

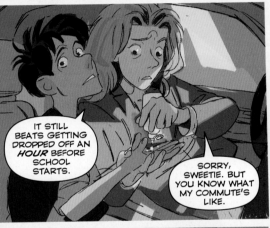

IT STILL BEATS GETTING DROPPED OFF AN **HOUR** BEFORE SCHOOL STARTS.

SORRY, SWEETIE. BUT YOU KNOW WHAT MY COMMUTE'S LIKE.

NOW HUG ME.

I...LOVE YOU, TOO, MOM.

WHIT, WHAT'S ON YOUR MIND? AND DON'T TELL ME "NOTHING."

I **KNOW** THAT FROWN. I SEE IT IN THE **MIRROR** EVERY DAY. JUST SO YOU KNOW...

"...WHATEVER IS WRONG..."

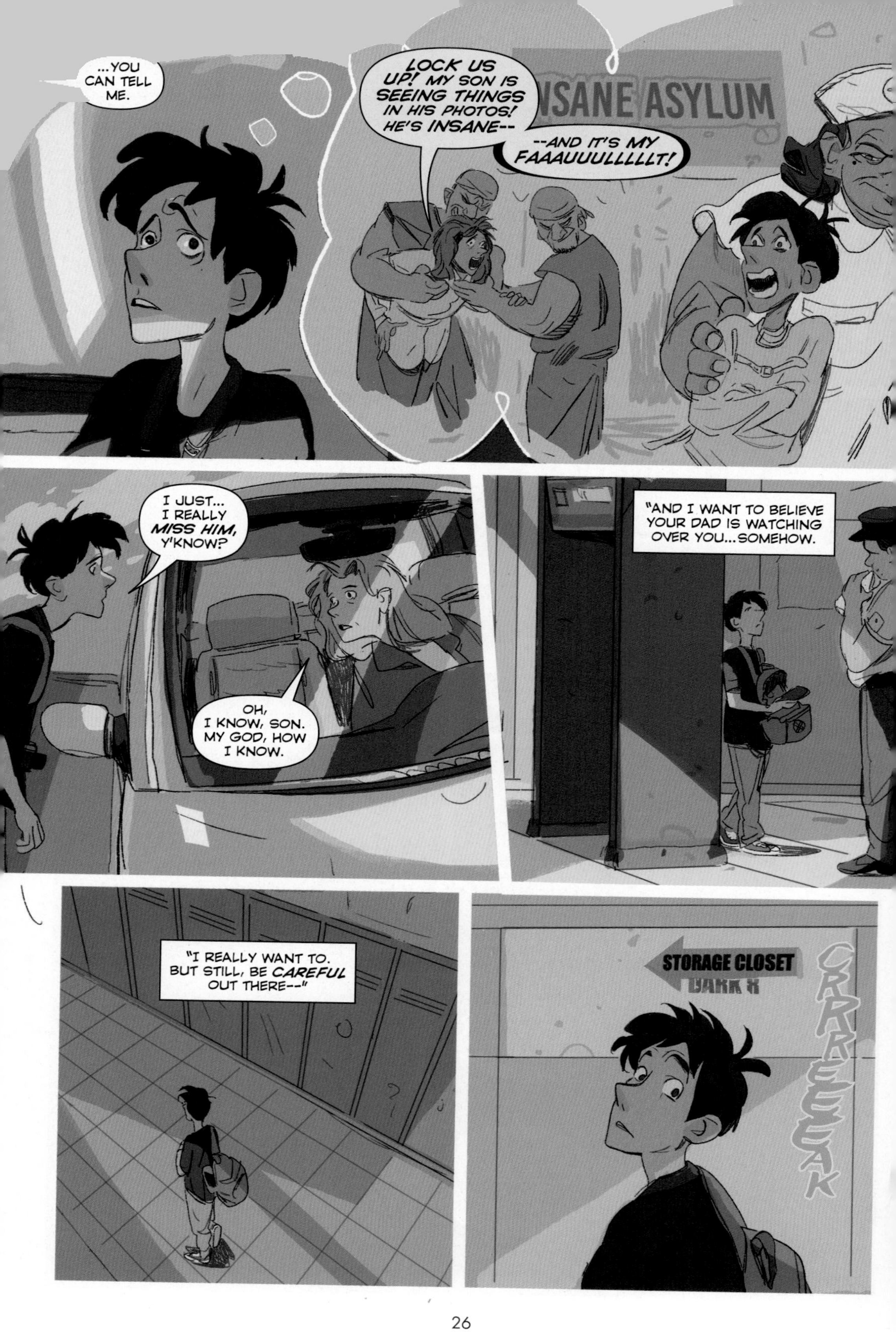
...YOU CAN TELL ME.
LOCK US UP! MY SON IS SEEING THINGS IN HIS PHOTOS! HE'S INSANE--
NSANE ASYLUM
--AND IT'S MY FAAAUUULLLLLLT!
I JUST... I REALLY MISS HIM, Y'KNOW?
OH, I KNOW, SON. MY GOD, HOW I KNOW.
"AND I WANT TO BELIEVE YOUR DAD IS WATCHING OVER YOU...SOMEHOW.
"I REALLY WANT TO. BUT STILL, BE CAREFUL OUT THERE--"
STORAGE CLOSET
CRRREEEAK

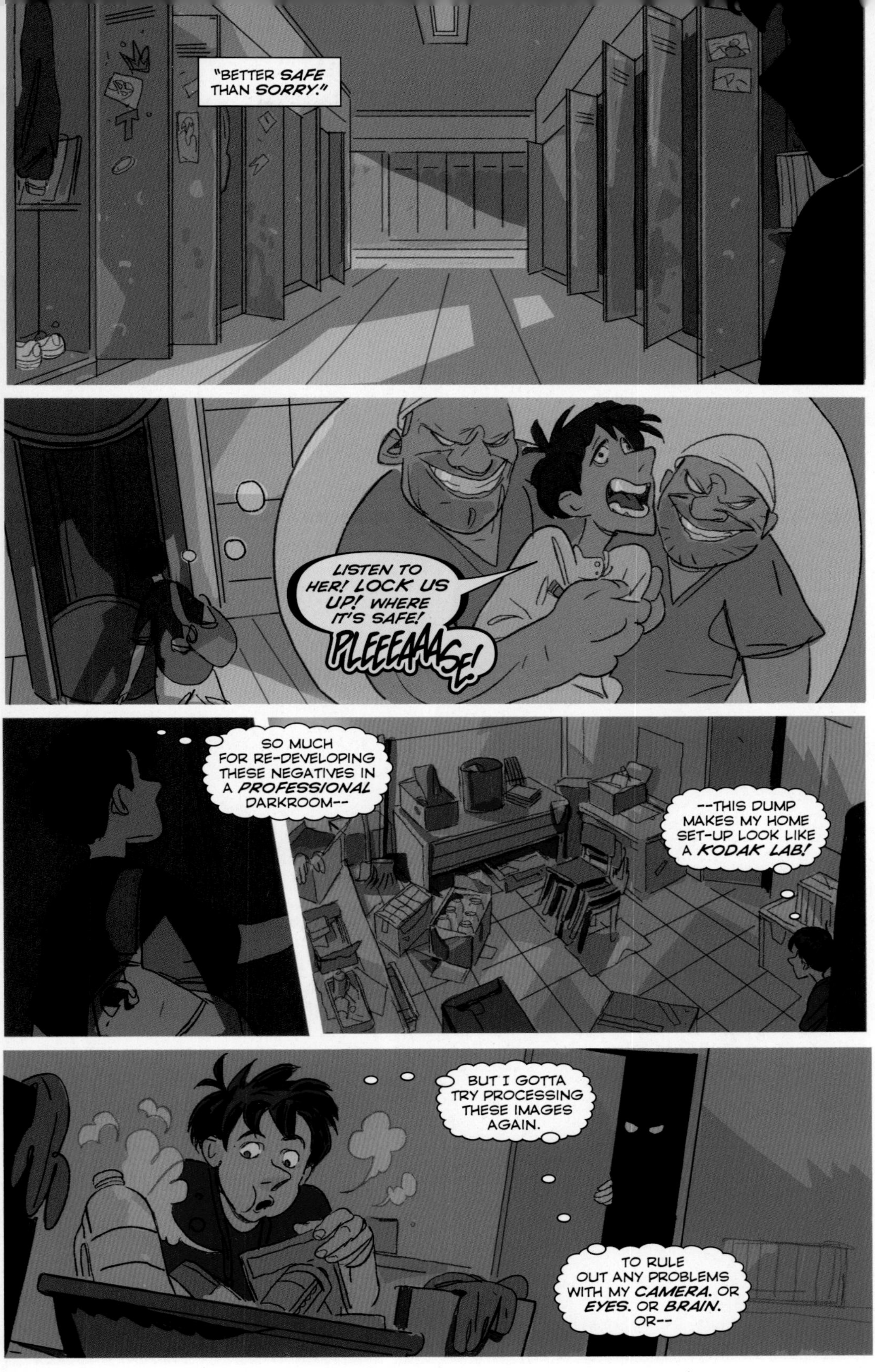
"BETTER SAFE THAN SORRY."
LISTEN TO HER! LOCK US UP! WHERE IT'S SAFE!
PLEEEAAAASE!
SO MUCH FOR RE-DEVELOPING THESE NEGATIVES IN A PROFESSIONAL DARKROOM--
--THIS DUMP MAKES MY HOME SET-UP LOOK LIKE A KODAK LAB!
BUT I GOTTA TRY PROCESSING THESE IMAGES AGAIN.
TO RULE OUT ANY PROBLEMS WITH MY CAMERA. OR EYES. OR BRAIN. OR--

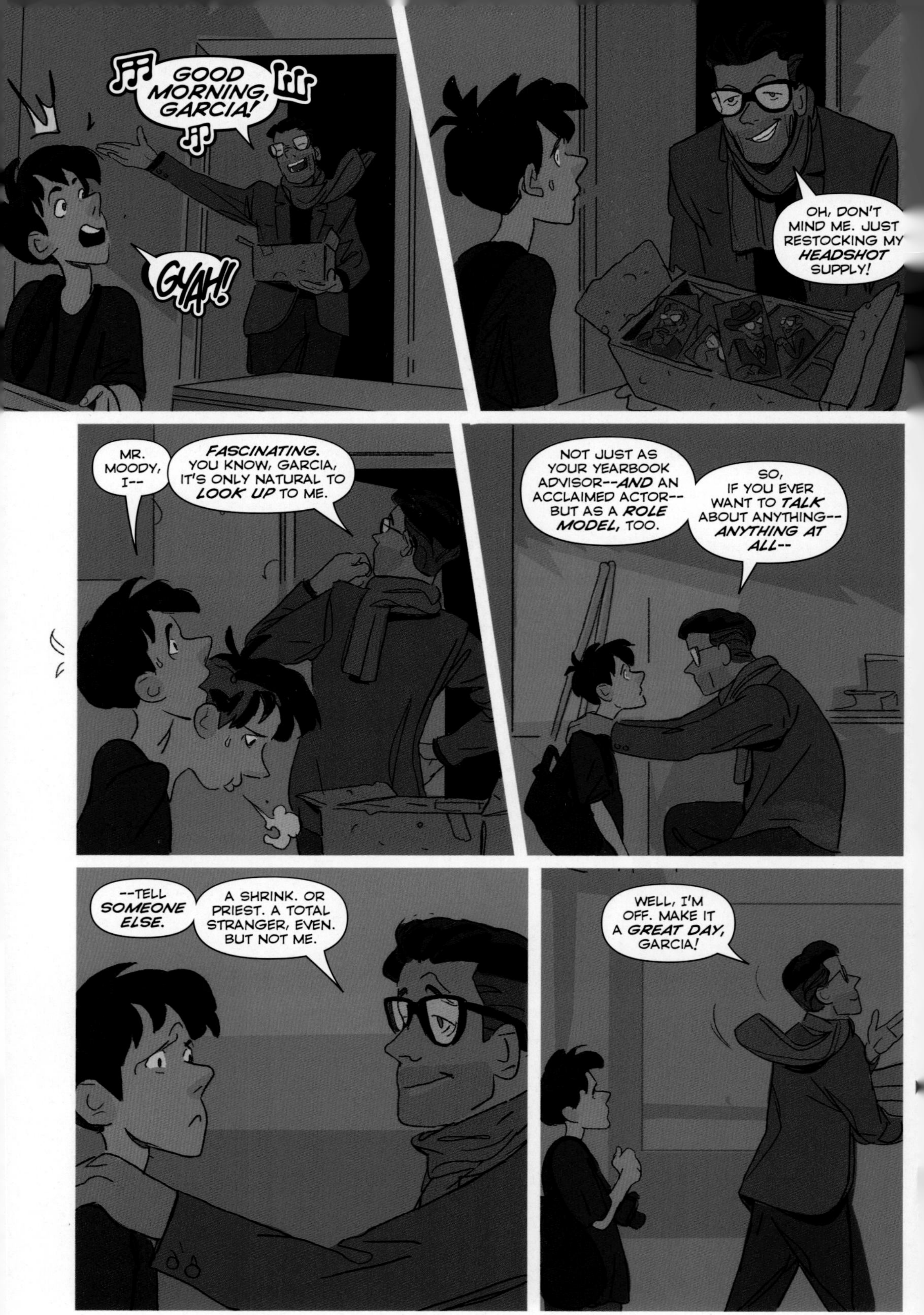
GOOD MORNING, GARCIA!
GYAH!
OH, DON'T MIND ME. JUST RESTOCKING MY *HEADSHOT* SUPPLY!
MR. MOODY, I--
FASCINATING. YOU KNOW, GARCIA, IT'S ONLY NATURAL TO *LOOK UP* TO ME.
NOT JUST AS YOUR YEARBOOK ADVISOR--*AND* AN ACCLAIMED ACTOR--BUT AS A *ROLE MODEL*, TOO.
SO, IF YOU EVER WANT TO *TALK* ABOUT ANYTHING--*ANYTHING AT ALL*--
--TELL *SOMEONE ELSE.*
A SHRINK. OR PRIEST. A TOTAL STRANGER, EVEN. BUT NOT ME.
WELL, I'M OFF. MAKE IT A *GREAT DAY,* GARCIA!

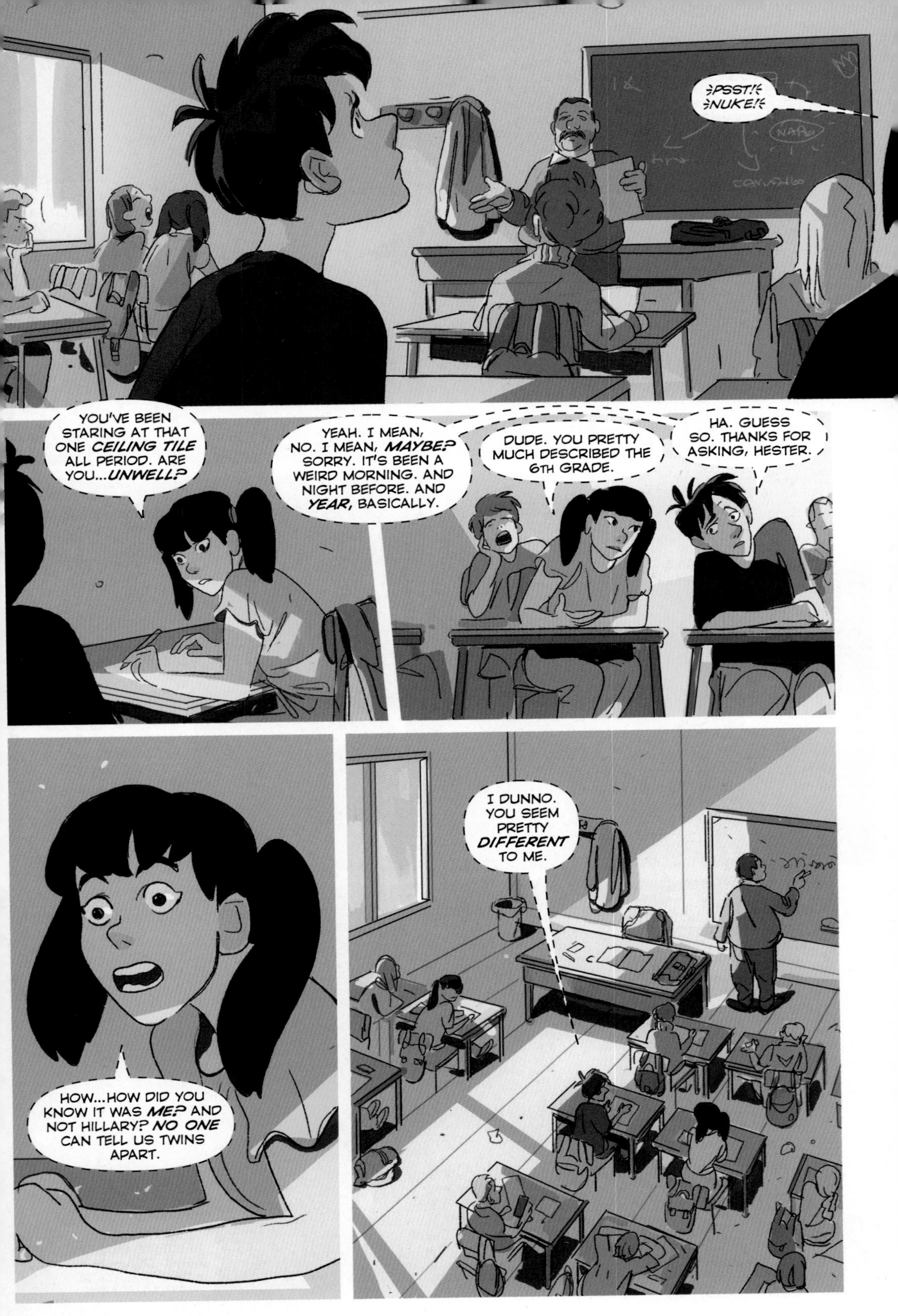

PSST! NUKE!
YOU'VE BEEN STARING AT THAT ONE CEILING TILE ALL PERIOD. ARE YOU...UNWELL?
YEAH. I MEAN, NO. I MEAN, MAYBE? SORRY. IT'S BEEN A WEIRD MORNING. AND NIGHT BEFORE. AND YEAR, BASICALLY.
DUDE. YOU PRETTY MUCH DESCRIBED THE 6TH GRADE.
HA. GUESS SO. THANKS FOR ASKING, HESTER.
HOW...HOW DID YOU KNOW IT WAS ME? AND NOT HILLARY? NO ONE CAN TELL US TWINS APART.
I DUNNO. YOU SEEM PRETTY DIFFERENT TO ME.

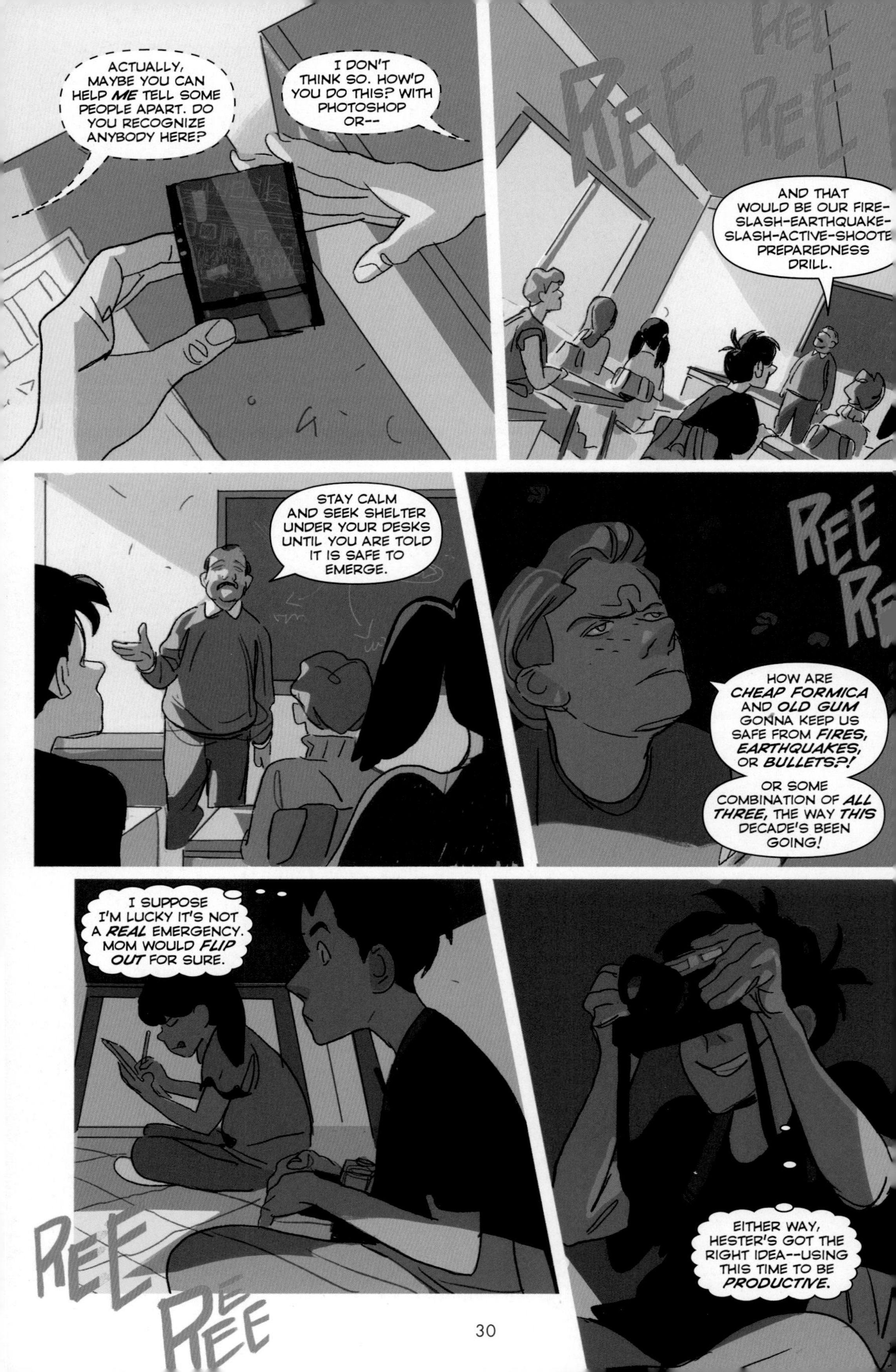

ACTUALLY, MAYBE YOU CAN HELP *ME* TELL SOME PEOPLE APART. DO YOU RECOGNIZE ANYBODY HERE?
I DON'T THINK SO. HOW'D YOU DO THIS? WITH PHOTOSHOP OR--
REE REE
AND THAT WOULD BE OUR FIRE-SLASH-EARTHQUAKE-SLASH-ACTIVE-SHOOTE PREPAREDNESS DRILL.
STAY CALM AND SEEK SHELTER UNDER YOUR DESKS UNTIL YOU ARE TOLD IT IS SAFE TO EMERGE.
REE
HOW ARE ***CHEAP FORMICA*** AND ***OLD GUM*** GONNA KEEP US SAFE FROM ***FIRES, EARTHQUAKES,*** OR ***BULLETS?!***
OR SOME COMBINATION OF ***ALL THREE,*** THE WAY ***THIS*** DECADE'S BEEN GOING!
I SUPPOSE I'M LUCKY IT'S NOT A ***REAL*** EMERGENCY. MOM WOULD ***FLIP OUT*** FOR SURE.
EITHER WAY, HESTER'S GOT THE RIGHT IDEA--USING THIS TIME TO BE ***PRODUCTIVE***.
REE REE REE

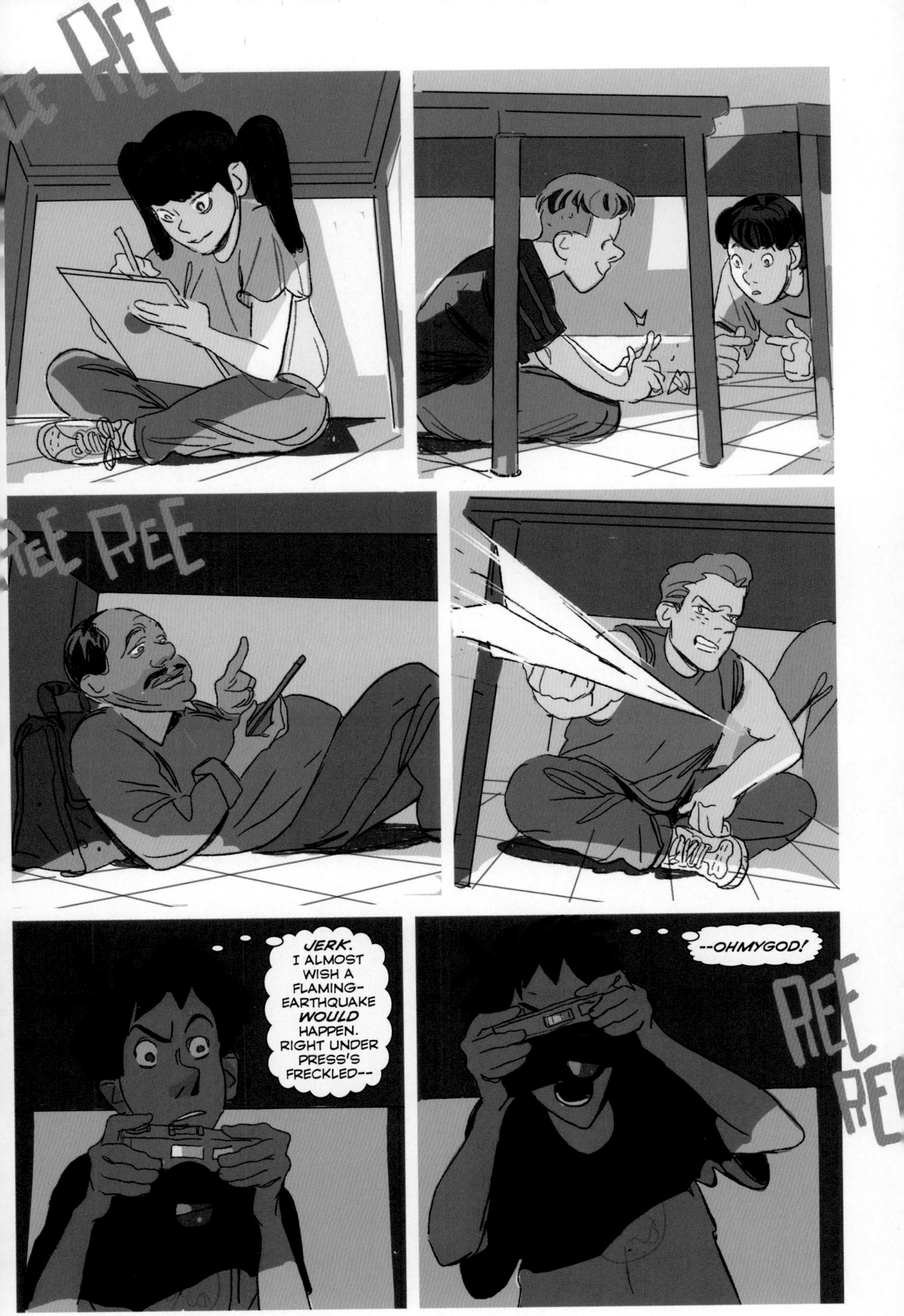
REE REE
REE REE
JERK. I ALMOST WISH A FLAMING-EARTHQUAKE WOULD HAPPEN. RIGHT UNDER PRESS'S FRECKLED--
--OHMYGOD!
REE
REE

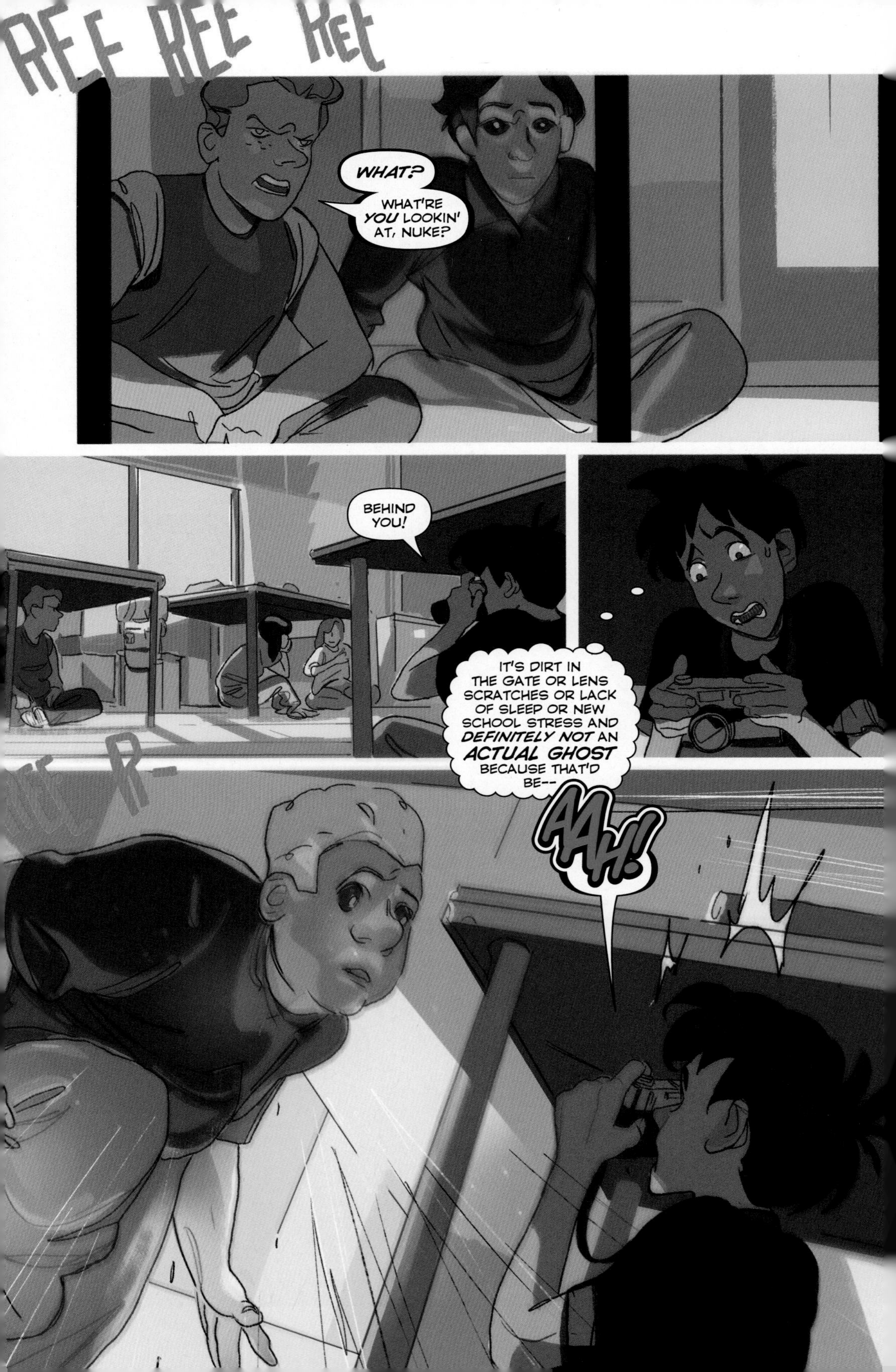
WHAT?
WHAT'RE YOU LOOKIN' AT, NUKE?
BEHIND YOU!
IT'S DIRT IN THE GATE OR LENS SCRATCHES OR LACK OF SLEEP OR NEW SCHOOL STRESS AND DEFINITELY NOT AN ACTUAL GHOST BECAUSE THAT'D BE--
AAH!

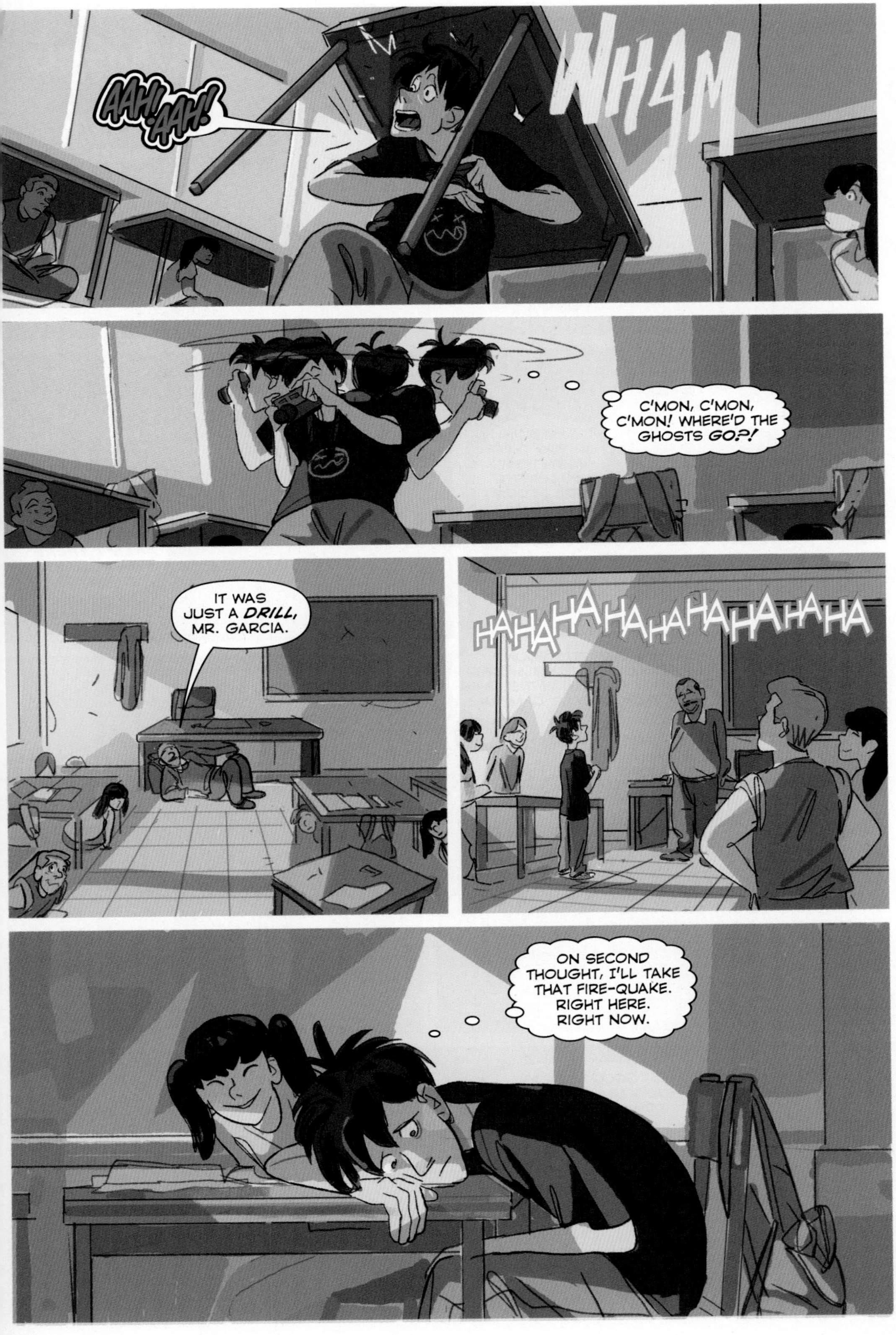
AAH! AAH!
WHAM
C'MON, C'MON, C'MON! WHERE'D THE GHOSTS GO?!
IT WAS JUST A DRILL, MR. GARCIA.
HAHAHAHAHAHAHAHAHAHAHAHAHA
ON SECOND THOUGHT, I'LL TAKE THAT FIRE-QUAKE. RIGHT HERE. RIGHT NOW.

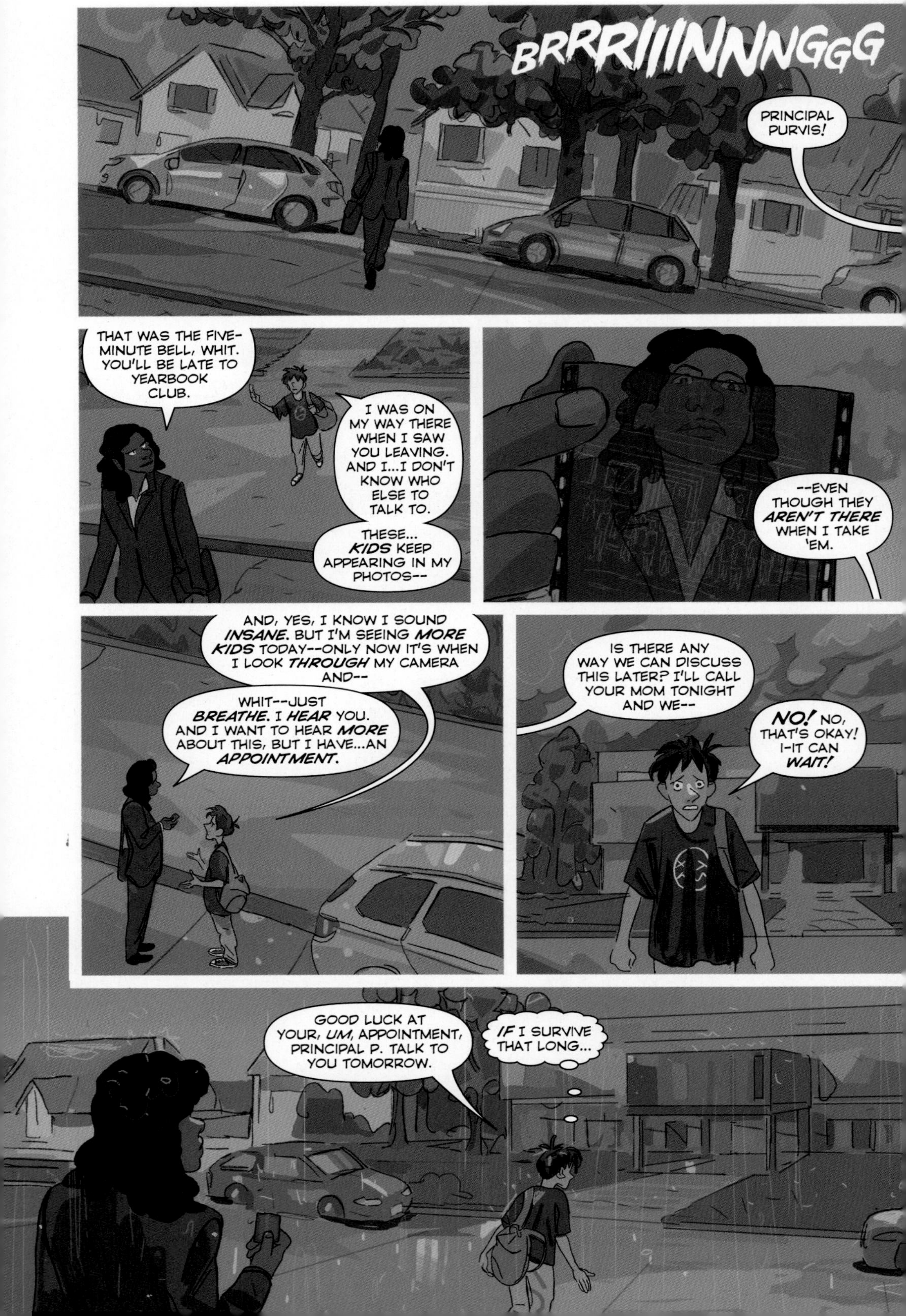
BRRRIIIINNNNGGG
PRINCIPAL PURVIS!
THAT WAS THE FIVE-MINUTE BELL, WHIT. YOU'LL BE LATE TO YEARBOOK CLUB.
I WAS ON MY WAY THERE WHEN I SAW YOU LEAVING. AND I...I DON'T KNOW WHO ELSE TO TALK TO.
THESE... KIDS KEEP APPEARING IN MY PHOTOS--
--EVEN THOUGH THEY AREN'T THERE WHEN I TAKE 'EM.
AND, YES, I KNOW I SOUND INSANE. BUT I'M SEEING MORE KIDS TODAY--ONLY NOW IT'S WHEN I LOOK THROUGH MY CAMERA AND--
WHIT--JUST BREATHE. I HEAR YOU. AND I WANT TO HEAR MORE ABOUT THIS, BUT I HAVE...AN APPOINTMENT.
IS THERE ANY WAY WE CAN DISCUSS THIS LATER? I'LL CALL YOUR MOM TONIGHT AND WE--
NO! NO, THAT'S OKAY! I-IT CAN WAIT!
GOOD LUCK AT YOUR, UM, APPOINTMENT, PRINCIPAL P. TALK TO YOU TOMORROW.
IF I SURVIVE THAT LONG...

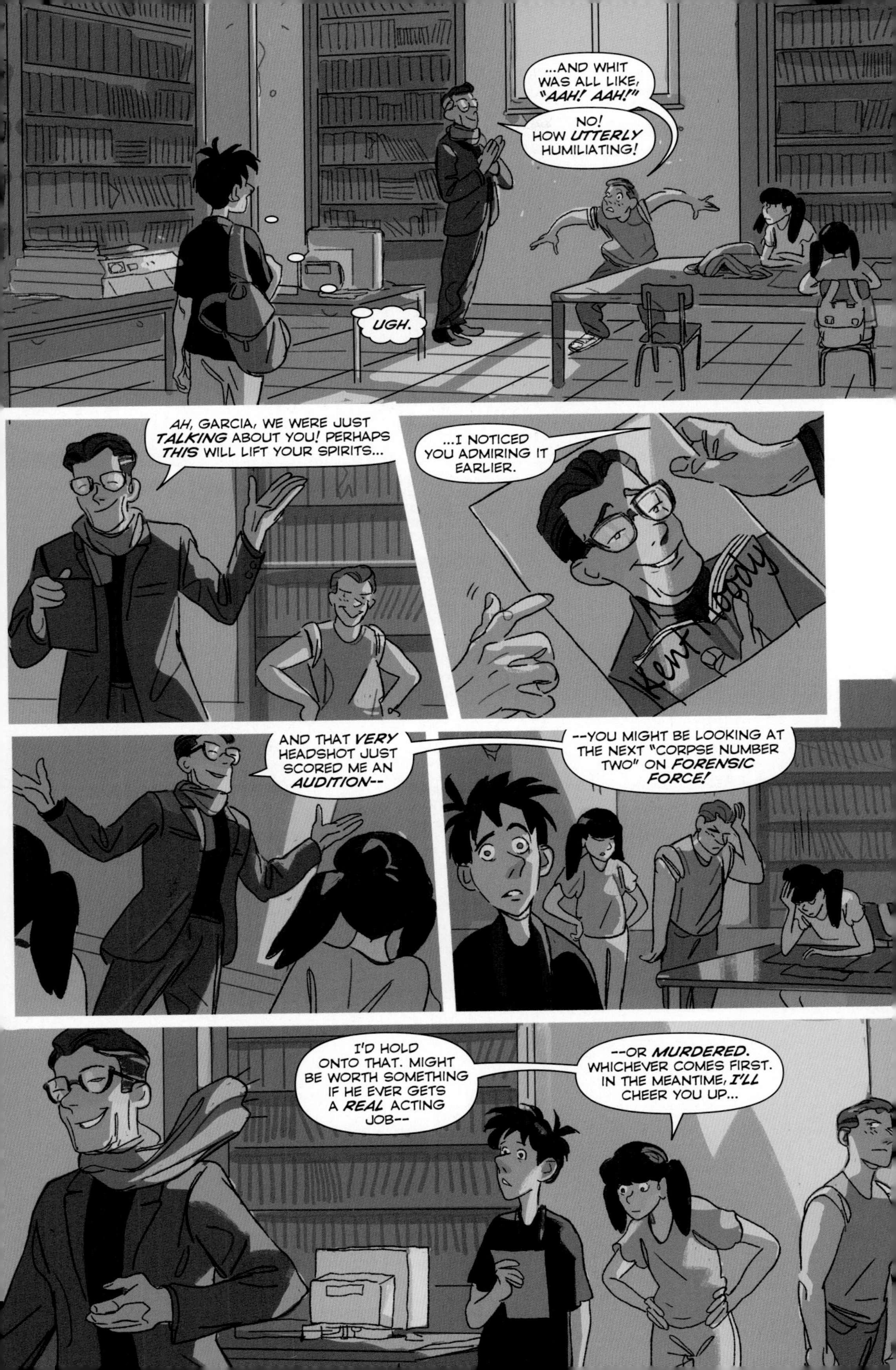
...AND WHIT WAS ALL LIKE, "AAH! AAH!"
NO! HOW UTTERLY HUMILIATING!
UGH.
AH, GARCIA, WE WERE JUST TALKING ABOUT YOU! PERHAPS THIS WILL LIFT YOUR SPIRITS...
...I NOTICED YOU ADMIRING IT EARLIER.
Kent Moody
AND THAT VERY HEADSHOT JUST SCORED ME AN AUDITION--
--YOU MIGHT BE LOOKING AT THE NEXT "CORPSE NUMBER TWO" ON FORENSIC FORCE!
I'D HOLD ONTO THAT. MIGHT BE WORTH SOMETHING IF HE EVER GETS A REAL ACTING JOB--
--OR MURDERED. WHICHEVER COMES FIRST. IN THE MEANTIME, I'LL CHEER YOU UP...

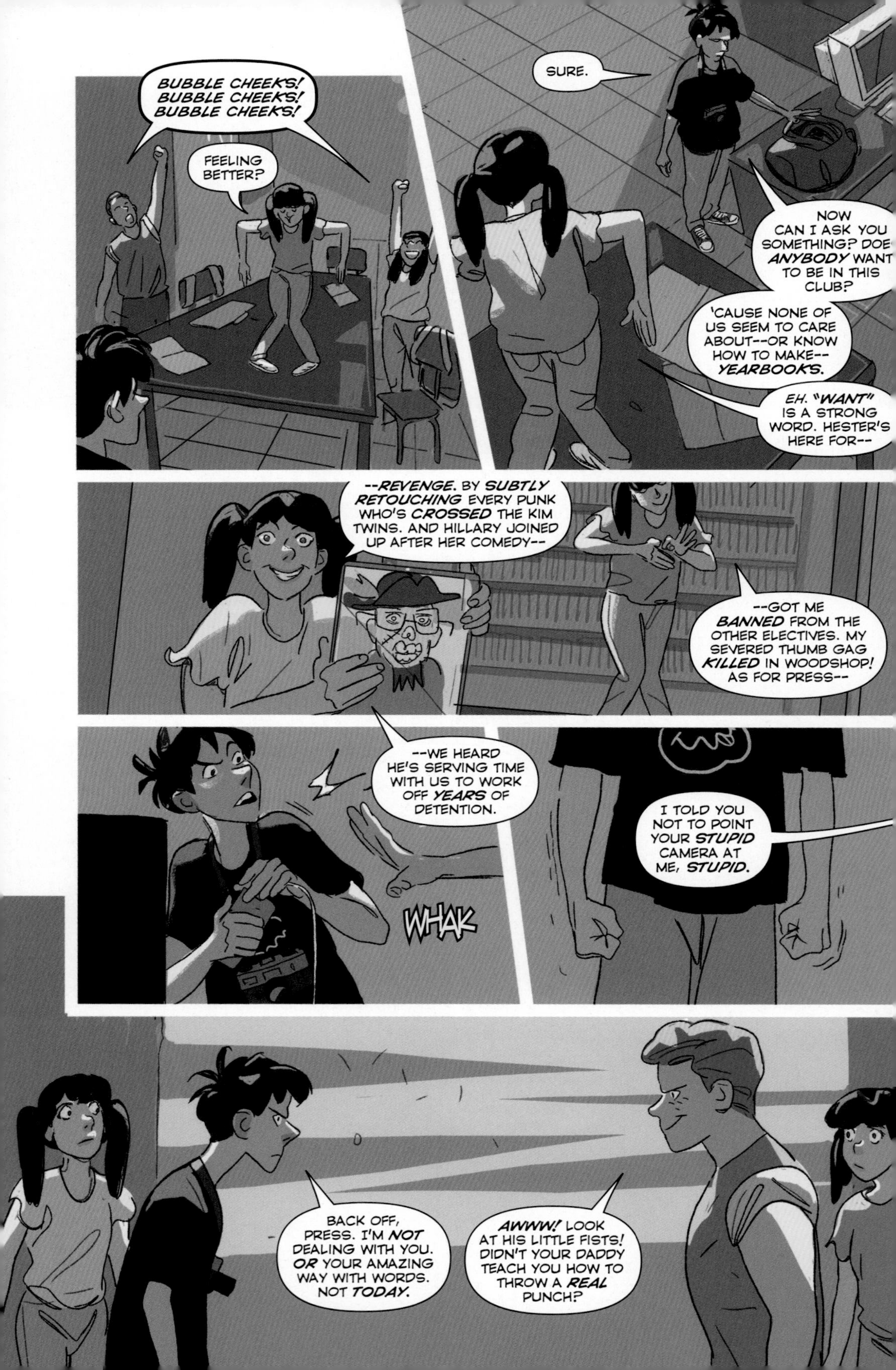

BUBBLE CHEEKS! BUBBLE CHEEKS! BUBBLE CHEEKS!
FEELING BETTER?
SURE.
NOW CAN I ASK YOU SOMETHING? DOE ANYBODY WANT TO BE IN THIS CLUB?
'CAUSE NONE OF US SEEM TO CARE ABOUT--OR KNOW HOW TO MAKE-- YEARBOOKS.
EH. "WANT" IS A STRONG WORD. HESTER'S HERE FOR--
--REVENGE. BY SUBTLY RETOUCHING EVERY PUNK WHO'S CROSSED THE KIM TWINS. AND HILLARY JOINED UP AFTER HER COMEDY--
--GOT ME BANNED FROM THE OTHER ELECTIVES. MY SEVERED THUMB GAG KILLED IN WOODSHOP! AS FOR PRESS--
--WE HEARD HE'S SERVING TIME WITH US TO WORK OFF YEARS OF DETENTION.
WHAK
I TOLD YOU NOT TO POINT YOUR STUPID CAMERA AT ME, STUPID.
BACK OFF, PRESS. I'M NOT DEALING WITH YOU. OR YOUR AMAZING WAY WITH WORDS. NOT TODAY.
AWWW! LOOK AT HIS LITTLE FISTS! DIDN'T YOUR DADDY TEACH YOU HOW TO THROW A REAL PUNCH?

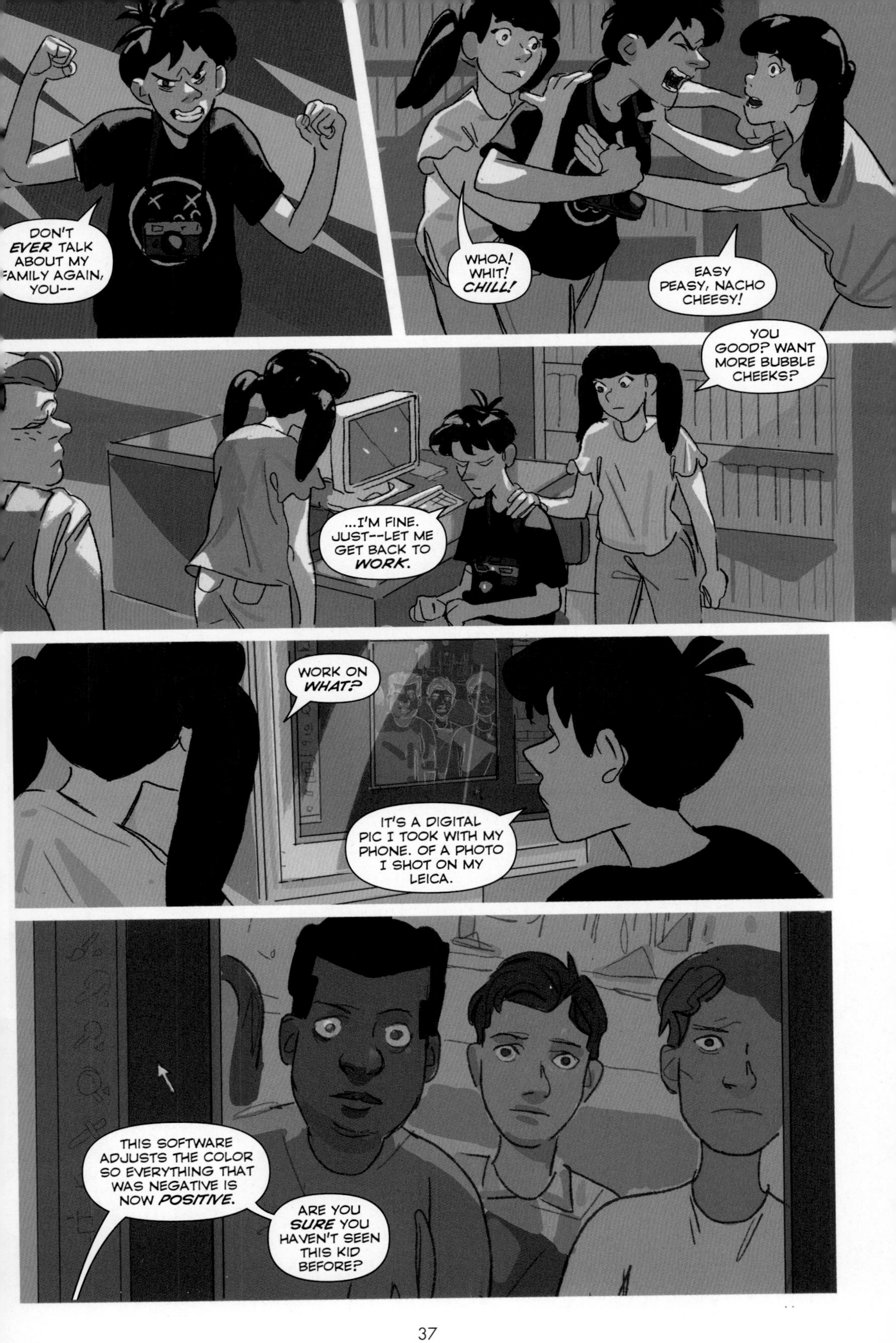
DON'T *EVER* TALK ABOUT MY FAMILY AGAIN, YOU--
WHOA! WHIT! *CHILL!*
EASY PEASY, NACHO CHEESY!
YOU GOOD? WANT MORE BUBBLE CHEEKS?
...I'M FINE. JUST--LET ME GET BACK TO *WORK*.
WORK ON *WHAT?*
IT'S A DIGITAL PIC I TOOK WITH MY PHONE. OF A PHOTO I SHOT ON MY LEICA.
THIS SOFTWARE ADJUSTS THE COLOR SO EVERYTHING THAT WAS NEGATIVE IS NOW *POSITIVE*.
ARE YOU *SURE* YOU HAVEN'T SEEN THIS KID BEFORE?

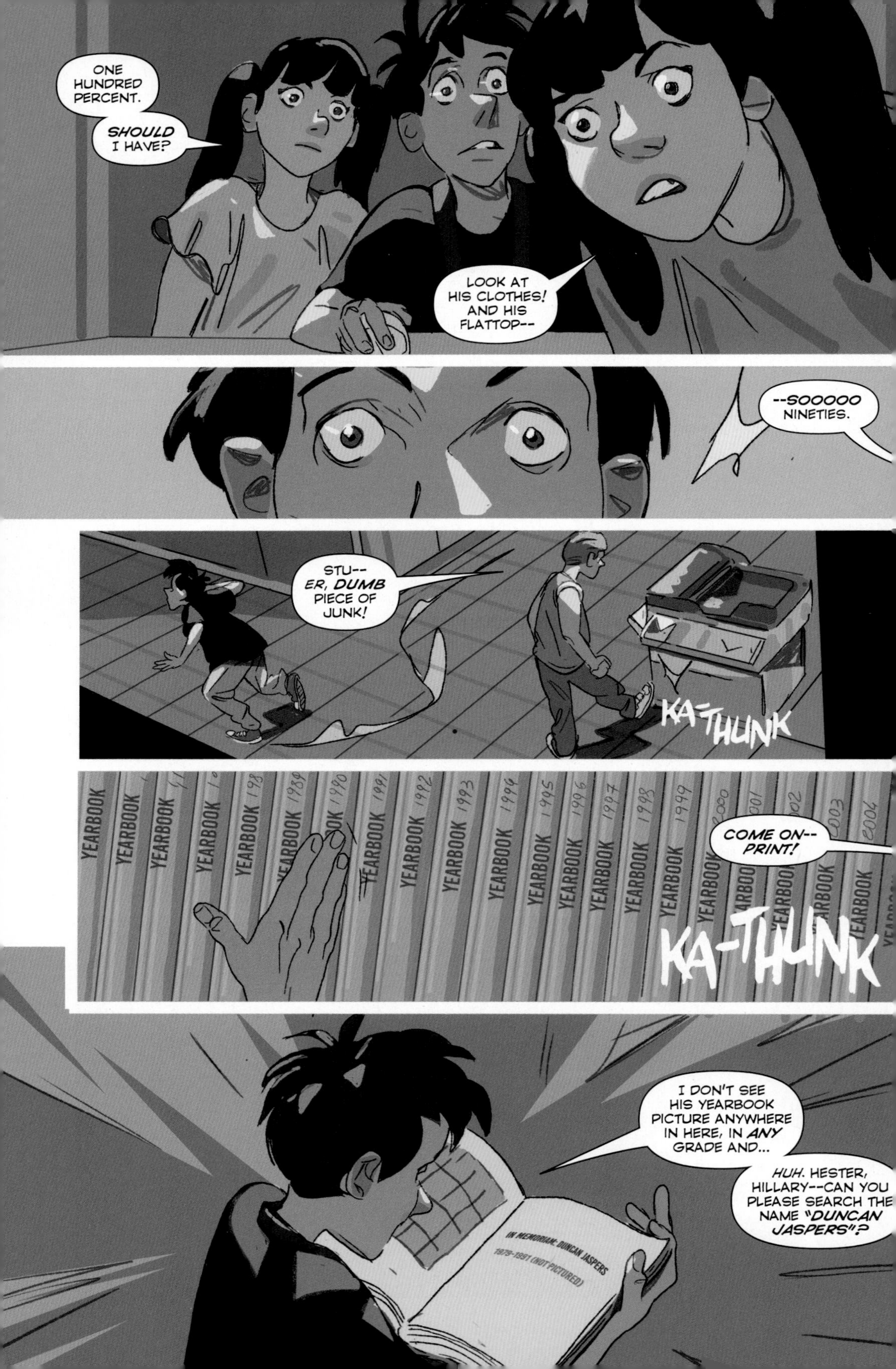
ONE HUNDRED PERCENT.
SHOULD I HAVE?
LOOK AT HIS CLOTHES! AND HIS FLATTOP--
--SOOOOO NINETIES.
STU-- *ER, DUMB* PIECE OF JUNK!
KA-THUNK
COME ON-- PRINT!
KA-THUNK
I DON'T SEE HIS YEARBOOK PICTURE ANYWHERE IN HERE, IN *ANY* GRADE AND...
HUH. HESTER, HILLARY--CAN YOU PLEASE SEARCH THE NAME *"DUNCAN JASPERS"?*
IN MEMORIAM: DUNCAN JASPERS
1979-1991 (NOT PICTURED)

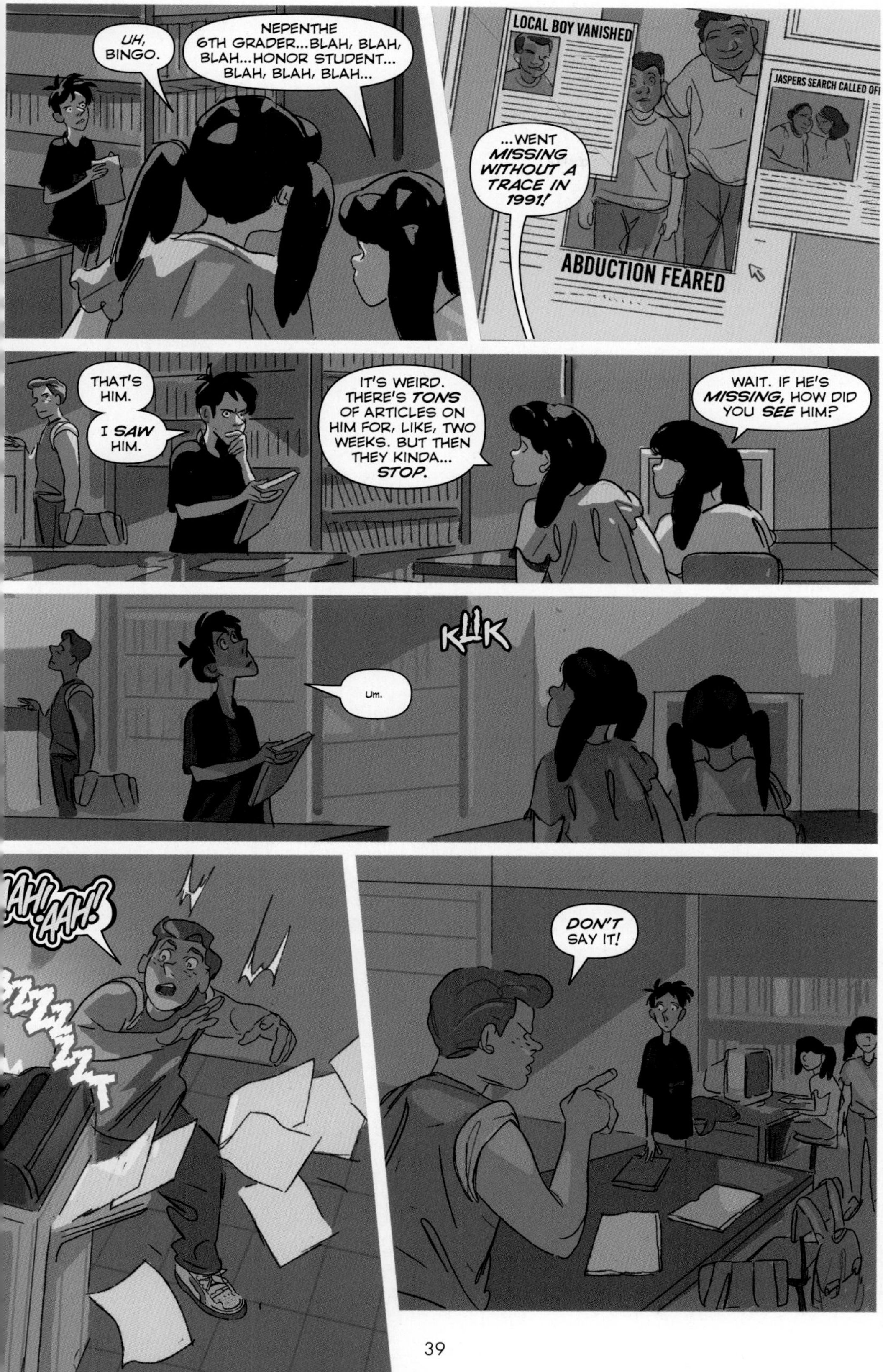
UH, BINGO.
NEPENTHE 6TH GRADER...BLAH, BLAH, BLAH...HONOR STUDENT... BLAH, BLAH, BLAH...
LOCAL BOY VANISHED
JASPERS SEARCH CALLED OFF
...WENT MISSING WITHOUT A TRACE IN 1991!
ABDUCTION FEARED
THAT'S HIM.
I SAW HIM.
IT'S WEIRD. THERE'S TONS OF ARTICLES ON HIM FOR, LIKE, TWO WEEKS. BUT THEN THEY KINDA... STOP.
WAIT. IF HE'S MISSING, HOW DID YOU SEE HIM?
KLIK
Um.
AAH! AAH!
DON'T SAY IT!

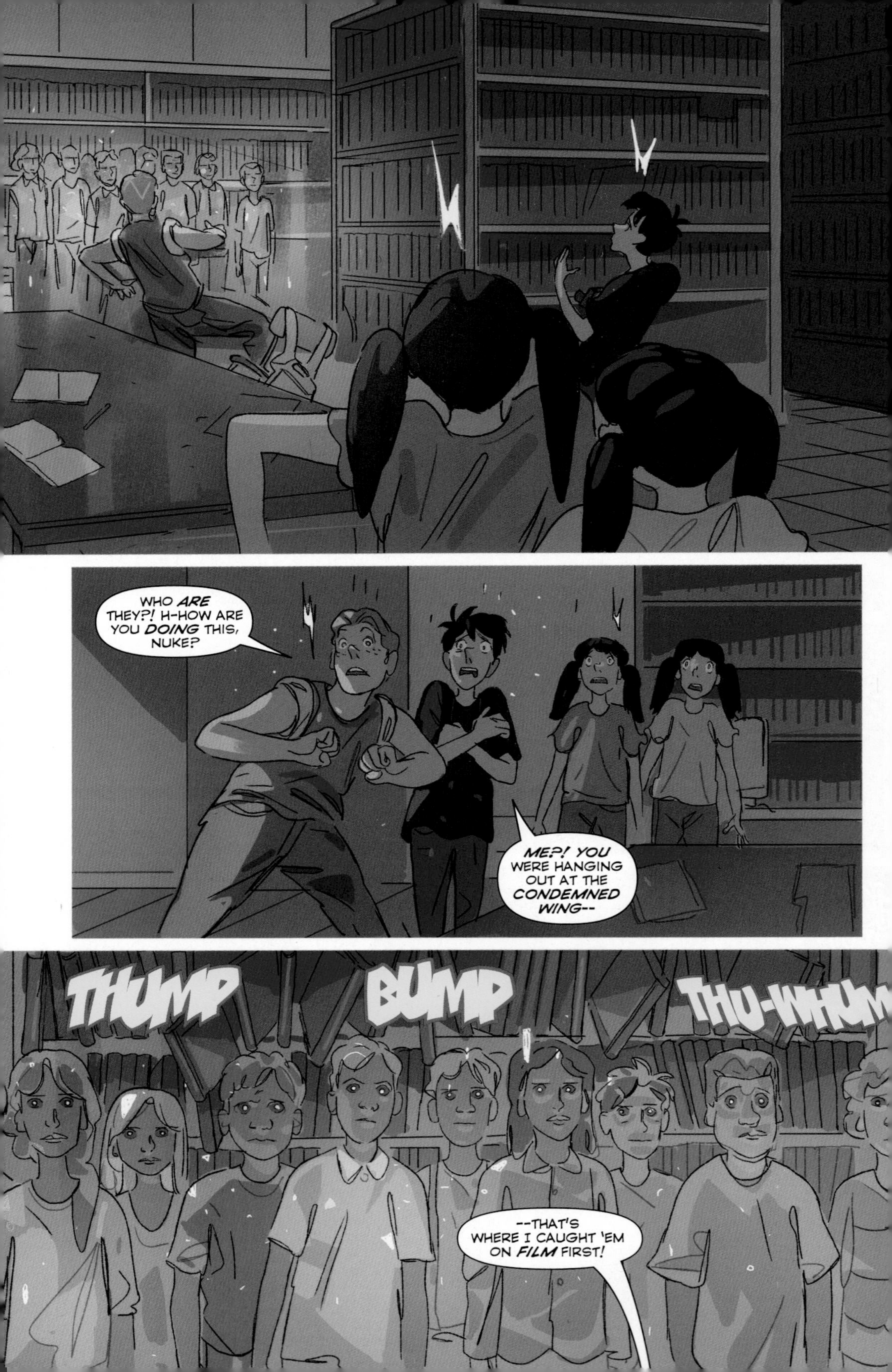
WHO ARE THEY?! H-HOW ARE YOU DOING THIS, NUKE?
ME?! YOU WERE HANGING OUT AT THE CONDEMNED WING--
THUMP
BUMP
THU-WHUM
--THAT'S WHERE I CAUGHT 'EM ON FILM FIRST!

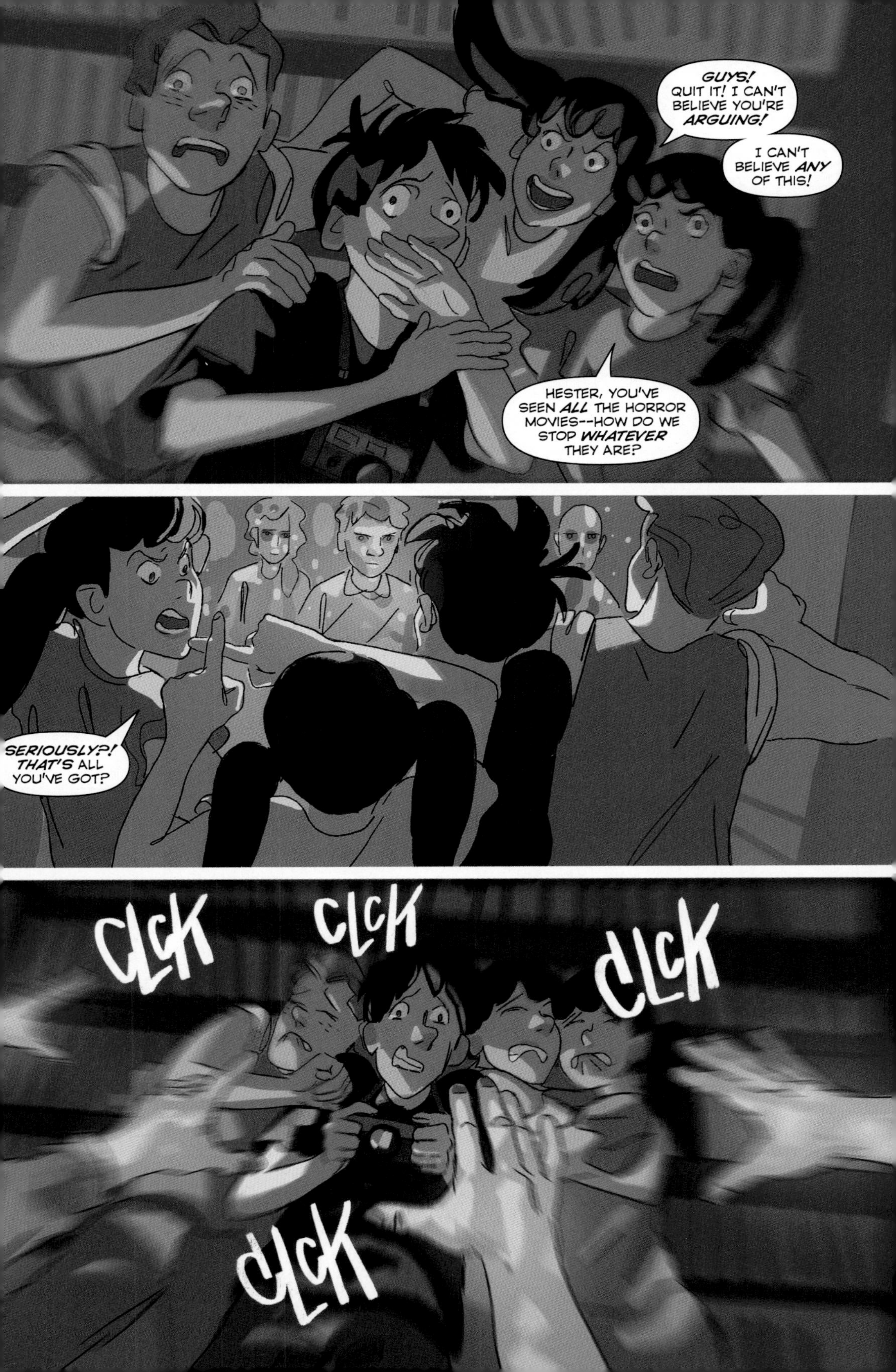
GUYS! QUIT IT! I CAN'T BELIEVE YOU'RE ARGUING!
I CAN'T BELIEVE ANY OF THIS!
HESTER, YOU'VE SEEN ALL THE HORROR MOVIES--HOW DO WE STOP WHATEVER THEY ARE?
SERIOUSLY?! THAT'S ALL YOU'VE GOT?
CLCK
CLCK
CLCK
CLCK

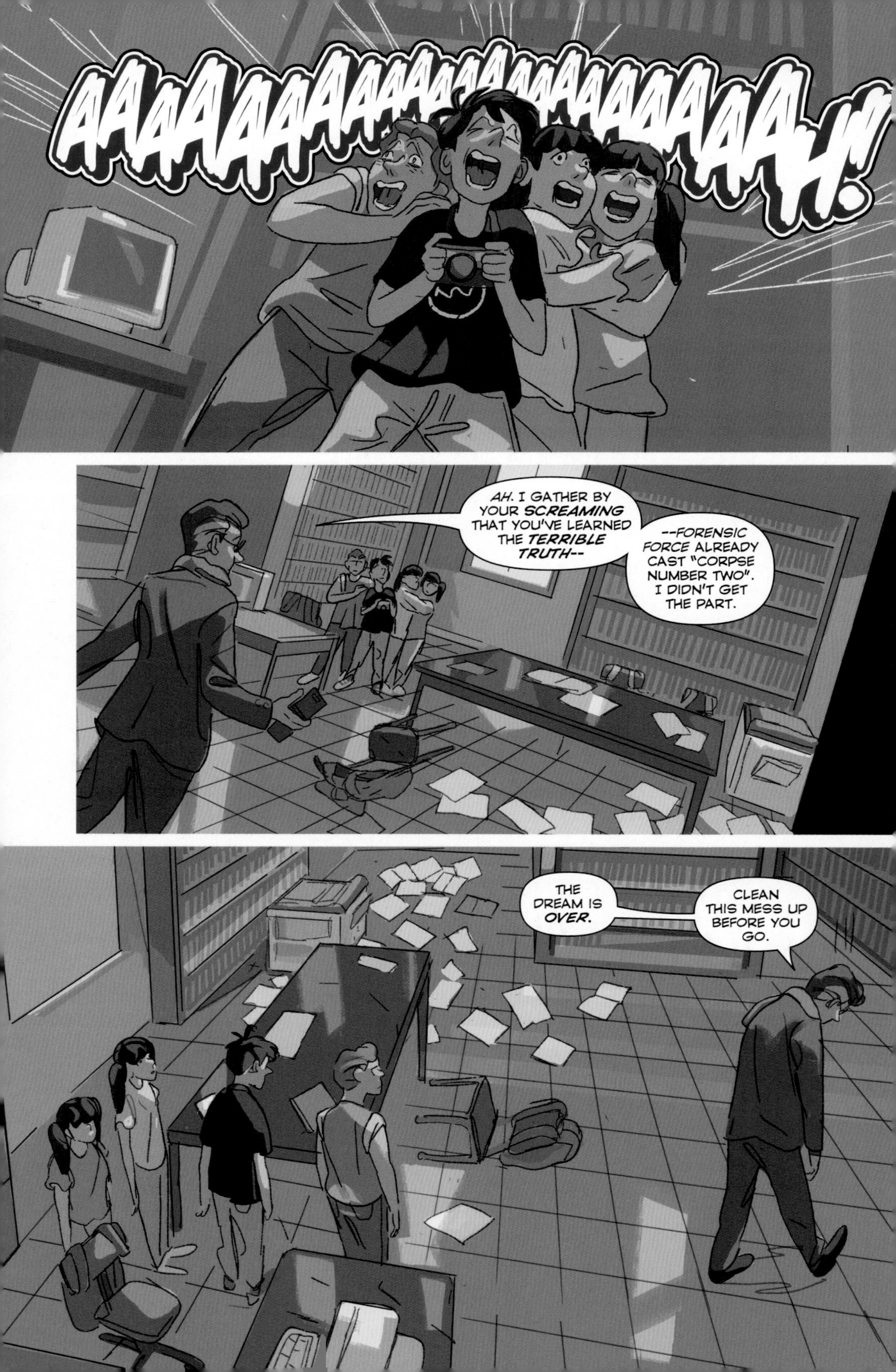
AAAAAAAAAAAAAAAAAAAAAAAH!
AH. I GATHER BY YOUR SCREAMING THAT YOU'VE LEARNED THE TERRIBLE TRUTH--
--FORENSIC FORCE ALREADY CAST "CORPSE NUMBER TWO". I DIDN'T GET THE PART.
THE DREAM IS OVER.
CLEAN THIS MESS UP BEFORE YOU GO.

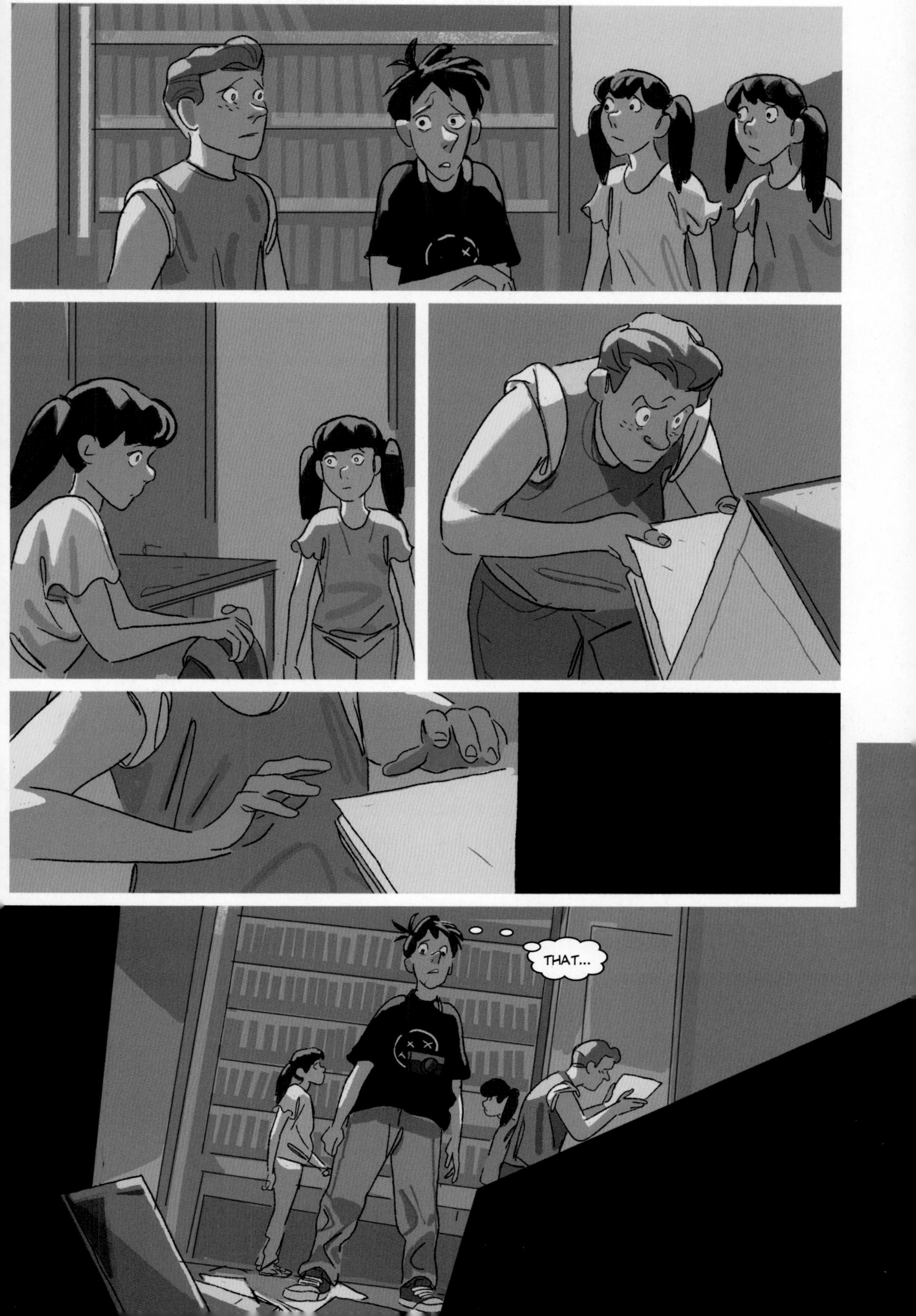
THAT...

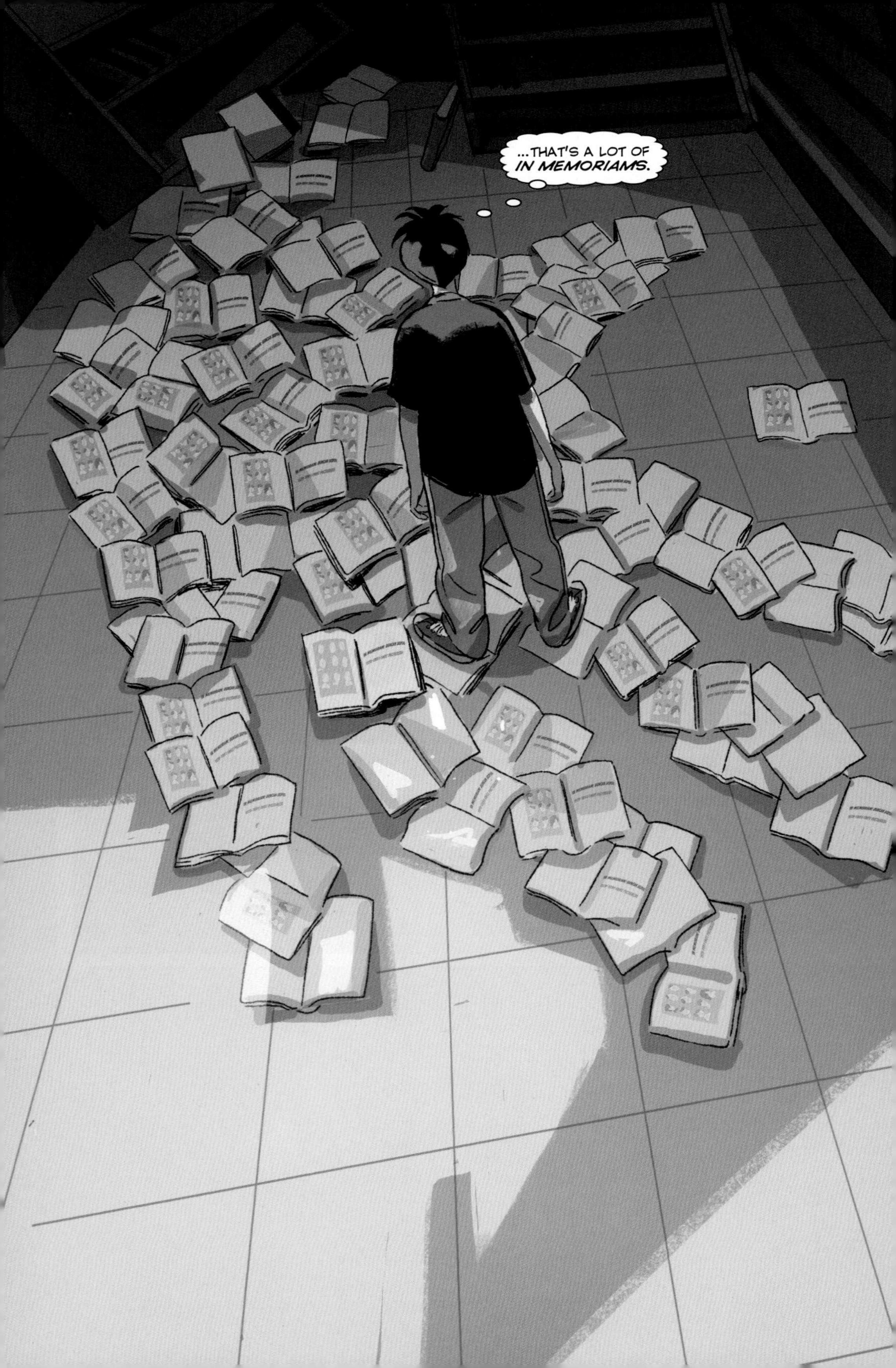
...THAT'S A LOT OF
IN MEMORIAMS.

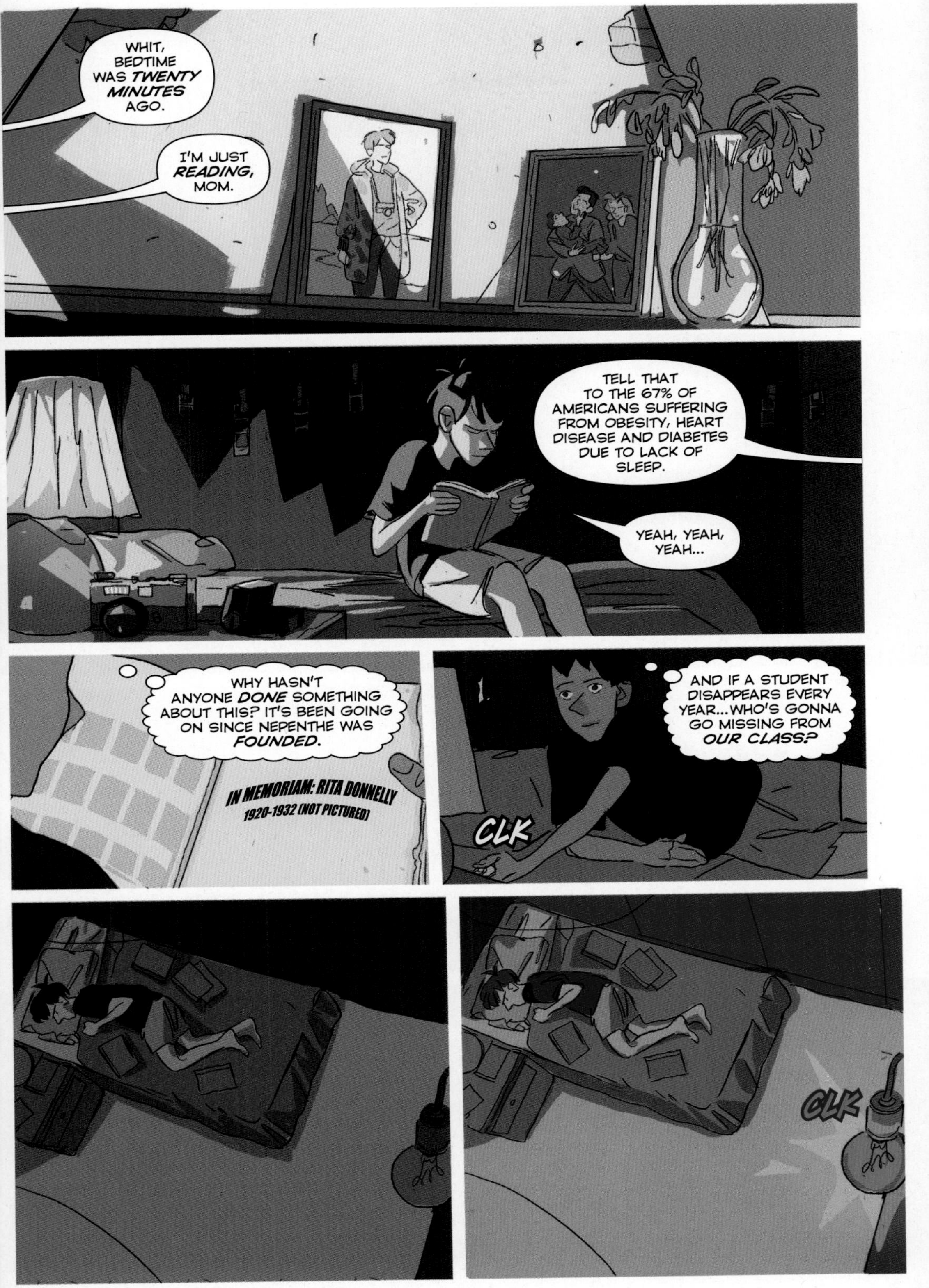

WHIT, BEDTIME WAS TWENTY MINUTES AGO.
I'M JUST READING, MOM.
TELL THAT TO THE 67% OF AMERICANS SUFFERING FROM OBESITY, HEART DISEASE AND DIABETES DUE TO LACK OF SLEEP.
YEAH, YEAH, YEAH...
WHY HASN'T ANYONE DONE SOMETHING ABOUT THIS? IT'S BEEN GOING ON SINCE NEPENTHE WAS FOUNDED.
IN MEMORIAM: RITA DONNELLY
1920-1932 (NOT PICTURED)
AND IF A STUDENT DISAPPEARS EVERY YEAR...WHO'S GONNA GO MISSING FROM OUR CLASS?
CLK
CLK

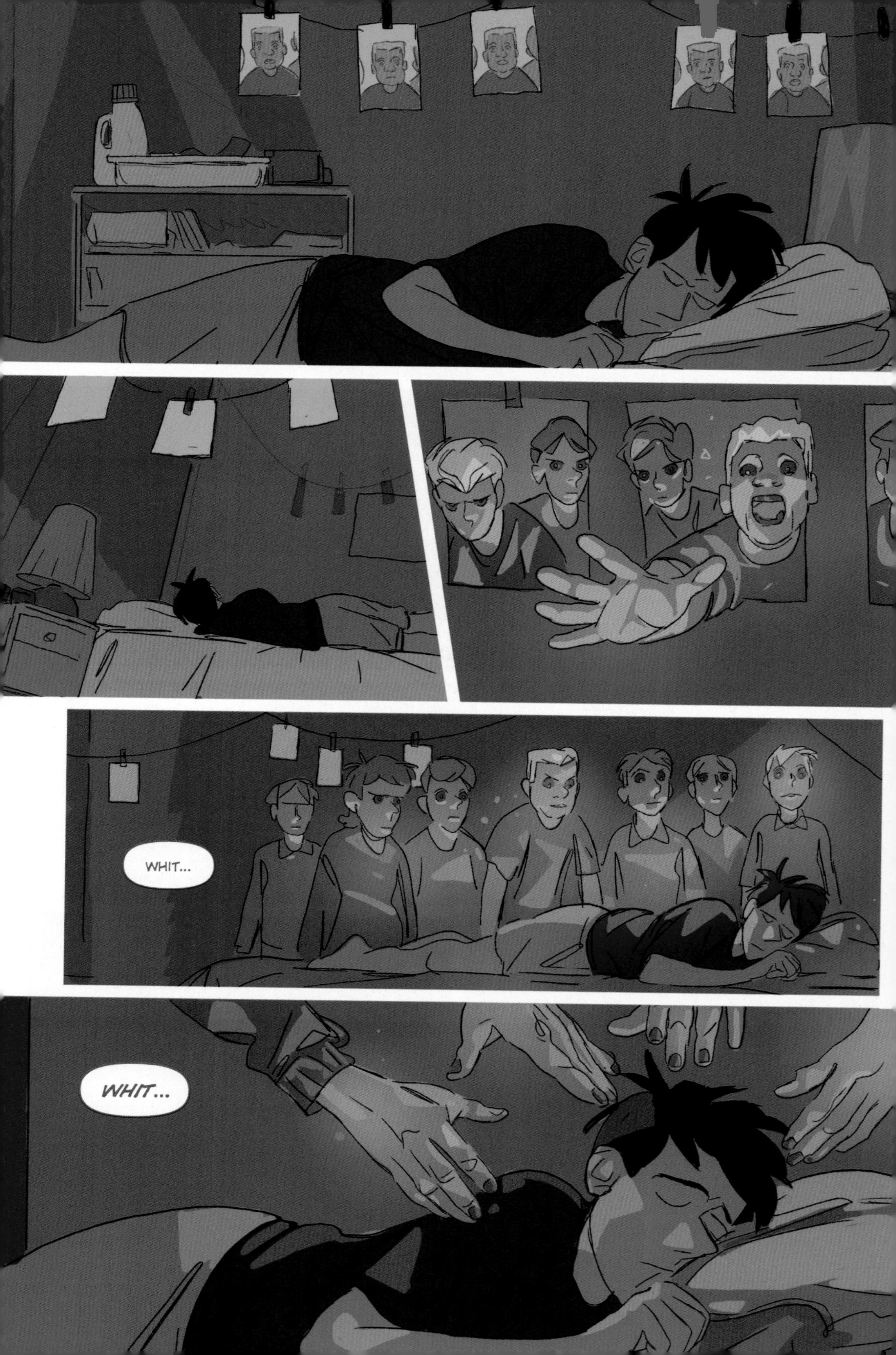
WHIT...
WHIT...

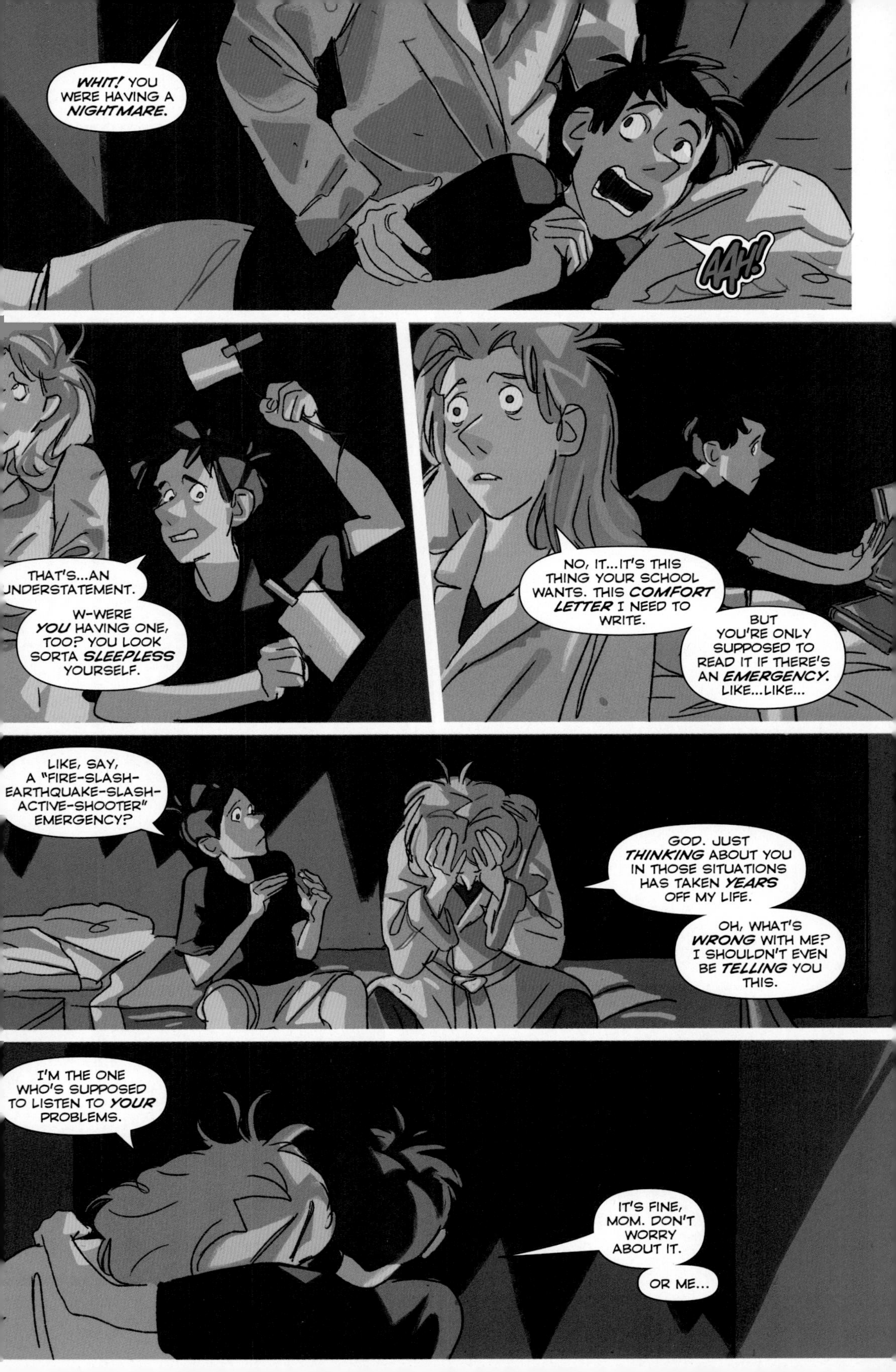
WHIT! YOU WERE HAVING A NIGHTMARE.
AAH!
THAT'S...AN UNDERSTATEMENT.
W-WERE YOU HAVING ONE, TOO? YOU LOOK SORTA SLEEPLESS YOURSELF.
NO, IT...IT'S THIS THING YOUR SCHOOL WANTS. THIS COMFORT LETTER I NEED TO WRITE.
BUT YOU'RE ONLY SUPPOSED TO READ IT IF THERE'S AN EMERGENCY. LIKE...LIKE...
LIKE, SAY, A "FIRE-SLASH-EARTHQUAKE-SLASH-ACTIVE-SHOOTER" EMERGENCY?
GOD. JUST THINKING ABOUT YOU IN THOSE SITUATIONS HAS TAKEN YEARS OFF MY LIFE.
OH, WHAT'S WRONG WITH ME? I SHOULDN'T EVEN BE TELLING YOU THIS.
I'M THE ONE WHO'S SUPPOSED TO LISTEN TO YOUR PROBLEMS.
IT'S FINE, MOM. DON'T WORRY ABOUT IT.
OR ME...

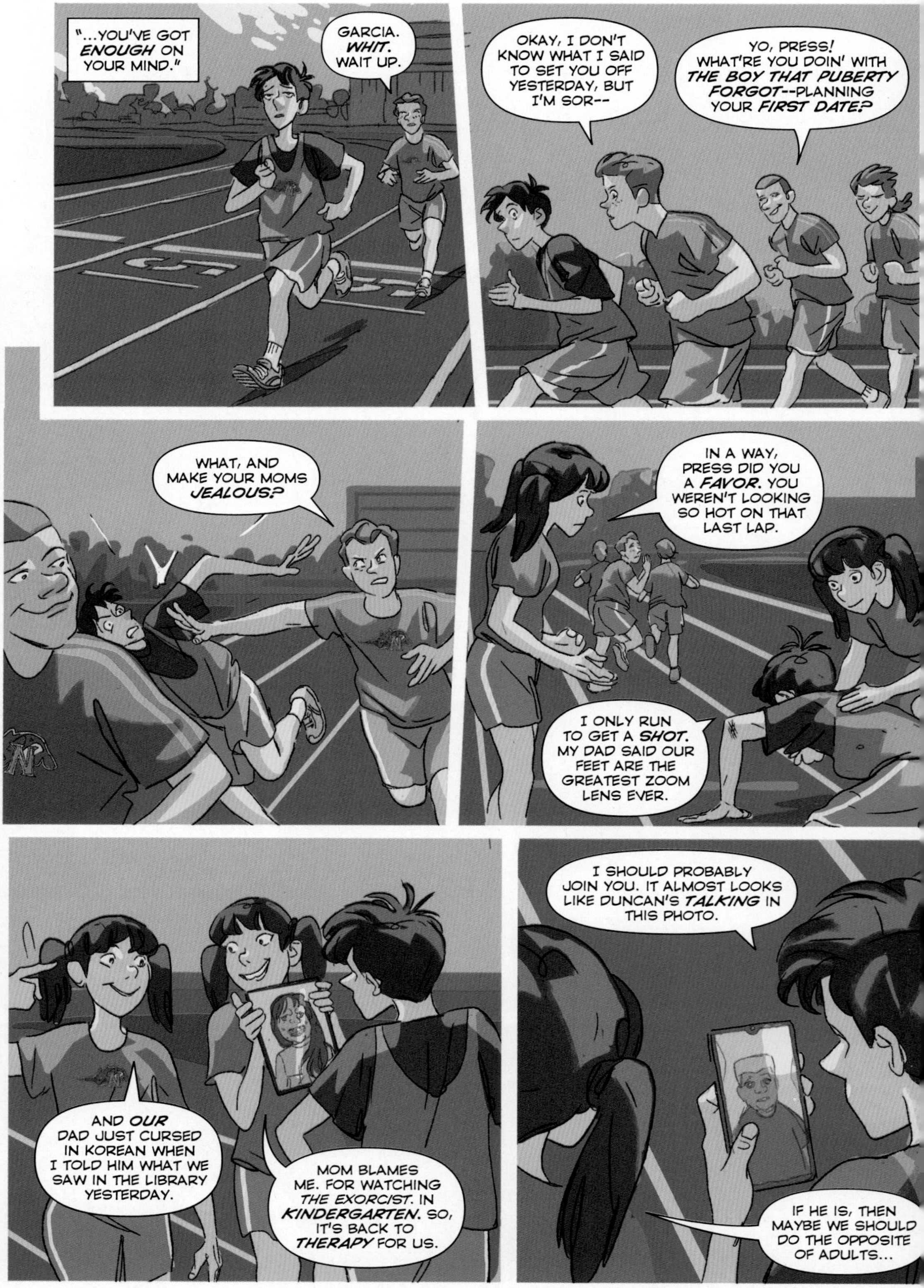
"...YOU'VE GOT ENOUGH ON YOUR MIND."
GARCIA. WHIT. WAIT UP.
OKAY, I DON'T KNOW WHAT I SAID TO SET YOU OFF YESTERDAY, BUT I'M SOR--
YO, PRESS! WHAT'RE YOU DOIN' WITH THE BOY THAT PUBERTY FORGOT--PLANNING YOUR FIRST DATE?
WHAT, AND MAKE YOUR MOMS JEALOUS?
IN A WAY, PRESS DID YOU A FAVOR. YOU WEREN'T LOOKING SO HOT ON THAT LAST LAP.
I ONLY RUN TO GET A SHOT. MY DAD SAID OUR FEET ARE THE GREATEST ZOOM LENS EVER.
AND OUR DAD JUST CURSED IN KOREAN WHEN I TOLD HIM WHAT WE SAW IN THE LIBRARY YESTERDAY.
MOM BLAMES ME. FOR WATCHING THE EXORCIST. IN KINDERGARTEN. SO, IT'S BACK TO THERAPY FOR US.
I SHOULD PROBABLY JOIN YOU. IT ALMOST LOOKS LIKE DUNCAN'S TALKING IN THIS PHOTO.
IF HE IS, THEN MAYBE WE SHOULD DO THE OPPOSITE OF ADULTS...

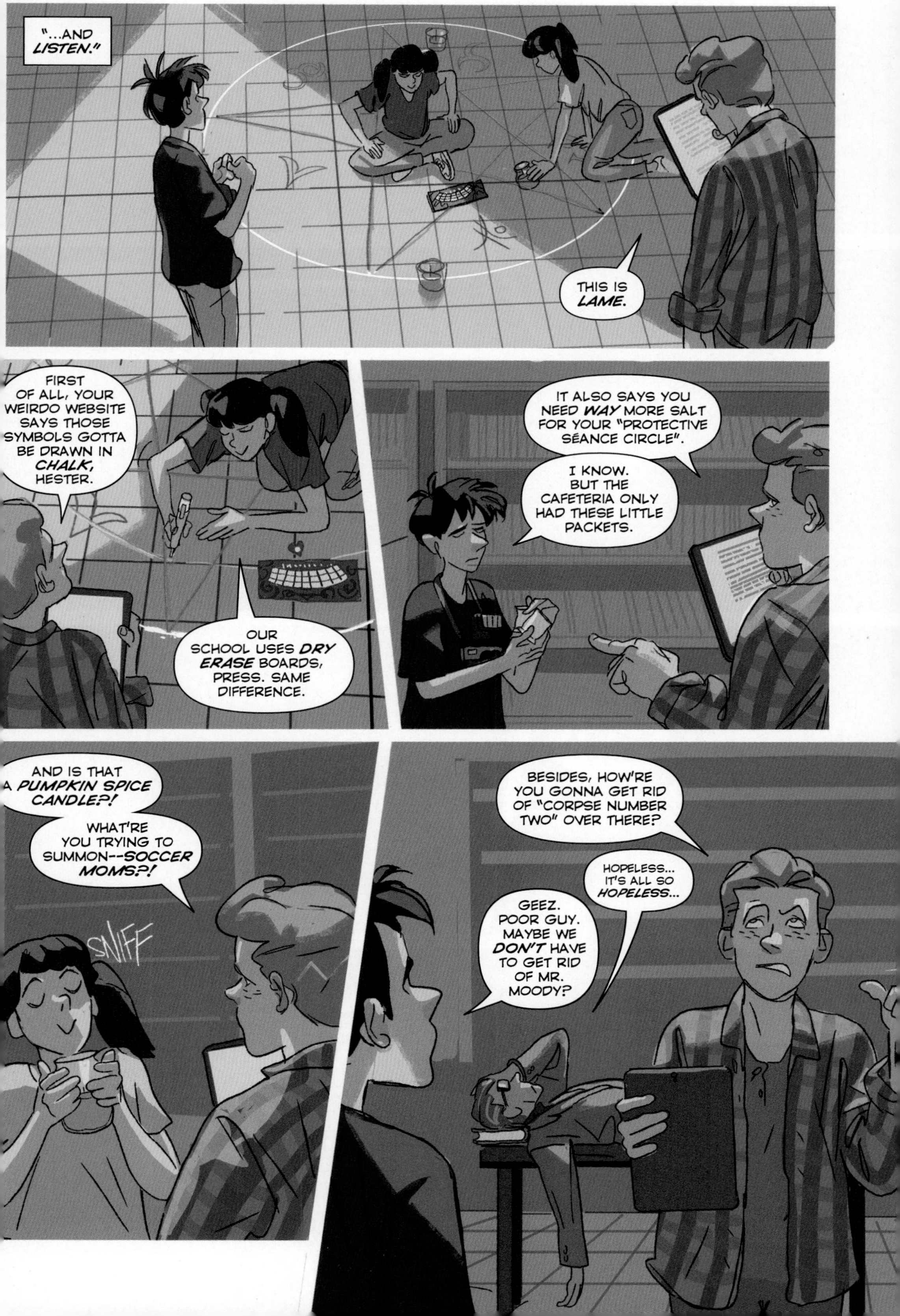
"...AND LISTEN."
THIS IS LAME.
FIRST OF ALL, YOUR WEIRDO WEBSITE SAYS THOSE SYMBOLS GOTTA BE DRAWN IN CHALK, HESTER.
OUR SCHOOL USES DRY ERASE BOARDS, PRESS. SAME DIFFERENCE.
IT ALSO SAYS YOU NEED WAY MORE SALT FOR YOUR "PROTECTIVE SÉANCE CIRCLE".
I KNOW. BUT THE CAFETERIA ONLY HAD THESE LITTLE PACKETS.
AND IS THAT A PUMPKIN SPICE CANDLE?!
WHAT'RE YOU TRYING TO SUMMON--SOCCER MOMS?!
SNIFF
BESIDES, HOW'RE YOU GONNA GET RID OF "CORPSE NUMBER TWO" OVER THERE?
HOPELESS... IT'S ALL SO HOPELESS...
GEEZ. POOR GUY. MAYBE WE DON'T HAVE TO GET RID OF MR. MOODY?

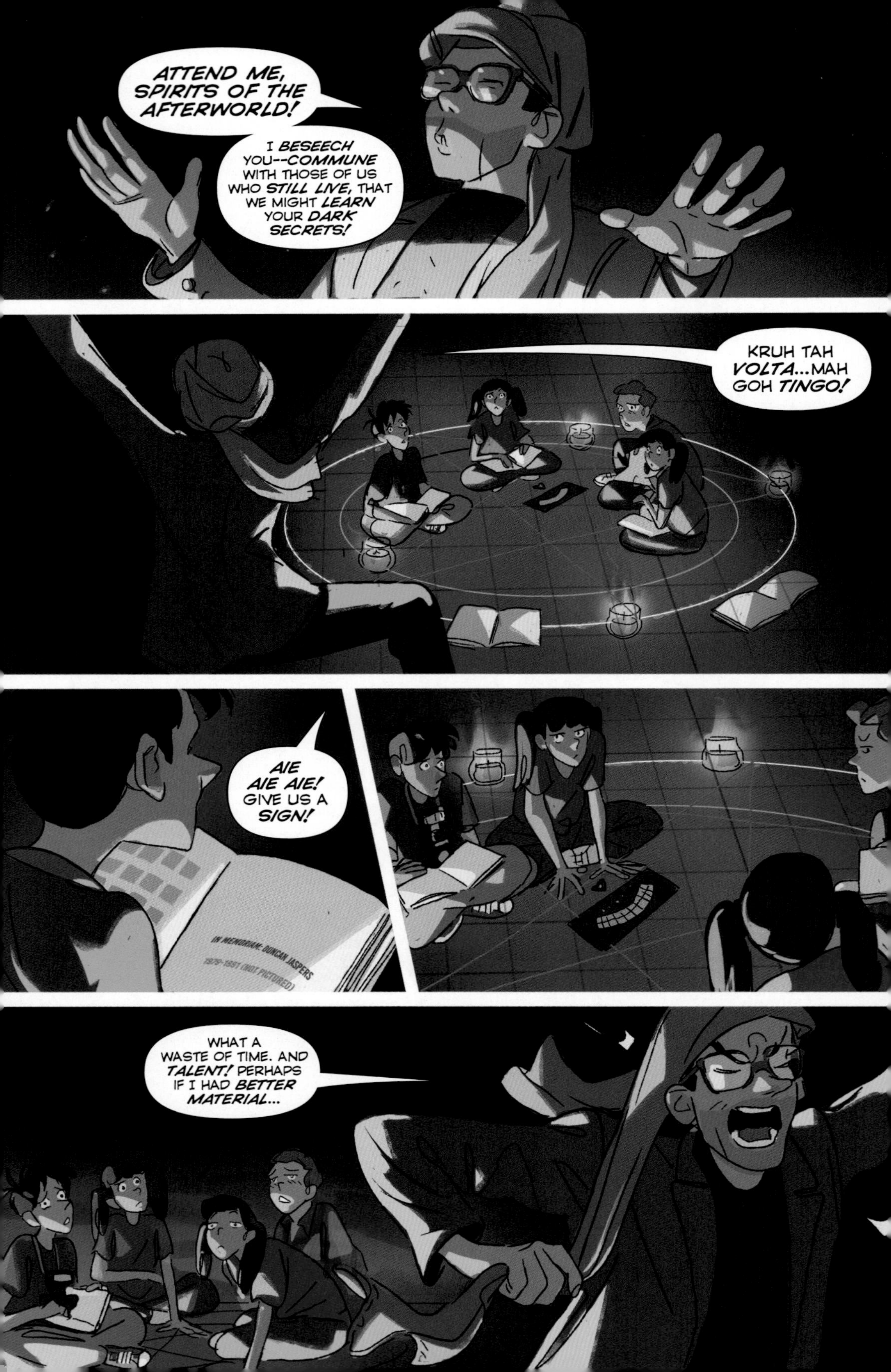
ATTEND ME, SPIRITS OF THE AFTERWORLD!
I *BESEECH* YOU--*COMMUNE* WITH THOSE OF US WHO *STILL LIVE,* THAT WE MIGHT *LEARN* YOUR *DARK SECRETS!*
KRUH TAH *VOLTA*...MAH GOH *TINGO!*
AIE AIE AIE! GIVE US A *SIGN!*
IN MEMORIAM: DUNCAN JASPERS
1975-1991 (NOT PICTURED)
WHAT A WASTE OF TIME. AND *TALENT!* PERHAPS IF I HAD *BETTER MATERIAL*...

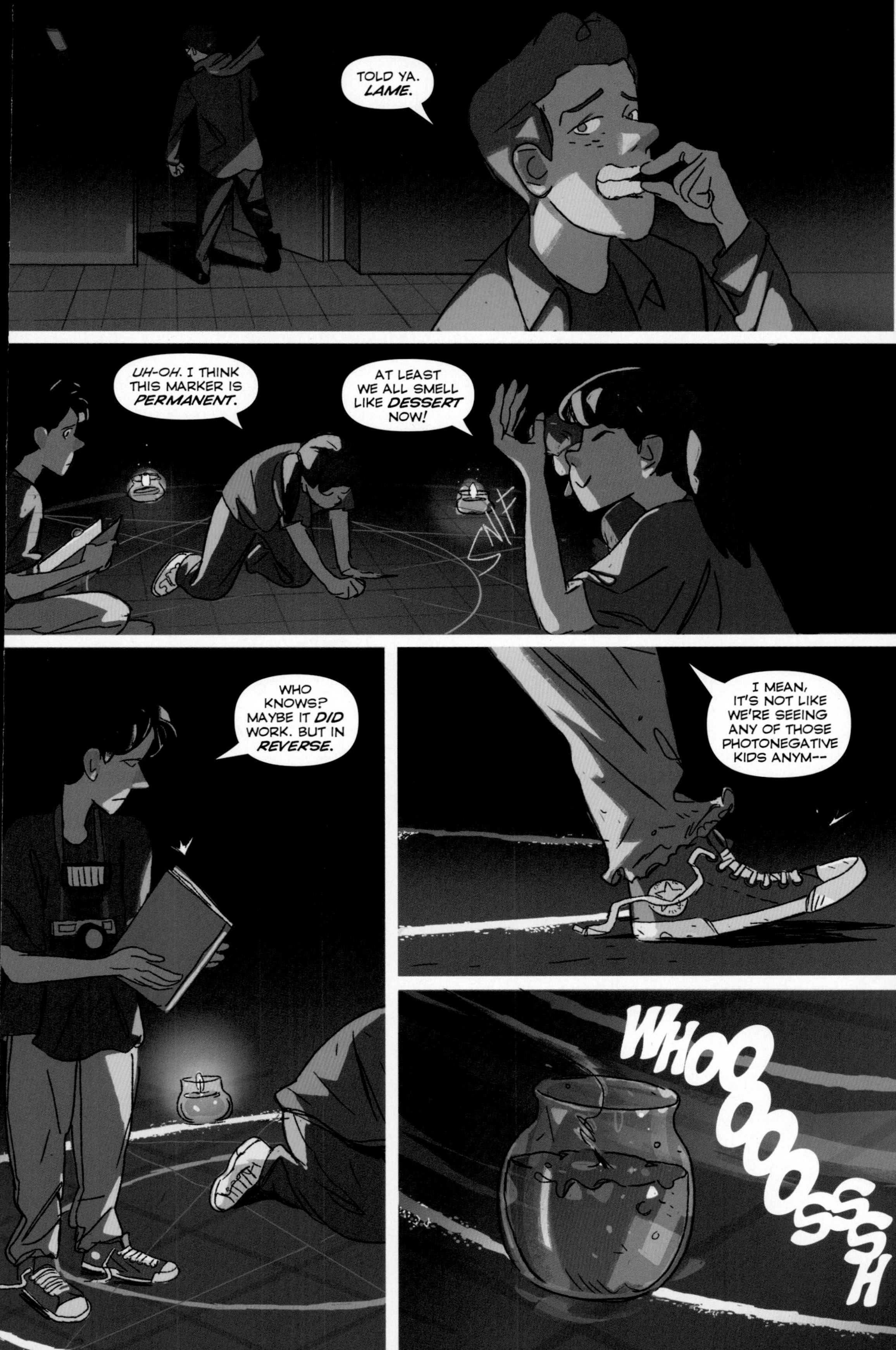
TOLD YA. LAME.
UH-OH. I THINK THIS MARKER IS PERMANENT.
AT LEAST WE ALL SMELL LIKE DESSERT NOW!
SNIF
WHO KNOWS? MAYBE IT DID WORK. BUT IN REVERSE.
I MEAN, IT'S NOT LIKE WE'RE SEEING ANY OF THOSE PHOTONEGATIVE KIDS ANYM--
WHOOOOOSSSH

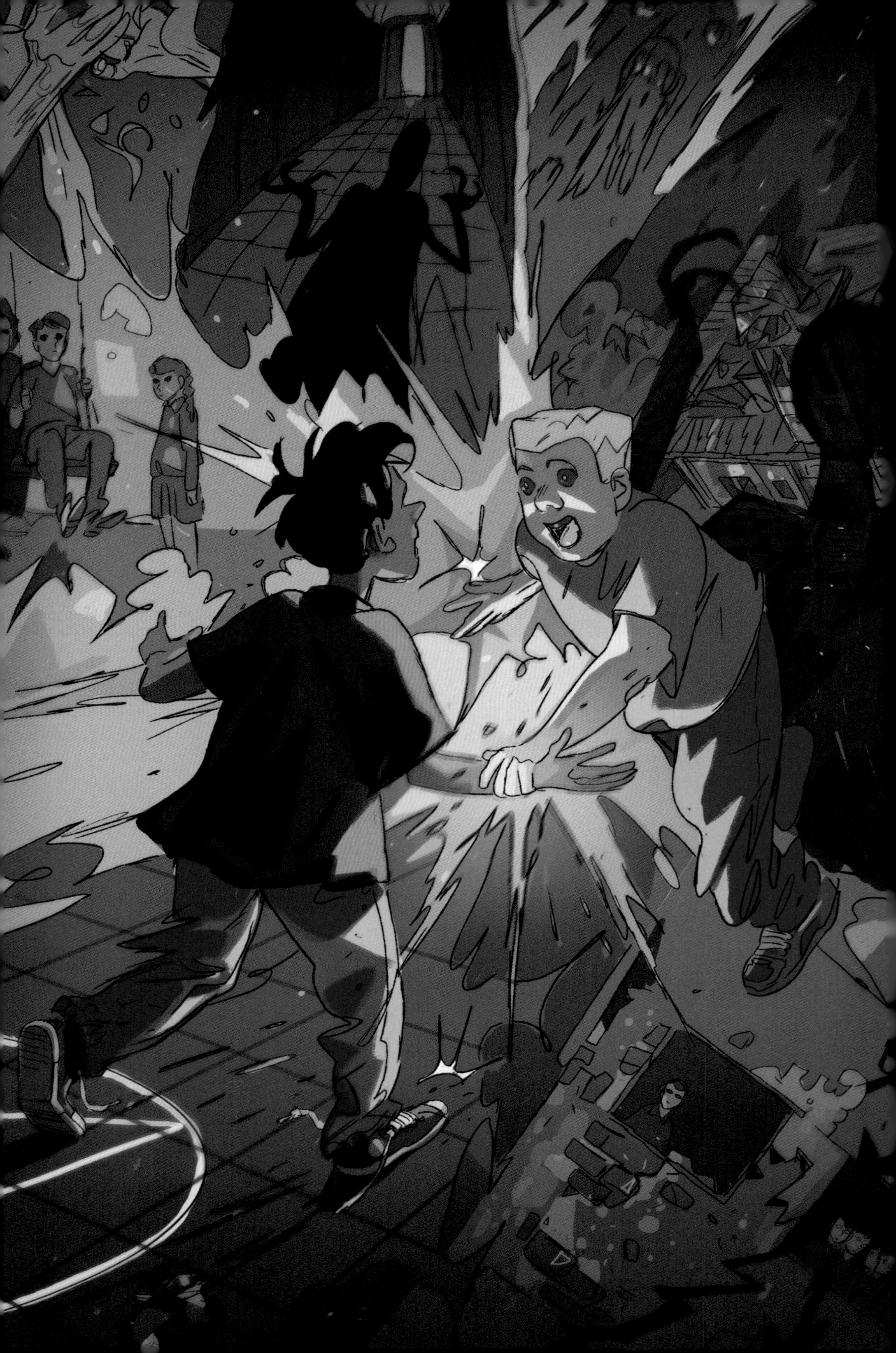

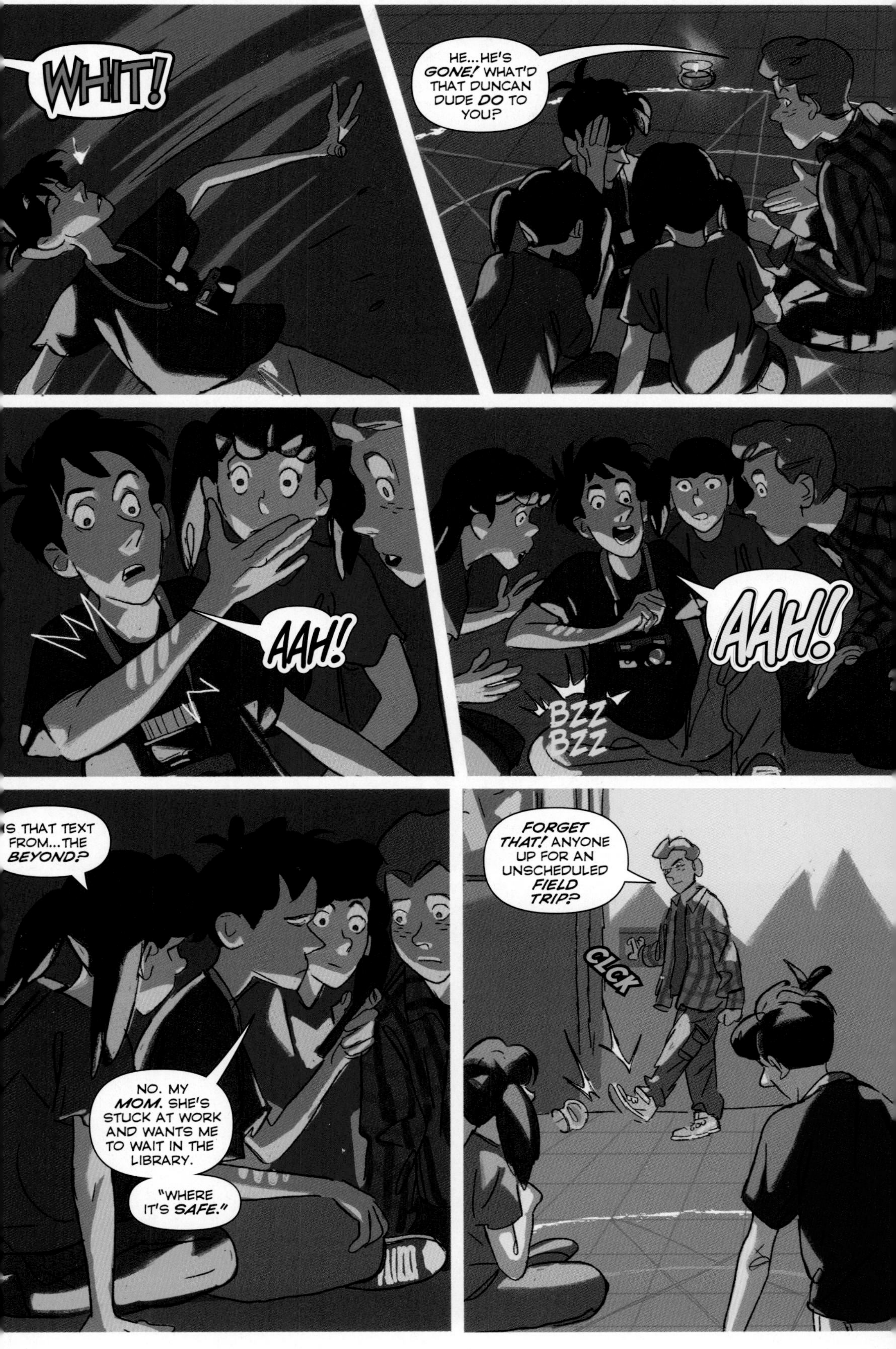
WHIT!
HE...HE'S GONE! WHAT'D THAT DUNCAN DUDE DO TO YOU?
AAH!
AAH!
BZZ BZZ
S THAT TEXT FROM...THE BEYOND?
NO. MY MOM. SHE'S STUCK AT WORK AND WANTS ME TO WAIT IN THE LIBRARY.
"WHERE IT'S SAFE."
FORGET THAT! ANYONE UP FOR AN UNSCHEDULED FIELD TRIP?
CLCK

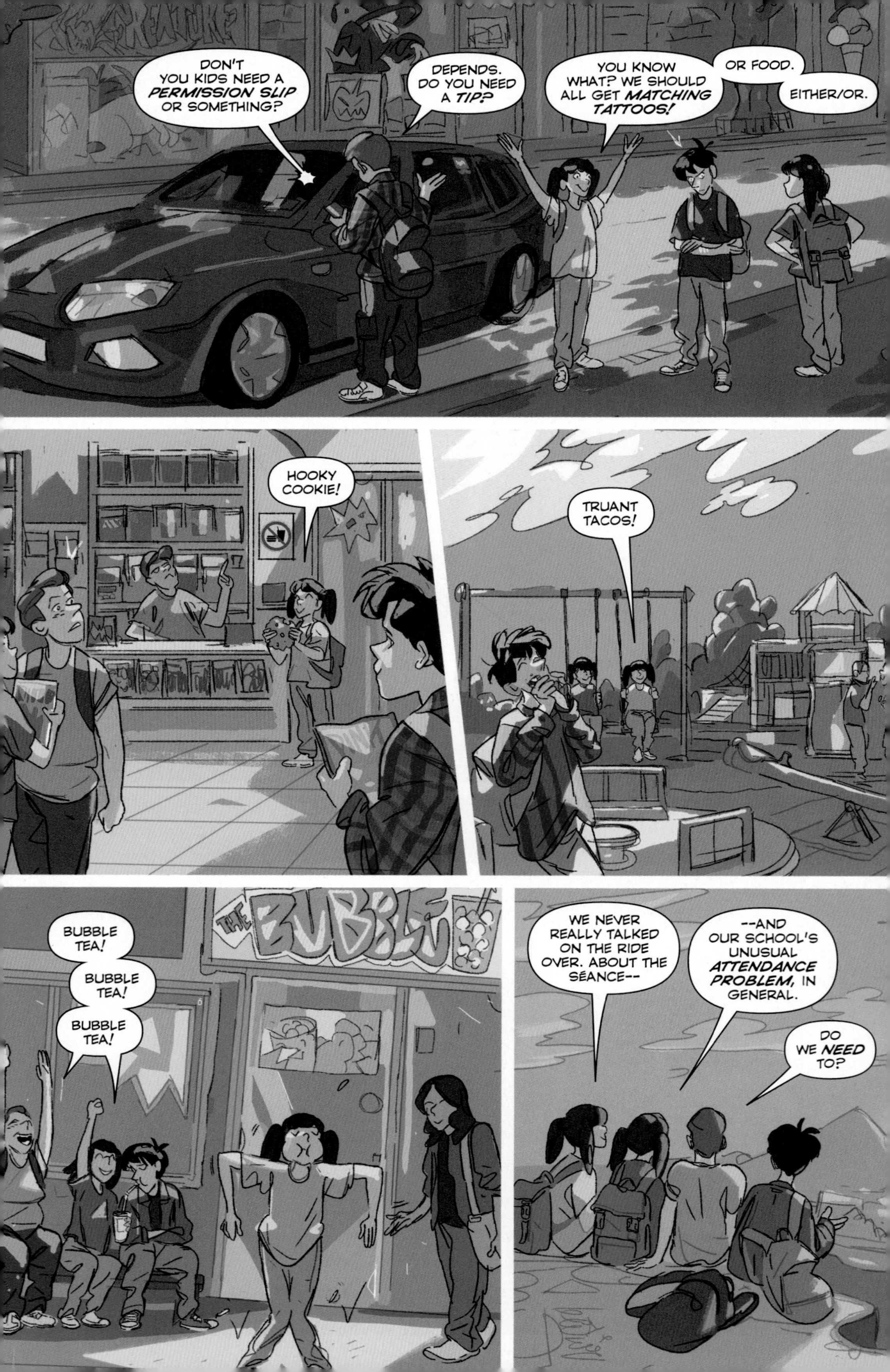
DON'T YOU KIDS NEED A *PERMISSION SLIP* OR SOMETHING?
DEPENDS. DO YOU NEED A *TIP?*
YOU KNOW WHAT? WE SHOULD ALL GET *MATCHING TATTOOS!*
OR FOOD.
EITHER/OR.
HOOKY COOKIE!
TRUANT TACOS!
THE BUBBLE
BUBBLE TEA!
BUBBLE TEA!
BUBBLE TEA!
WE NEVER REALLY TALKED ON THE RIDE OVER. ABOUT THE SÉANCE--
--AND OUR SCHOOL'S UNUSUAL *ATTENDANCE PROBLEM,* IN GENERAL.
DO WE *NEED* TO?

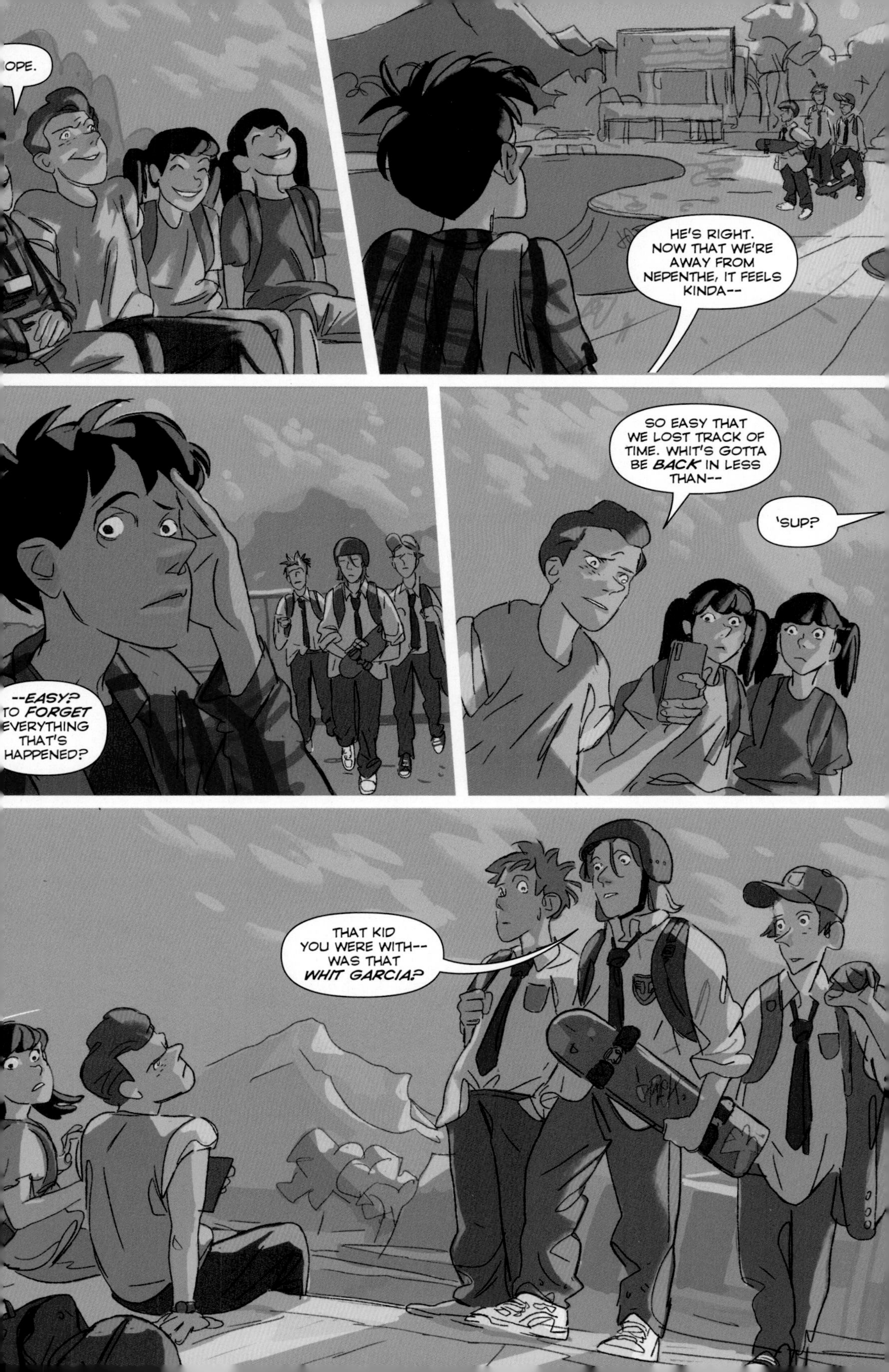

OPE.
HE'S RIGHT. NOW THAT WE'RE AWAY FROM NEPENTHE, IT FEELS KINDA--
--EASY? TO FORGET EVERYTHING THAT'S HAPPENED?
SO EASY THAT WE LOST TRACK OF TIME. WHIT'S GOTTA BE BACK IN LESS THAN--
'SUP?
THAT KID YOU WERE WITH-- WAS THAT WHIT GARCIA?

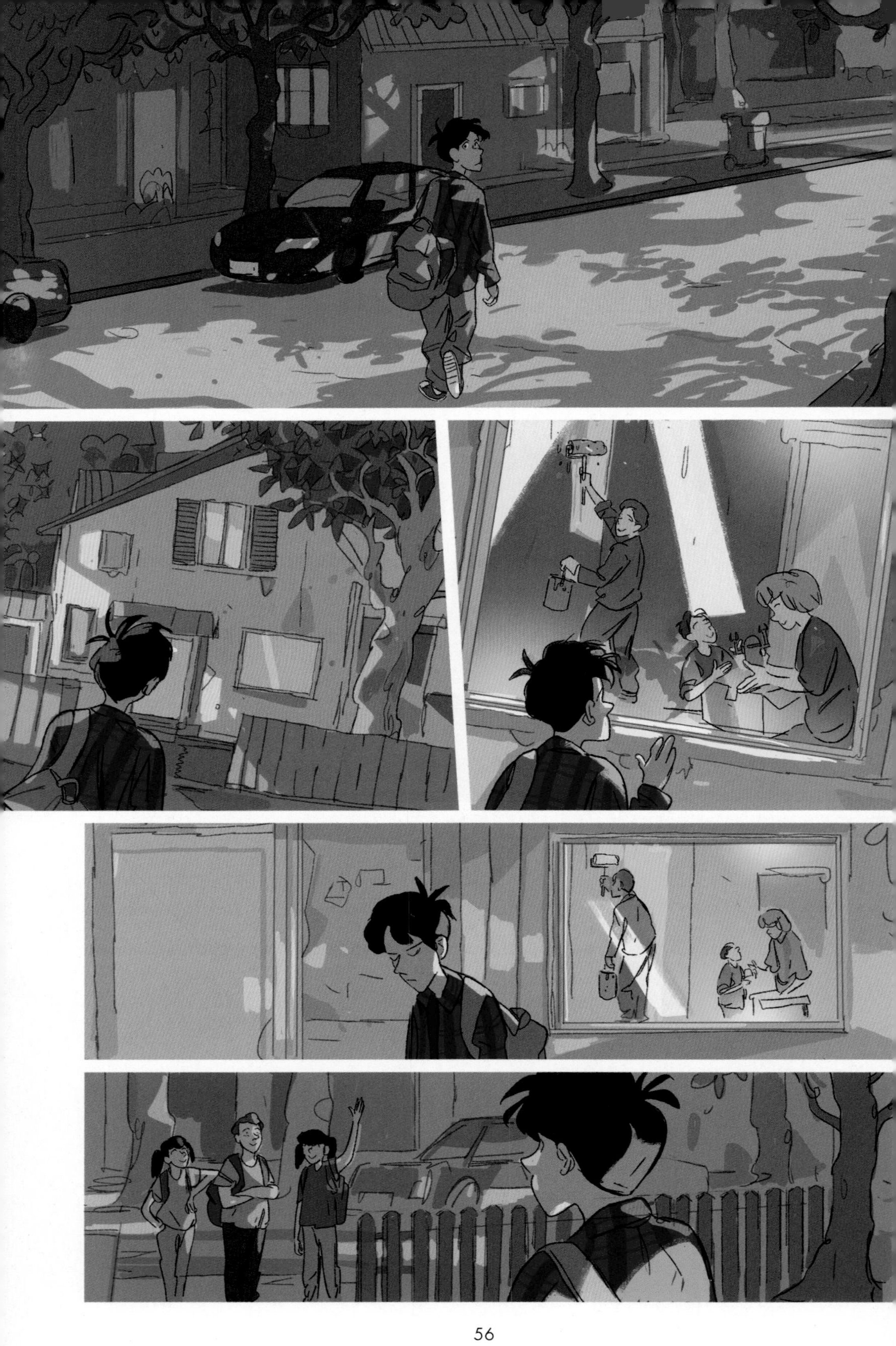

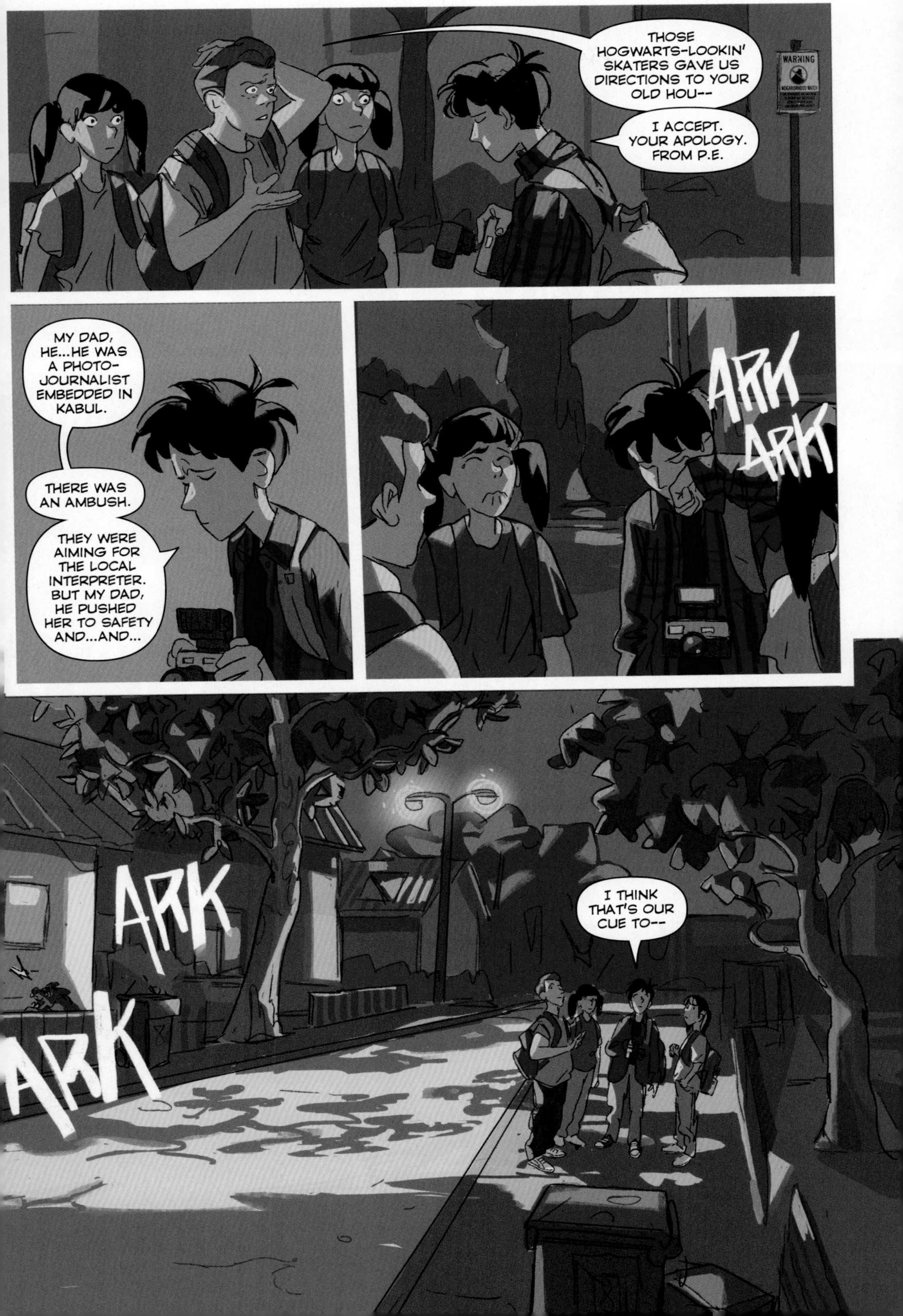

THOSE HOGWARTS-LOOKIN' SKATERS GAVE US DIRECTIONS TO YOUR OLD HOU--
I ACCEPT. YOUR APOLOGY. FROM P.E.
WARNING
MY DAD, HE...HE WAS A PHOTO-JOURNALIST EMBEDDED IN KABUL.
THERE WAS AN AMBUSH.
THEY WERE AIMING FOR THE LOCAL INTERPRETER. BUT MY DAD, HE PUSHED HER TO SAFETY AND...AND...
ARK
ARK
ARK
ARK
I THINK THAT'S OUR CUE TO--

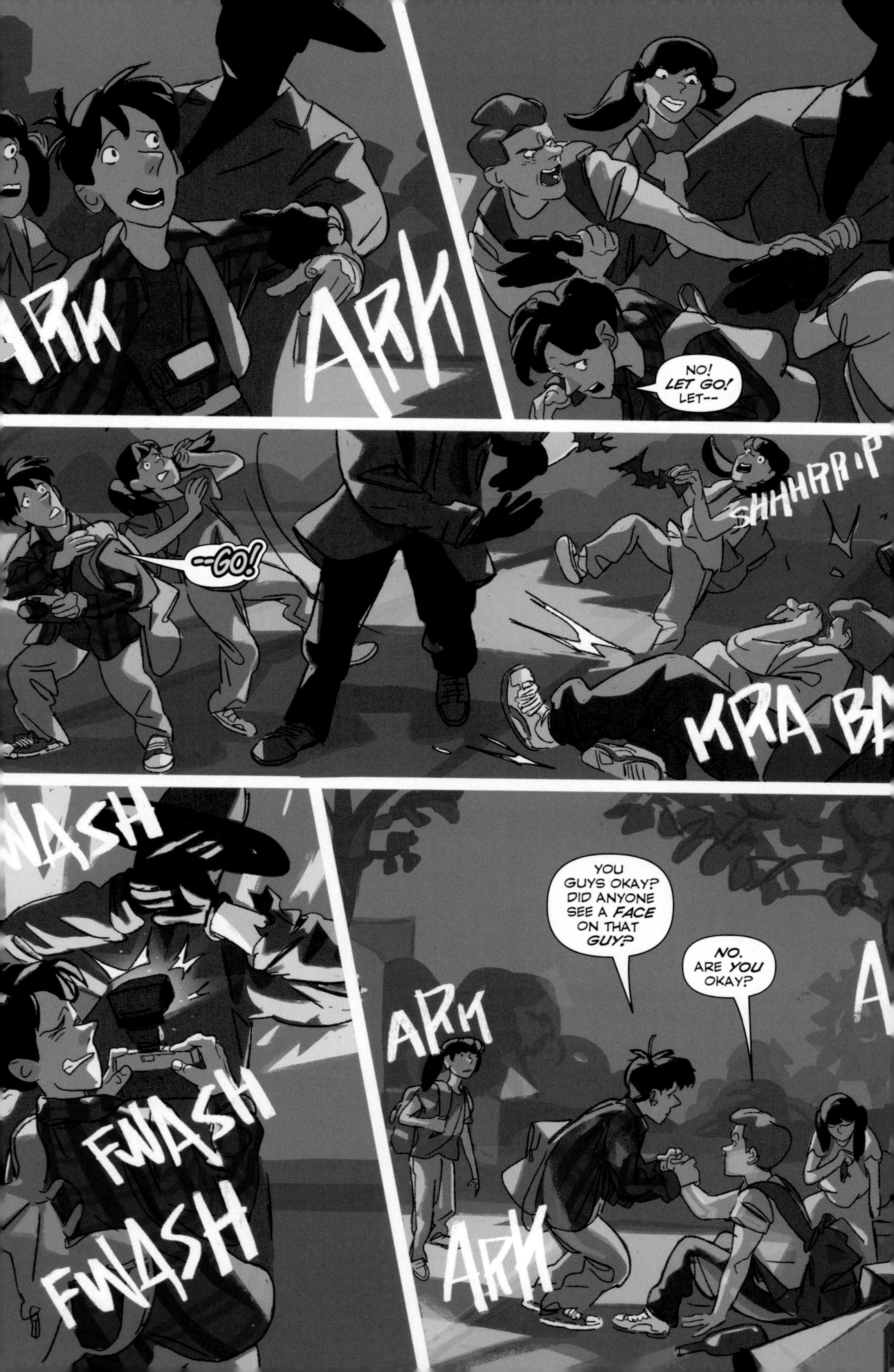
ARK
ARK
NO! LET GO! LET--
--GO!
SHHHRRRIP
KRA BA
WASH
FWASH
FWASH
YOU GUYS OKAY? DID ANYONE SEE A FACE ON THAT GUY?
NO. ARE YOU OKAY?
ARK
ARK

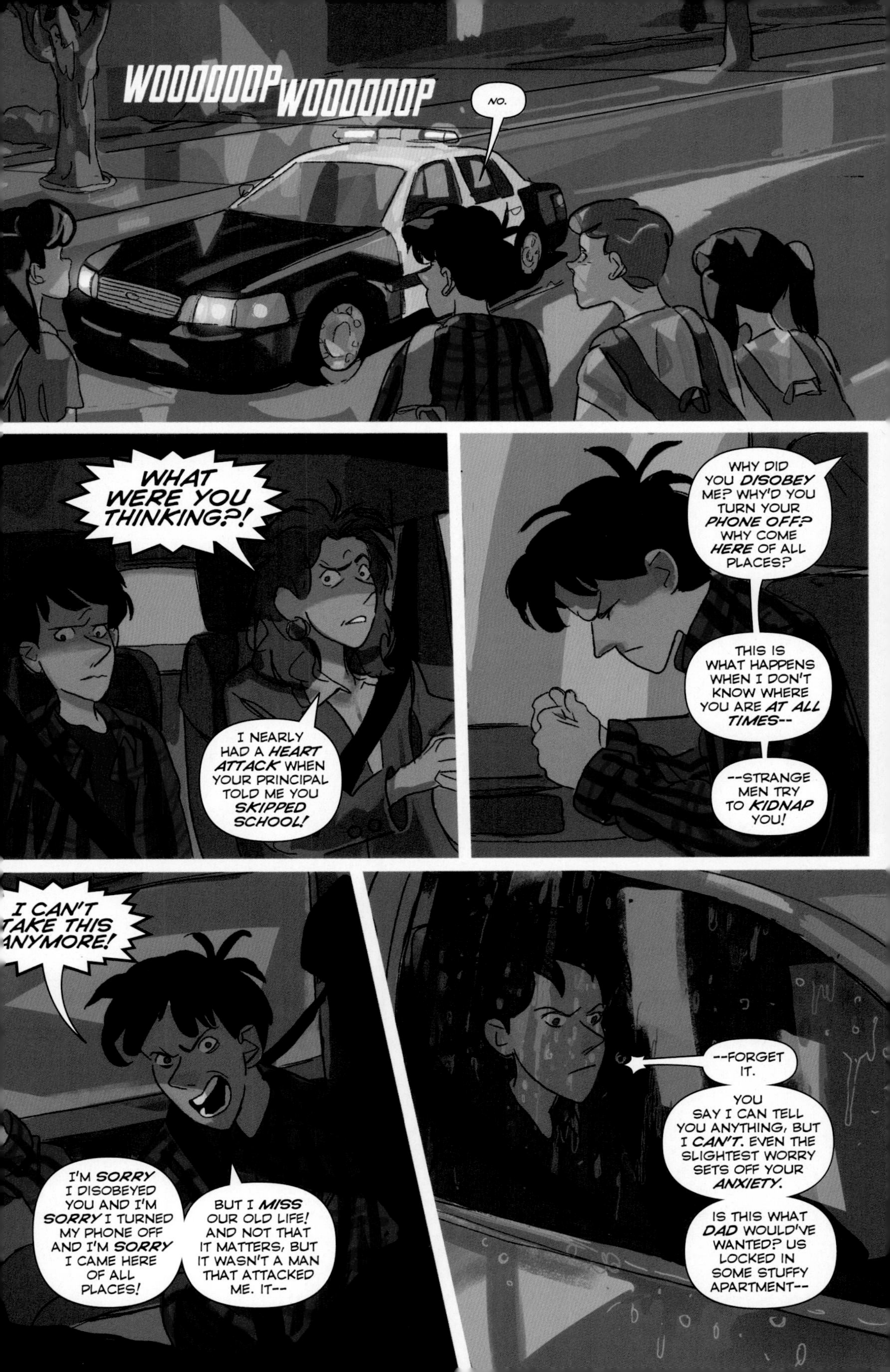
WOOOOOOP WOOOOOOP
NO.
WHAT WERE YOU THINKING?!
I NEARLY HAD A HEART ATTACK WHEN YOUR PRINCIPAL TOLD ME YOU SKIPPED SCHOOL!
WHY DID YOU DISOBEY ME? WHY'D YOU TURN YOUR PHONE OFF? WHY COME HERE OF ALL PLACES?
THIS IS WHAT HAPPENS WHEN I DON'T KNOW WHERE YOU ARE AT ALL TIMES--
--STRANGE MEN TRY TO KIDNAP YOU!
I CAN'T TAKE THIS ANYMORE!
I'M SORRY I DISOBEYED YOU AND I'M SORRY I TURNED MY PHONE OFF AND I'M SORRY I CAME HERE OF ALL PLACES!
BUT I MISS OUR OLD LIFE! AND NOT THAT IT MATTERS, BUT IT WASN'T A MAN THAT ATTACKED ME. IT--
--FORGET IT.
YOU SAY I CAN TELL YOU ANYTHING, BUT I CAN'T. EVEN THE SLIGHTEST WORRY SETS OFF YOUR ANXIETY.
IS THIS WHAT DAD WOULD'VE WANTED? US LOCKED IN SOME STUFFY APARTMENT--

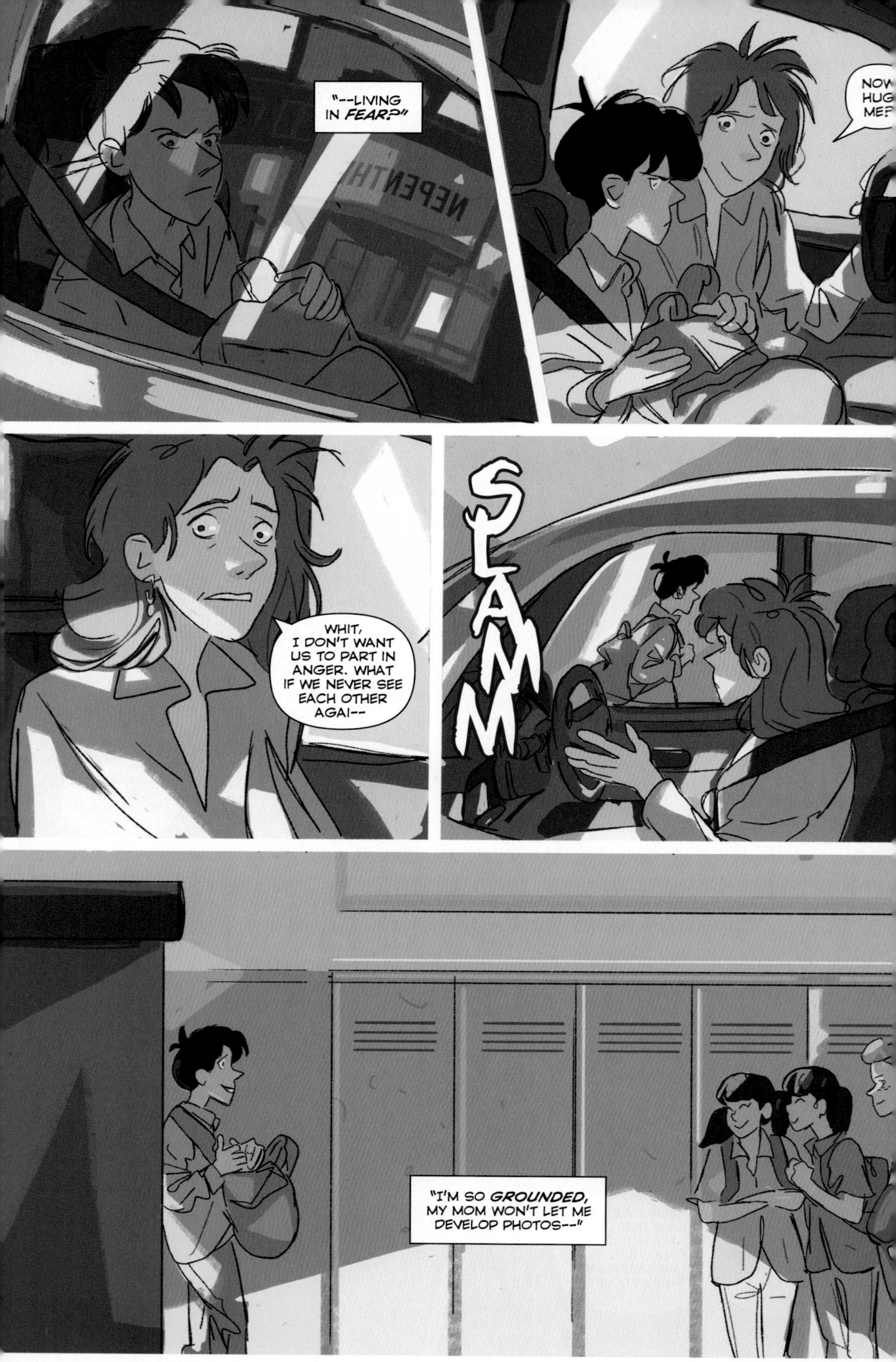
"--LIVING IN *FEAR?*"
NEPENTH
NOW HUG ME?
WHIT, I DON'T WANT US TO PART IN ANGER. WHAT IF WE NEVER SEE EACH OTHER AGAI--
SLAM
"I'M SO *GROUNDED*, MY MOM WON'T LET ME DEVELOP PHOTOS--"

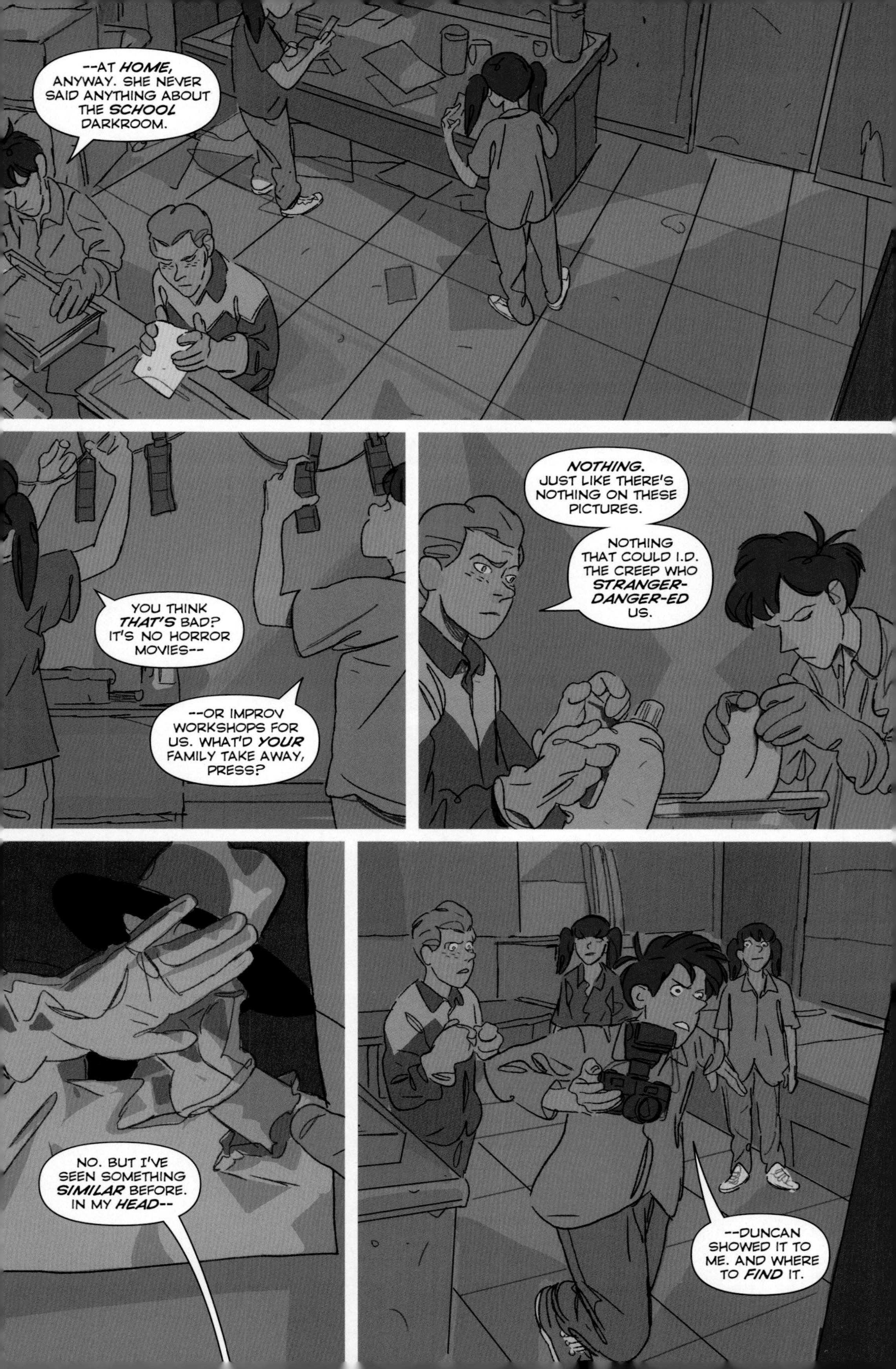
--AT HOME, ANYWAY. SHE NEVER SAID ANYTHING ABOUT THE SCHOOL DARKROOM.
YOU THINK THAT'S BAD? IT'S NO HORROR MOVIES--
--OR IMPROV WORKSHOPS FOR US. WHAT'D YOUR FAMILY TAKE AWAY, PRESS?
NOTHING. JUST LIKE THERE'S NOTHING ON THESE PICTURES.
NOTHING THAT COULD I.D. THE CREEP WHO STRANGER-DANGER-ED US.
NO. BUT I'VE SEEN SOMETHING SIMILAR BEFORE. IN MY HEAD--
--DUNCAN SHOWED IT TO ME. AND WHERE TO FIND IT.

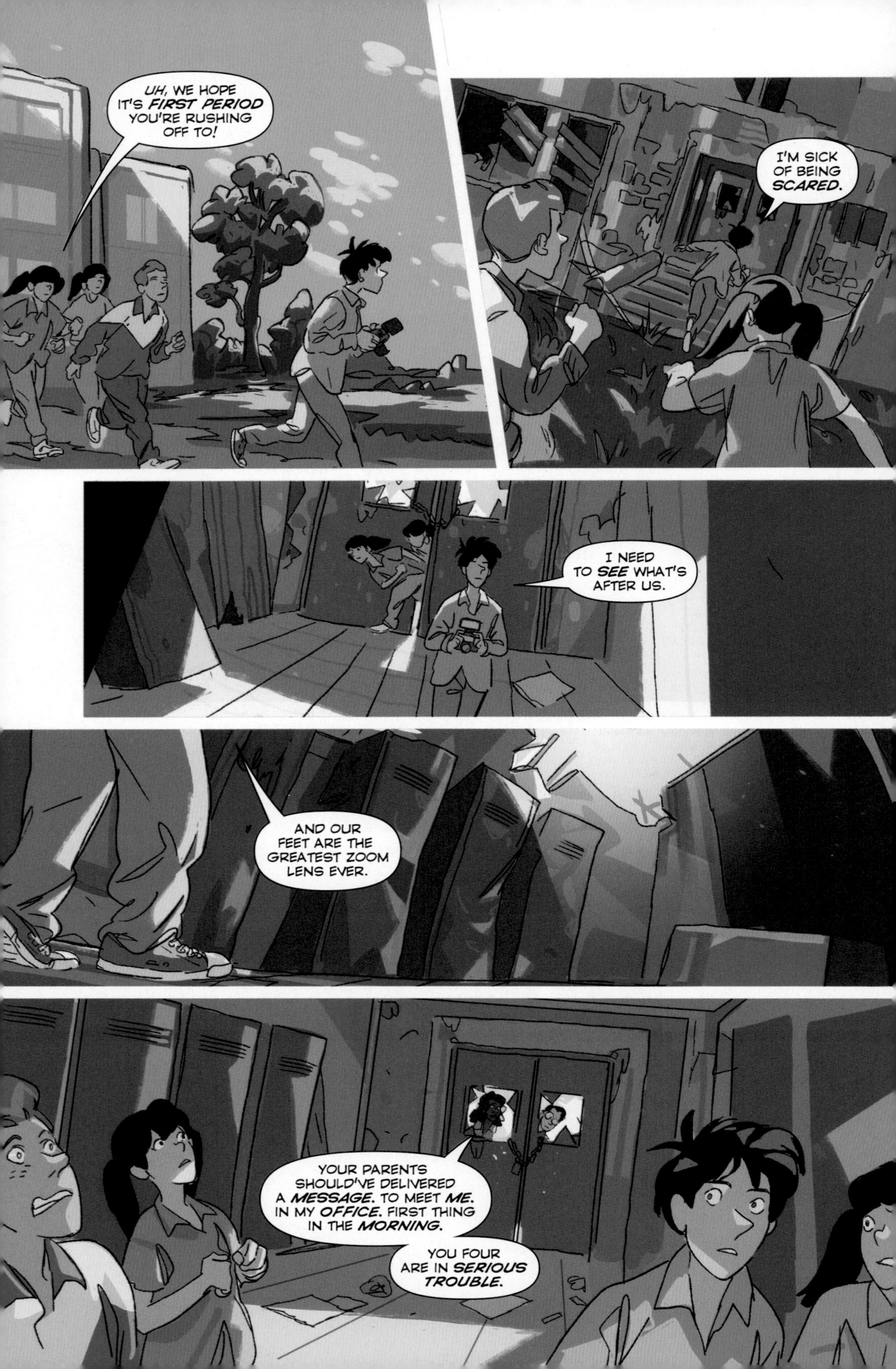

UH, WE HOPE IT'S FIRST PERIOD YOU'RE RUSHING OFF TO!
I'M SICK OF BEING SCARED.
I NEED TO SEE WHAT'S AFTER US.
AND OUR FEET ARE THE GREATEST ZOOM LENS EVER.
YOUR PARENTS SHOULD'VE DELIVERED A MESSAGE. TO MEET ME. IN MY OFFICE. FIRST THING IN THE MORNING.
YOU FOUR ARE IN SERIOUS TROUBLE.

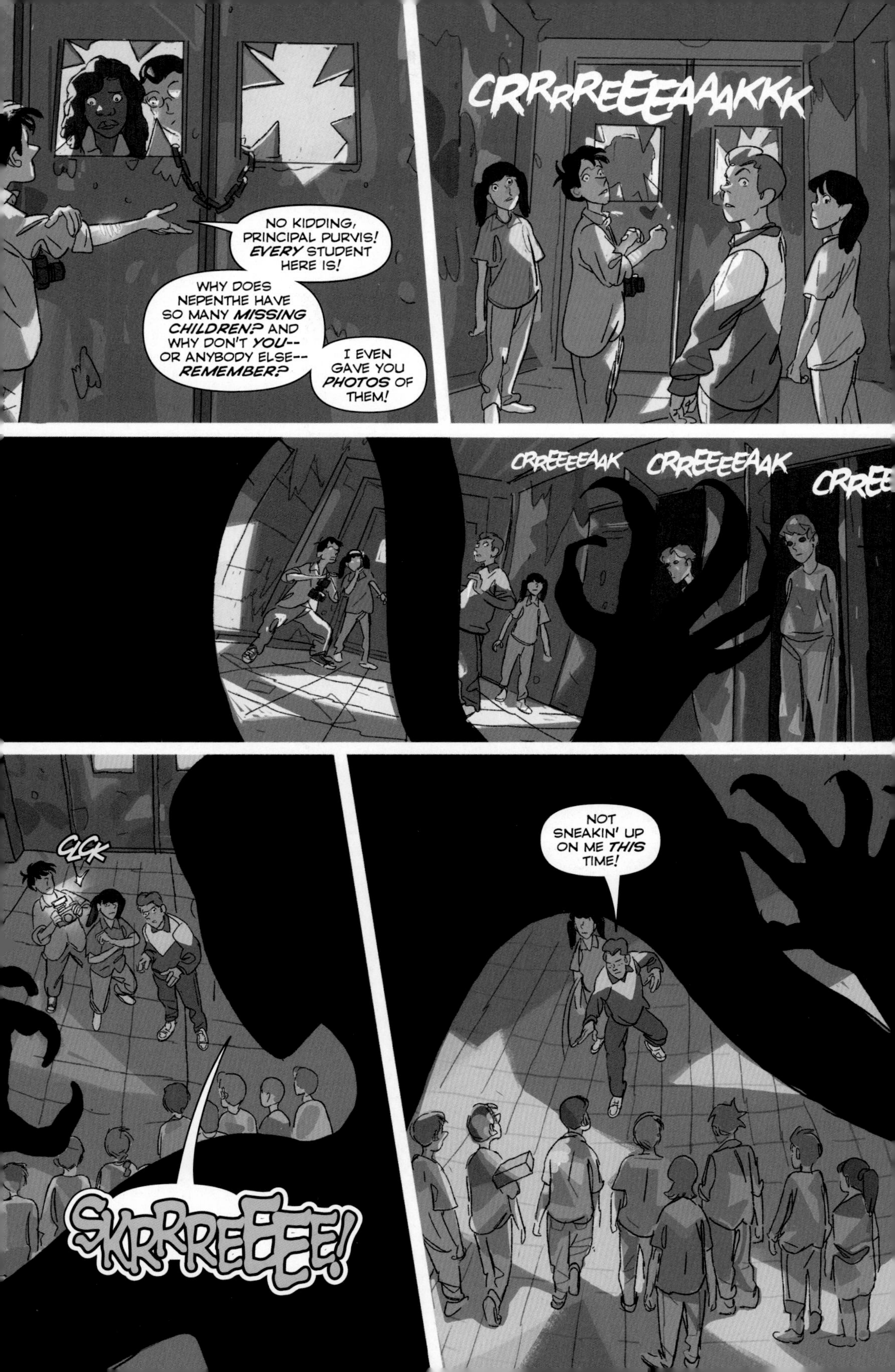
NO KIDDING, PRINCIPAL PURVIS! EVERY STUDENT HERE IS!
WHY DOES NEPENTHE HAVE SO MANY MISSING CHILDREN? AND WHY DON'T YOU--OR ANYBODY ELSE--REMEMBER?
I EVEN GAVE YOU PHOTOS OF THEM!
CRRRREEEEAAAKKKK
CRREEEEAAK
CRREEEEAAK
CRREE
CLCK
SKRRREEEEE!
NOT SNEAKIN' UP ON ME THIS TIME!

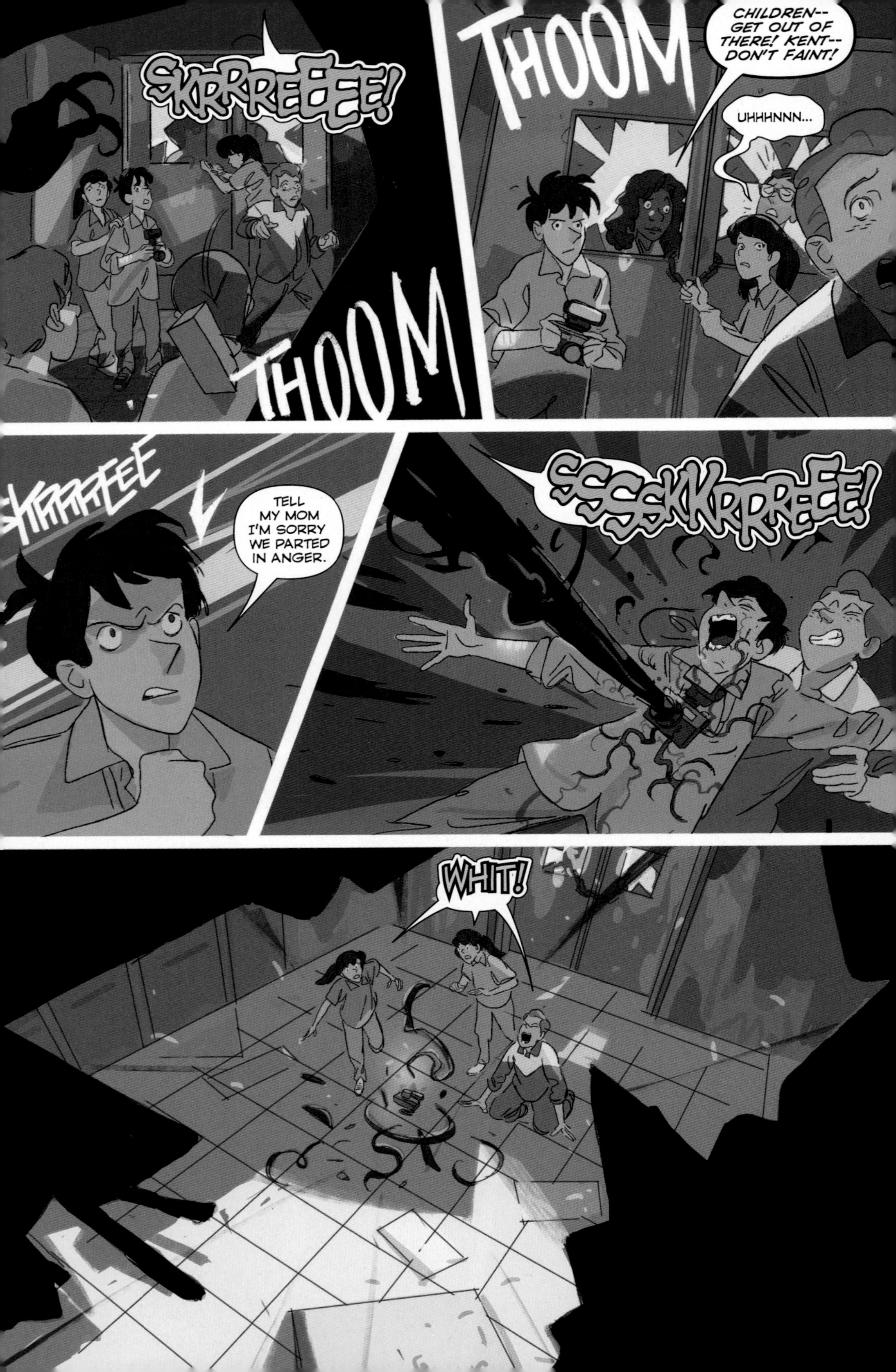

SKRRREEEE!
THOOM
THOOM
CHILDREN-- GET OUT OF THERE! KENT-- DON'T FAINT!
UHHHNNN...
TELL MY MOM I'M SORRY WE PARTED IN ANGER.
SSSSKKRRREEE!
WHIT!

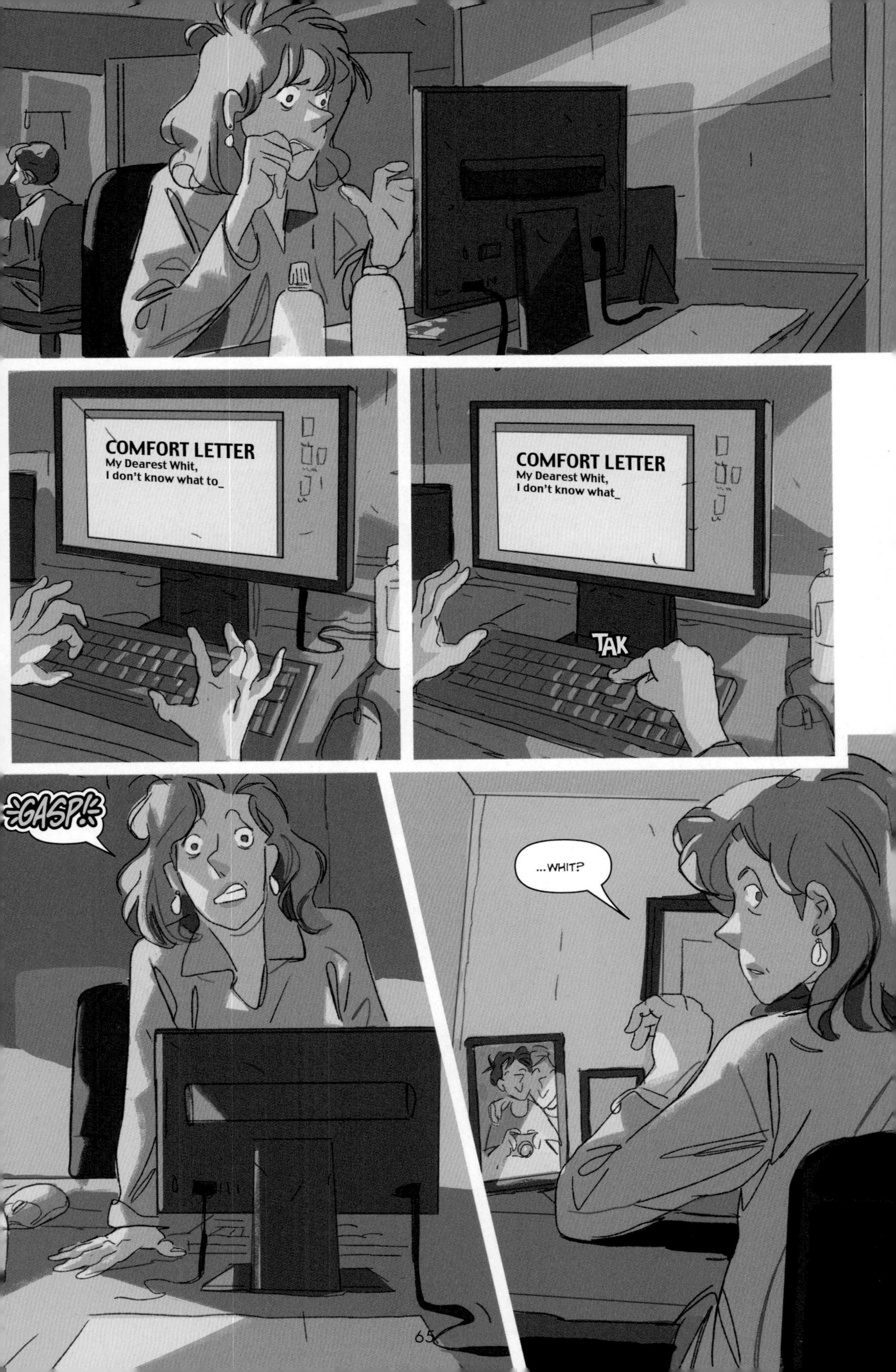
COMFORT LETTER
My Dearest Whit,
I don't know what to_
COMFORT LETTER
My Dearest Whit,
I don't know what_
TAK
GASP!
...WHIT?

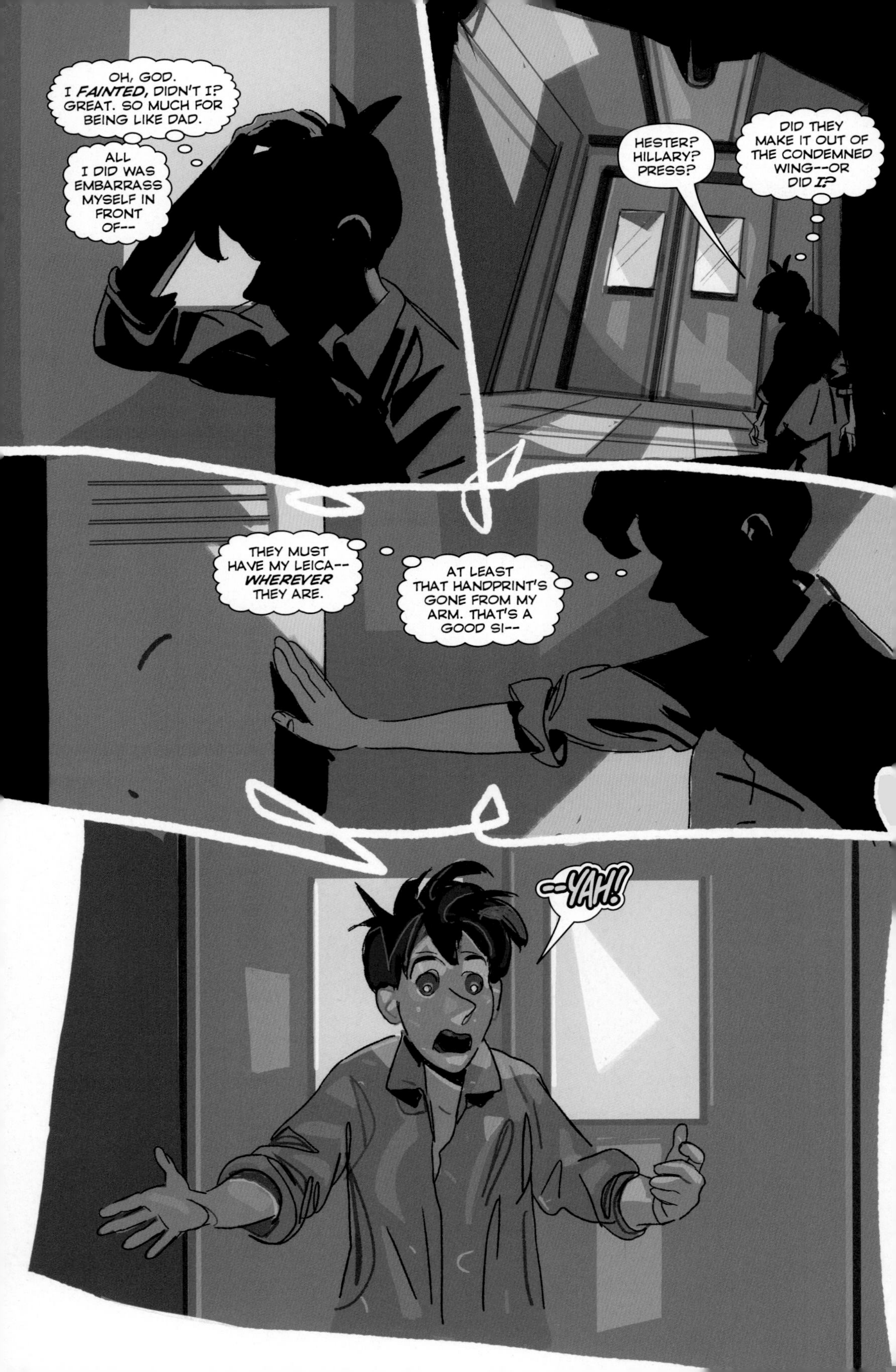
OH, GOD. I FAINTED, DIDN'T I? GREAT. SO MUCH FOR BEING LIKE DAD.
ALL I DID WAS EMBARRASS MYSELF IN FRONT OF--
HESTER? HILLARY? PRESS?
DID THEY MAKE IT OUT OF THE CONDEMNED WING--OR DID I?
THEY MUST HAVE MY LEICA--WHEREVER THEY ARE.
AT LEAST THAT HANDPRINT'S GONE FROM MY ARM. THAT'S A GOOD SI--
--YAH!

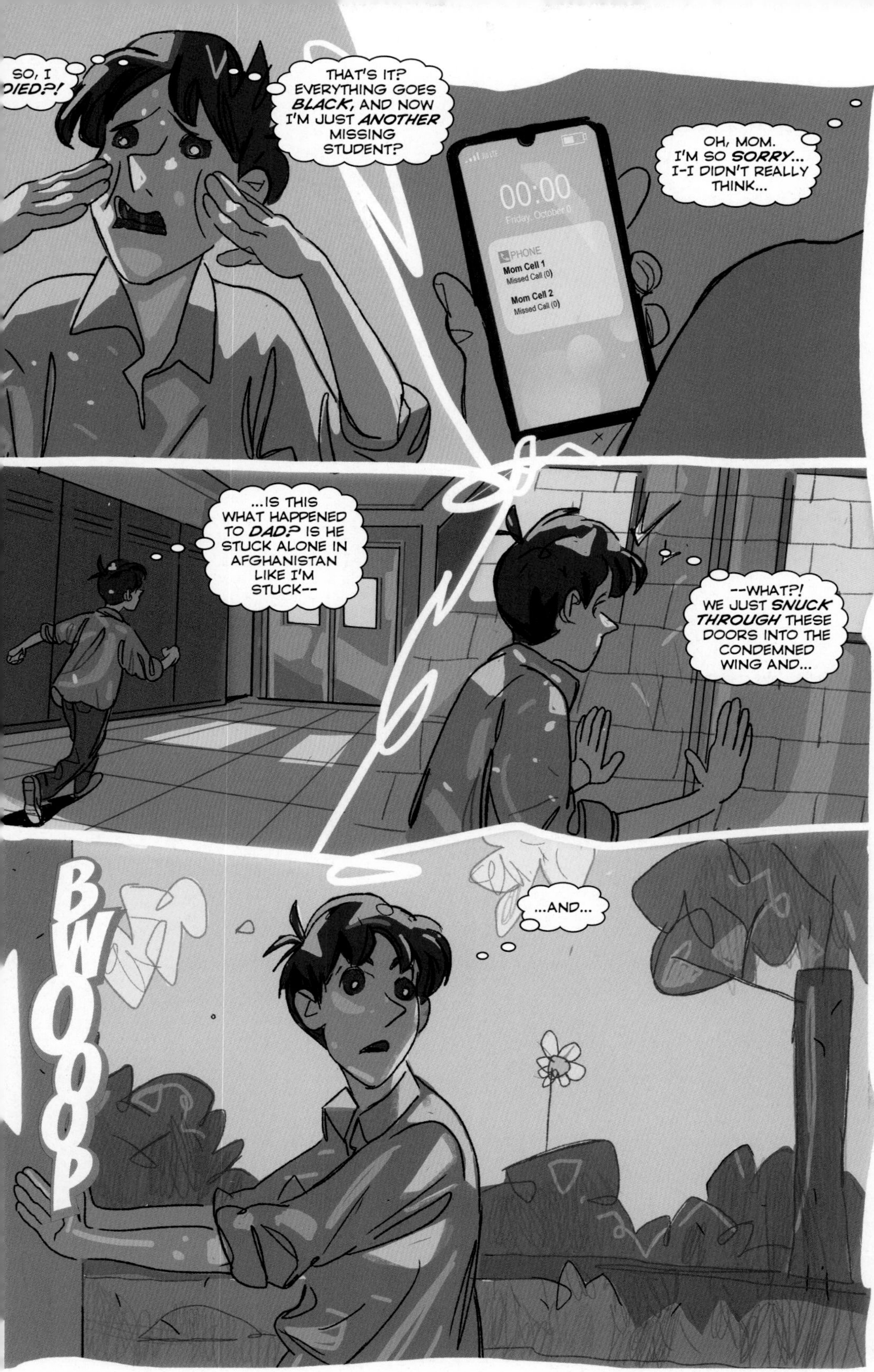
SO, I DIED?!
THAT'S IT? EVERYTHING GOES BLACK, AND NOW I'M JUST ANOTHER MISSING STUDENT?
00:00
Friday, October 0
PHONE
Mom Cell 1
Missed Call (0)
Mom Cell 2
Missed Call (0)
OH, MOM. I'M SO SORRY... I-I DIDN'T REALLY THINK...
...IS THIS WHAT HAPPENED TO DAD? IS HE STUCK ALONE IN AFGHANISTAN LIKE I'M STUCK--
--WHAT?! WE JUST SNUCK THROUGH THESE DOORS INTO THE CONDEMNED WING AND...
BWOOOP
...AND...

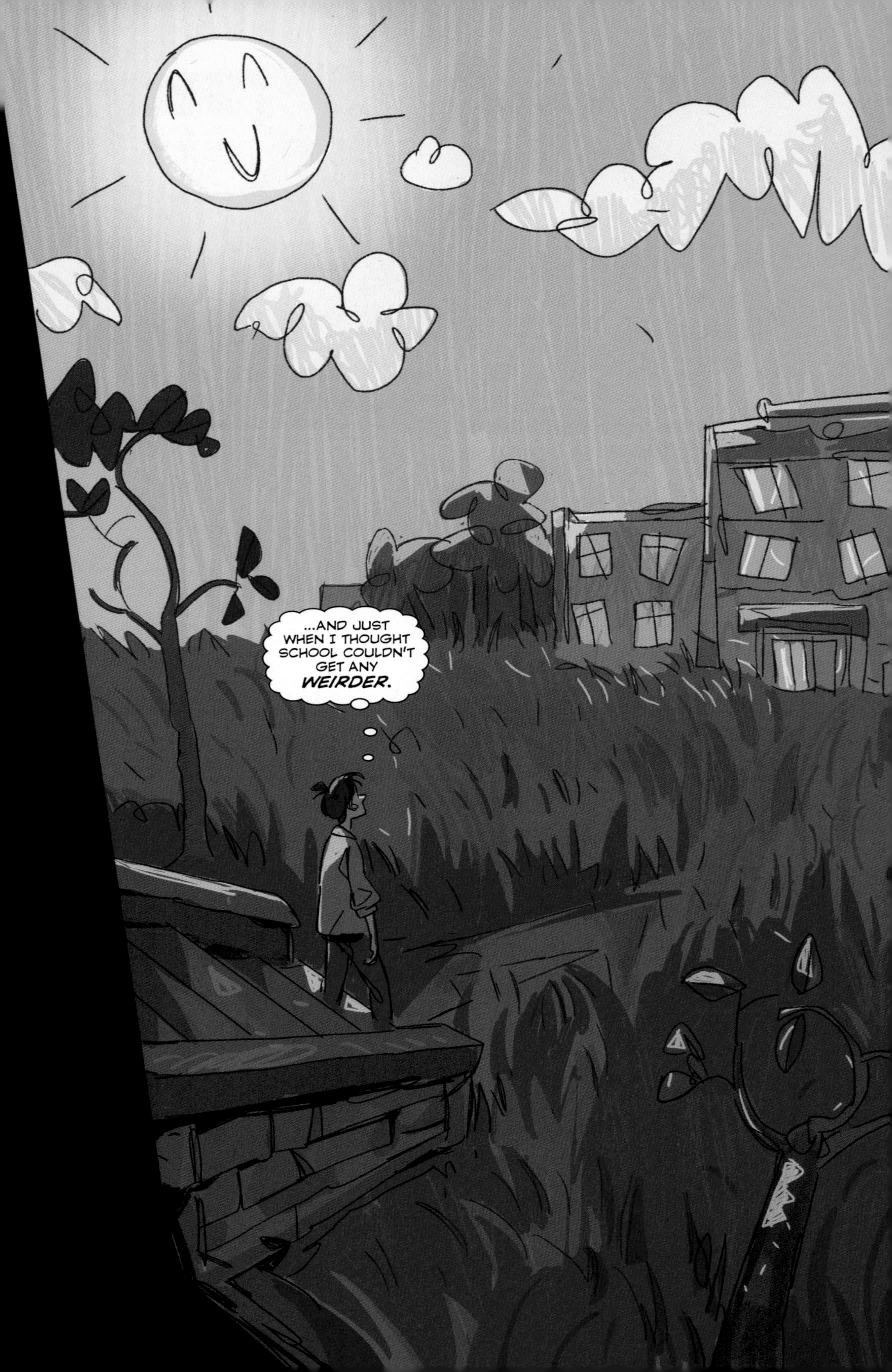
...AND JUST WHEN I THOUGHT SCHOOL COULDN'T GET ANY *WEIRDER*.

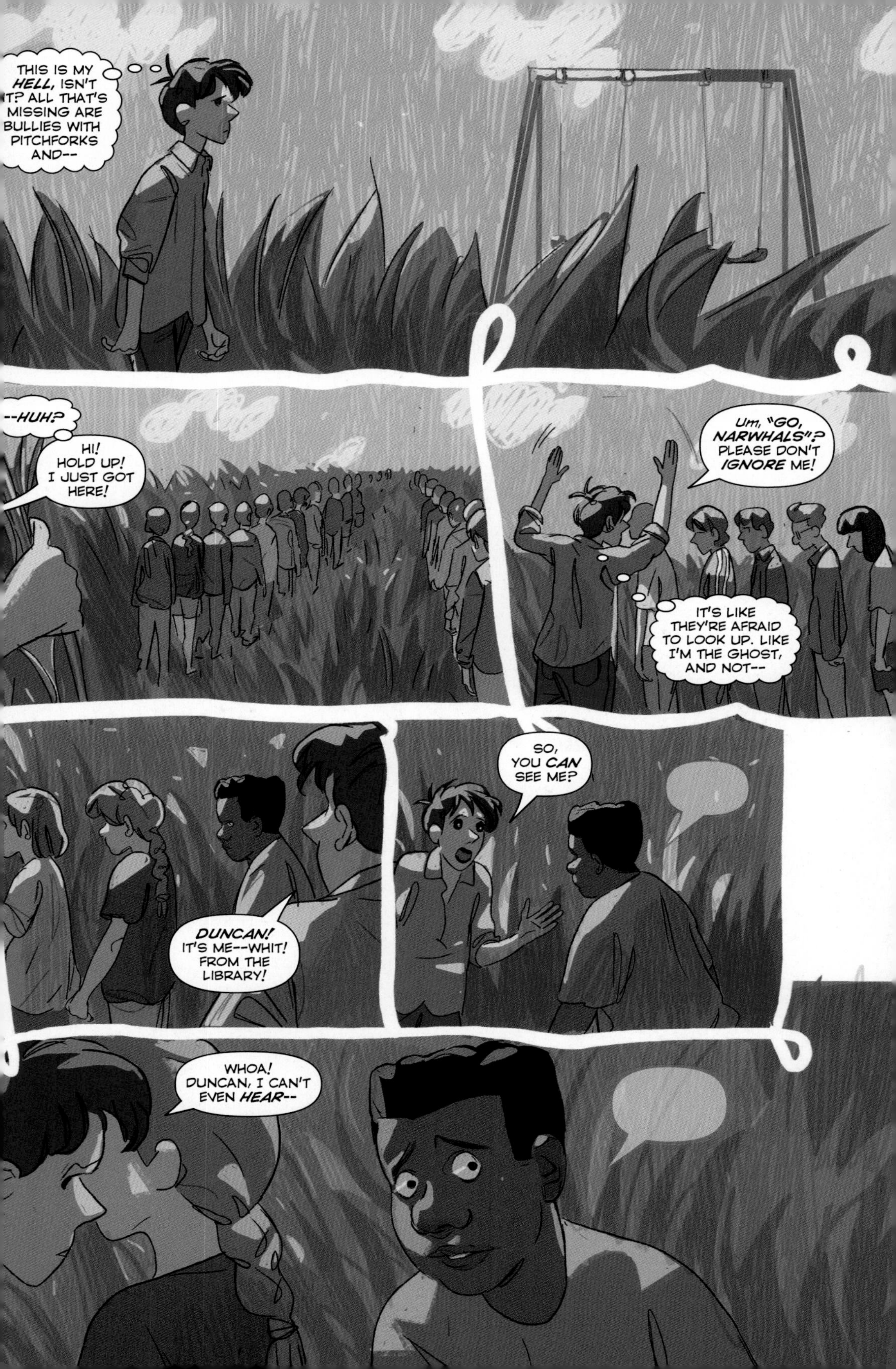
THIS IS MY *HELL*, ISN'T IT? ALL THAT'S MISSING ARE BULLIES WITH PITCHFORKS AND--
--*HUH?*
HI! HOLD UP! I JUST GOT HERE!
Um, "GO, NARWHALS"? PLEASE DON'T *IGNORE* ME!
IT'S LIKE THEY'RE AFRAID TO LOOK UP. LIKE I'M THE GHOST, AND NOT--
DUNCAN! IT'S ME--WHIT! FROM THE LIBRARY!
SO, YOU *CAN* SEE ME?
WHOA! DUNCAN, I CAN'T EVEN *HEAR*--

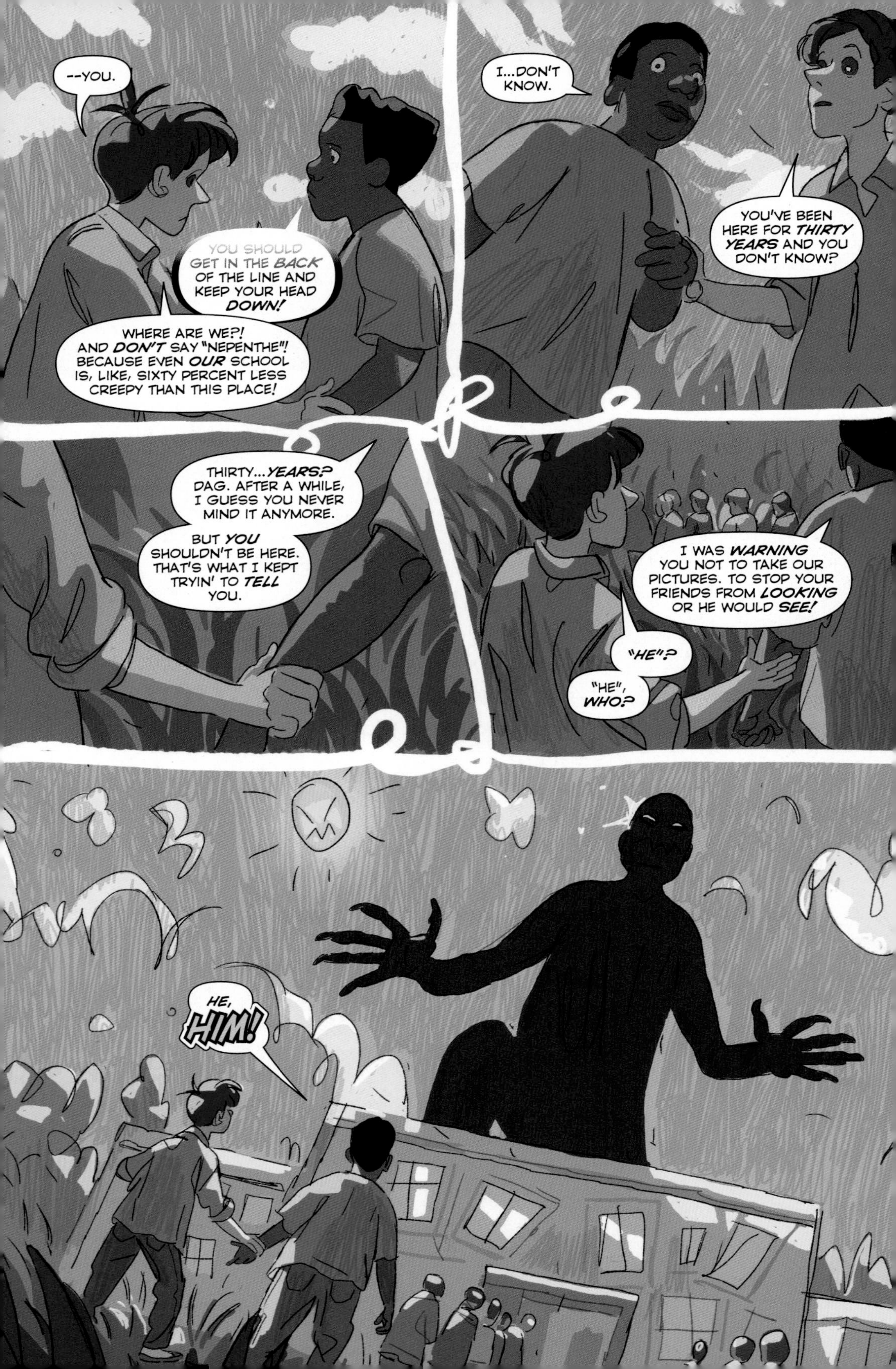
--YOU.
YOU SHOULD GET IN THE BACK OF THE LINE AND KEEP YOUR HEAD DOWN!
WHERE ARE WE?! AND DON'T SAY "NEPENTHE"! BECAUSE EVEN OUR SCHOOL IS, LIKE, SIXTY PERCENT LESS CREEPY THAN THIS PLACE!
I...DON'T KNOW.
YOU'VE BEEN HERE FOR THIRTY YEARS AND YOU DON'T KNOW?
THIRTY...YEARS? DAG. AFTER A WHILE, I GUESS YOU NEVER MIND IT ANYMORE.
BUT YOU SHOULDN'T BE HERE. THAT'S WHAT I KEPT TRYIN' TO TELL YOU.
I WAS WARNING YOU NOT TO TAKE OUR PICTURES. TO STOP YOUR FRIENDS FROM LOOKING OR HE WOULD SEE!
"HE"?
"HE", WHO?
HE, HIM!

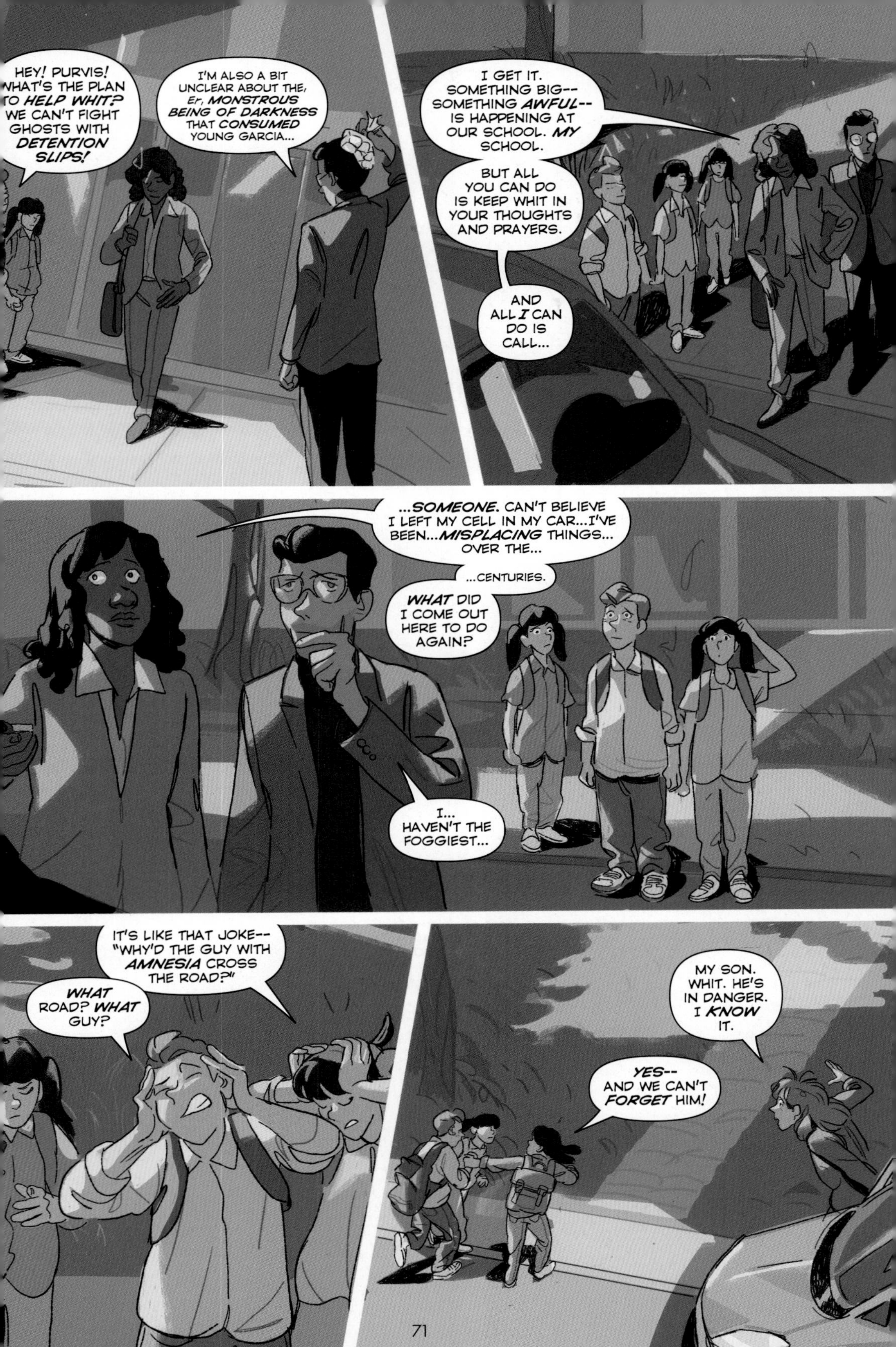
HEY! PURVIS! WHAT'S THE PLAN TO HELP WHIT? WE CAN'T FIGHT GHOSTS WITH DETENTION SLIPS!
I'M ALSO A BIT UNCLEAR ABOUT THE, Er, MONSTROUS BEING OF DARKNESS THAT CONSUMED YOUNG GARCIA...
I GET IT. SOMETHING BIG-- SOMETHING AWFUL-- IS HAPPENING AT OUR SCHOOL. MY SCHOOL.
BUT ALL YOU CAN DO IS KEEP WHIT IN YOUR THOUGHTS AND PRAYERS.
AND ALL I CAN DO IS CALL...
...SOMEONE. CAN'T BELIEVE I LEFT MY CELL IN MY CAR...I'VE BEEN...MISPLACING THINGS... OVER THE...
...CENTURIES.
WHAT DID I COME OUT HERE TO DO AGAIN?
I... HAVEN'T THE FOGGIEST...
IT'S LIKE THAT JOKE-- "WHY'D THE GUY WITH AMNESIA CROSS THE ROAD?"
WHAT ROAD? WHAT GUY?
MY SON. WHIT. HE'S IN DANGER. I KNOW IT.
YES-- AND WE CAN'T FORGET HIM!

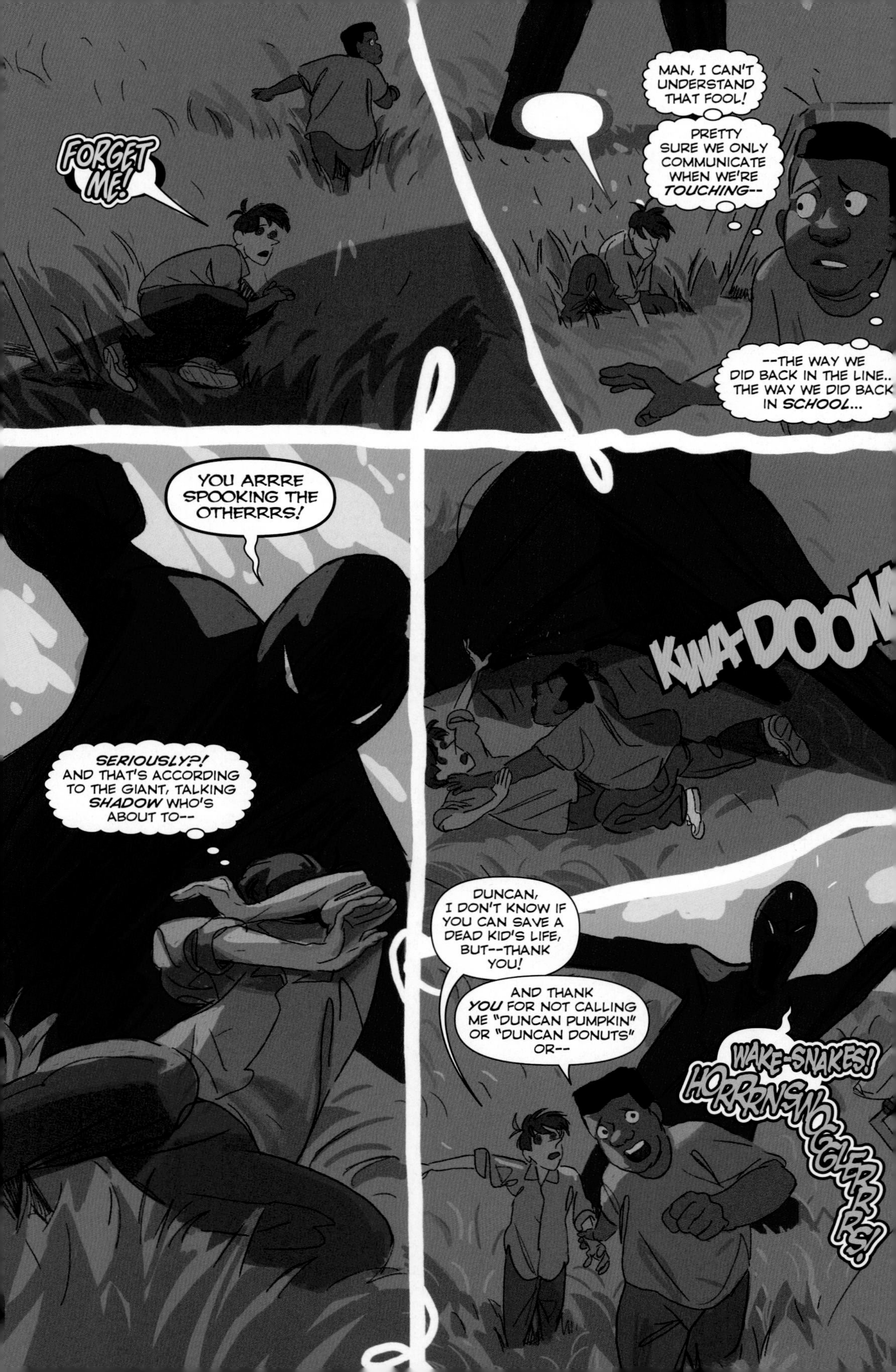
FORGET ME!
MAN, I CAN'T UNDERSTAND THAT FOOL!
PRETTY SURE WE ONLY COMMUNICATE WHEN WE'RE *TOUCHING*--
--THE WAY WE DID BACK IN THE LINE.. THE WAY WE DID BACK IN *SCHOOL*...
YOU ARRRE SPOOKING THE OTHERRRS!
SERIOUSLY?! AND THAT'S ACCORDING TO THE GIANT, TALKING *SHADOW* WHO'S ABOUT TO--
KWA-DOOM
DUNCAN, I DON'T KNOW IF YOU CAN SAVE A DEAD KID'S LIFE, BUT--THANK YOU!
AND THANK *YOU* FOR NOT CALLING ME "DUNCAN PUMPKIN" OR "DUNCAN DONUTS" OR--
WAKE-SNAKES! HORRRNSNOGGLERRRRS!

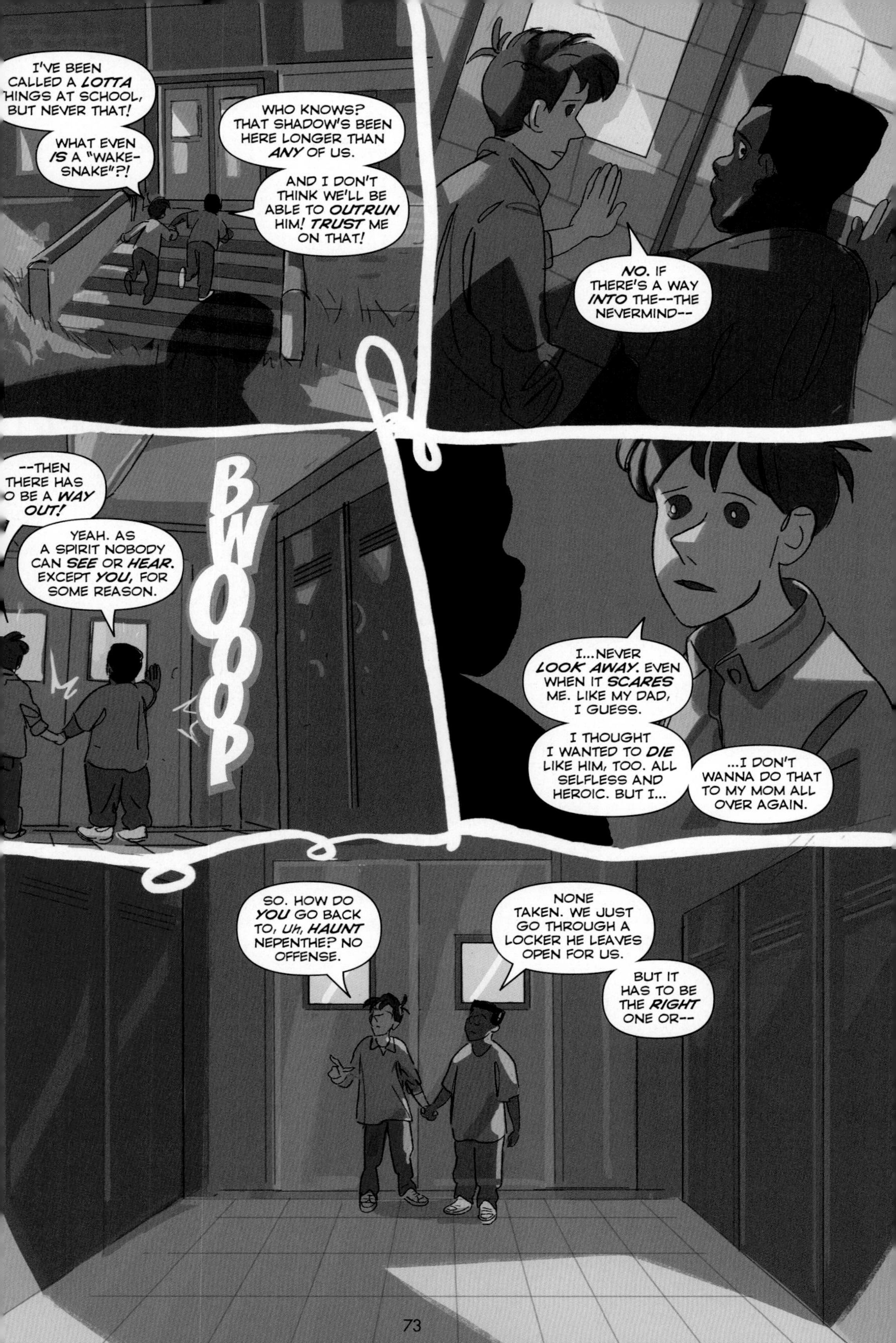
I'VE BEEN CALLED A LOTTA THINGS AT SCHOOL, BUT NEVER THAT!
WHAT EVEN IS A "WAKE-SNAKE"?!
WHO KNOWS? THAT SHADOW'S BEEN HERE LONGER THAN ANY OF US.
AND I DON'T THINK WE'LL BE ABLE TO OUTRUN HIM! TRUST ME ON THAT!
NO. IF THERE'S A WAY INTO THE--THE NEVERMIND--
--THEN THERE HAS TO BE A WAY OUT!
YEAH. AS A SPIRIT NOBODY CAN SEE OR HEAR. EXCEPT YOU, FOR SOME REASON.
BWOOOP
I...NEVER LOOK AWAY. EVEN WHEN IT SCARES ME. LIKE MY DAD, I GUESS.
I THOUGHT I WANTED TO DIE LIKE HIM, TOO. ALL SELFLESS AND HEROIC. BUT I...
...I DON'T WANNA DO THAT TO MY MOM ALL OVER AGAIN.
SO. HOW DO YOU GO BACK TO, Uh, HAUNT NEPENTHE? NO OFFENSE.
NONE TAKEN. WE JUST GO THROUGH A LOCKER HE LEAVES OPEN FOR US.
BUT IT HAS TO BE THE RIGHT ONE OR--

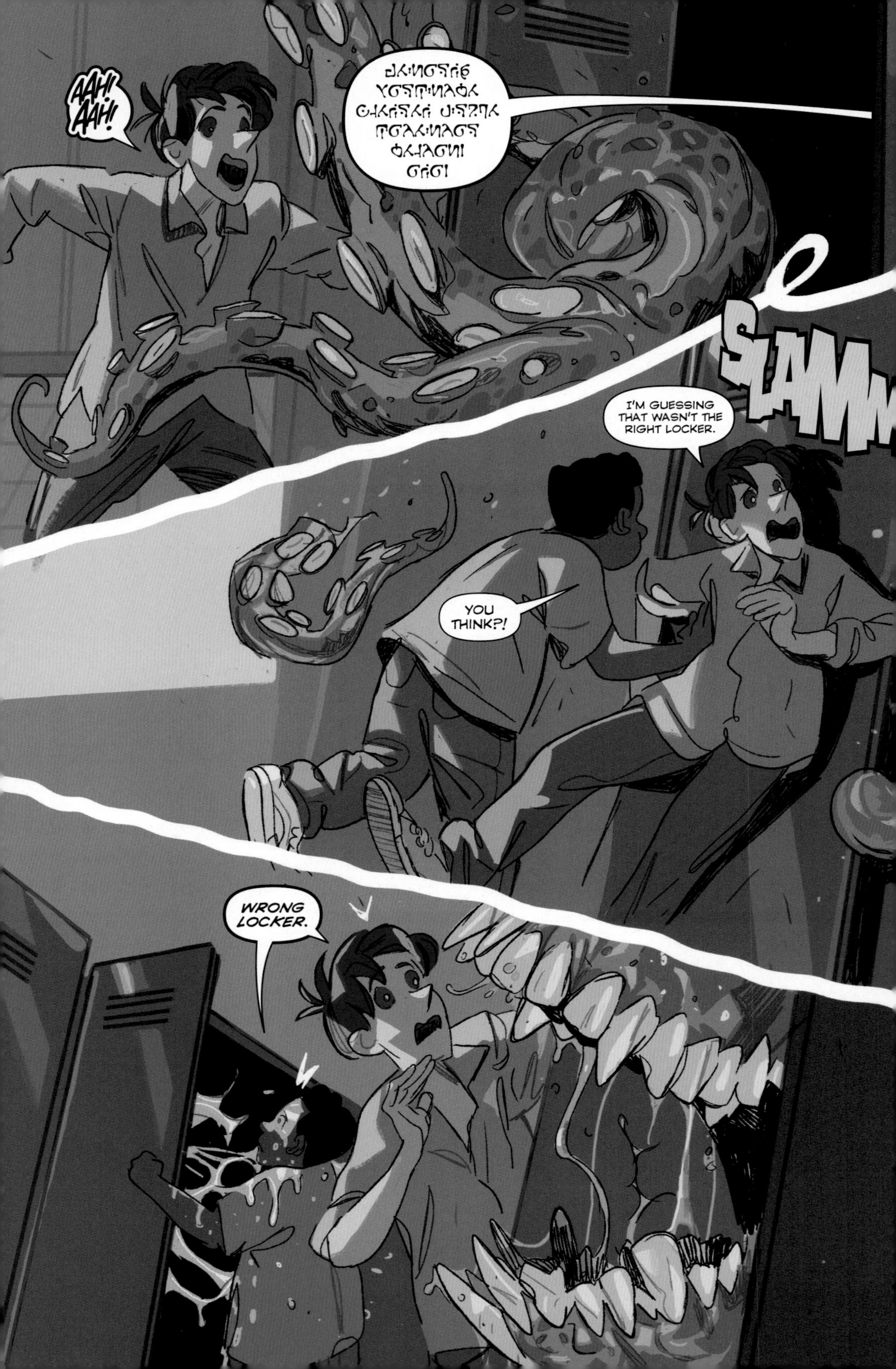
AAH! AAH!
SLAMM
I'M GUESSING THAT WASN'T THE RIGHT LOCKER.
YOU THINK?!
WRONG LOCKER.

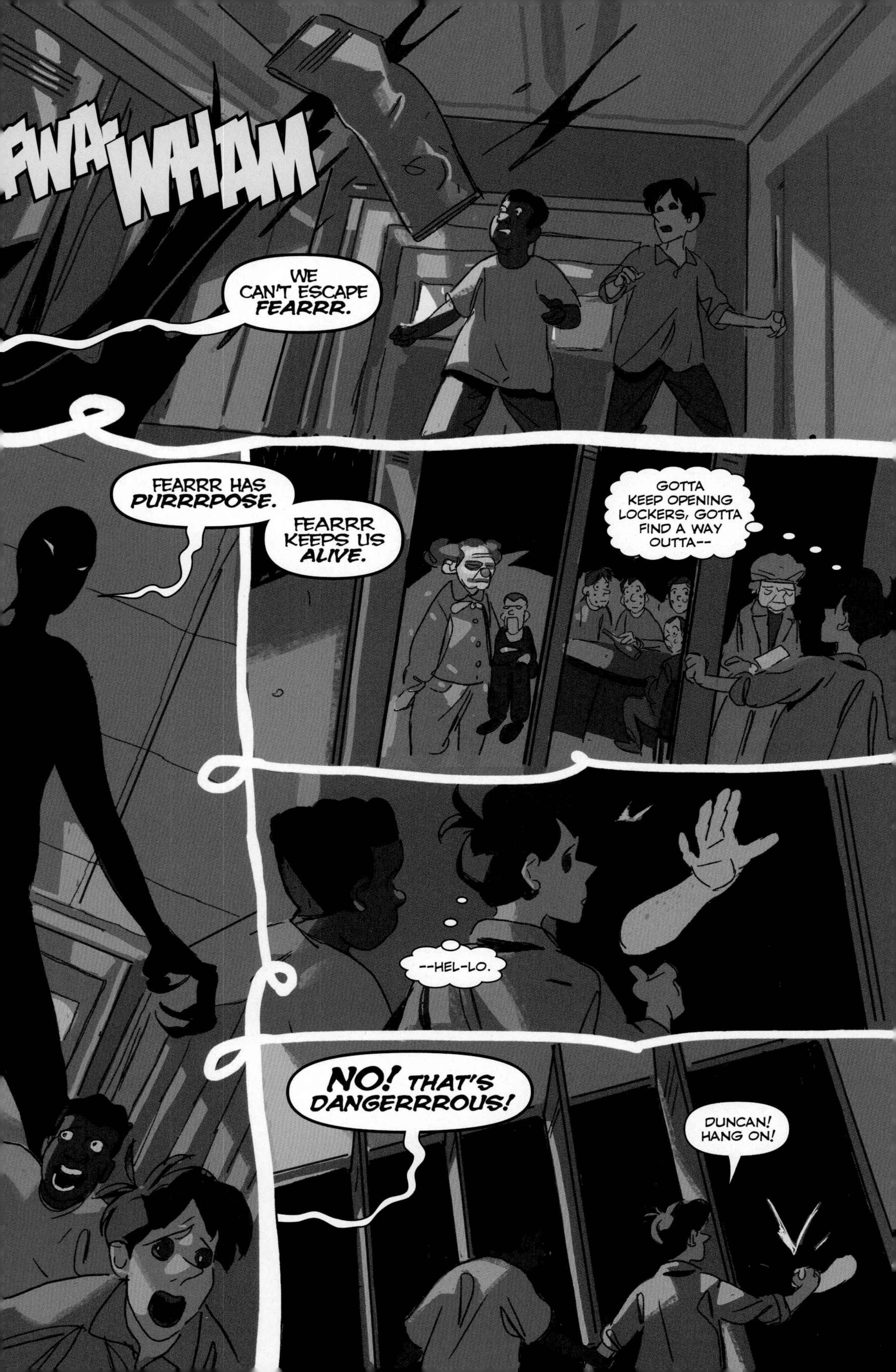
FWA-WHAM
WE CAN'T ESCAPE FEARRR.
FEARRR HAS PURRRPOSE.
FEARRR KEEPS US ALIVE.
GOTTA KEEP OPENING LOCKERS, GOTTA FIND A WAY OUTTA--
--HEL-LO.
NO! THAT'S DANGERRROUS!
DUNCAN! HANG ON!

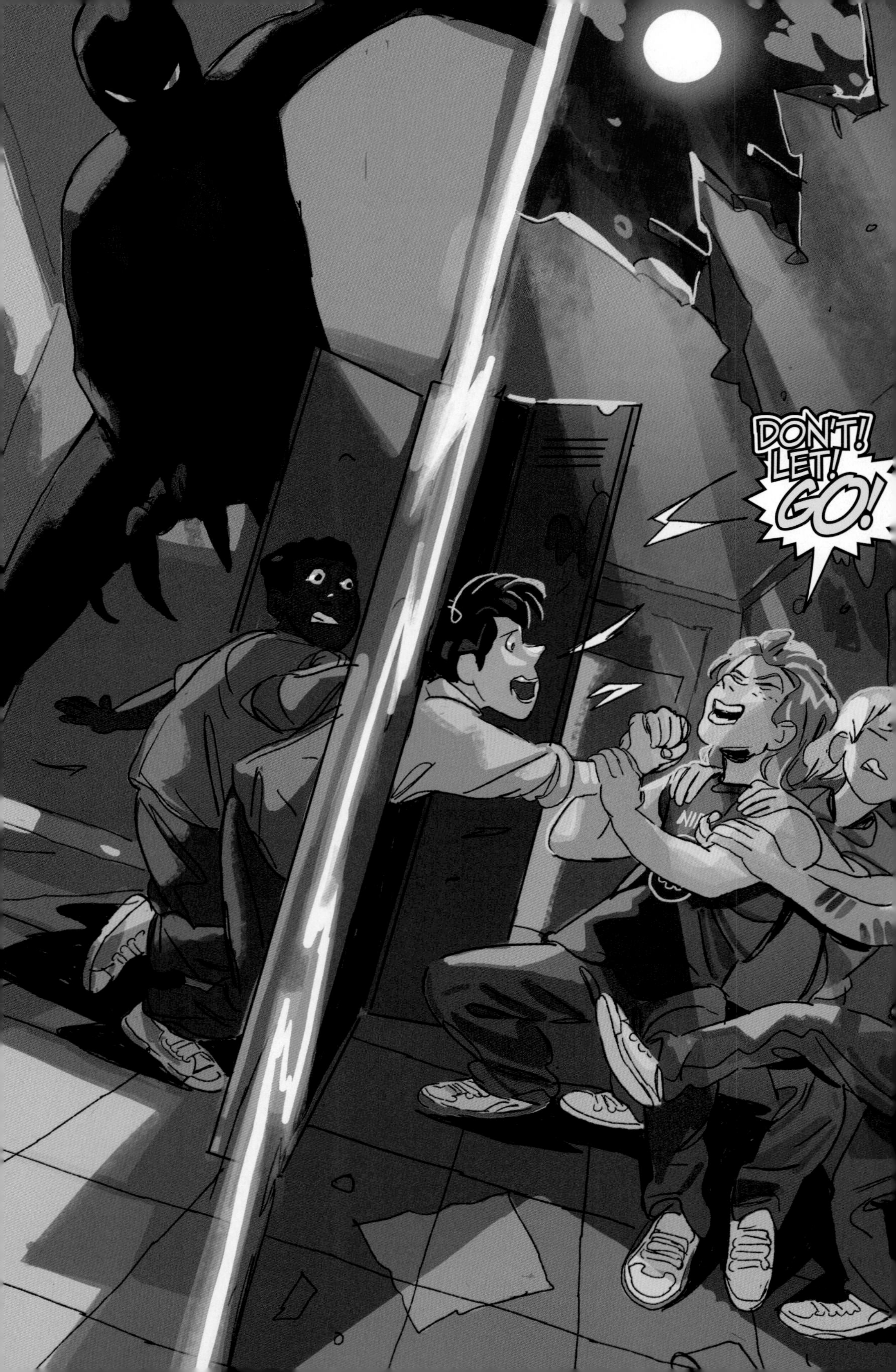
DON'T! LET! GO!

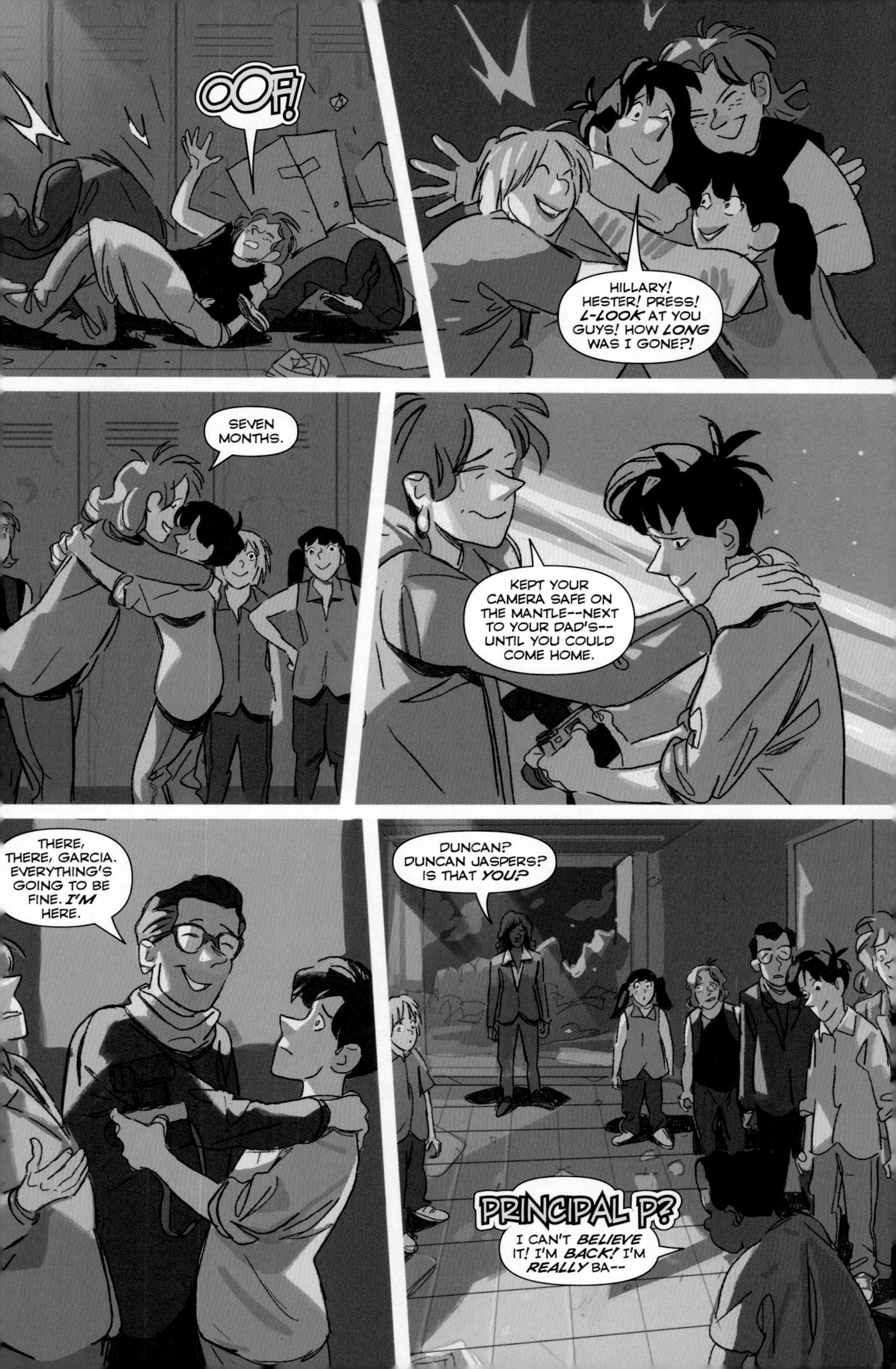
OOF!
HILLARY! HESTER! PRESS! L-LOOK AT YOU GUYS! HOW LONG WAS I GONE?!
SEVEN MONTHS.
KEPT YOUR CAMERA SAFE ON THE MANTLE--NEXT TO YOUR DAD'S--UNTIL YOU COULD COME HOME.
THERE, THERE, GARCIA. EVERYTHING'S GOING TO BE FINE. I'M HERE.
DUNCAN? DUNCAN JASPERS? IS THAT YOU?
PRINCIPAL P?
I CAN'T BELIEVE IT! I'M BACK! I'M REALLY BA--

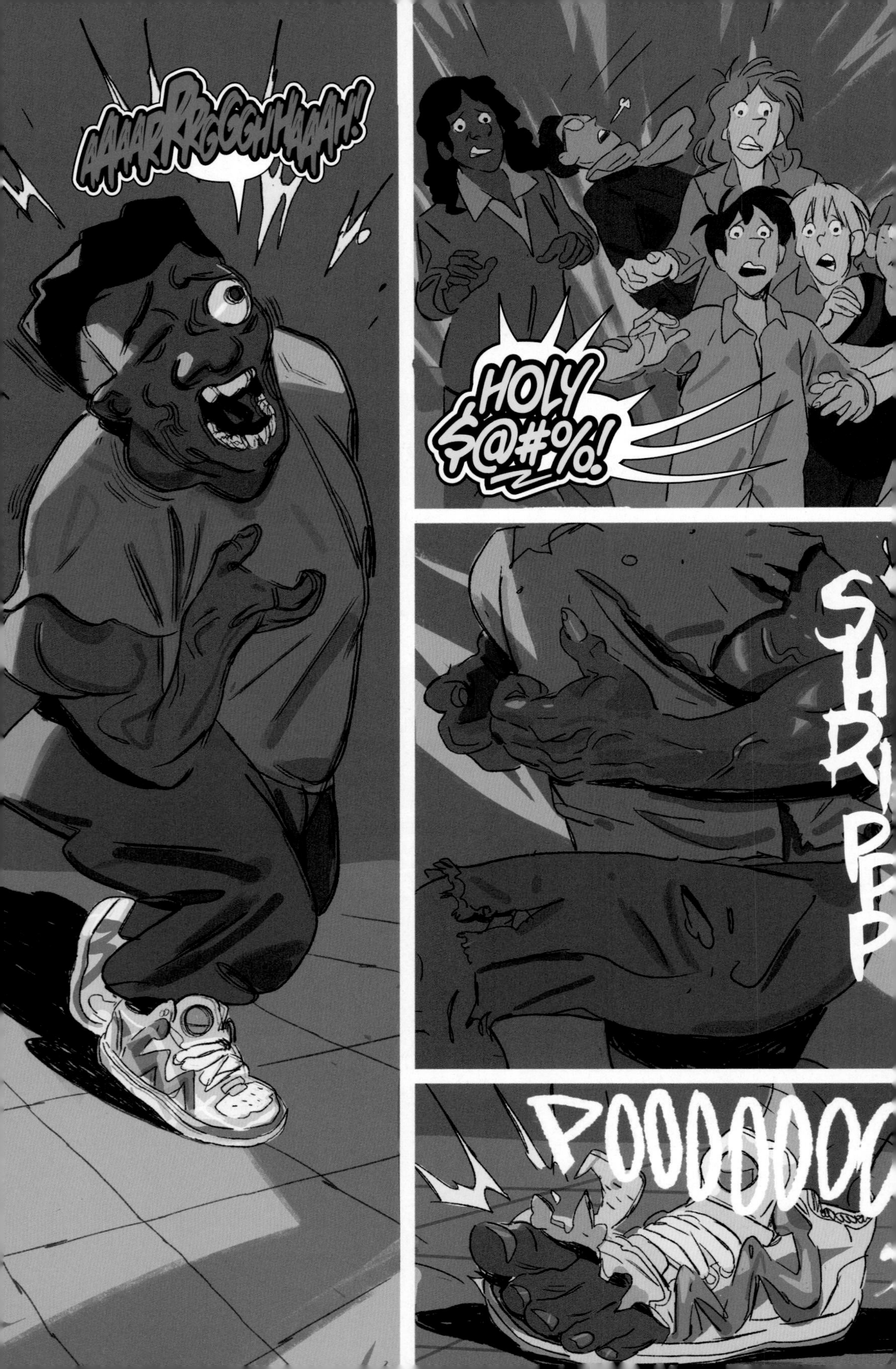
AAAARRRGGGHHAAAAH!
HOLY $@#%!
SHRIPPP
POOOOOOC

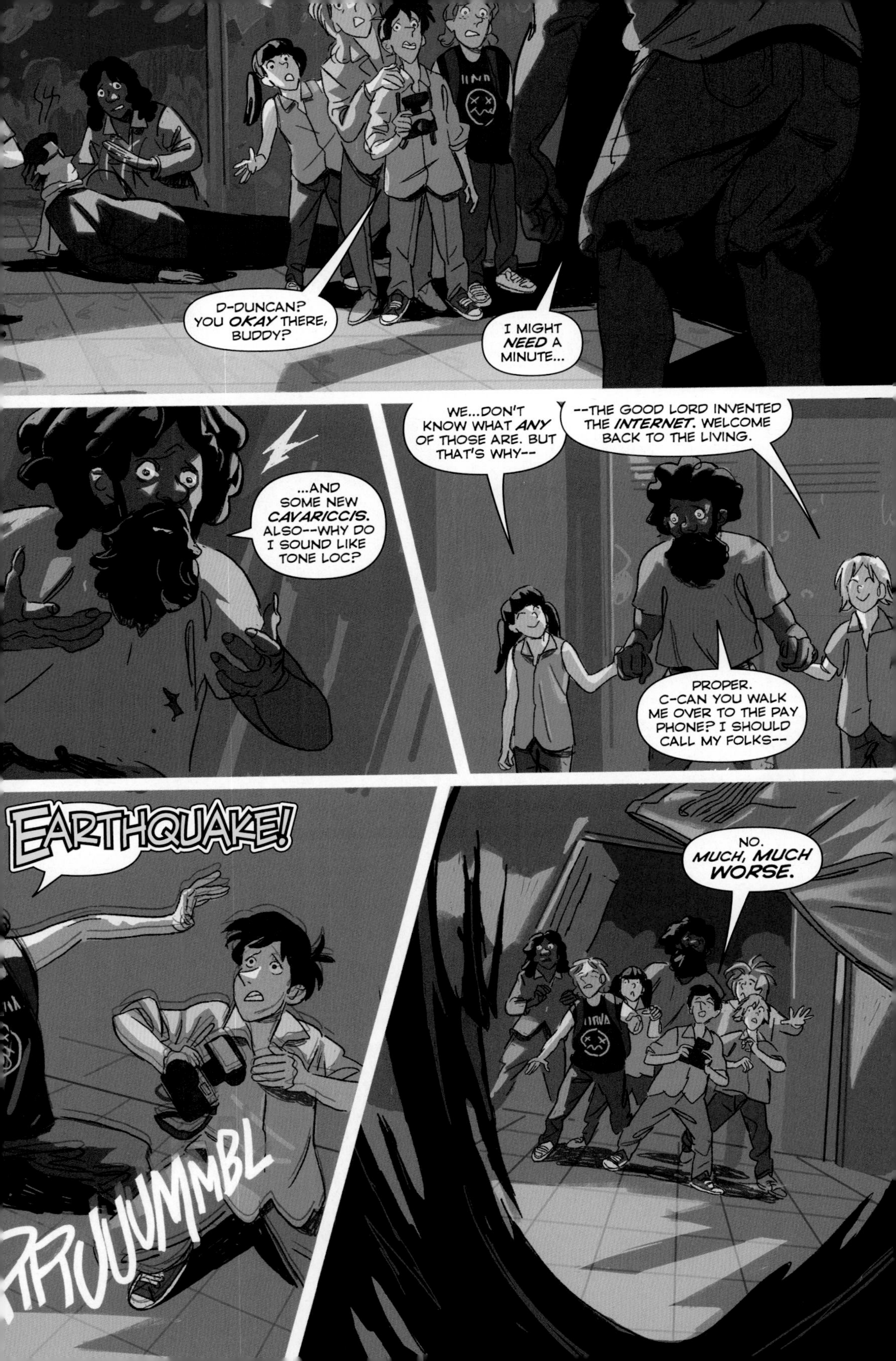
D-DUNCAN? YOU OKAY THERE, BUDDY?
I MIGHT NEED A MINUTE...
...AND SOME NEW CAVARICCIS. ALSO--WHY DO I SOUND LIKE TONE LOC?
WE...DON'T KNOW WHAT ANY OF THOSE ARE. BUT THAT'S WHY--
--THE GOOD LORD INVENTED THE INTERNET. WELCOME BACK TO THE LIVING.
PROPER. C-CAN YOU WALK ME OVER TO THE PAY PHONE? I SHOULD CALL MY FOLKS--
EARTHQUAKE!
RRUUUMMBL
NO. MUCH, MUCH WORSE.

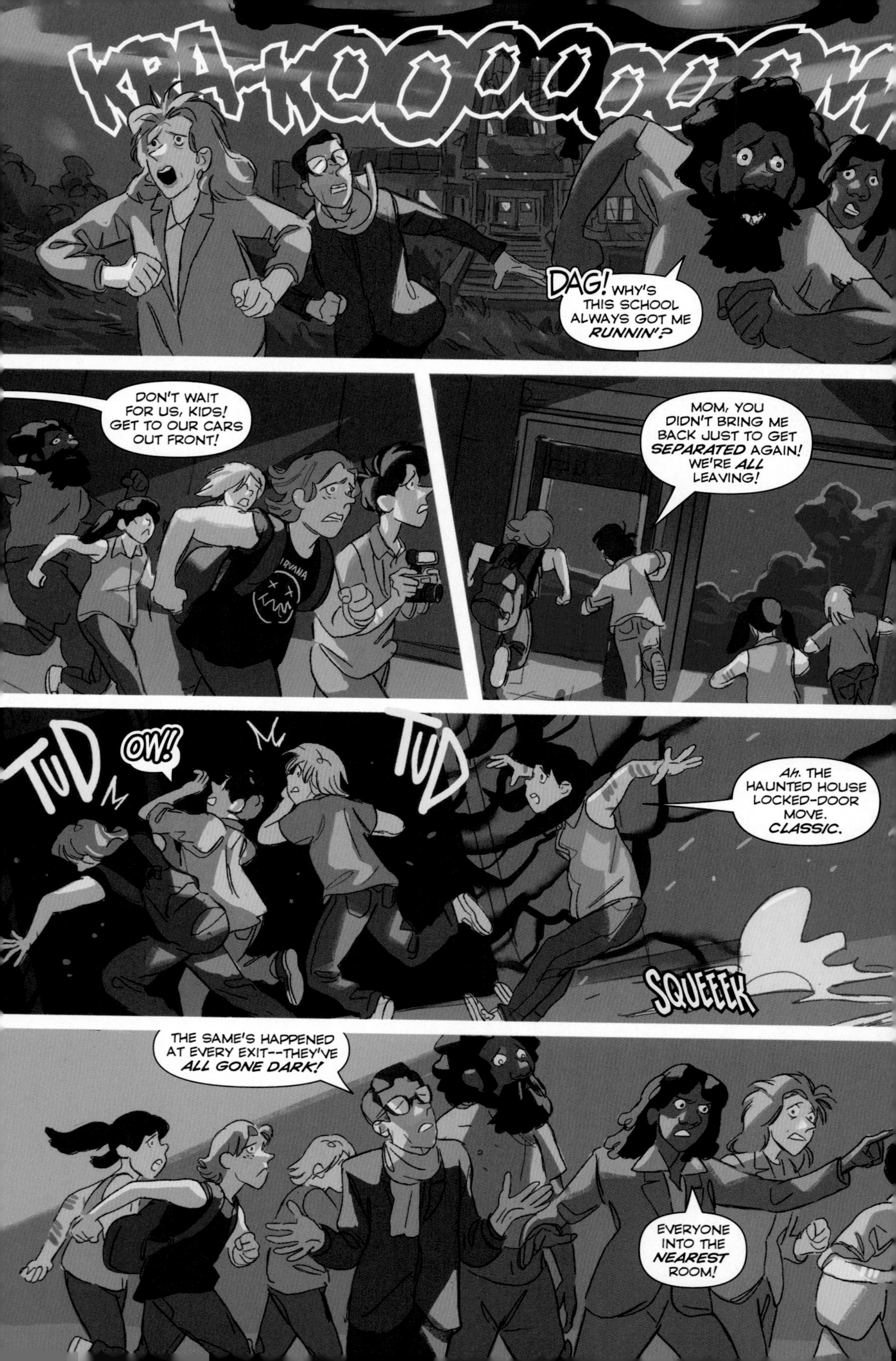
KRA-KOOOOOOOM
DAG! WHY'S THIS SCHOOL ALWAYS GOT ME RUNNIN'?
DON'T WAIT FOR US, KIDS! GET TO OUR CARS OUT FRONT!
MOM, YOU DIDN'T BRING ME BACK JUST TO GET SEPARATED AGAIN! WE'RE ALL LEAVING!
TUD
OW!
TUD
AH. THE HAUNTED HOUSE LOCKED-DOOR MOVE. CLASSIC.
SQUEEEK
THE SAME'S HAPPENED AT EVERY EXIT--THEY'VE ALL GONE DARK!
EVERYONE INTO THE NEAREST ROOM!

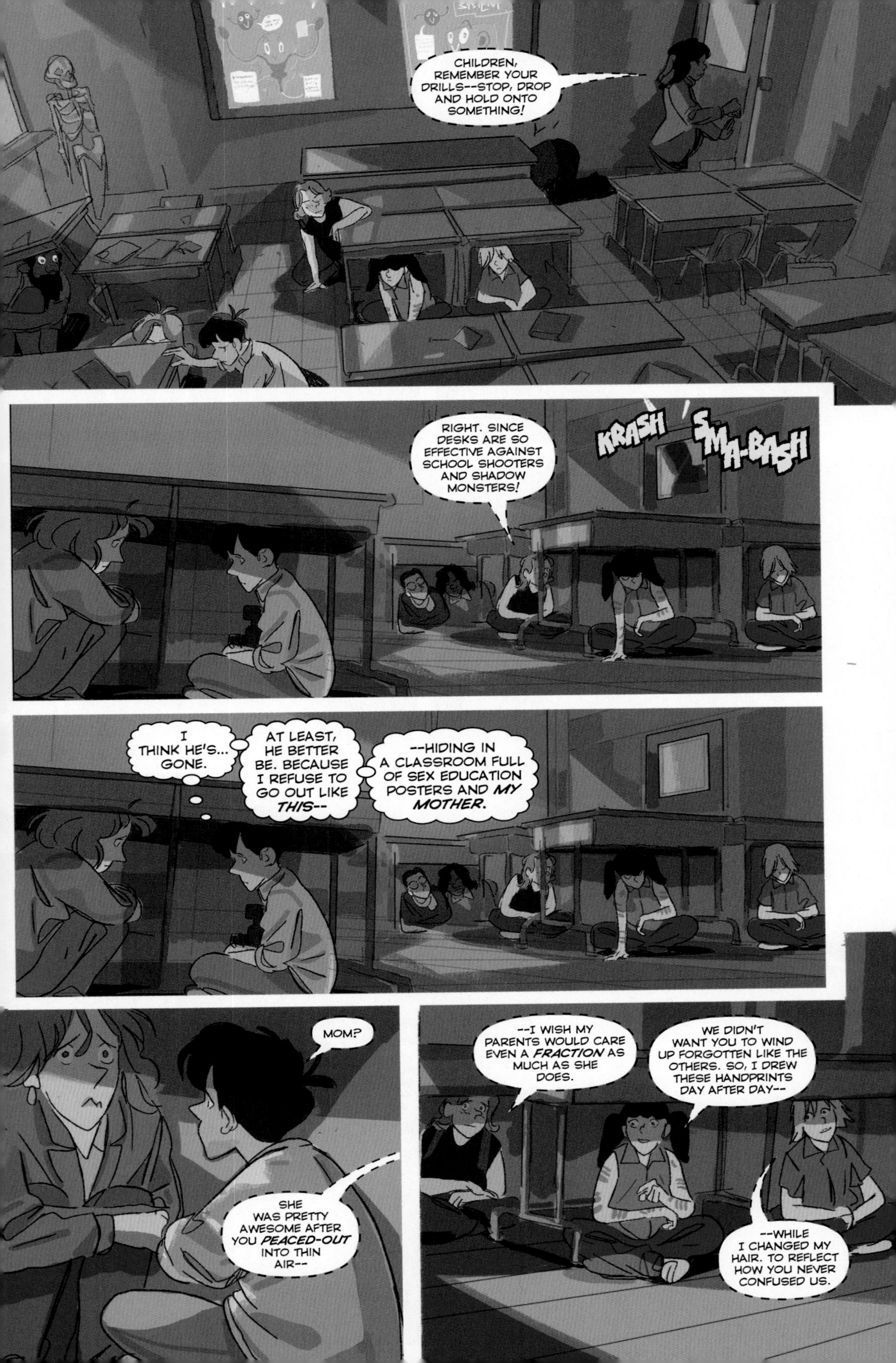
CHILDREN, REMEMBER YOUR DRILLS--STOP, DROP AND HOLD ONTO SOMETHING!
RIGHT. SINCE DESKS ARE SO EFFECTIVE AGAINST SCHOOL SHOOTERS AND SHADOW MONSTERS!
KRASH
SMA-BASH
I THINK HE'S... GONE.
AT LEAST, HE BETTER BE. BECAUSE I REFUSE TO GO OUT LIKE THIS--
--HIDING IN A CLASSROOM FULL OF SEX EDUCATION POSTERS AND MY MOTHER.
MOM?
SHE WAS PRETTY AWESOME AFTER YOU PEACED-OUT INTO THIN AIR--
--I WISH MY PARENTS WOULD CARE EVEN A FRACTION AS MUCH AS SHE DOES.
WE DIDN'T WANT YOU TO WIND UP FORGOTTEN LIKE THE OTHERS. SO, I DREW THESE HANDPRINTS DAY AFTER DAY--
--WHILE I CHANGED MY HAIR. TO REFLECT HOW YOU NEVER CONFUSED US.

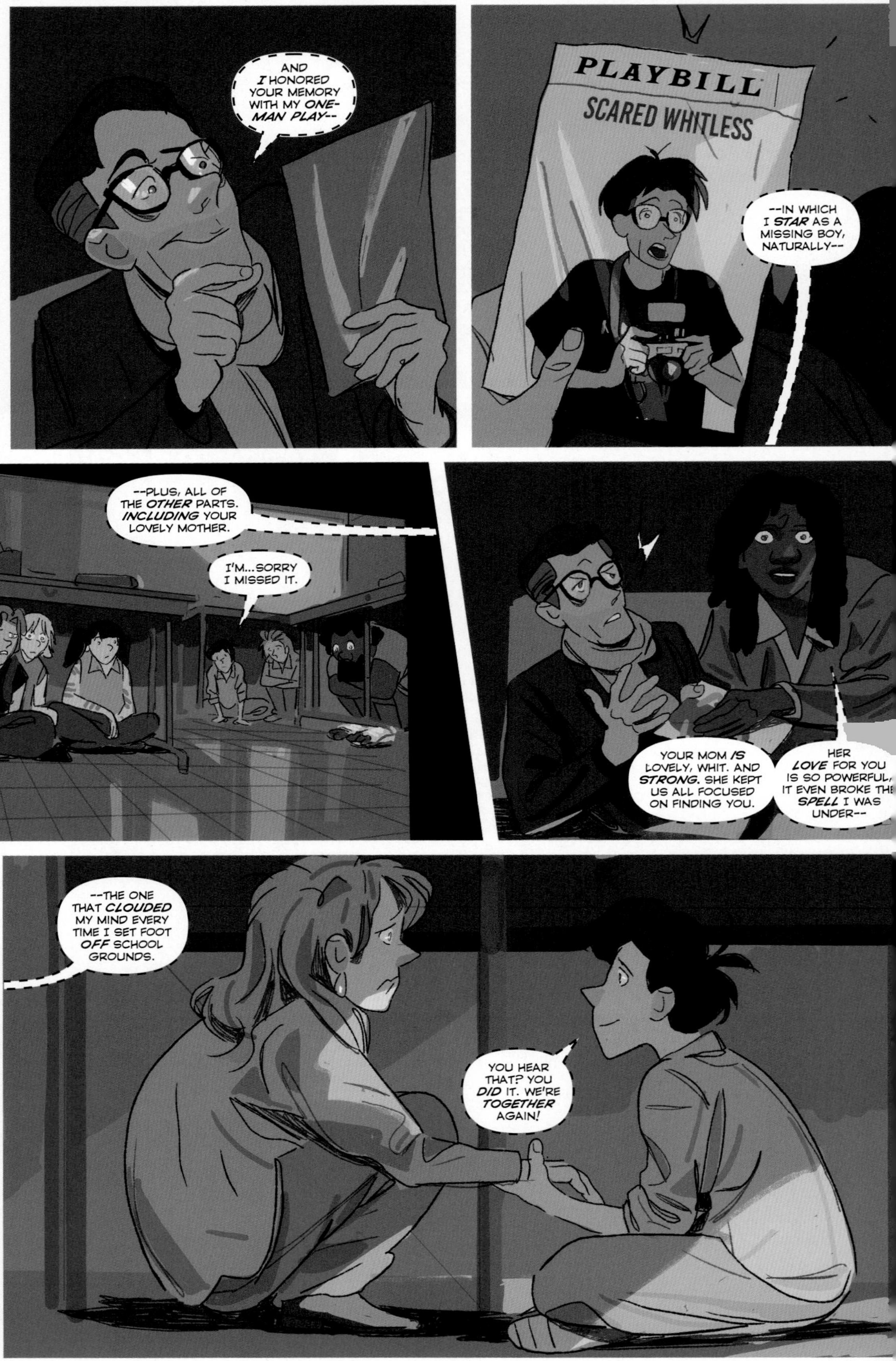

AND *I* HONORED YOUR MEMORY WITH MY *ONE-MAN PLAY*--
PLAYBILL
SCARED WHITLESS
--IN WHICH I *STAR* AS A MISSING BOY, NATURALLY--
--PLUS, ALL OF THE *OTHER* PARTS. *INCLUDING* YOUR LOVELY MOTHER.
I'M...SORRY I MISSED IT.
YOUR MOM *IS* LOVELY, WHIT. AND *STRONG*. SHE KEPT US ALL FOCUSED ON FINDING YOU.
HER *LOVE* FOR YOU IS SO POWERFUL, IT EVEN BROKE THE *SPELL* I WAS UNDER--
--THE ONE THAT *CLOUDED* MY MIND EVERY TIME I SET FOOT *OFF* SCHOOL GROUNDS.
YOU HEAR THAT? YOU *DID* IT. WE'RE *TOGETHER* AGAIN!

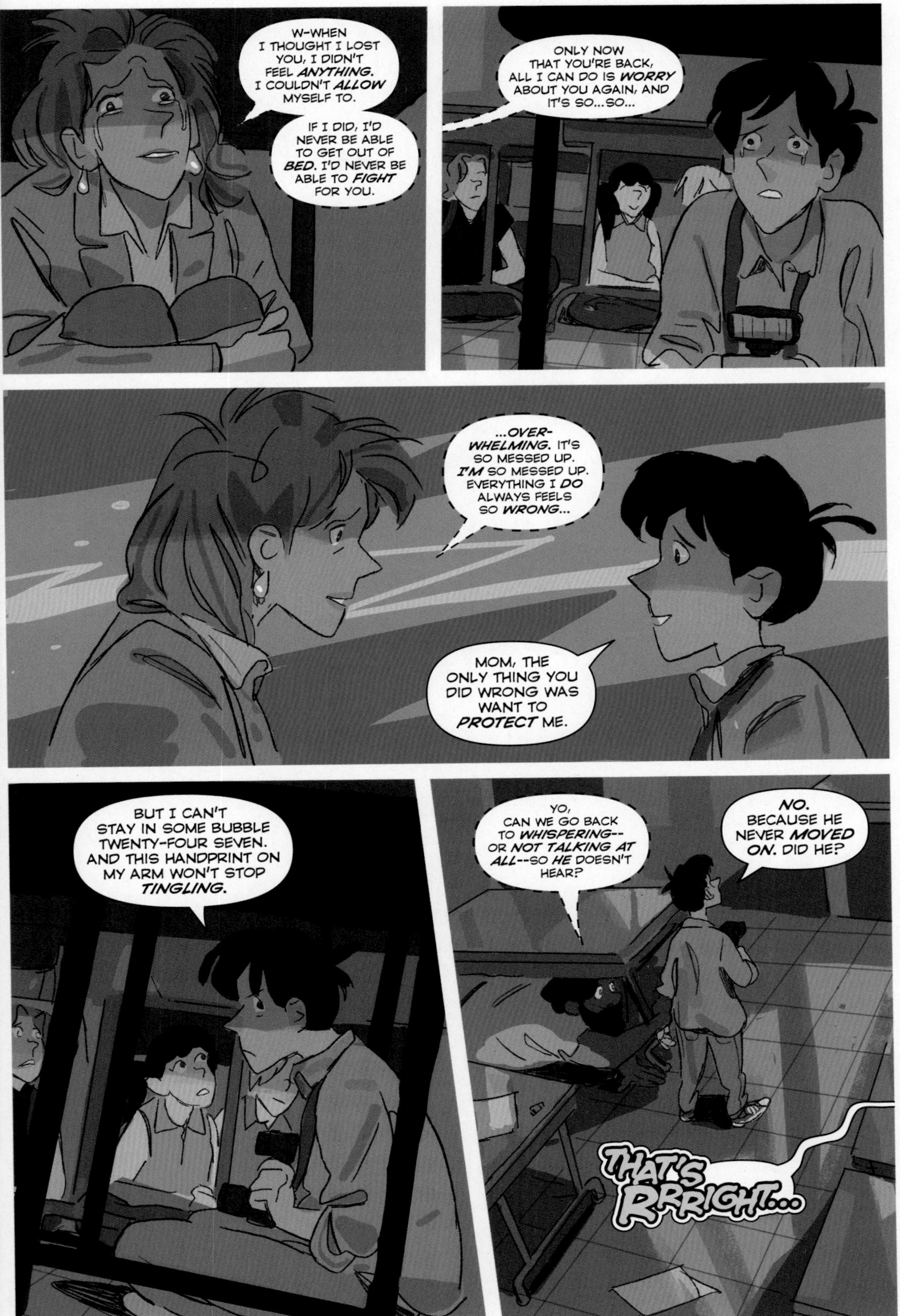
W-WHEN I THOUGHT I LOST YOU, I DIDN'T FEEL ANYTHING. I COULDN'T ALLOW MYSELF TO.
IF I DID, I'D NEVER BE ABLE TO GET OUT OF BED. I'D NEVER BE ABLE TO FIGHT FOR YOU.
ONLY NOW THAT YOU'RE BACK, ALL I CAN DO IS WORRY ABOUT YOU AGAIN, AND IT'S SO...SO...
...OVER-WHELMING. IT'S SO MESSED UP. I'M SO MESSED UP. EVERYTHING I DO ALWAYS FEELS SO WRONG...
MOM, THE ONLY THING YOU DID WRONG WAS WANT TO PROTECT ME.
BUT I CAN'T STAY IN SOME BUBBLE TWENTY-FOUR SEVEN. AND THIS HANDPRINT ON MY ARM WON'T STOP TINGLING.
YO, CAN WE GO BACK TO WHISPERING-- OR NOT TALKING AT ALL--SO HE DOESN'T HEAR?
NO. BECAUSE HE NEVER MOVED ON. DID HE?
THAT'S RRRIGHT...

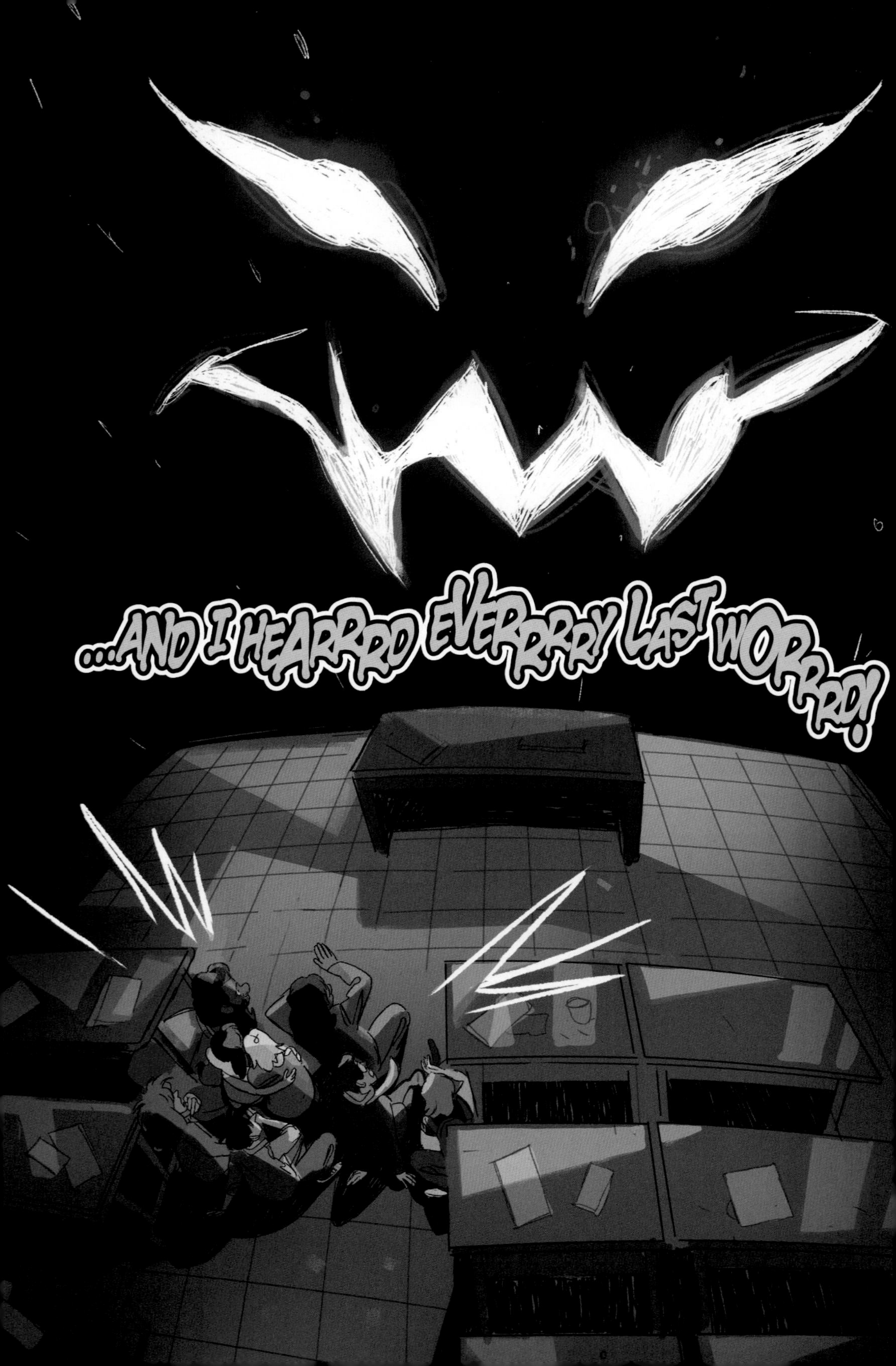
...AND I HEARRRD EVERRRRY LAST WORRRD!

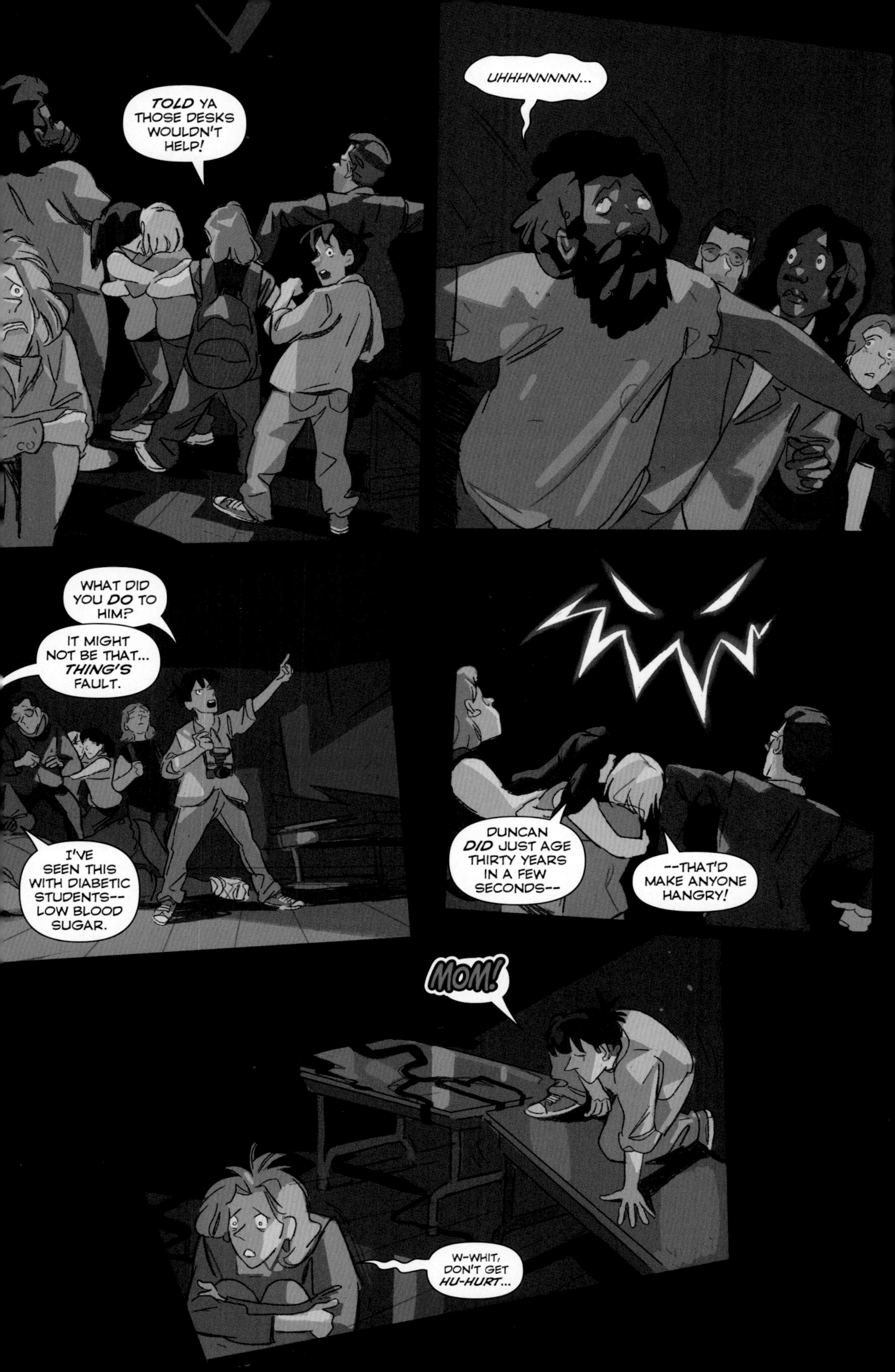
TOLD YA THOSE DESKS WOULDN'T HELP!
UHHHNNNNN...
WHAT DID YOU DO TO HIM?
IT MIGHT NOT BE THAT... THING'S FAULT.
I'VE SEEN THIS WITH DIABETIC STUDENTS-- LOW BLOOD SUGAR.
DUNCAN DID JUST AGE THIRTY YEARS IN A FEW SECONDS--
--THAT'D MAKE ANYONE HANGRY!
MOM!
W-WHIT, DON'T GET HU-HURT...

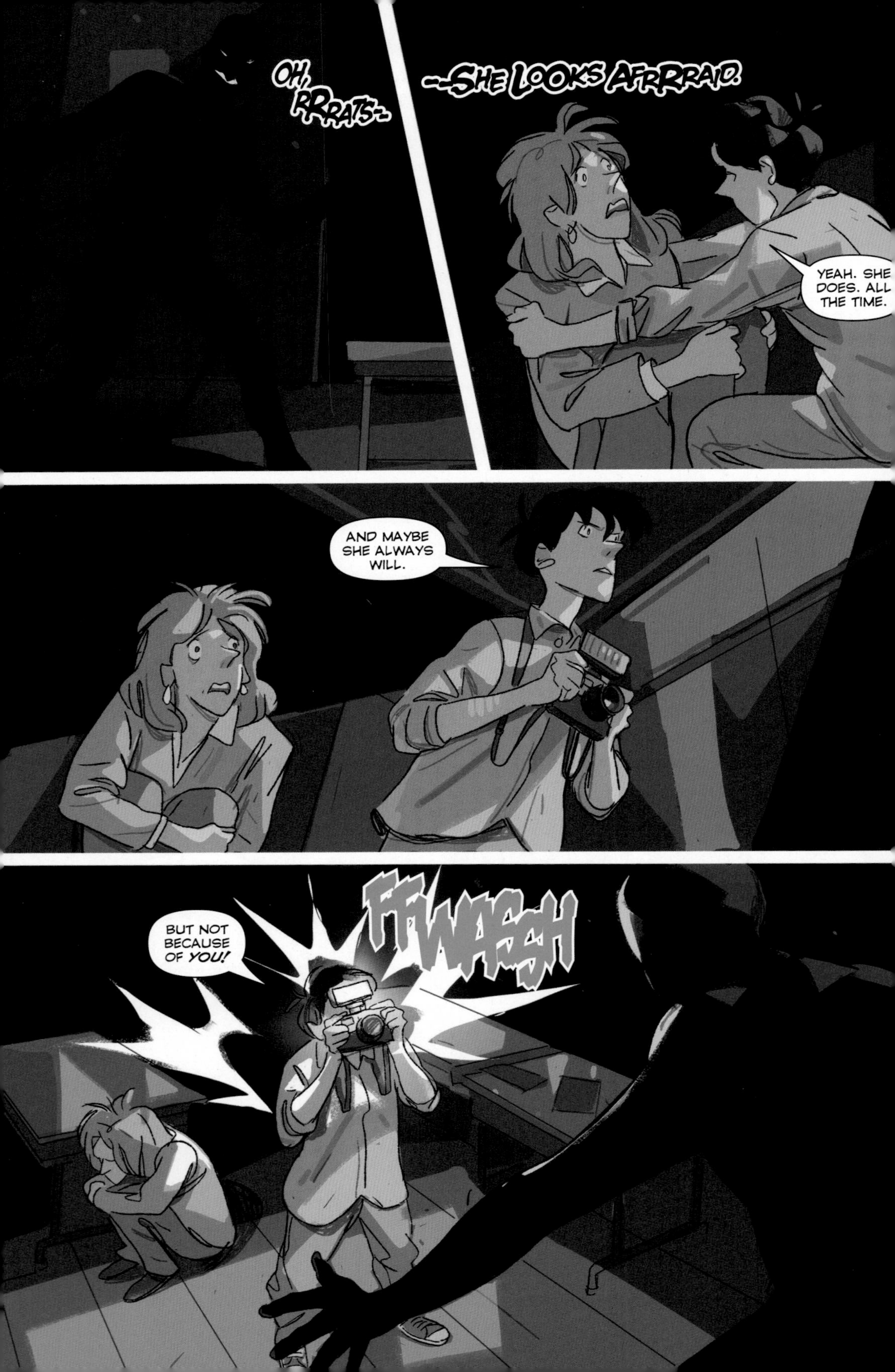
OH, RRRATS--
--SHE LOOKS AFRRRAID.
YEAH. SHE DOES. ALL THE TIME.
AND MAYBE SHE ALWAYS WILL.
BUT NOT BECAUSE OF YOU!
FFWASSH

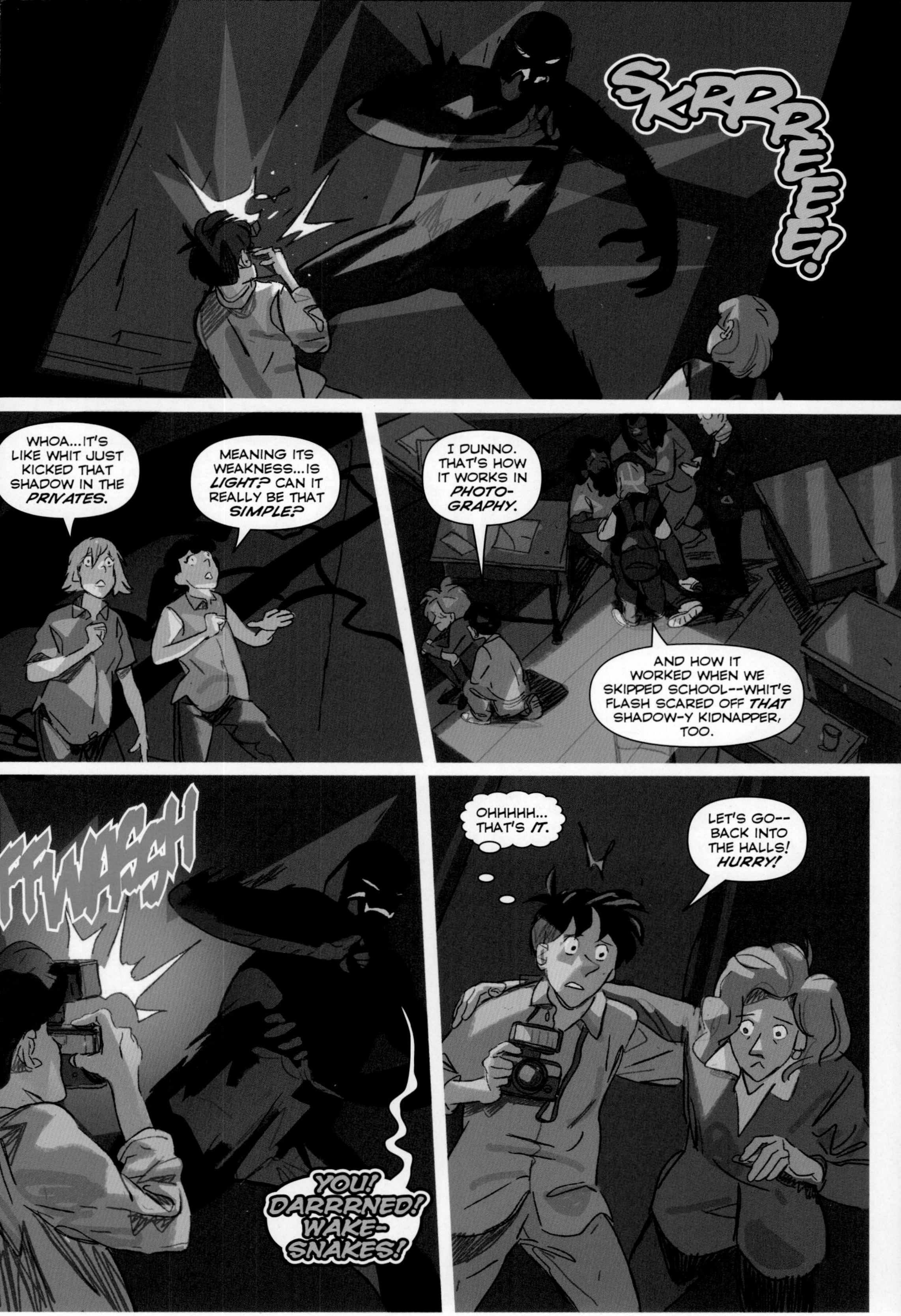
SKRRREEEE!
WHOA...IT'S LIKE WHIT JUST KICKED THAT SHADOW IN THE PRIVATES.
MEANING ITS WEAKNESS...IS LIGHT? CAN IT REALLY BE THAT SIMPLE?
I DUNNO. THAT'S HOW IT WORKS IN PHOTOGRAPHY.
AND HOW IT WORKED WHEN WE SKIPPED SCHOOL--WHIT'S FLASH SCARED OFF THAT SHADOW-Y KIDNAPPER, TOO.
FFWASH
YOU! DARRRNED! WAKE-SNAKES!
OHHHHH... THAT'S IT.
LET'S GO-- BACK INTO THE HALLS! HURRY!

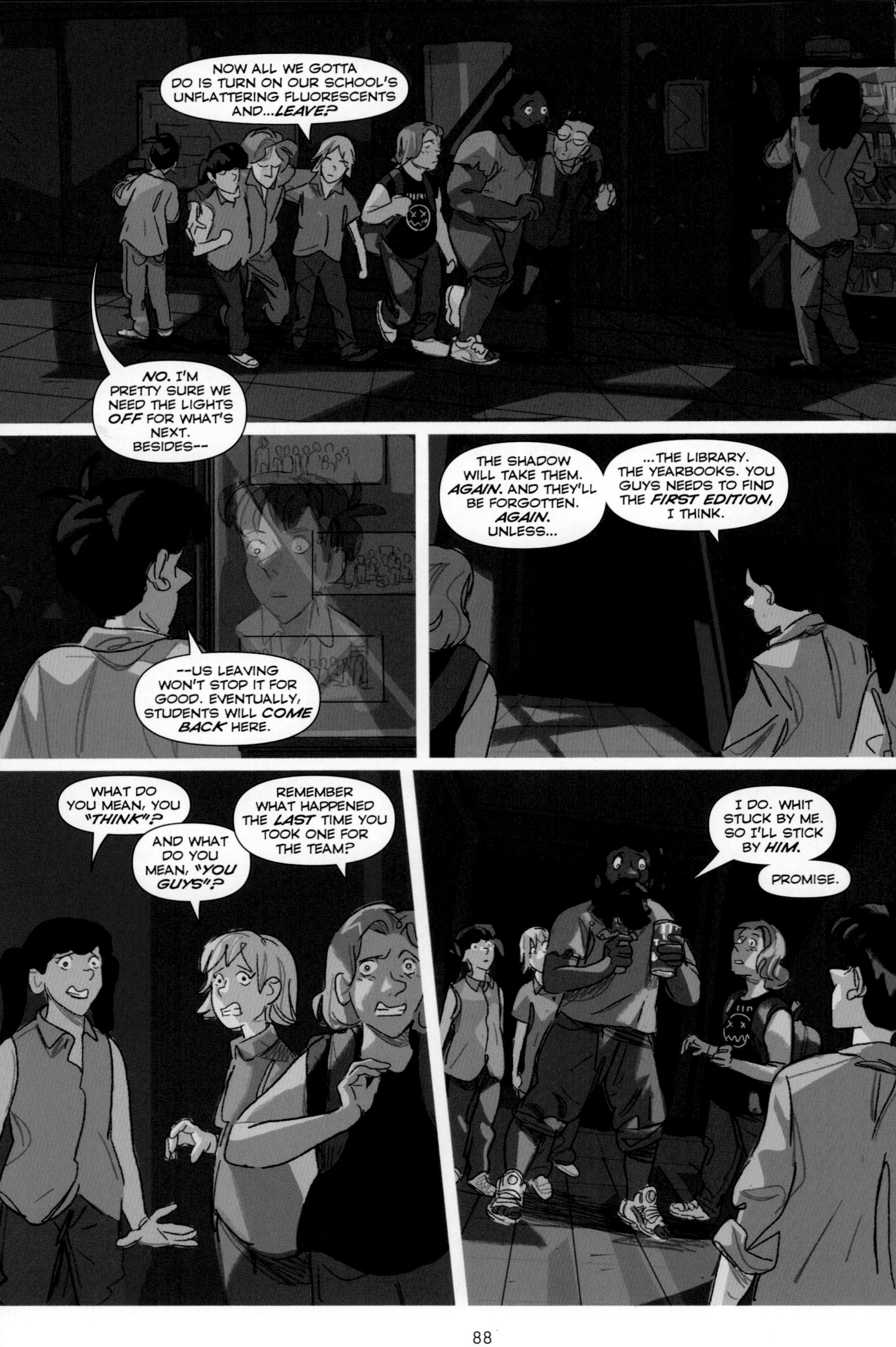
NOW ALL WE GOTTA DO IS TURN ON OUR SCHOOL'S UNFLATTERING FLUORESCENTS AND...*LEAVE?*
NO. I'M PRETTY SURE WE NEED THE LIGHTS *OFF* FOR WHAT'S NEXT. BESIDES--
--US LEAVING WON'T STOP IT FOR GOOD. EVENTUALLY, STUDENTS WILL *COME BACK* HERE.
THE SHADOW WILL TAKE THEM. *AGAIN.* AND THEY'LL BE FORGOTTEN. *AGAIN.* UNLESS...
...THE LIBRARY. THE YEARBOOKS. YOU GUYS NEEDS TO FIND THE *FIRST EDITION,* I THINK.
WHAT DO YOU MEAN, YOU *"THINK"?*
AND WHAT DO YOU MEAN, *"YOU GUYS"?*
REMEMBER WHAT HAPPENED THE *LAST* TIME YOU TOOK ONE FOR THE TEAM?
I DO. WHIT STUCK BY ME. SO I'LL STICK BY *HIM.*
PROMISE.

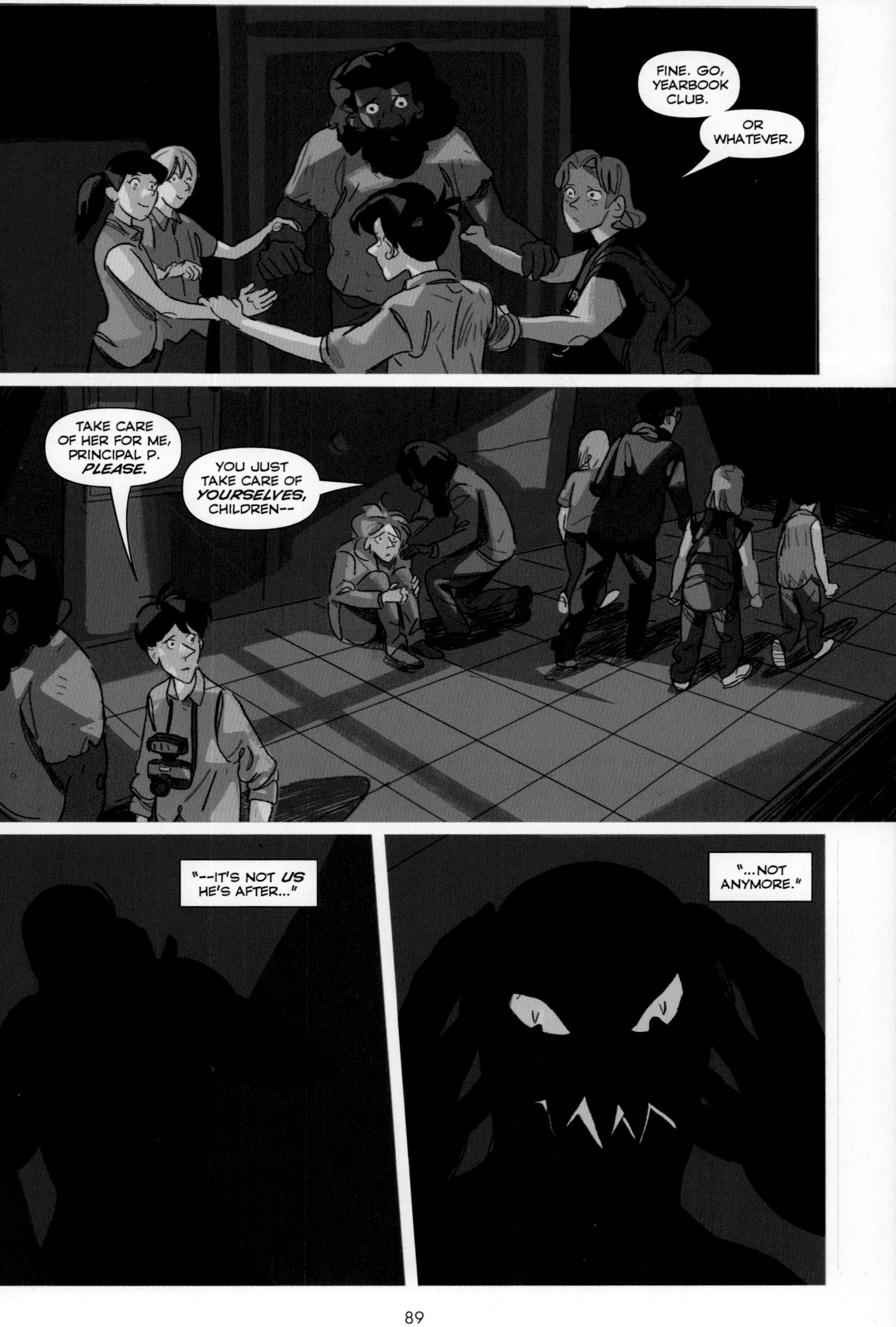
FINE. GO, YEARBOOK CLUB.
OR WHATEVER.
TAKE CARE OF HER FOR ME, PRINCIPAL P. *PLEASE*.
YOU JUST TAKE CARE OF ***YOURSELVES,*** CHILDREN--
"--IT'S NOT *US* HE'S AFTER..."
"...NOT ANYMORE."

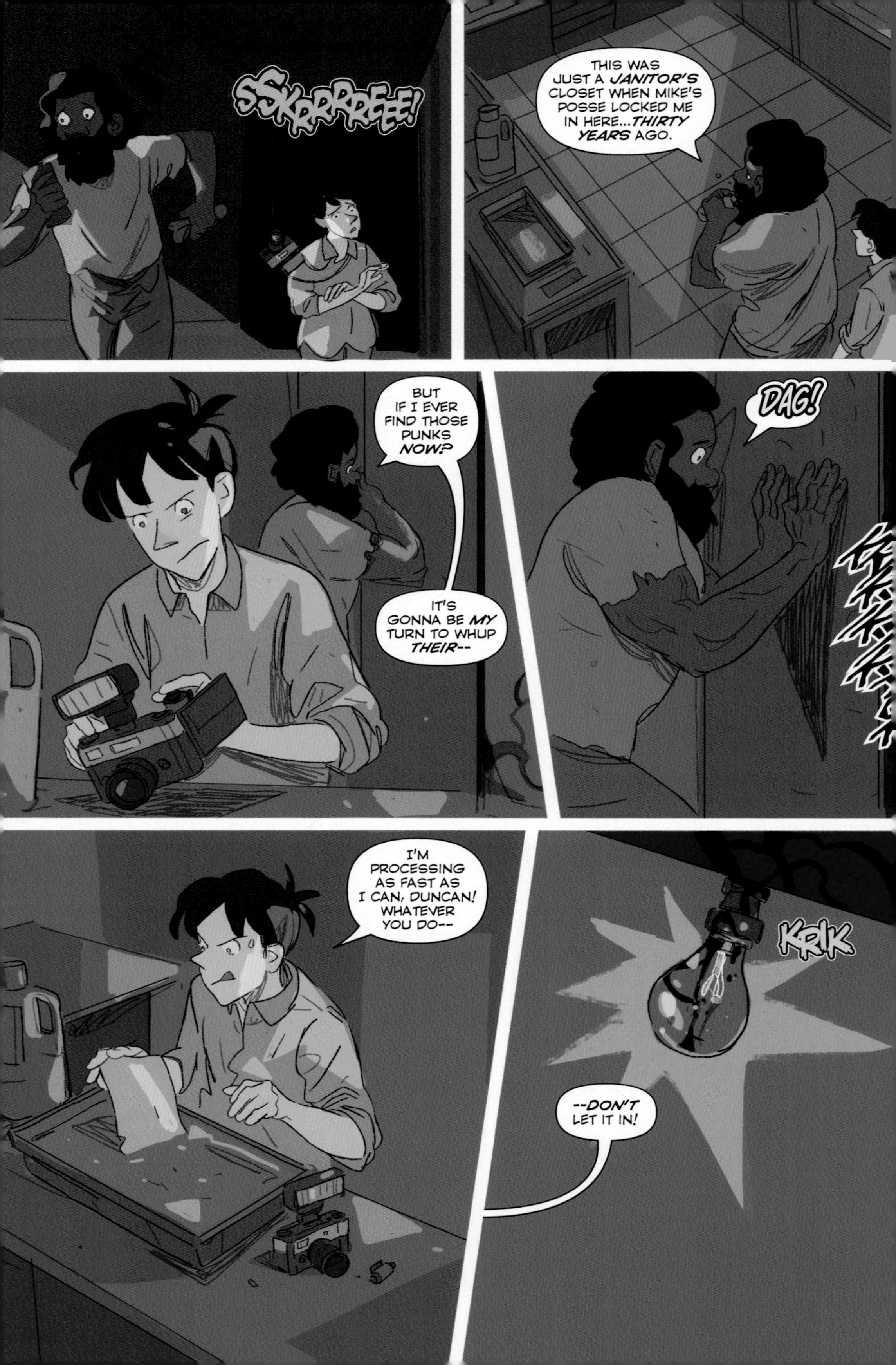
SSKRRRREEE!
THIS WAS JUST A JANITOR'S CLOSET WHEN MIKE'S POSSE LOCKED ME IN HERE...THIRTY YEARS AGO.
BUT IF I EVER FIND THOSE PUNKS NOW?
IT'S GONNA BE MY TURN TO WHUP THEIR--
DAG!
I'M PROCESSING AS FAST AS I CAN, DUNCAN! WHATEVER YOU DO--
KRIK
--DON'T LET IT IN!

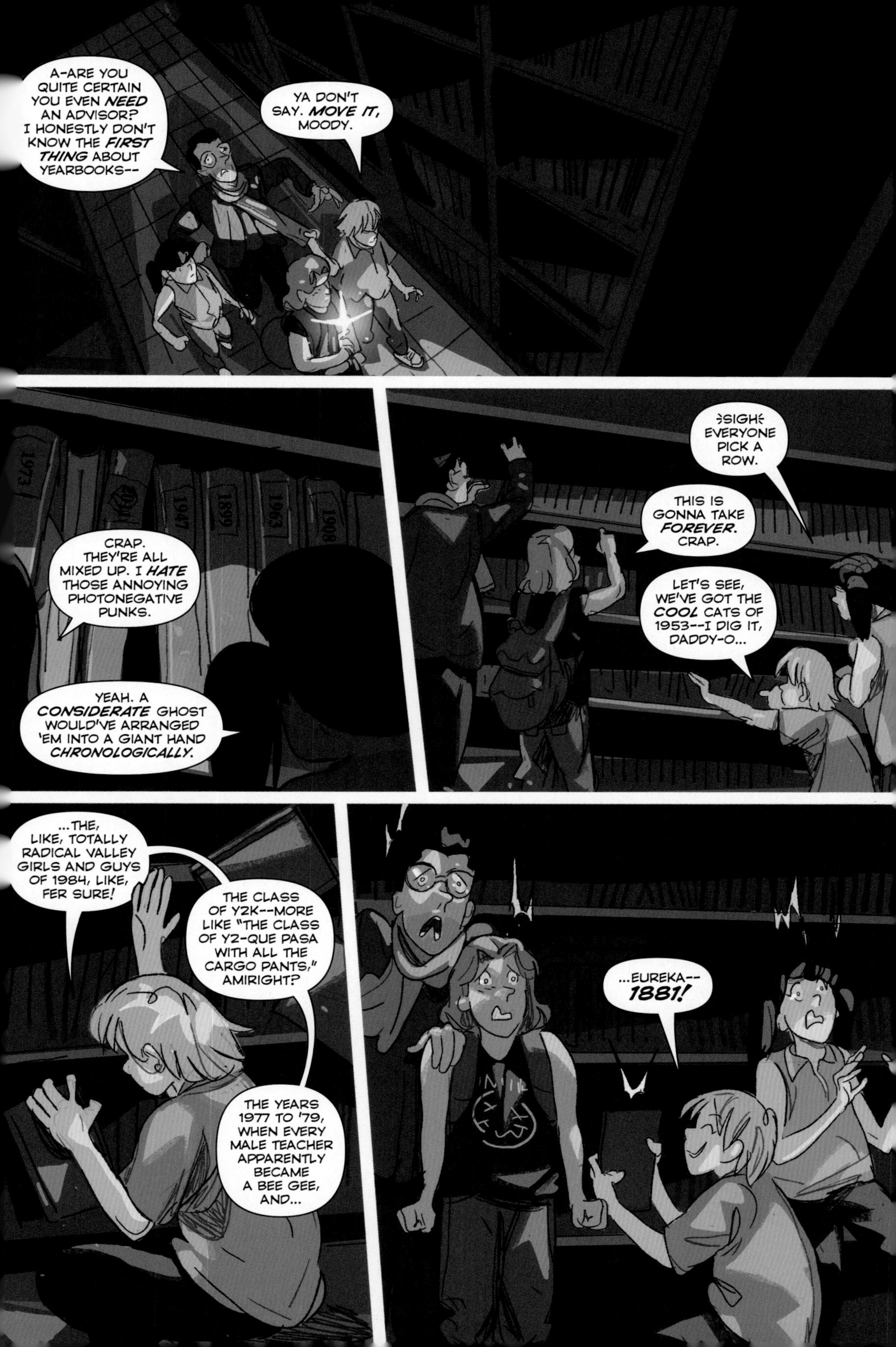
A-ARE YOU QUITE CERTAIN YOU EVEN NEED AN ADVISOR? I HONESTLY DON'T KNOW THE FIRST THING ABOUT YEARBOOKS--
YA DON'T SAY. MOVE IT, MOODY.
1973
1947
1899
1963
1908
CRAP. THEY'RE ALL MIXED UP. I HATE THOSE ANNOYING PHOTONEGATIVE PUNKS.
YEAH. A CONSIDERATE GHOST WOULD'VE ARRANGED 'EM INTO A GIANT HAND CHRONOLOGICALLY.
SIGH EVERYONE PICK A ROW.
THIS IS GONNA TAKE FOREVER. CRAP.
LET'S SEE, WE'VE GOT THE COOL CATS OF 1953--I DIG IT, DADDY-O...
...THE, LIKE, TOTALLY RADICAL VALLEY GIRLS AND GUYS OF 1984, LIKE, FER SURE!
THE CLASS OF Y2K--MORE LIKE "THE CLASS OF Y2-QUE PASA WITH ALL THE CARGO PANTS," AMIRIGHT?
THE YEARS 1977 TO '79, WHEN EVERY MALE TEACHER APPARENTLY BECAME A BEE GEE, AND...
...EUREKA-- 1881!

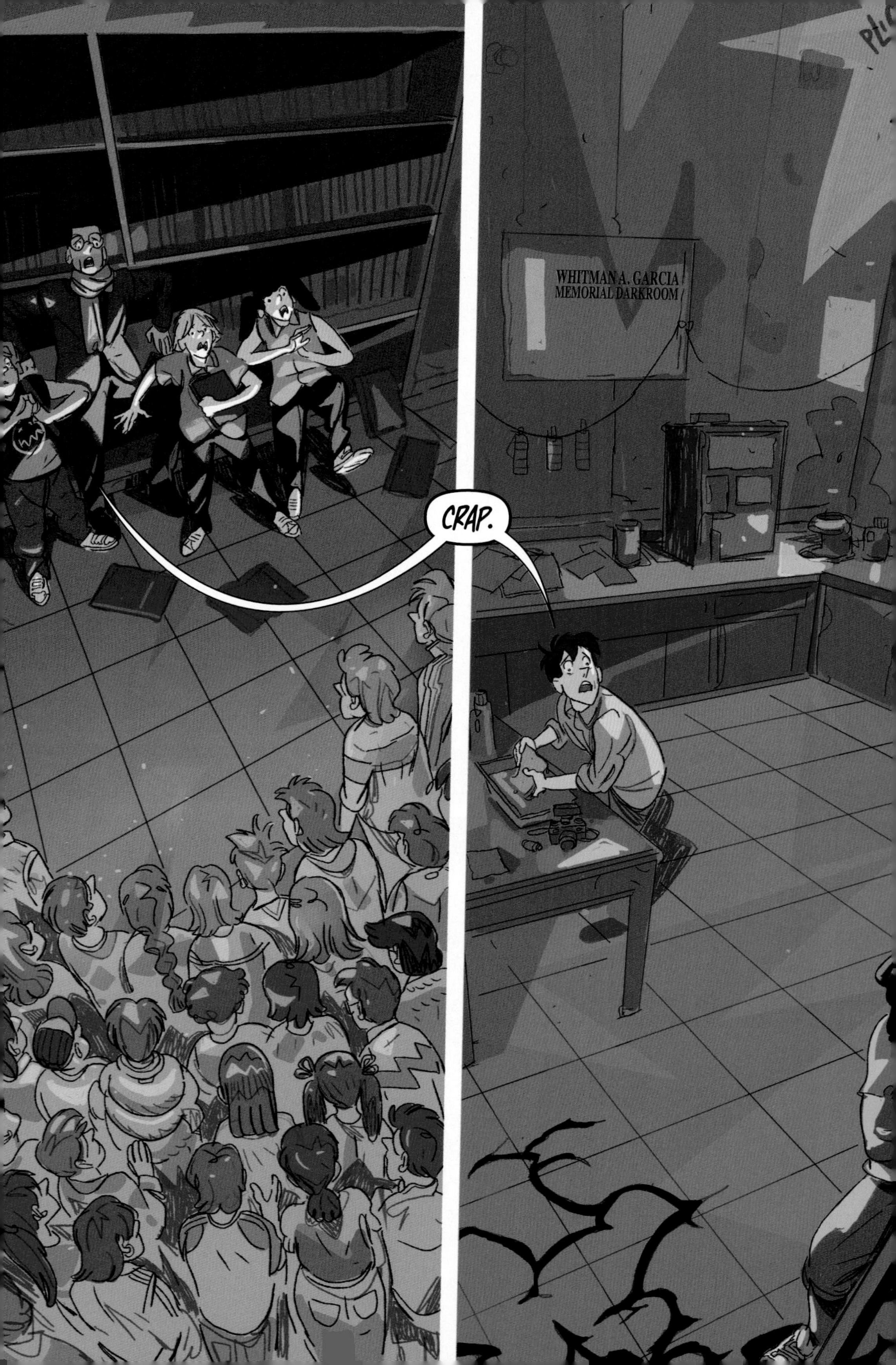
WHITMAN A. GARCIA
MEMORIAL DARKROOM
CRAP.

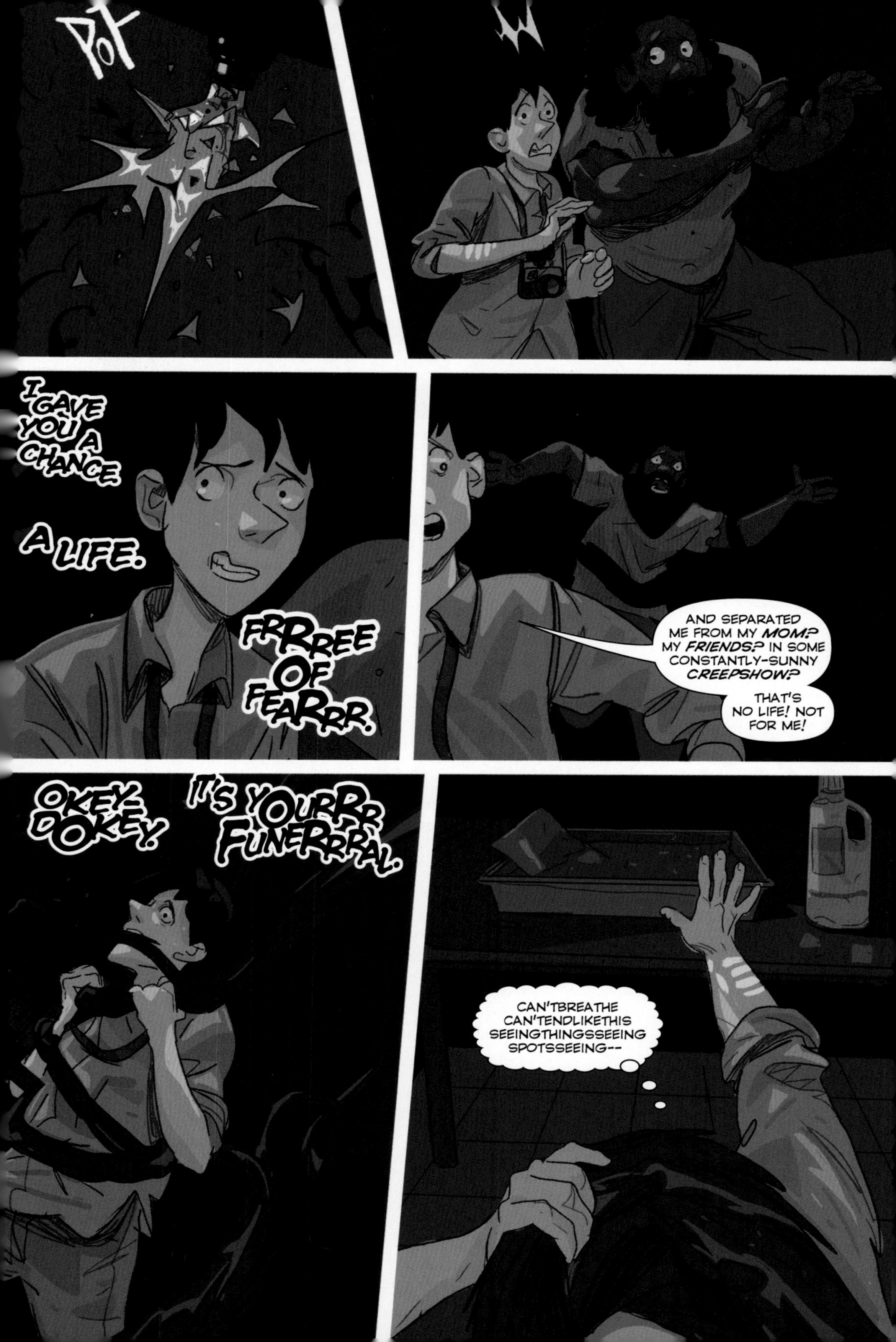
POK
I GAVE YOU A CHANCE.
A LIFE.
FRRRREE OF FEARRRR.
AND SEPARATED ME FROM MY MOM? MY FRIENDS? IN SOME CONSTANTLY-SUNNY CREEPSHOW?
THAT'S NO LIFE! NOT FOR ME!
OKEY-DOKEY.
IT'S YOURRRR FUNERRRRAL.
CAN'TBREATHE CAN'TENDLIKETHIS SEEINGTHINGSSEEING SPOTSSEEING--

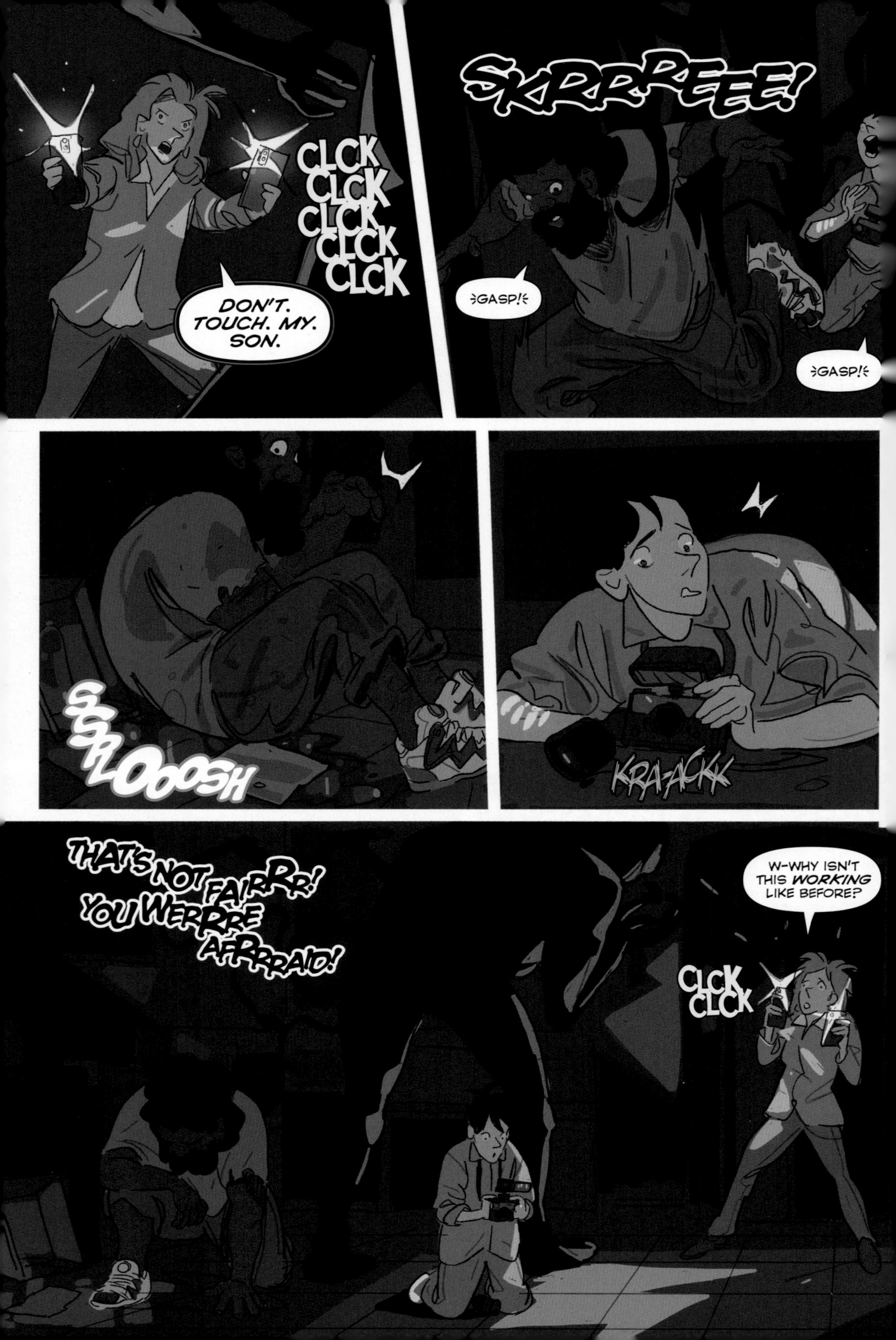
CLCK
CLCK
CLCK
CLCK
CLCK
DON'T. TOUCH. MY. SON.
SKRRREEE!
GASP!
GASP!
SSPLOOOOSH
KRA-ACKK
THAT'S NOT FAIRRR! YOU WERRRE AFRRRRAID!
W-WHY ISN'T THIS WORKING LIKE BEFORE?
CLCK
CLCK

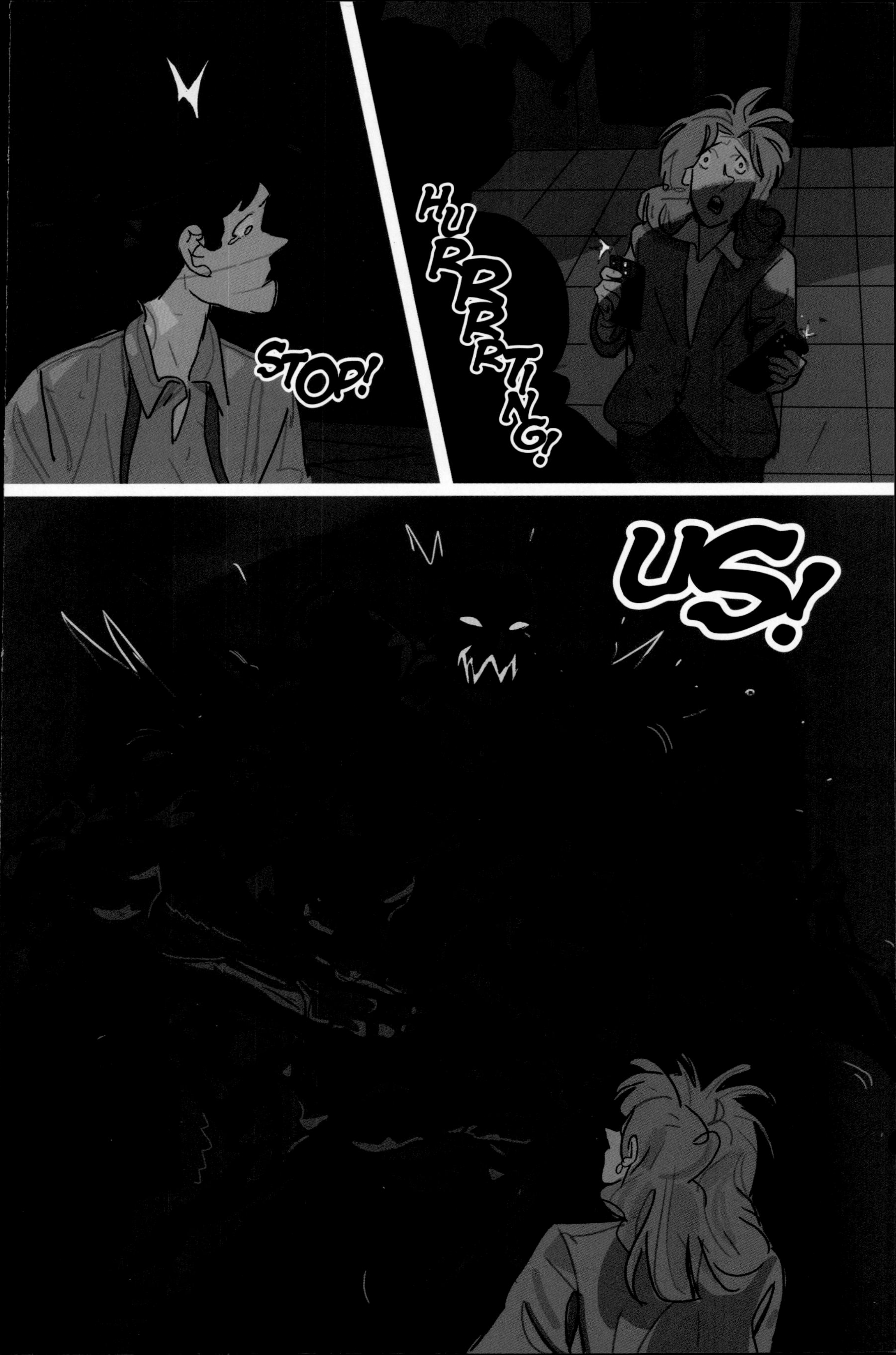
STOP!
HURRRRTING!
US!

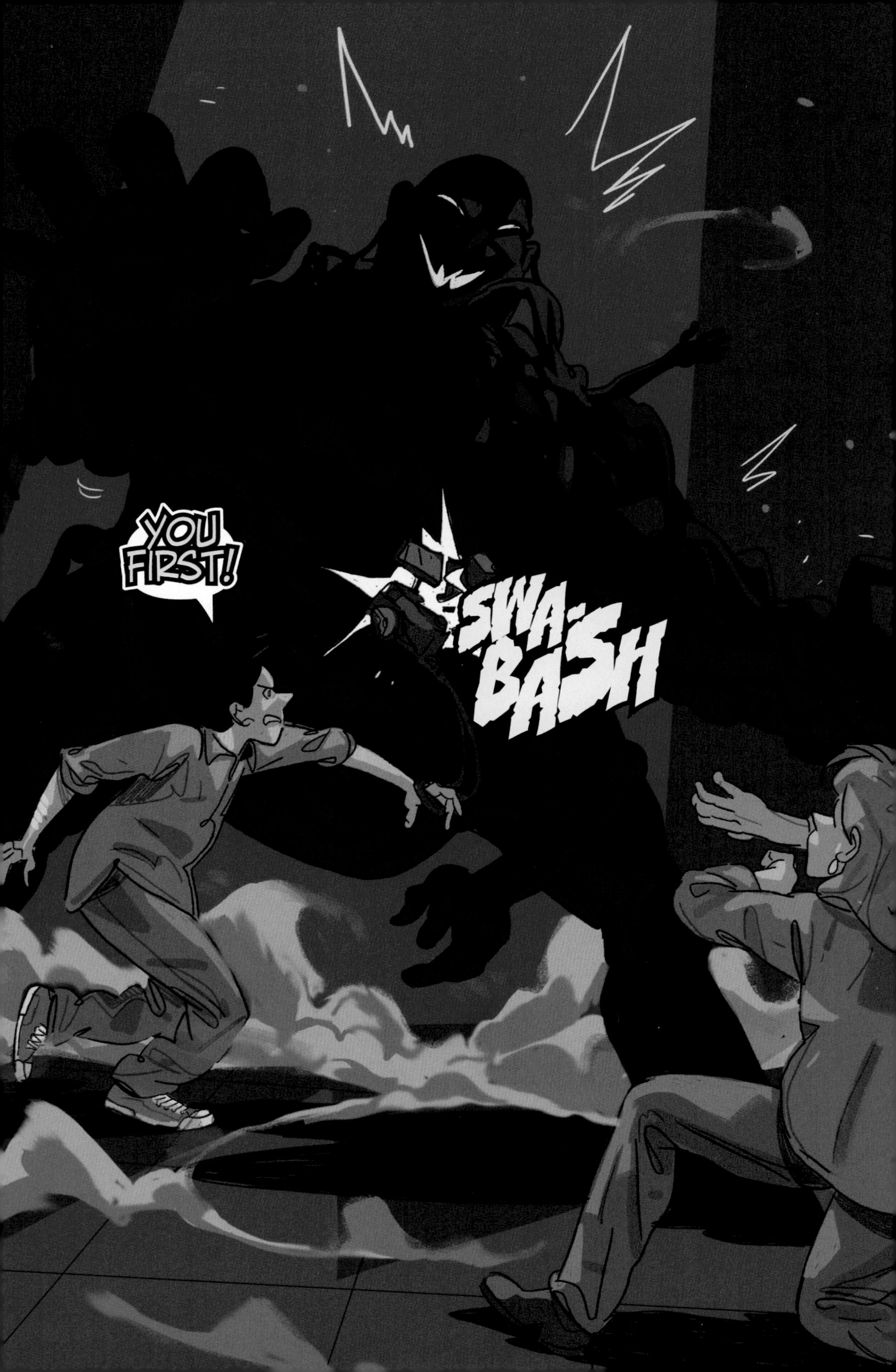
YOU FIRST!
SWA-BASH

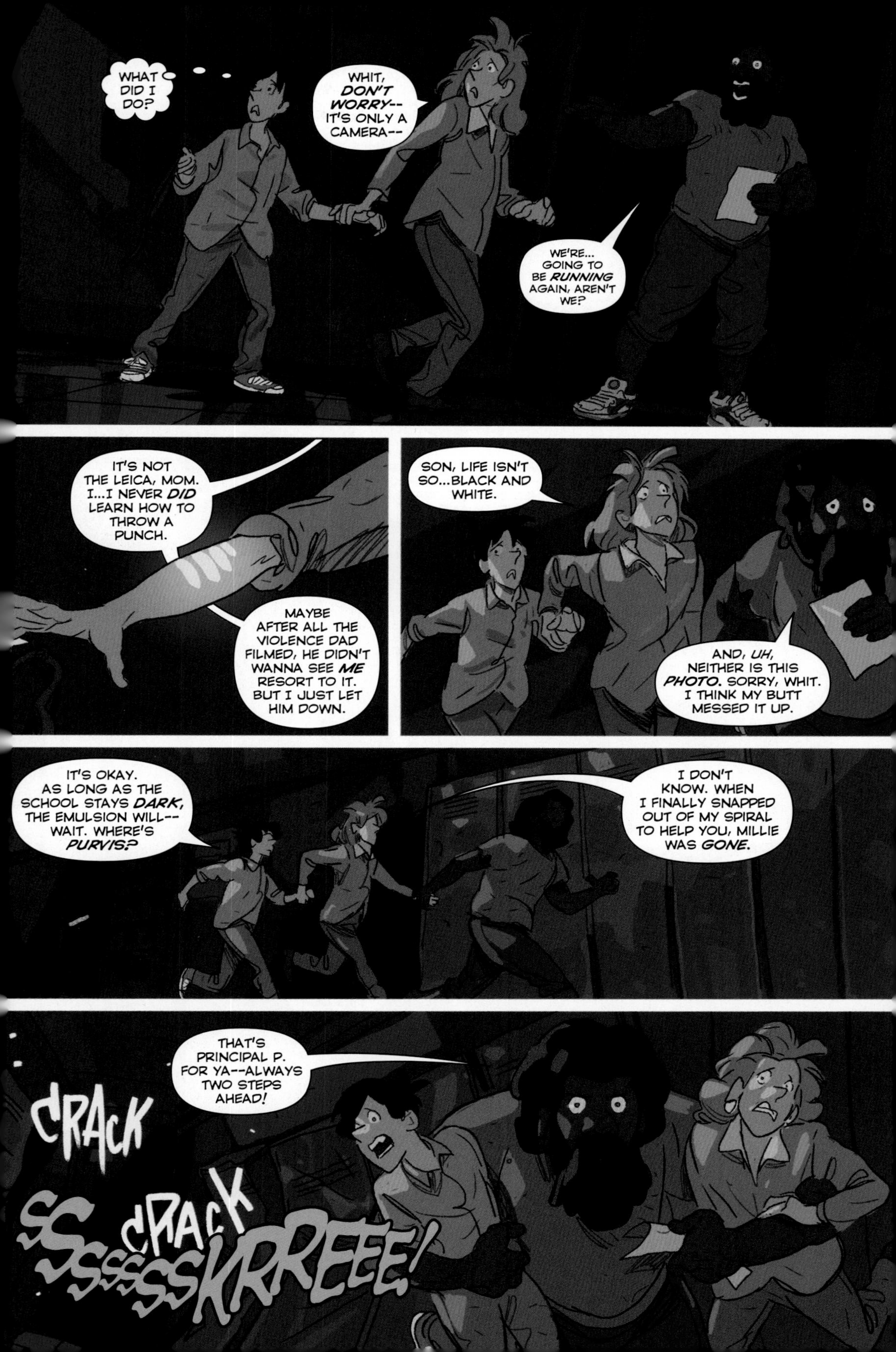
WHAT DID I DO?
WHIT, DON'T WORRY-- IT'S ONLY A CAMERA--
WE'RE... GOING TO BE RUNNING AGAIN, AREN'T WE?
IT'S NOT THE LEICA, MOM. I...I NEVER DID LEARN HOW TO THROW A PUNCH.
MAYBE AFTER ALL THE VIOLENCE DAD FILMED, HE DIDN'T WANNA SEE ME RESORT TO IT. BUT I JUST LET HIM DOWN.
SON, LIFE ISN'T SO...BLACK AND WHITE.
AND, UH, NEITHER IS THIS PHOTO. SORRY, WHIT. I THINK MY BUTT MESSED IT UP.
IT'S OKAY. AS LONG AS THE SCHOOL STAYS DARK, THE EMULSION WILL--WAIT. WHERE'S PURVIS?
I DON'T KNOW. WHEN I FINALLY SNAPPED OUT OF MY SPIRAL TO HELP YOU, MILLIE WAS GONE.
THAT'S PRINCIPAL P. FOR YA--ALWAYS TWO STEPS AHEAD!
CRACK
CRACK
SSSSSSKRREEE!

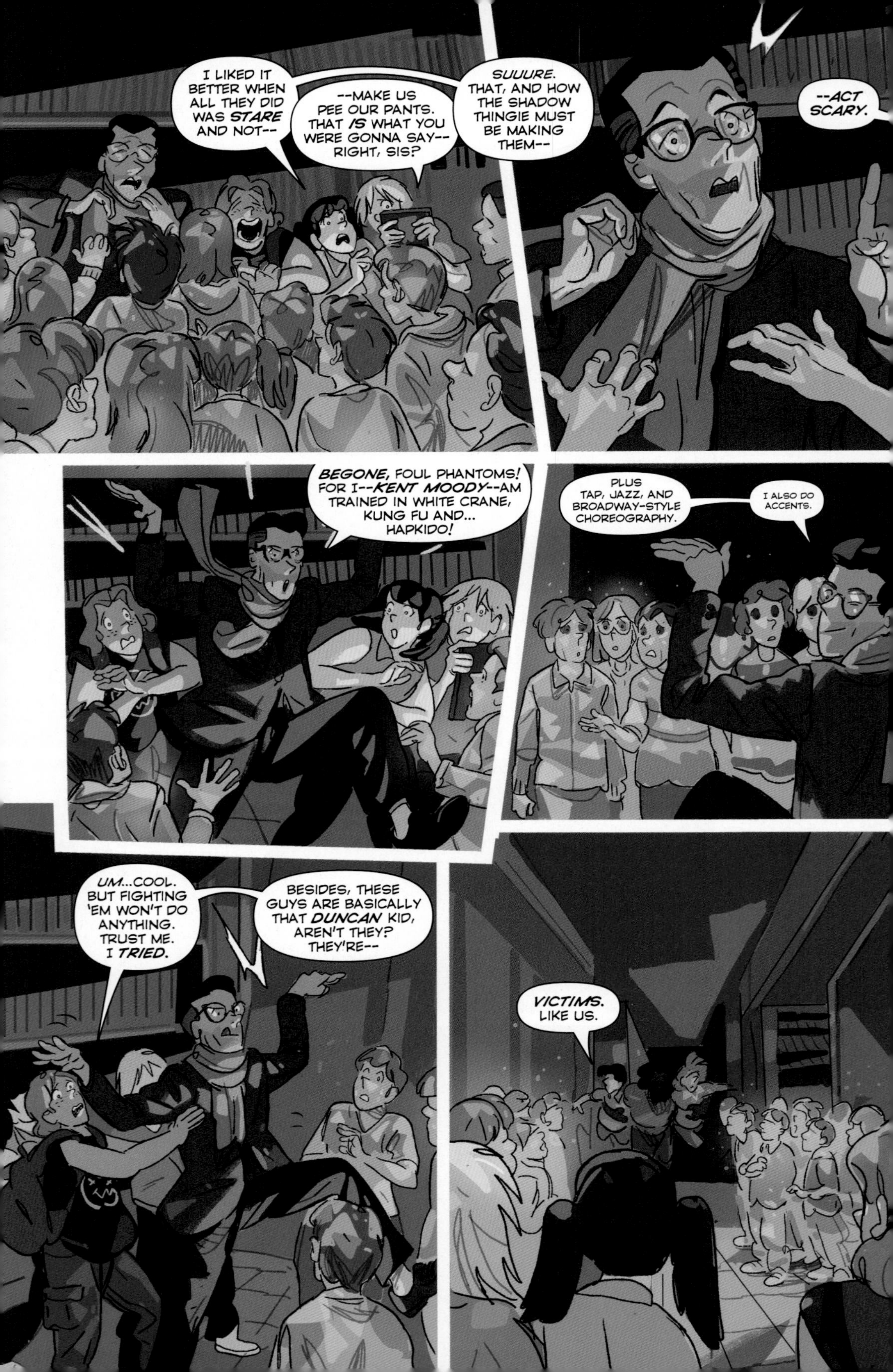
I LIKED IT BETTER WHEN ALL THEY DID WAS *STARE* AND NOT--
--MAKE US PEE OUR PANTS. THAT *IS* WHAT YOU WERE GONNA SAY--RIGHT, SIS?
SUUURE. THAT, AND HOW THE SHADOW THINGIE MUST BE MAKING THEM--
--*ACT SCARY.*
BEGONE, FOUL PHANTOMS! FOR I--*KENT MOODY*--AM TRAINED IN WHITE CRANE, KUNG FU AND... HAPKIDO!
PLUS TAP, JAZZ, AND BROADWAY-STYLE CHOREOGRAPHY.
I ALSO DO ACCENTS.
UM...COOL. BUT FIGHTING 'EM WON'T DO ANYTHING. TRUST ME. I *TRIED.*
BESIDES, THESE GUYS ARE BASICALLY THAT *DUNCAN* KID, AREN'T THEY? THEY'RE--
VICTIMS. LIKE US.

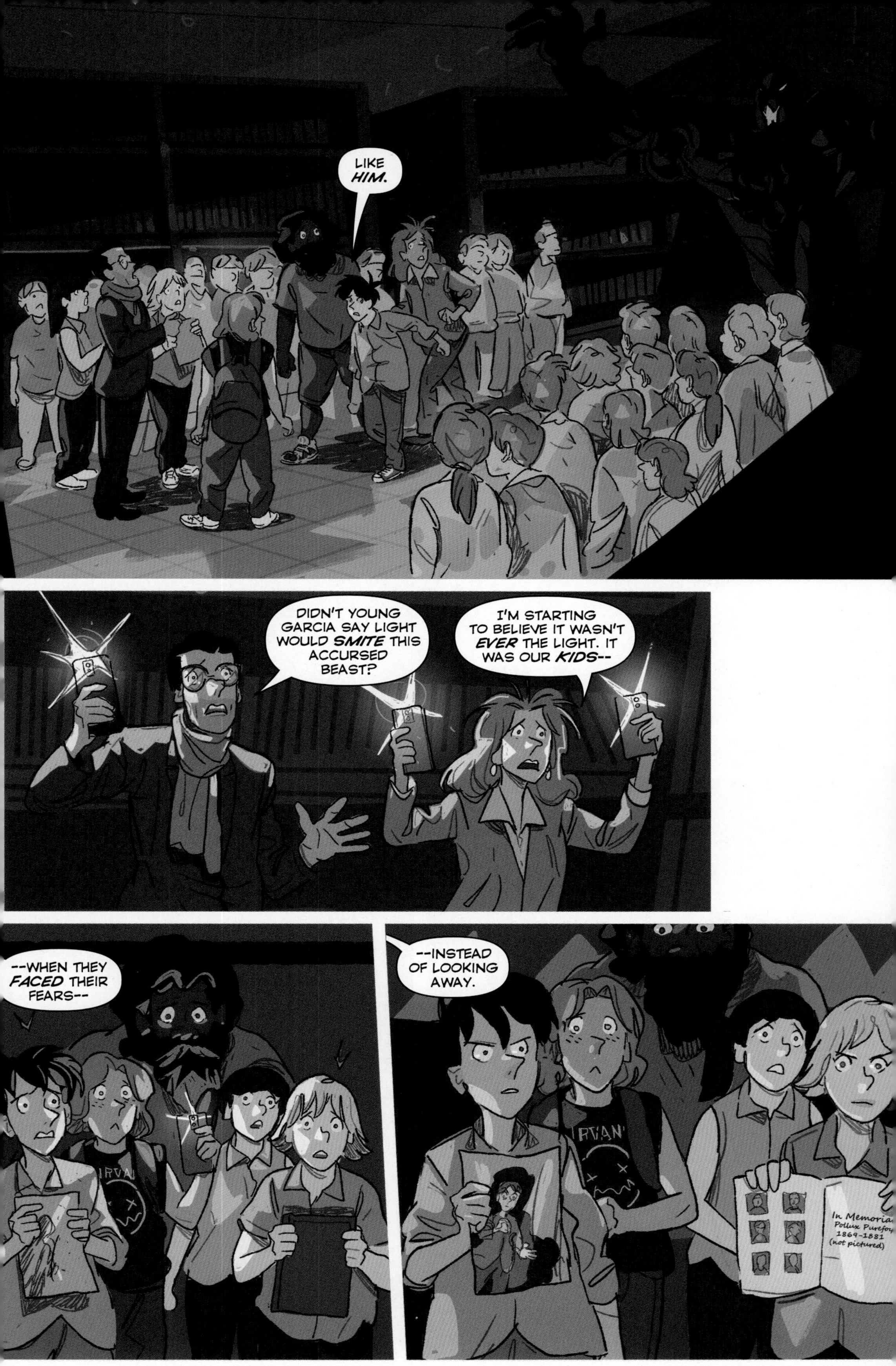
LIKE *HIM.*
DIDN'T YOUNG GARCIA SAY LIGHT WOULD *SMITE* THIS ACCURSED BEAST?
I'M STARTING TO BELIEVE IT WASN'T *EVER* THE LIGHT. IT WAS OUR *KIDS*--
--WHEN THEY *FACED* THEIR FEARS--
--INSTEAD OF LOOKING AWAY.
In Memoria
Pollux Purefoy
1869-1881
(not pictured)

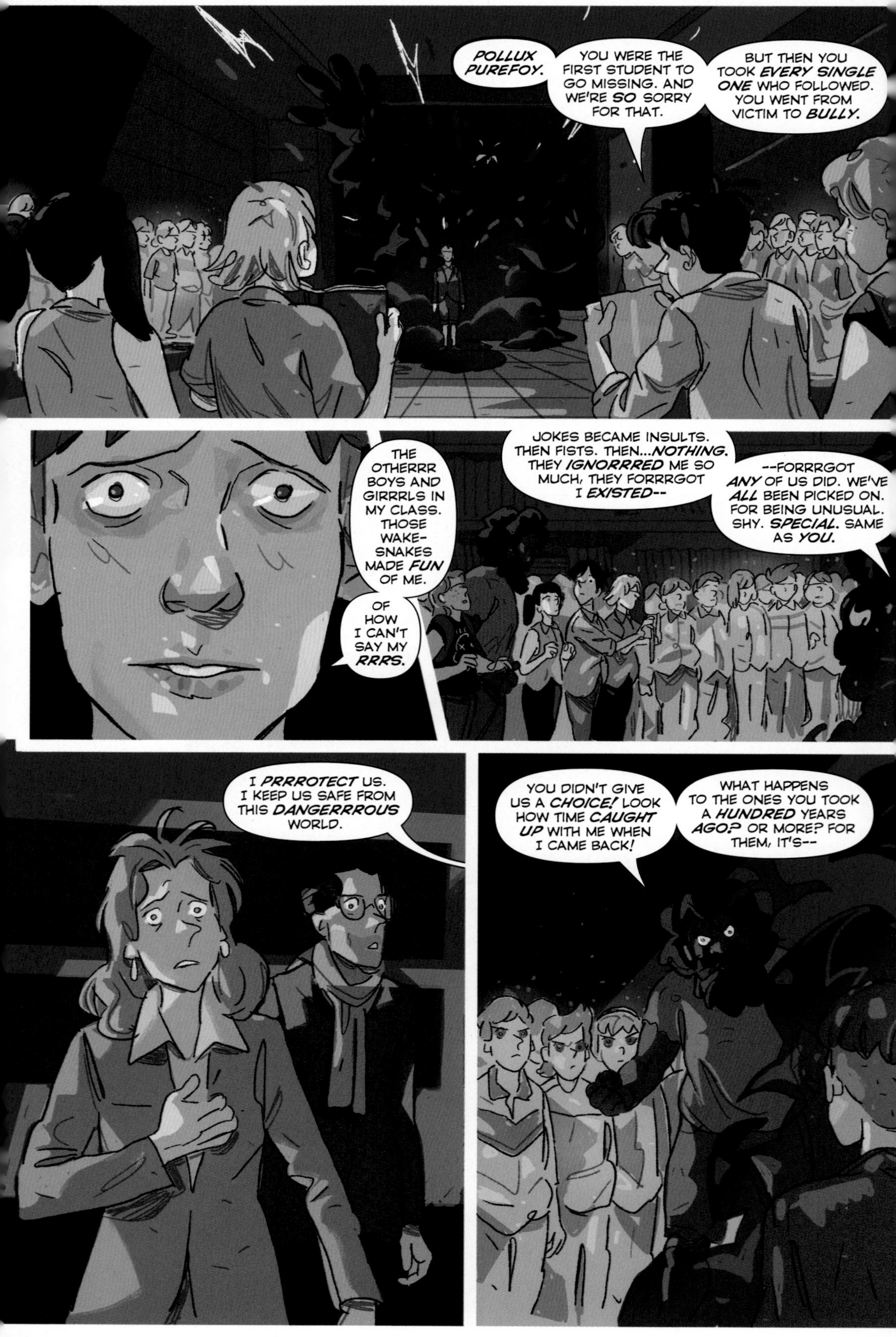
POLLUX PUREFOY.
YOU WERE THE FIRST STUDENT TO GO MISSING. AND WE'RE SO SORRY FOR THAT.
BUT THEN YOU TOOK EVERY SINGLE ONE WHO FOLLOWED. YOU WENT FROM VICTIM TO BULLY.
THE OTHERRR BOYS AND GIRRRLS IN MY CLASS. THOSE WAKE-SNAKES MADE FUN OF ME.
OF HOW I CAN'T SAY MY RRRS.
JOKES BECAME INSULTS. THEN FISTS. THEN...NOTHING. THEY IGNORRRED ME SO MUCH, THEY FORRRGOT I EXISTED--
--FORRRGOT ANY OF US DID. WE'VE ALL BEEN PICKED ON. FOR BEING UNUSUAL. SHY. SPECIAL. SAME AS YOU.
I PRRROTECT US. I KEEP US SAFE FROM THIS DANGERRROUS WORLD.
YOU DIDN'T GIVE US A CHOICE! LOOK HOW TIME CAUGHT UP WITH ME WHEN I CAME BACK!
WHAT HAPPENS TO THE ONES YOU TOOK A HUNDRED YEARS AGO? OR MORE? FOR THEM, IT'S--

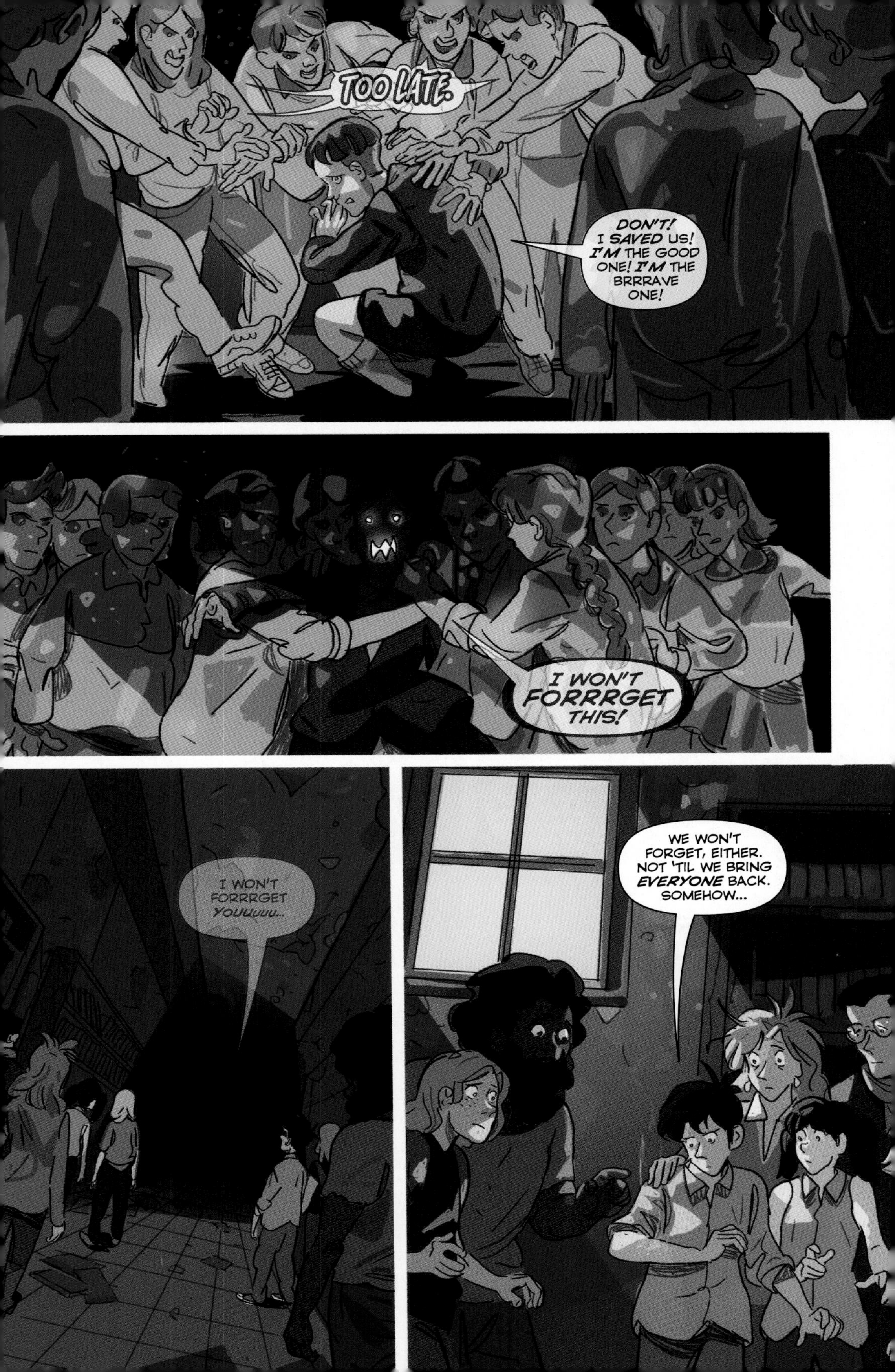
TOO LATE.
DON'T! I SAVED US! I'M THE GOOD ONE! I'M THE BRRRAVE ONE!
I WON'T FORRRGET THIS!
I WON'T FORRRGET YOUuuuu...
WE WON'T FORGET, EITHER. NOT 'TIL WE BRING EVERYONE BACK. SOMEHOW...

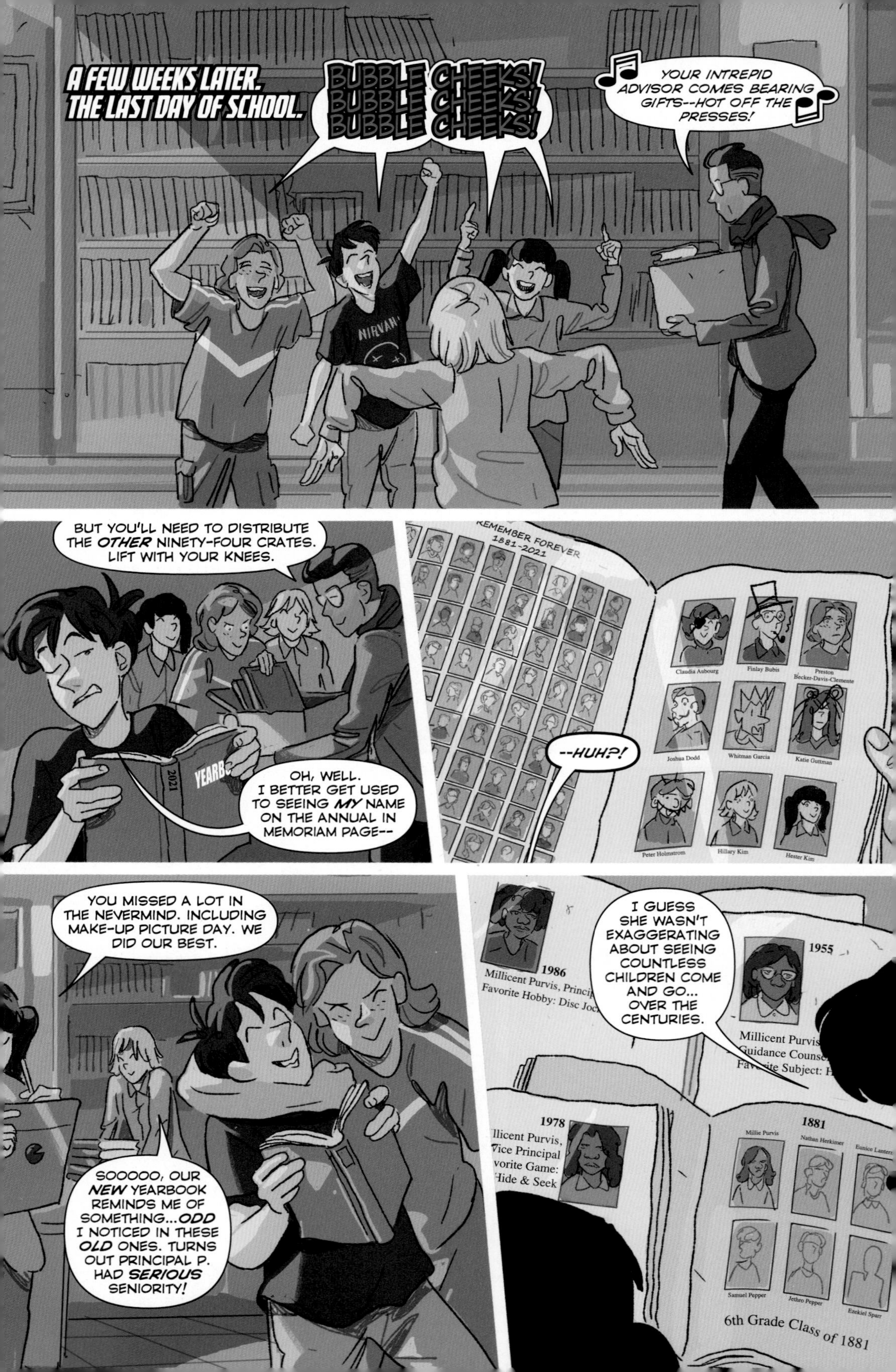
A FEW WEEKS LATER. THE LAST DAY OF SCHOOL.
BUBBLE CHEEKS! BUBBLE CHEEKS! BUBBLE CHEEKS!
YOUR INTREPID ADVISOR COMES BEARING GIFTS--HOT OFF THE PRESSES!
NIRVANA
BUT YOU'LL NEED TO DISTRIBUTE THE OTHER NINETY-FOUR CRATES. LIFT WITH YOUR KNEES.
YEARB
2021
OH, WELL. I BETTER GET USED TO SEEING MY NAME ON THE ANNUAL IN MEMORIAM PAGE--
REMEMBER FOREVER 1881-2021
--HUH?!
Claudia Aubourg
Finlay Bubis
Preston Becker-Davis-Clemente
Joshua Dodd
Whitman Garcia
Katie Guttman
Peter Holmstrom
Hillary Kim
Hester Kim
YOU MISSED A LOT IN THE NEVERMIND. INCLUDING MAKE-UP PICTURE DAY. WE DID OUR BEST.
SOOOOO, OUR NEW YEARBOOK REMINDS ME OF SOMETHING...ODD I NOTICED IN THESE OLD ONES. TURNS OUT PRINCIPAL P. HAD SERIOUS SENIORITY!
1986
Millicent Purvis, Princip
Favorite Hobby: Disc Jock
I GUESS SHE WASN'T EXAGGERATING ABOUT SEEING COUNTLESS CHILDREN COME AND GO... OVER THE CENTURIES.
1955
Millicent Purvis
Guidance Counse
Fav ite Subject: H
1978
illicent Purvis,
ice Principal
avorite Game:
Hide & Seek
1881
Millie Purvis
Nathan Herkimer
Eunice Lantern
Samuel Pepper
Jethro Pepper
Ezekiel Sparr
6th Grade Class of 1881

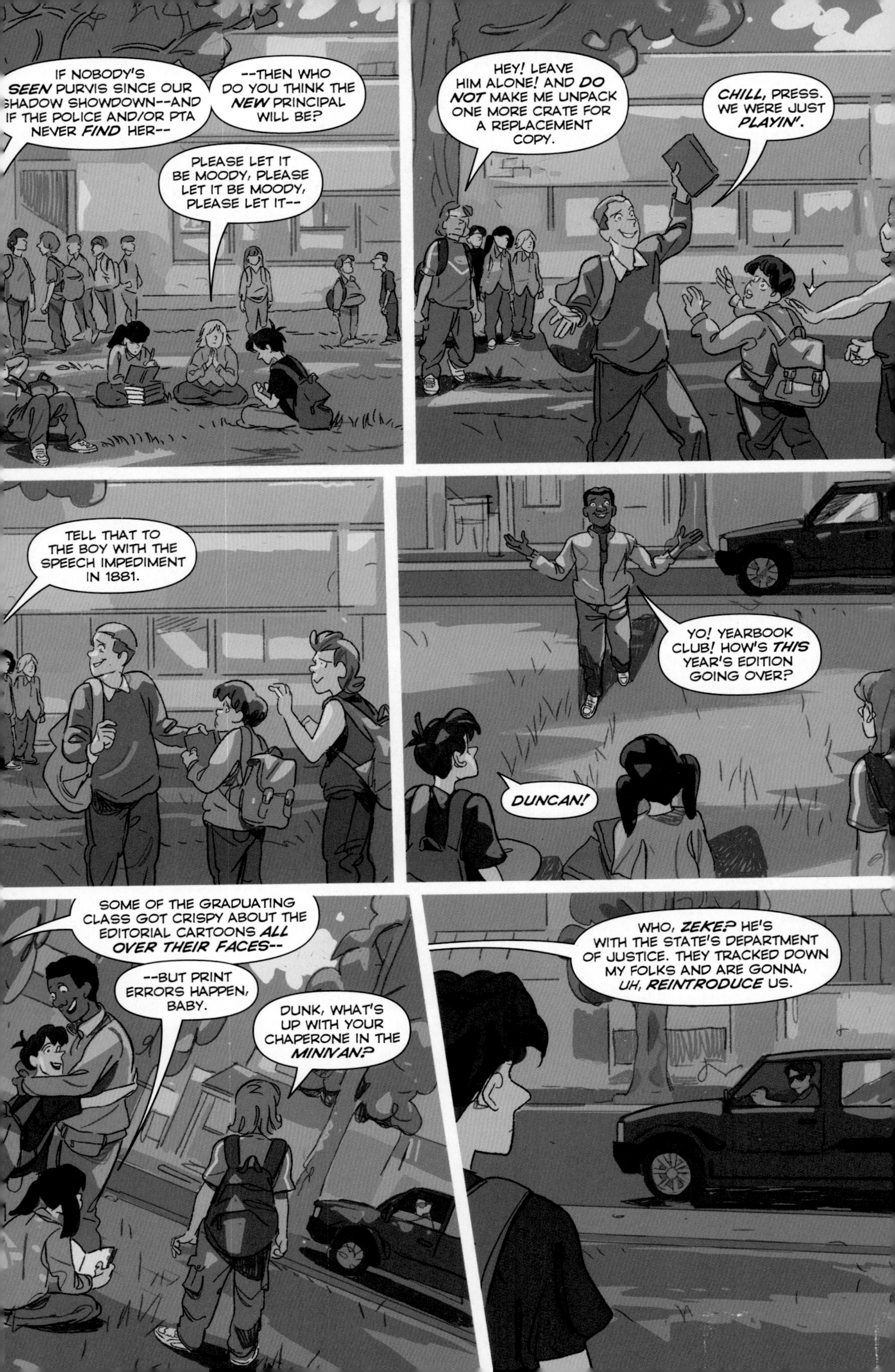
IF NOBODY'S SEEN PURVIS SINCE OUR SHADOW SHOWDOWN--AND IF THE POLICE AND/OR PTA NEVER FIND HER--
--THEN WHO DO YOU THINK THE NEW PRINCIPAL WILL BE?
PLEASE LET IT BE MOODY, PLEASE LET IT BE MOODY, PLEASE LET IT--
HEY! LEAVE HIM ALONE! AND DO NOT MAKE ME UNPACK ONE MORE CRATE FOR A REPLACEMENT COPY.
CHILL, PRESS. WE WERE JUST PLAYIN'.
TELL THAT TO THE BOY WITH THE SPEECH IMPEDIMENT IN 1881.
YO! YEARBOOK CLUB! HOW'S THIS YEAR'S EDITION GOING OVER?
DUNCAN!
SOME OF THE GRADUATING CLASS GOT CRISPY ABOUT THE EDITORIAL CARTOONS ALL OVER THEIR FACES--
--BUT PRINT ERRORS HAPPEN, BABY.
DUNK, WHAT'S UP WITH YOUR CHAPERONE IN THE MINIVAN?
WHO, ZEKE? HE'S WITH THE STATE'S DEPARTMENT OF JUSTICE. THEY TRACKED DOWN MY FOLKS AND ARE GONNA, UH, REINTRODUCE US.

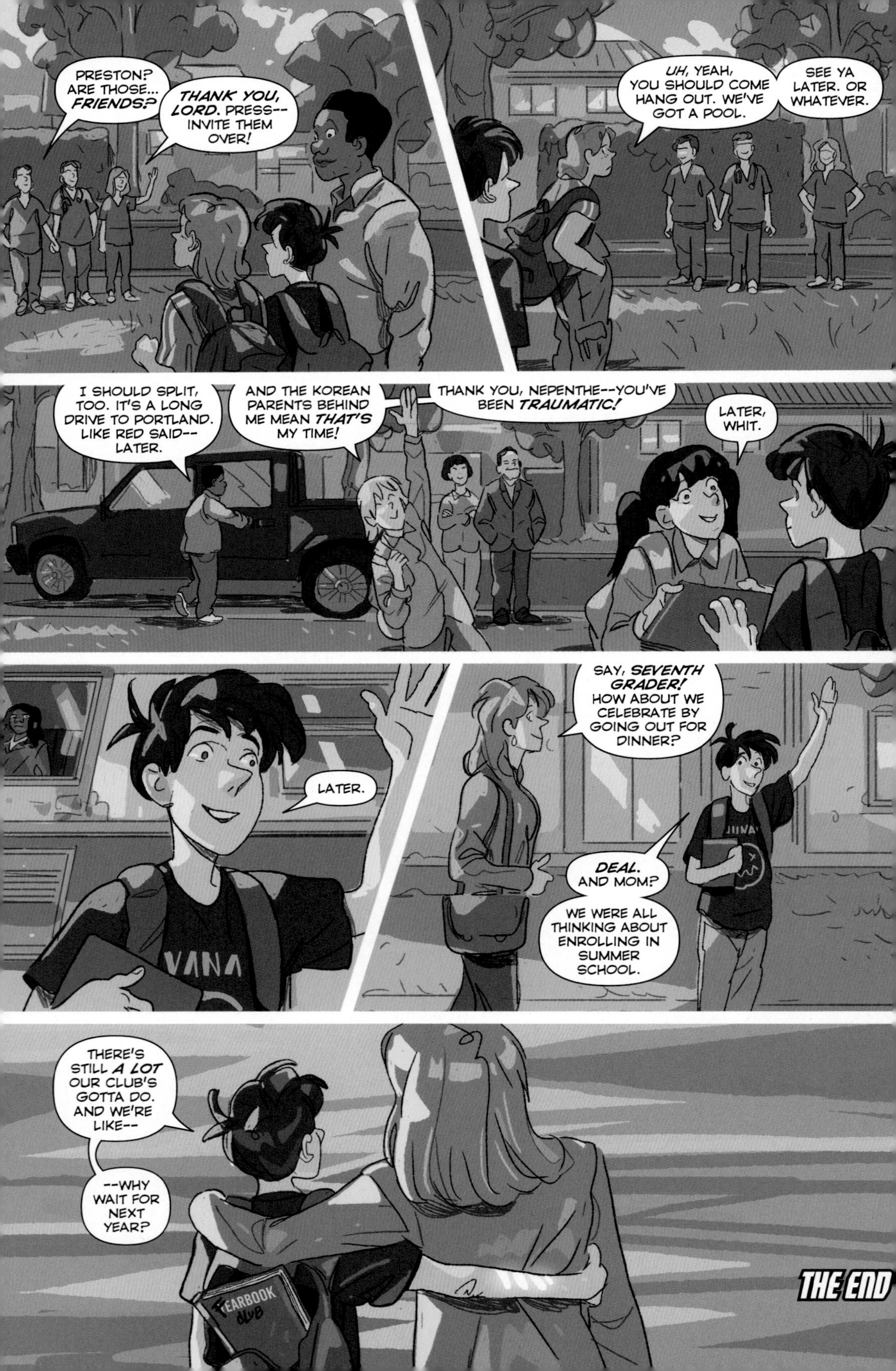
PRESTON? ARE THOSE... FRIENDS?
THANK YOU, LORD. PRESS-- INVITE THEM OVER!
UH, YEAH, YOU SHOULD COME HANG OUT. WE'VE GOT A POOL.
SEE YA LATER. OR WHATEVER.
I SHOULD SPLIT, TOO. IT'S A LONG DRIVE TO PORTLAND. LIKE RED SAID-- LATER.
AND THE KOREAN PARENTS BEHIND ME MEAN THAT'S MY TIME!
THANK YOU, NEPENTHE--YOU'VE BEEN TRAUMATIC!
LATER, WHIT.
LATER.
SAY, SEVENTH GRADER! HOW ABOUT WE CELEBRATE BY GOING OUT FOR DINNER?
DEAL. AND MOM?
WE WERE ALL THINKING ABOUT ENROLLING IN SUMMER SCHOOL.
THERE'S STILL A LOT OUR CLUB'S GOTTA DO. AND WE'RE LIKE--
--WHY WAIT FOR NEXT YEAR?
FEARBOOK CLUB
THE END

LETTER TO THE WEIRDO CLUB

Hey. You. Yeah, YOU — the weirdo reading this comic.

I mean, this graphic novel. Sorry. I'm still not used to calling them that, as I am quite old.

I'm also sorry for calling you a 'weirdo'. If it makes you feel any better, I'm weird, too. Only I think that's actually a good thing — a badge of pride, celebrating how we're different. Distinct. You know, special.

Which is why I'm inviting you to join our private club, weirdo.

Let's face it — this world sure is scary. And middle school? Even scarier. So, in order to survive it, we need all the friends we can get, right? Look, 6th through 8th grade was pretty much a blur for me. But here's what I do recall from those nightmarish 1990s: Young Ricky's acne, braces, love-handles and aviator frame glasses. Not sunglasses, mind you. Aviator reading glasses — the kind a middle-aged pharmacist might wear.

And worst of all? I loved comics. Graphic novels. Whatever. You get the point.

It wasn't that I was unpopular (although I definitely wasn't popular). Or that I was particularly bullied (I endured my fair share, yet others had it way worse). It was more like I was...nothing. Like I didn't belong to any one group. I certainly wasn't going to be mistaken for a jock. And my grades weren't good enough to make me a nerd, either. Most days, I felt like I could just disappear, and nobody would ever notice I was gone.

Maybe you feel the same way sometimes. And who could blame you? Not me.

Yeah, my childhood had its issues. But what your generation has to deal with? The environment? Civil unrest? Pandemics? Social media? Talk about scary. Honestly, I don't know how you do it. You are so much braver than I'll ever be. That said, even the most courageous of us can succumb to our doubts — our anxieties — every now and then. And that's okay. We all experience fear.

The question is: What do we do with it? Do we ignore fear (which, by the way, never works)? Do we collapse under the crushing weight of it? Or do we try to understand it so that we might move past — or, at the very least, cope with — our fear?

Well, everyone who had a hand in making FEARBOOK CLUB truly hopes you choose that last option. Just like we hope our spooky ghost story gives you some insights that you can apply to whatever frightens you in the real world. I promise you, even if your existence seems terrifying right now, it will get better. Those aviator glasses that caused me so much pre-teen pain? They're now — no joke — in style. (I'm still waiting for love handles to start trending, though.)

Maybe that means people like us are ahead of the curve. Maybe those things that we think of as our faults today will become our assets tomorrow. And maybe those dopes who dismissed us for being special simply weren't special enough.

But who cares about them? After all, you and I are part of a club, remember?

Meaning that lots of us would miss you if you disappeared. So, please don't do that, okay? You will always belong — and you will always find family — in our shared community of comics. Graphic novels. Whatever. You get the point.

And the point is this: No fear is too great when we face it with friends.

Stay brave, stay yourself, and see you in the funny pages, weirdo.

RAH!
November 2021

INTERVIEW WITH ARTIST
MARCO MATRONE

SEISMIC PRESS: At what age did you first start drawing? Did it come naturally or was it something you needed to work on constantly?

MARCO MATRONE: For as long as I can remember, drawing has always been a part of me. As a child, I was very fond of animals, and they were the first thing I started to draw. It has always been my source of fun, and it still is! This doesn't mean that I didn't take drawing seriously over the years, to the contrary. If you are passionate about something, you have the duty to commit to it, explore it and study it to understand it better.

SP: When you were Whit's age, what did you want to do when you grew up?

MM: Like many kids at Whit's age, I couldn't make up my mind. It was such a confusing period for me because you are in a phase of growth in which your internal and external transformations are so fast that you don't allow yourself to have fixed points. I've always known I would have liked to have a job in the creative arts, but I also dreamt of becoming a nature photographer around the world, and looking back now, it would have been a great experience— but I love what I do!

WHIT

SP: Were you in any clubs or play any sports when you were in school?

MM: There are no sports clubs in Italy like in America, but sports have always been important to me. Since I was a child, I have loved playing football (soccer for my American friends). My family has been lucky enough to own a football pitch where we played with friends and cousins every day.

SP: Did any childhood friends or experiences influence you when illustrating FEARBOOK CLUB?

MM: It was not a particular event or experience, but the whole vibe I tried to create was inspired by the feelings and sensations that I experienced growing up. The discomfort towards some of the other classmates, the shyness and the sometimes conflicting relationship you have with your parents at that age, are all contributing elements of experiences that have helped me enrich and characterize the world of FEARBOOK CLUB.

SP: Any advice for young adults who want to become a comic artist?

MM: Before becoming a cartoonist, you need to become a storyteller. The very first piece of advice is to observe a lot. Learn to tell a story by consuming all sorts of content to understand how different people, places and cultures tell stories. Next, you should never give up on the first sign of difficulty. When you try to make your dreams come true, it's rarely easy — that's why it holds its value — which is why you have to keep trying and put a lot of effort into it. The last piece of advice is perhaps the most important: be humble. To fulfill your potential, you need to accept and understand criticism. This is the only way you can really grow, otherwise, you remain stuck. (P.S. this last piece of advice applies to everything in life.)

SP: What was the most challenging aspect for you when you were Whit's age?

MM: That was a difficult period for me. I struggled to build any relationship with my classmates, and I lost interest in studying. It all felt like a nightmare, so I didn't like to go to school. But this slowly changed. I started to make friends and build genuine relationships, and even my interest in studying came back! As I said before, it's such a difficult age because our bodies and minds change so quickly, but as soon as we start to understand ourselves, everything falls into place. Take the time to understand who you truly are—not what the world tells you to be. You, and the world, will be better off if you are the person you truly are meant to be.

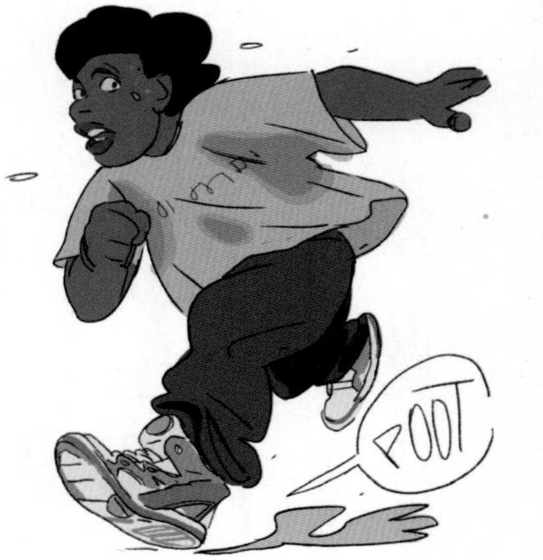
POOT

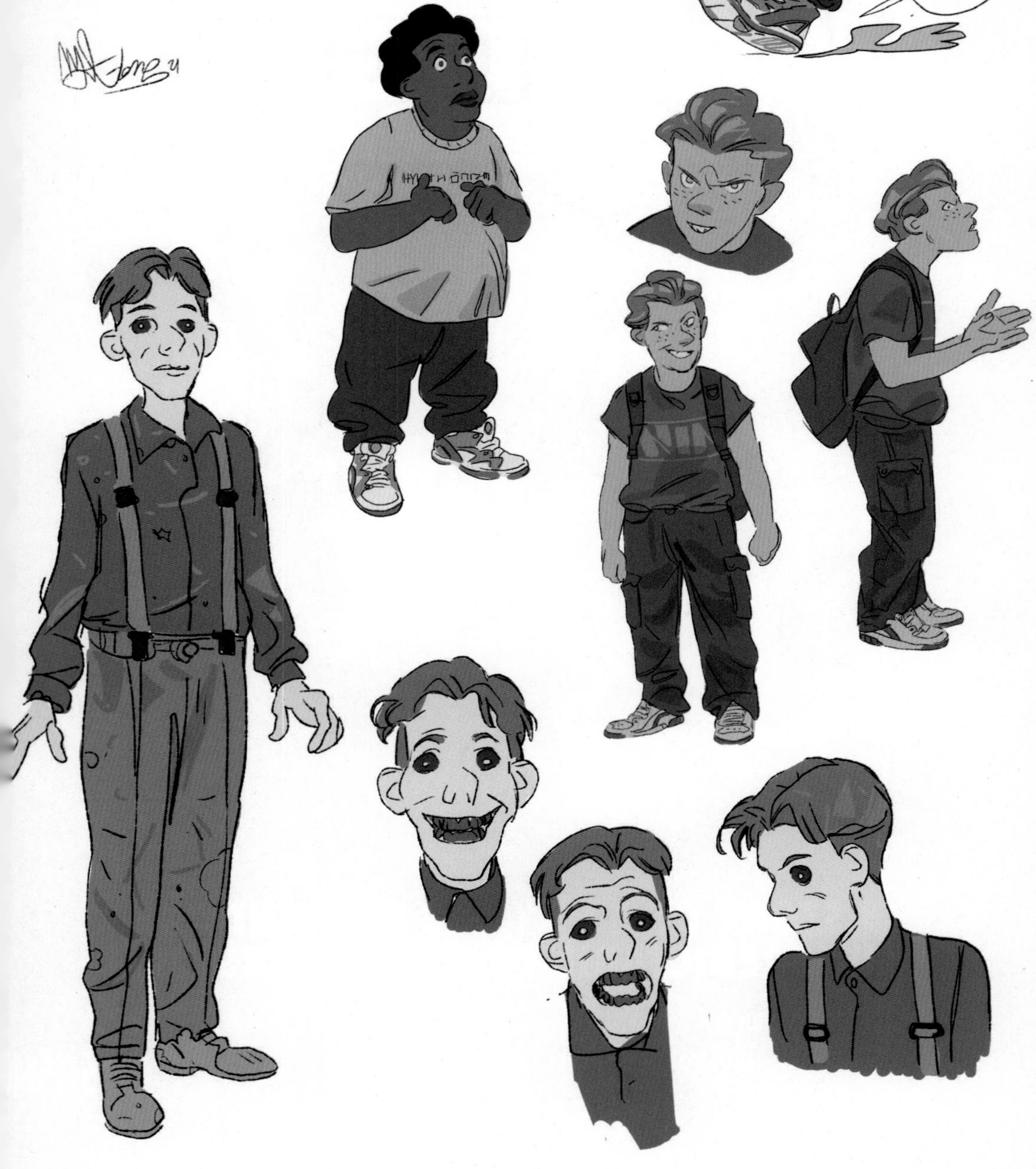

Have something to say?! SPEAK SEISMICALLY

SAY IT HERE
@SeismicComics

OR HERE
@SeismicPress

OR EVEN HERE
@SeismicPress

SEE WHAT WE'RE SAYING?

SEISMIC™
PRESS

ABOUT THE CREATORS

RICHARD ASHLEY HAMILTON
writer

Richard Ashley Hamilton is the award-winning screenwriter and author best known for his storytelling across DreamWorks Animation's *How to Train Your Dragon, Trollhunters* and *3Below* franchises. He wrote on the Daytime Emmy-winning first season of *Dragons: Race to the Edge* and the Lumiere award-winning *How to Train Your Dragon: Hidden World Tour* VR experience.

But in his heart, Richard remains a lifelong comics fan and has written for Dark Horse Comics, Simon & Schuster and more. Richard currently writes his YA graphic novel series, *SCOOP*, for Insight Comics and FEARBOOK CLUB for the Seismic Press imprint at AfterShock Comics.

MARCO MATRONE
artist

Marco Matrone is an Italian illustrator and colorist with work experience across industries, including colorist for the game *Sword and Sorcery* by Ares Games, illustrations for *Last Kaiju* published by Magic Press and concept and storyboard artist on the animated film *Yaya and Lennie: The Walking Liberty* from Mad Animation studios.

DAVE SHARPE
letterer

Upon graduating from the Joe Kubert School in 1990, he went on to work at Marvel Comics as an in-house letterer, eventually running their lettering department in the late 90s and early 00s. Over the years, Dave has lettered hundreds of comics, such as *Spider-Girl, She-Hulk* and *The Defenders* for Marvel, and *Green Lantern, Harley Quinn* and *Batgirl* for DC Comics. Dave now works on both *X-O Manowar* and *Faith* for Valiant Comics in addition to his lettering duties on several AfterShock titles.